MARVELOUS

ALSO BY MOLLY GREELEY

The Clergyman's Wife

The Heiress

MARVELOUS

A Novel

MOLLY GREELEY

wm
WILLIAM MORROW
An Imprint of HarperCollins*Publishers*

This book is a work of fiction. References to real people, events, establishments, organizations, or locales are intended only to provide a sense of authenticity, and are used fictitiously. All other characters, and all incidents and dialogue, are drawn from the author's imagination and are not to be construed as real.

HarperCollins books may be purchased for educational, business, or sales promotional use. For information, please email the Special Markets Department at SPsales@harpercollins.com.

FIRST EDITION

Designed by Bonni Leon-Berman

Library of Congress Cataloging-in-Publication Data has been applied for.

ISBN 978-0-06-324409-2

22 23 24 25 26 LBC 5 4 3 2 1

To Ashley,
who knows just how long ago this story began;
and to Stu,
who listened patiently to each and every ending.

In all things of nature there is something of the marvelous.

—*Aristotle*

AUTHOR'S NOTE

In the Château de Blois hangs a portrait of a girl. She is forever eight years old and crowned with flowers, with lace about her throat. Her face is covered all over in hair, and her painted hands hold the story with which she was born:

> *Don Pietro, a wild man discovered in the Canary Islands, was conveyed to his most serene highness Henri the king of France, and from there came to His Excellency the Duke of Parma. From whom came I, Antonietta, and now I can be found nearby at the court of the Lady Isabella Pallavicina, the honorable Marchesa of Soragna.*

The story held by the girl in the painting is almost certainly familiar to you, though you may not recognize it in the words above. The story has changed, you see, rather dramatically over the years, the centuries. When it was finally written down and bound in leather, it had already become something else, a tale thick with magic, the sort wielded by witches and fairies in their shadowed hollows; by magicians in their towers. The very air in the version you likely know hums with this magic; it eddies around the ankles of the two people who inhabit the story, the animal-husband and his beautiful bride. He is fearsome or noble, depending upon the telling—sometimes both at once, a marvel of contradictions in appearance and temperament. She is always beautiful, dutiful, good. Perhaps courageous, if you squint.

They are the only two people who inhabit the story, the only two people in the castle in the forest, the castle that does not exist as usual castles exist, on this plane, dug solid into the earth, built of stones and mortar and the good honest labor of muscles and minds. The castle in the story you probably know is insubstantial; a dream-world that comes and goes as it wishes, its stones so much milkweed fluff. The usual rules do not apply in this castle: a man lost might stumble upon it, his toes purpling with cold; might wade through snowdrifts up the great curving stairs, past gargoyles half-buried by the storm and rosebushes heavy with blossoms, bold with red, despite the season. He might find a meal and respite there, might be served wine and soup by servants made of wind. If he leaves and tries to return, he will not find the castle again, for it will be gone, entirely vanished, the forest closing around, trees pulling up their roots like tentacles, like feet, and moving upon them to crowd their trunks together, to hide the emptiness where the castle briefly rested.

But there is no history here, no weight. All is gossamer. The witch or fairy or magician transforms a man into a beast, and love transforms him back. In and out of forms, as the castle in which he imprisons himself slips in and out of time and earth-space. None of it is real.

But the girl in the painting—and her parents, who are centered in the story you know—they were real.

Part One

La Bestia

CAPODIMONTE, ITALY
1618

Catherine

It happens in the trembling time between night and day, long after the passing of midnight but well before the cock wakes to crow. The waiting hours. The witching hours. A fitting time for a man long assumed to be born of witchcraft to die.

Many years ago, Catherine spent these same hours with her newborn babes, all four of whom wakened without fail at the same gray and blurry time of morning-night, mouths opening and throats keening for the breast; and then, when their hunger was sated, their eyes opening too, looking around at the darkness. Though she is past sixty now, Catherine's arms still remember the weight of each infant; the center of her back, the ache of rocking. Her ears and throat hold the memory of cradle songs passed down to her by her mother, which devolved into broken, tuneless humming as the hours passed, and still her children stayed awake and watchful, as if to keep their mother safe from monsters in the night. That frayed-string feeling of waiting for the sun to paint the horizon all the colors of peaches, when at last they consented to sleep again and she, too, could finally rest.

She does not want to rest now. She woke after a short sleep, as she has so often before, with a fragment of a dream ready on her lips, a fragment that unthreaded itself and slithered away when she saw how he exhaled, eyes closed, through his open mouth, and heard the great pauses between one breath and the next. And then she could not sleep at all, waiting with him through the hours for his final exhalation.

Her mind skims now from those early days of motherhood—days that lasted for years and years, when she sometimes hated the man beside her for the completeness of his sleep, his deep insensibility to the world while he dreamed—it skims from there to the early days of love, when they lay together and fought sleep just for joy of one another's wakeful presence, and for irrational fear of the parting sleep would bring. Now it is only she who struggles to stay awake, though her body subtly shakes with weariness and her eyelids draw down and down, like those of a corpse being gently closed by loving fingers.

A little earlier, she pushed open the window curtains, and in the light of the moon Petrus lies stiller than he ever did in sleep, and ageless, the silver of moonbeams brightening the silver of all his hair. Catherine lies upon her side facing him, facing his stillness. Holds herself nearly as still.

Soon enough will come peach-tinted morning, and the necessity of announcing his leaving to their children and grandchildren. Madeleine and Henri, asleep now in their own homes, will wake and come to see their father, only to find instead the sealike sadness of his loss; and it will be Catherine who must comfort them. Then the washing of his body, and the wrapping. She will tuck bay leaves and rosemary sprigs between his body and his shroud to keep back the creeping scent of decay.

She is strangely aware of her fingers now, at their fleshy tips, a restless sensation. Instinctively, she reaches for Petrus to alleviate it, puts her hand over his where it rests at his side. Moves her whole hand lightly up and down the length of his, that she might feel the familiar whisper against her palm of the fine hairs that cover the backs of his hands and creep up the tops of his fingers. His nails have grown long and ragged, and guilt stuffs her throat with sand. She must trim them before anyone else sees.

MADELEINE IS PREDICTABLY WET in her grief when she arrives to find her parents hand-clasped, her father's fingers growing stiff. With a wail she clutches at Catherine's legs like the child she has not been for decades, and Catherine pulls herself from the muck of the sleep that must have closed over her despite her best efforts. She sits, releasing Petrus's hand without thinking, gathers her daughter into her arms and onto her lap, where Madeleine's full-grown weight is both burden and delight. Catherine presses their cheeks together, furrowed flesh to long soft hair, and lets her daughter cry.

But after a moment, she turns her head to look back at Petrus. Her own grief rushes up very suddenly from her chest, catching in the slender opening of her throat, and she makes a terrible strangled sound, and would reach for him again, would apologize for letting him go at all; but no—there is no need. For she can see, in the bright of morning: he is more obviously gone than he was while they lay together in the in-between.

THE REST OF THE day is predictable, and predictably exhausting. Catherine prepares Petrus's body with help from Madeleine, along with Girolama, her son Henri's wife. Girolama is silent in the face of the weeping of her sister by marriage, Madeleine's facial hair flattening against her cheeks as if she has been standing in a pour of rain.

Catherine clips her husband's fingernails and toenails, washes and combs his body, listens to her daughter's mournful wails, and feels detached from all of it, her earlier grief stuffed back down deep among her dark insides. Never before, in all the times she prepared someone she loved at death, has she felt so far away from her task, her hands working entirely on their own. She thinks of Maman, over whose body she wept as helplessly as Madeleine weeps now for her father. Of Ercole, whom she cradled in his shroud, swaying and singing to him as she had every night of his brief life, raising her voice in spikes of fury to drown the voices of anyone who tried to take him from her. Of Henri and Girolama's dear Giacomo, dead before his second birthday, how terrible, how unnatural, it seemed to stitch his shroud closed over his round-faced sweetness. The feet, which carried him running before he was twelve months old, stilled; the voice, which was so joyfully raucous, silenced.

Every single time, a knife stab. But she was *there* in every instance. When it was Girolama who would not release her son, who stroked his softly furred back for hours as if he merely lay sleeping, it was Catherine who kept others from disturbing her. When it was her own child dead, she was present for every slicing wound. She honored them with her pain.

She pauses, palms pressed to the tall arches of Petrus's feet, and breathes to anchor herself here, in these last moments with this well-known flesh, though already it begins to turn unfamiliar as death makes itself comfortable. She tries to *feel*, knowing that if she does not, she will wake in the night reaching for his toes with her own.

The last thing she does, once all the rest is finished, is to take up a sharp knife, the best of the kitchen knives, with its handle of bone and its blade whetted to a keen cutting edge. Petrus kept it so for her, knowing that it was her favorite knife, that it sliced through meat like a sword through an enemy. She takes the knife now, feels the familiar weight of it in her hand, and looks at him where he lies. Soon he will be stitched into a shroud, but now he is there for her to look at, and she takes her time choosing where to cut. His head, she decides at last; his head, as if he were any other man, as if it were the only possible place to do this. She moves to his head, looks not into his face but at the hair that grows so thickly from his scalp; takes a soft lock of it between her fingers; slices it off with the knife he sharpened for her when he sat there, just *there* beside the hearth, the grating sound of the whet stone, the calm concentration on his face. So many nights.

She puts the knife carefully away and ties the lock with a bit of ribbon, knotting it firmly, that not a single hair might escape.

CATHERINE LIES EASILY TO the priest when he comes to sit with them in their grief. How terribly unfortunate, he says, gently admonishing that she was too stricken by shock and sadness to send for him in time to administer the last rites.

Yes, Catherine hears herself say. *I should have, Padre.*

In this one thing, she honors her husband. If she cannot manage tears or wailing, she has at least kept the church's hand from his brow, though it would have given her some comfort to know he was blessed before passing on to whatever awaits the dead. *Heaven*, she still likes to think, though Petrus had reason to think otherwise. Wherever he is now, she imagines his quick, conspiratorial smile at her complicity in keeping the priest from him, and something bittersweet fills her mouth.

THE SUN FALLS IN a brilliant flare to sleep, and, together with Madeleine, Catherine sits beside her husband's body. Untouched plates of white beans in herbs and oil sit congealing beside them both, left there by Girolama. Earlier, Henri came to sit beside his father, his face running with tears as easily as Madeleine's. But he went away again to his own home, leaving the women alone with the body.

Her other daughter should be here, Catherine thinks. The thought is a little knife-stab of its own. *Antoinette—*

But she cannot think of her youngest girl just now. She will not.

Instead, she sings. Her voice is not what it once was, age stretching it thinner even than it was when she sang to their children, but Petrus would not mind. After a moment, Madeleine joins her, Madeleine who never sings, for embarrassment of how her voice cracks like plaster on both the highest and the lowest notes. The song is a *ninnananna* that Catherine's mother used to sing to her when she was small, an old, old tune that must have soothed thousands of babes to sleep. The firelight flickers lower and lower, and they sing in deepening shadow until their voices grow hoarse, heedless of the rasping, with no one but themselves and the dead to hear it. When at last they fall silent, the creases of Catherine's face are filled, like the many branches of a river, with wet.

"Another," Madeleine says, and then begins without awaiting a reply, her voice straining to reach like a child wavering on her toes, fingers stretching toward the sugar on a high shelf. Catherine pauses a moment, listening. From far away, she almost hears something, sweet and improbable as songbirds after dark—the echoing voices of their collective lost. Even Petrus, in that instant, seems about to stir.

There! There is Antoinette, who shouted even when she meant to whisper; Giacomo's trill; Maman's hum. Papa, too, who never sang, only spoke, long and often; but whose voice in music Catherine knows all the same. All of them a distant, joyous, discordant racket.

Madeleine trips a little on a note, as if perhaps she can hear them, too.

SHE IS VEILED DURING the funeral Mass, pretending to watch and listen to the priest from behind a skim of gossamer black. This is to the good, for the film of it hides the wandering of her thoughts, which dart like startled sheep from one side of her mind to the other. Long ago, at the beginning of their marriage, she had clutched at the daily Mass, which all courtiers were expected to attend, as if it were a rope thrown as she slipped beneath a roiling sea. Those mornings the rituals and rhythms she had known since infanthood were soothing, as soothing as her mother's songs when she was a child.

Now, she does not want to hear the priest's intonations, does not want to think about the reason they are here; about Petrus's death. She will dissolve if she does, all her bones turning liquid, her spine running in drips down the bench and making a murky pool on the floor.

She thinks instead of things that make her smile, safe, behind her veil, in the knowledge that no one can see her clearly. Petrus's love of melon, eager as a little boy's, though the juice ran sticky down his beard. How he taught her to read, long after their children were grown, in spite of her protests that there was no reason, no *point*; and how he kept his frustrations with her slowness at fifty tucked into his cheeks like a squirrel with a walnut, too big to be hidden, though he tried anyway. The way he slept, noisily, all rumbles—he made her think of a bear in its winter cave; though that was not a comparison he would have appreciated, and so she kept it safe inside herself. She liked his rumbles, once she knew him better, just as she learned to like, to treasure, the soft hairy bristle over his flesh and muscle and bone. Strange to think how two people can be such utter strangers to one another and then so intertwined, as threads of silk weave together to make cloth. The cloth of their life together has unraveled in the days since his death, and she'd have thought she would unravel, as well, all the fibrous parts of her pulling in opposite directions until there was nothing left. But here she still is.

Catherine looks down at her hands. They are still soft, though the skin now is lightly spotted, stretching thin as onionskins across the backs. She remembers when Petrus would not take her hands for fear of frightening her; remembers when she was frightened. It seems so long ago—another man, another woman. Another life entirely.

THE FUNERAL MASS GOES on and on, the warmth of the day bringing out the odors in people's clothing. Or perhaps Catherine's mind is drifting, perhaps she is gone from this place, gone away to someplace where time moves differently, where hours stretch slow and aching in the space of ten breaths here in the church. Under the concealing fall of her veil, she holds a little pouch of fawn leather, unadorned, the throat of it pulled tight by a darker leather thong. The lock of Petrus's hair is inside, and she cups the bag between both palms, a prayer.

Also in the bag is a folded bit of paper, creased, the ink faded. She has nothing left of her mother but the thimble from her sewing kit; even the hair powder she had once used, one of the few things that escaped being sold after the sinking of Papa's ship, is long gone. Catherine had brought that powder, which smelled so like her mother that it made her weep, with her to Château de Fontainebleau, to her wedding; she wore it in her hair until none of it was left. And though she made more powder, doing her best to reproduce her mother's recipe, it never smelled quite the same.

But she does have this one bit of her father—this letter, this paper, his words, his slanted hand, his love in ink. When she cups the bag, she can hear the paper rustle, just a little. She inhales, breathing in again the bodily odors of all the people around her, and oh, how she longs suddenly to be small again, to have known no sorrow, to have her father smiling into her face, palms full of rose petals that would one day be turned into scents for women's wrists and throats, into powder, like Maman's, for their hair. *Smell, ma petite belle. Breathe them in. Would your mother like them?*

She rises at the end of the interminable Mass, all the words and rhythms that have comforted her all her life, and which she clung to so desperately for their familiarity in the midst of so much overwhelming strangeness when she arrived at court as a bride, sounding hollow now as poorly cast bells. Henri reaches her first from his seat a little down the bench, and offers her his arm; his wife remained behind at their home, laying out the food.

Catherine finds herself faltering a little as they walk, round stones in the dirt street catching under her feet. She tightens her grip on her son's arm, and feels really old for the first time in her life. Madeleine detaches herself from her husband and takes Catherine's other arm in a firm grip; together, her two children steer her toward the funeral feast.

The other mourners straggle out behind them, mumbling to keep their voices at an appropriate, funereal level. There are more of them than Catherine expected. Most, she suspects, will have come because Petrus enjoyed the patronage of the Duke of Parma, under whose protection the whole village rests. Only a few have come because they knew and loved Petrus himself; but then, he made himself difficult to know.

She finds herself looking back, as if her other children might have joined them—Ercole floating alongside from wherever it is the dead do go, Antoinette, grown now and richly dressed, following at a sedater pace than she would have set in childhood. Come from wherever she is now.

GARACHICO, ISLAND OF TENERIFE

1547

Pedro

It was other children who taught him to bark when he was little more than a babe, to raise his piping voice, doglike, to the fat moon. They surrounded him and urged him on with their laughter until he felt like a dog in truth, and sometimes they ran down the town's streets, always a little behind him, all yipping and growling in play. He thought them his pack.

It wasn't until he was a little older, his limbs lengthening and hardening and all the softness gone from his feet, that he understood that the laughter was jeering, and that the pack encircled him not as their leader, but as their prey. They poked him with sticks; sometimes they threw stones. When he was still small and round he thought this was how boys always played. Now he knows differently, knows enough to recognize the difference in the way they play together and the way they play with him.

LA BESTIA, THEY CALL him. The boys, and everyone else: fishermen and merchants, priests and slaves, beggars and the wealthy families who live in the best houses in the town. Women cross themselves when they see him; children are sometimes frightened, sometimes taunting, and sometimes want to pet him, for the hair that covers him like a pelt is very soft. It is thickest on his head and face, and covers his shoulders, chest, and back like a cape drawn in against a breeze.

Isabel tells him not to mind the taunts. And she never calls him

La Bestia. She calls him Pedro, because that is his name, given to him by his mother and father.

HE DOES NOT KNOW who his mother and father are. Or even if they still *are*, rather than *were*. Sometimes at night when the town is dark and quiet as a womb and all he can hear is the wind over the hills and occasional muffled laughter of drunken men stumbling home from the taverns, their voices echoing through the narrow winding streets, Pedro wonders whether one of them might be his father. Whether his mother waits up at night for her husband to return. Whether the two of them miss him, Pedro.

Isabel's mouth, usually soft and generous, turns thin and puckered when Pedro asks about his parents. She will tell him only that his mother was Guanche, like Isabel herself, and that his father was a Spaniard, like Isabel's own husband.

"One of them who came over years after our leaders surrendered to their soldiers," she says, bending low over her work, a necklace of clay beads that she has painted bright with the dyes of plants. "No doubt he meant to make his fortune from our rich land."

"And did he?" Pedro asks, but Isabel just shakes her head, makes an irritable sound at the back of her throat, and will not answer; and from this he understands that they are probably still here, still in Garachico. He might pass them every day and not know it.

But *they*—they must always, *always* know him. There is a small, hard satisfaction in that, in knowing that his hairy face is unmistakable; that if they are still here, they can never forget him.

"Are they hairy, like me?" he asks on another day. He has come in from the rain, and his hair is all sodden, pressed flat to his skull and dripping puddles on the floor.

He knows that she must know his parents. He is old enough now, nearly nine summers behind him, to realize that since he was not abandoned immediately after his birth, news of him, a hairy infant, must have traveled swiftly through the town. When Manuel brought him to her, Isabel must have known who abandoned him, and why, for the shame of bringing something so monstrous into the world must have been hard to bear. The only question is why they did not give him up sooner.

Isabel, who had snatched up a rag and begun rubbing it briskly over his head, pauses now. She knows, without asking, whom he means.

"No," she says, after a very long silence, during which Pedro stares down at the spreading damp. His feet, in their secondhand shoes, shift against the floor. Isabel catches his chin in her hand, tugs his face up and stoops to meet his eyes. Her smile is small and sad.

"There is no one like you," she says. "You are very special."

IT WAS ISABEL GONZALES who gave Pedro *ahoren* from her own pot when he was small and hungry and alone, the fine fern-root and barley flour dissolved in goat's milk so it was thin enough to drink; and her grandson Manuel who showed him, when he was bigger, how to gather limpets and winkles and mussels when the tide was low. Pedro has become so good at gathering that he is able to supply Isabel and Manuel with an abundance of shellfish, freeing them from the task and letting him feel he has truly earned himself a place by their hearth. He glows with his ability to help them, to provide.

Manuel brought Pedro home when he was just a babe—"Squalling and scrawny, left for the church to take in or dispose of," he said. The clipped way he spoke about it later told Pedro that he thought it more likely Pedro would be disposed of than given shelter, had the priest been the one to discover him. Dropped from the cliffs into the sea, the waves swallowing him whole, the fact of him gone in an instant.

Instead, it was Manuel who found him, hardly more than a child himself, then, hearing Pedro's cries when he was passing the church in the night, on his way back from a night of mischief making with his friends, warm with cheap wine. The wind that whipped along the street, the creaking of the trees overhead, the rumble he could hear coming in from the sea—all of these must have aroused in him a strange, bruising tenderness, for he stopped at the church, picked up the child that lay on its step, hands fisted and face screwed in fury, and cradled him against his chest, carrying him home to the house he shared with his grandmother, Pedro's hungry cries startling her from her slumber.

"Only a few weeks old, you were," she says, whenever Pedro begs for the story of his coming to her. "Without all that hair, you'd have been the tiniest sack of bones." She tells him how his mouth opened and closed around her finger as if it were a teat; how his tongue muscle thrust her finger away, disgusted, when it yielded no milk. How she laughed and cried together, the clench of sudden love butting up against the fear that he might not survive, this small draggled creature thrust so unexpectedly into her arms.

THEY HAVE LIVED TOGETHER all the years since then, among the dusty streets and bright-painted houses. The tolling of the church bell calling them, all unwilling, to prayer. Their house is small and cramped, for all that the only sticks of furniture are the chairs and table built by Isabel's husband so many years before, the plain bedstead he used to share with her. There are pegs by the door for hats and for Pedro's woven palm bag, and shoved against the wall are his and Manuel's pallets, stuffed with straw and only slightly softened by flock, bits of wool and fabric cut up fine. Pedro likes to sleep with the small, humped shapes of his wooden menagerie dozing beside his pallet.

Manuel made the toys for him from spare bits of wood, during idle hours that could have been spent instead lazing with friends or wooing women. Instead, he chose to spend the time whittling for Pedro—the flash of knife, the curls of wood falling to the floor between Manuel's sun-browned feet, leaving in their wake a horse with its tail carved in motion; a dog, tongue lolling; a pig, fat and round and fitting perfectly into the hollow of Pedro's palm. A goat with wee sharp horns and swollen teats, her two kids gamboling behind her. Pedro loves to run his fingers over the little grooves in the animals' bodies from the knife scrapes, the spindly delicacy of their legs and horns.

Manuel's careless hand on Pedro's head, not to pet him or test the texture of the hair there but to ruffle it in affection. Isabel's playful scolding over the mess of wood scraps; her gentle glance when Pedro kneels in the dust, playing with the animals with the sun hot on his head and shoulders and the seabirds wheeling above. At night, he falls asleep warm and fed, toys beside him, the smiles of the only two people who matter filling his head and his nighttime breath mingling with theirs in the house's single room.

Every day, Isabel combs the hair on his head and face with her own wooden comb, the one her long-ago husband carved in a pattern of flowers that look just like the bright yellow *ranúnculo* that sprout wild all over the island in autumn. The hair on his cheeks droops especially long; though there is no looking glass in Isabel's home, Pedro can feel its length with his fingers, and if he looks down he can see it, soft and brown.

Isabel's own hair is white and wispy as the clouds that are pushed across the blue, blue sky by the ocean winds. Her skin is roughly lined like the bark of a dragon tree, and she has little humps of skin, darker than the rest, in clusters on her cheeks and throat. The largest of these has a hair growing from it, long and black as a spider's fine leg. Pedro's chest feels warm looking at that hair, growing, proud and unapologetic, where it oughtn't.

ISABEL SCOLDS HIM WHENEVER he turns up with scrapes from his encounters with other boys. She prods at his swollen cheekbone, making him wince. "Cruel children," she mutters, and then a few words that Pedro does not understand but whose meaning is unmistakable when paired with her scowl, white brows pressed together over the long straight bone of her nose. These are words she shouldn't say; they come from a language that is now forbidden, the secret language of Isabel's girlhood, which she stubbornly refuses to forget. Her own name wasn't hers until after the island was finally overcome—her father, a goatherd, slaughtered like one of his own goats, and her brothers put on a great ship and taken away. Her new name—Isabel—may be a Christian name, and she may have been baptized by a priest's holy water, but she still worships silently the god of her parents and grandparents.

Yet to Manuel, her grandson by blood, and to Pedro, whom she calls *el nieto de mi corazón*—the grandson of her heart—she will not speak the name of her god or any of his intermediaries. She fears the boys will be clumsy and say the names aloud where someone else might hear.

The bell of the new whitewashed church calls them to Mass every Sunday. Manuel, whose skill as a builder means he never lacks for work in their growing port town, points out the fine details to Pedro and Isabel—from the fitted beams in the ceiling to the graceful stone arches—as they wait for the service to begin.

Pedro sits cushioned between Isabel and Manuel and listens to the priest while ignoring the sideways stares from the other benches. He recites the Latin prayers in a whisper, tries to feel their holiness on his tongue though he cannot understand them with his ears. The priest's Spanish sermons at least are comprehensible, and Pedro sits straight and still as he speaks. His mind strains to fill with all the mysteries the priests have deciphered from their heavy holy book.

But no matter how closely he listens, the priest's stories never answer the one question that drifts in an endless whirlpool through his head. Perhaps, he thinks, he can ask the priest himself one day, when he is older and feeling brave.

Instead, Pedro begs Isabel for stories of her god, and even of the evil spirits who, Isabel says, caused all manner of illness and accident; but she refuses.

"Evil did not cause you, *cariño mio*," she says, understanding at once his unspoken worry.

PEDRO OFTEN GOES DOWN to the sea to harvest shellfish for their supper; but he also helps by scouring the beach for shells that Isabel can use in her work. Almost everything from Isabel's girlhood has long since been forbidden by the Spanish who conquered the island, but the rulers have not entirely quelled admiration for traditional artistry. Isabel sits most days in the shade, stringing clay beads and shells into adornments that she can sell; it is Pedro's job to make sure her pile of shells is always heaped high.

Today, Pedro hurries through the twisting streets. He keeps his head low, eyes on his feet as they scurry forward. If he stops even for a moment he is as likely to receive a coin as a kick; the merchants shoo him away when he lingers too long outside their shops and stalls, afraid that his strangeness will deter custom. Although thanks to Isabel he is no beggar, the wealthy always seem to assume he is one, anyway; they offer him coin if he lets them touch the fur of his cheek. Once, one gentleman cut a long lock of his hair to bring home to his wife.

A pity, the gentleman said, rubbing the hairs between his fingers, *that a little beast like you can't be skinned like a goat. What a handsome coat you have.*

Pedro gives these coins to Isabel, and she takes them, though with a furious look when he explains how he came to have them. He much prefers the look she gives him when he brings her his gleanings from the sea.

The sea is once again his destination, and he does not look up at all until he reaches it, even when he passes the monastery where monks' voices thrum through the windows. At the beach he removes his shoes and places them on the sand, high enough that the tide cannot snatch them away. The sand is soft and black; Pedro amuses himself for a short while by marching up and down the shore, neck twisted so he can see the line of his own small shallow footprints before the waves lap them away. When he has tired of this, he finally crouches down to work.

Always, the sea is generous. It daily offers an abundance of shells that have been abandoned by their occupants: large, spiny shells with insides as pink and smooth as palms; the rough dark shells of mussels; the curled shells of sea snails, as small and delicate as a fingernail. He picks through them all, putting the best ones into the sack Isabel made for him for just this purpose, woven tightly from the fibers of palm leaves.

Two fishermen are at work far down the beach; one of them waves to Pedro, and Pedro lifts his hand in response, smiling with all his teeth. They are too far away to see him properly; he must look like any ordinary boy to them.

He is still smiling when he throws the bag over his shoulder and makes for his favorite spot, a nook within one of the twisted rocks overlooking the sea. These rocks were formed, Manuel told him, long ago by fire from the tallest mountain in the area. Hills loom high around the town, but as far as Pedro knows, only this one ever belches fire.

He used to fit perfectly inside this nook, nestled close enough to the water that when the tide was in, he could feel the spray on his face as the waves rushed forth. The sea is a deeper blue than the sky and filled with just as many mysteries; not just the fish and eels, crabs and urchins, but deeper mysteries of the sort that sailors like to describe, particularly to small boys with large eyes and eager questions.

These sailors, accustomed to all manner of extraordinary sights in the strange lands to which they journey, often seem less shocked than other people by Pedro's appearance. They speak of monsters that lurk in the deepest parts of the sea, many-armed and many-toothed, all the more fearsome because they come from a place where humans cannot go.

Pedro finds his nook, and though he has grown a little older, a little longer, and doesn't fit quite as well as he used to, he still curls into it as best he can, like a winkle into its shell, and looks out over the water, his head full of sea monsters.

HE IS DOZING IN his nook when a true sea monster comes for him. It snatches him up in its tentacles; covers his mouth so he cannot scream; rushes with him into the waves, great splashes of water soaking his clothes against his body. He bucks and struggles within the monster's grip, but its arms are immovable.

Then suddenly the waves are gone—Pedro thrashes, tries to bite the thing that holds him, finds himself smacked hard enough that if it weren't for the monster's tight grip his head would have snapped on his neck.

He stops moving instantly, but not for the smack itself; because the smack was delivered not by a slimy tentacle, but by a human palm.

Pedro

Pedro has always known to be wary of pirates, those lawless sailors who came sometimes to the island and stole whatever they wished, then slipped away again in their fast ships. Everyone knows to be wary of pirates. But there has not been an attack for years, at least not in their port; the danger seemed, until this moment, as imaginary as the danger of being swallowed by a sea creature.

Now he is curled in a ship's damp hold, cheek pressed to a coil of half-rotted rope. He listens to the slapping of water against the sides of the ship, and the voices of the men above. They speak some tongue Pedro cannot understand.

A man in a brown jerkin brings him hard bread and some fresh water, speaks to him in that strange ugly language, and looks angry when Pedro cannot respond. Pedro spills half the water down his chin in fear.

ALL THROUGH THE SEA voyage, he is ill. He retches and retches, though there is little enough in his belly to bring up. The man in the brown jerkin shouts at him and makes him clean the mess, but the stench of vomit lingers, mingling with the smell of damp and the slick green-black mold that grows in ever-widening spots on the hold walls.

In between bouts of sickness he lies on his side, eyes closed against the terrible sight of the ship's walls heaving up and down with the waves, hands over his ears to keep out the sounds of men from above—the thump of their footsteps, the creaking of the wood, their voices raised in laughter and in anger—and drifts in and out of a restless sleep. In his sleep, he returns to the island, to his nook. The beach riddled with stones and shells. The water rushing in and out, offering treasures and taking them back again.

Inside the ship, his eyes adjust to the dimness, to the shadows that creep and shift and cast out tendrils of themselves like tentacles, reaching for him, beckoning to him until he has pulled his legs as close to his belly as he can, clutched his arms around them, tucked his head down so that he occupies as little space as possible, so that he is more difficult to reach. He is surrounded by bulging sacks—supplies, he wonders, or items stolen from his town of Garachico, and from other towns, as well? Pedro stares at the sacks but dares not open them, though his heart pounds against his chest and his fingers curl into fists. Like other children, he was brought up on stories of pirate attacks, which left so many Guanche families in fragments and so many churches and rich houses looted. These pirates did not come only for him—they must have come for many treasures. The church's silver candlesticks; wealthy ladies' jewels. Manuel has teased Pedro for years about how soundly he sleeps—could he have slept that day through the screams from an attack?

No, he thinks. *No, no, no.* But still his fists long to *punch*. Instead, he puts his palm into his own mouth to stopper the screams trying to hurl themselves into the world.

He weeps when he thinks of Isabel—stringing beads and waiting for him to return home. This thought is more substantial than his imaginings of what could have happened to the town during a pirate attack, and the tears stream and stream, mixing with snot from his nose and saliva from his open, grieving mouth. Manuel will calm her when Isabel grows worried about Pedro's absence; Manuel will promise to find Pedro, without knowing how impossible the promise will be to keep. He will scour the port and the streets and climb the neighboring hills. He will ask and ask whether anyone has seen the hairy boy—the little beast. At last, perhaps, he will search the shore for a small washed-up body. But he will not find even that, only the bag of perfect shells and a pair of empty shoes.

WHEN THE SHIP DOCKS at last, Pedro is thin and shaky from days and days of vomiting, his tongue dry and sticky. There was no sense of day and night in the ship's hold, but he was given one meal each day, and he kept count of those—eighteen in all. Eighteen days away from home.

He is bundled roughly up the stairs, his wrists tied tight with rope. He cries out a question, but the man just shoves him up the last steps to the deck, where he stands, eyes squeezed shut against the dazzling sun and shoulders hunched against the stares of the other men, their tongues muttering and their throats laughing. His blood whooshes, loud but not loud enough to deaden other sounds. The tall mast creaks, seabirds scream above their heads, and the sea air blows cool over his face, fresh and salty as it was at home. He keeps his eyes closed and inhales it in great gulps. The salt that runs from between his lids makes the men laugh louder.

There are people all around. Eyes everywhere. Pedro is used to having eyes upon him, but these press hard, encircling him like cage bars.

Isabel, he thinks, and tries very hard not to snivel, though he has never been so frightened, not even when the boys pelted him with rocks. Not even when the new priest sketched the sign of the cross like a barrier before his own chest, eyes as wide as if he had just spied a demon, when Pedro came forward for the holy communion. *Isabel, Isabel.*

There are other people in this square, men and women and even children, bound and drooping. Most have Moor-dark skin; others look like they should be pale, except that the sun has burned them until they appear almost cooked, red-brown and crispy. But none of *them* draws the attention that Pedro does; the man in the brown jerkin smiles with half his mouth, pulls up Pedro's shirt to show his hairy back. Fingers brush, marveling, at his spine. Pedro tries to keep his head down, eyes upon his own bare feet, but the man will not let him, squeezing the sides of Pedro's jaw until his mouth opens. Pedro's own breathing rattles inside his ears, half-drowning the excited murmurs of the men who surround him, peering at his teeth.

He longs to run away; Manuel used to say Pedro darted like a fish. But the man in the brown jerkin holds his chin in one hand, and keeps his other hand on Pedro's shoulder, gripping tight. So Pedro's eyes dart instead, from face to avid face.

He is too dulled by terror to notice when he is finally bought, a price negotiated, coins clinking into the pirate's fat purse. He only knows that suddenly there is a new hand upon him, less rough, plump fingers with a gold ring. A voice speaks to him, the words lost to the harsh rustle of his own frantic breaths, and Pedro looks up into a pair of pale blue eyes.

"Come," the man says again, and this time Pedro understands the word, and could sob for the understanding.

THE MAN DOES NOT ask Pedro's name, or give his own. He speaks Spanish badly and with a strange accent, and calls Pedro his wild boy, which makes Pedro want to bite. But the man feeds him well, better even than his own two servants. He gives Pedro meat from his own plate and says, "We want you glossy," laughing and wiping grease from his fingers.

This journey is jolting, over land rather than sea, and Pedro dozes through much of it despite his fear, his eyes drooping closed to the sounds of the horses' hooves rhythmic upon the dusty, pitted roads. Though he is well-fed, his stomach recoils from food, rejecting much of what he eats as if he had drunk bad water; the blue-eyed man shouts in disgust the first time this happens, and begins demanding how long Pedro has been ill. Pedro forms a miserable curl. His belly doesn't want food; it is too frightened.

They make their beds in fields, at times, one or the other of the big servants standing watch for thieves; other times they all pile into a stable or room at an inn. The man who bought Pedro always gets the bed in the room; Pedro sleeps between the two manservants on the hard floor.

At one inn, in a town that teems with scuttling people as busy and numerous as ants, the man leaves Pedro alone with the servants, who chuckle and toss dice together on the floor of the room while Pedro watches. They do not speak Spanish but another language, enough of whose words are familiar that Pedro can cobble together a small understanding of their conversation, dull as it is—admiration for a serving girl they saw downstairs; irritation for the fleas that leap fearlessly among them all. Pedro scratches at his own flea bites and wonders where these men come from; on his island, there were people from many lands, but he never had reason to pay close attention to any tongues besides his own. He watches the dice fall and clatter, again and again.

When the man returns, it is with two of the inn's servants, who lug between them a rough wooden tub. As Pedro stares, they return again and again with buckets of steaming water. A serving girl scents the water with oil and herbs. And then the blue-eyed man who bought him directs Pedro to strip and get into the tub.

No, Pedro tries to say; but one servant is already pulling his shirt over his head, and then suddenly he is in the tub, the scalding water making him hiss. The blue-eyed man laughs a little at his reaction, then sets about briskly scrubbing him with harsh soap. The scented water turns quickly gray and murky.

After, he is dried and combed and stands naked before the man and his manservants, fists at his sides and heat that has nothing to do with the bath rushing up from his chest to his cheeks.

The blue-eyed man brought new clothes back with him from outside, and now he orders Pedro to dress. The hose are yellow as *ranúnculo*, the buttercups at home that send out their runners all along the island and twine, painted, along the edge of Isabel's comb. There is lace at the shirt's wrists and throat; the doublet is a deep green, stitched with silver thread. Pedro has never touched, let alone worn, clothes so fine; his fingers fumble with the lacings, and he looks down at himself in disbelief, then up, smiling shyly, to the man for approval.

But the man is frowning. "No," he says slowly, running a finger around his mouth in thought. "Take them off."

Tears prick, but Pedro obeys. When he is again bare, he looks back at the man, who nods and finally smiles.

"Yes," he says. "Wild as God made you. You are perfect."

WHEN THE BIG SERVANTS throw a blanket over him and bear him down the inn's dark stairway and out, blinking, into the bustle of the street outside, he finds a cart waiting, not the coach they had been using; and in the cart, a cage.

Pedro has learned not to ask questions, for the blue-eyed man never answers them, but he begins crying out questions now. "Where are you taking me?" he says, and then, when there is no answer, only the blanket whipped away and one servant lifting him up, the other holding open the cage's hinged door, he begins screaming: "No! *No!*" But as ever, the servants and the blue-eyed man—who has come out through the inn door dressed not in his dusty traveling clothes, but in a tooled leather doublet and bright trunk hose, a snowy plume in his hat—pretend to deafness. The only sign that Pedro is not voiceless and invisible are the curious glances and startled exclamations from passersby.

He kneels inside the cage and folds himself low over his genitals. He has grown accustomed, over the last endless weeks, to terror. It has become his only constant friend, buzzing with an almost-friendly familiarity inside his chest. But this is an entirely new terror; it roars inside his chest like the beast the people of Garachico said he was. The cage has bars of wood, round and oiled smooth, which are nonetheless too strong for Pedro to shift, no matter how he rattles them. They won't move—*they won't move*—and as the cart lurches forward, the servants perched to either side of the cage and the blue-eyed man on the seat in front with the driver, the roaring terror bursts between Pedro's ribs, up the tunnel of his throat and out of the hole of his mouth. He shouts and shouts, wordless and wild as the man wants him to be, his skin burning under the bristle of hair. But the cart rolls inexorably on, and his throat begins to ache, and the shouts turn to pleadings. First with the man who purchased him, who does not even turn around; then to the God who made him, and to his Son, and to the Holy Mother. When they do not respond he turns to Isabel's god—to the god and spirits of his mother's people.

But, of course, he never learned their names, and so they cannot hear him.

Pedro

He huddles, tense and shivering, in the center of the cage as the servants lift it from the cart. The cage is generous enough that he could kneel with his neck perfectly straight if he wished; instead, he makes himself as small as he can, a tight, furry ball, arms pressed hard to his ribs, sharp elbow-points in the hollows of his palms. He does not want to know where they are taking him; his eyes close. He pretends that he is in his nook.

The cage bumps a little with the servants' uneven steps. Pedro's heart bumps, too, each time he hears a gasp or exclamation from someone they pass. He focuses on the little wind that ruffles over his body through the cage bars.

And then, quite suddenly, the air changes, grows still and stagnant; and scented, too, like the air inside a church, as if the servants have carried him into a building, a closed-up place filled with the perfumes of the wealthy. The murmurs thicken around him. Pedro tightens his arms around himself, rocking slightly.

He is unprepared, when the servants set the cage down, for the cacophonous swelling of murmured voices to suddenly cease. There is a faint rustling, like fabric or tree leaves, from all sides; and then a single voice directly beside Pedro, speaking in the language of the pirates but gently, and in a tone of wonder. Almost against his will, Pedro opens his eyes, one after the other, to find himself eye to eye with a man crouched on the other side of the bars.

The man has a narrow face, and a beard that makes his chin look very pointed. His eyebrows tip up in the center; his eyelids droop down. There is a gold hoop in his ear, from which a pearl dangles. When Pedro looks at him, he makes a sound of delight and, gesturing excitedly, turns to say something to the man standing beside him.

It is the blue-eyed man who bought Pedro at the market, who does not look at Pedro at all, though Pedro reaches out, folding his fingers around the bars of his cage, peering up between them. All around are other people, men and women both, richly dressed in cloth of red and black and blue and gold, whispering to each other behind their hands. The whispers echo, for the ceiling of the room is very tall, and all their staring eyes fix upon Pedro. His blood surges high and fast as a wave dashing itself against a cliff; the muscles of his legs bunch, as if they would spring. He breathes through his mouth like a winded dog.

The bearded man stands from his crouch, and he and the man who bought Pedro speak together over the cage for several minutes, their tongues whirring. Pedro's fingers clench on the cage bars; his ears ache for something he can understand.

Then the man who brought Pedro here bows low before the bearded man. And then he is leaving—Pedro swings around to watch as he walks briskly down the long length of the room, the two big servants falling in behind him—a call sticks in Pedro's throat, choking him. But the blue-eyed man, who fed Pedro meat from his own knife and combed his hair as gently as Isabel once did, is gone.

Pedro has only a moment to stare after him before he is surrounded by all the people who whispered at the edges of the room before. They bend down, pushing their faces close to the cage; their mouths spill forth still more words that Pedro cannot understand; their fingers, heavy with rings, reach curiously through the cage bars. Pedro shrinks back, pulling all his limbs in tight; his head moves in little frantic shakes. "No," he says, a breeze of a word, and, "Please—I want to go home—"

One of the women hears and exclaims, pointing. Pedro pushes himself as far away from them as he can, the cage bars hard against his spine.

THEY PUT HIM INSIDE a windowless chamber, filled with odds and ends—trunks and tapestries, heavy carved chairs and silver platters, their stacked forms casting bulging shadows across the walls. The cage is set down with a jarring thump. Pedro sits very still but for his chest and shoulders, which rise and fall with his rapid breaths. The servants who bore him into the room bend to get a better look at him, but he does not look up until they leave, the door clunking into place behind them with terrible solidity.

HE IS STILL NAKED, and a little cold, when the storeroom door opens abruptly sometime the following day. His stomach aches, with hunger and fear both. He dreamed last night of goat's milk, hot from the teat.

The man who enters looks wary. He opens the cage with a key, looking as if he would like to leap back as Pedro, after a moment's hesitation, half-crawls from within, standing slowly. Muttering something Pedro cannot understand, the man slips a rope around his wrists, pulling it tight, tugging so Pedro follows as he leads him from the storeroom and into a maze of corridors. His shoes are loud upon the floors, Pedro's bare feet softly slapping. Pedro keeps his eyes on his toes against the tiles, his back rounding against the stares of the few people they pass.

There are men with swords at the door where they finally stop. The man with Pedro fiddles with his end of the rope. When he knotted it earlier around Pedro's wrists, his fingers grazed the back of Pedro's hand, and he hastily wiped them on his own hose. Pedro stares now at those fingers, long and white as bones. There is a buzzing inside his ears. He wills himself invisible.

The door opens, and the rope is tugged, and Pedro stumbles forward, his wristbones creaking, his back absorbing the whispers from the guards like thwacks. Voices speak, but Pedro cannot hear them; the buzzing rises, bees swarming. His head whirls upon his neck, as if he stole too many sips of wine.

And then one voice cuts through the rest—raised only slightly, but for some reason, everyone else in the room goes silent. Two feet in soft round shoes appear before Pedro, and he looks up, bound hands awkward over his nakedness.

The bearded man from the day before looks down at him. Like yesterday, he wears a pearl in one ear and shows no sign of fear at Pedro's nearness, only a look of wonder. As if Pedro is a saint, or something from a story the man remembers from childhood.

"I am told you can speak," he says, in Spanish that is perfect, almost without accent. Pedro feels an echoing expression of wonder come over his own face. "Is this true?"

"Yes," Pedro says. He has to force the word over his very dry tongue. At the sound, the man's eyebrows jump like delighted children, and his face, so long and solemn, suddenly transforms itself with a grin, his eyes rumpling at the corners.

"Well, now," he says. "Not such a savage, then, as I was told, if you can speak a Christian tongue. I swore I'd never again speak the language of my captors, but here we are."

But then something in his expression slackens. "You truly are just a child," he says. "I didn't realize—" He speaks over his shoulder to a group of men Pedro had not noticed, who huddle together, looking like goats in a storm despite their fine clothes. When he turns back to Pedro, he crouches so that their faces are level.

"A child," he says again, and the wonder is back in his voice, along with something else, something that makes Pedro think of Manuel's voice when he talks about the building of churches. Pedro is silent, fingers knotting. His joints ache, every one, from holding them tight and ready. The man continues to look at him, then says, "I was told you would have been a king in your own country, once upon a time. That your father was a great Guanche king, slain in the last battle with the Spanish. Tell me—from one king to another—are all your people so hairy as you?"

Bewildered, Pedro's eyes flick from the man's face, with its long, straight nose and neat beard, to his clothing. His hat, Pedro sees now, is sewn all over with pearls to match the one in his ear. Around his neck hangs a heavy chain, from which the largest pearl Pedro has ever seen dangles below a thick golden cross.

From one king to another. Nonsense words. Crazy words. Pedro opens his mouth to ask a question, then closes it again. The blue-eyed man who brought him here never answered any questions Pedro asked; surely questions would only anger *this* man, who says he is a king.

"N-no," Pedro says at last, stutter-tongued. For a moment, he is back on the beach, pirate hands clasped tight over his struggling limbs and seawater splashing. This man does not look like a pirate, but there is *something* in his face that matches the something in his voice, an eagerness at the thought of an entire island of hairy people. A king, or even a man rich enough to dress all over in pearls, could command ships to steal people. Pedro flounders up out of the wet, wrenches away from the hard fingers.

"No," he says again, and then stops, flustered. How is one meant to address a king? Or a madman? But the man just watches him, apparently unconcerned by Pedro's confusion. So Pedro tries again. "They are not—we are not—" He shakes his head. "I am the only one like me."

In his head, he hears Isabel's voice, warm and wry and very far away: *You are very special.* His throat catches, as if around a small spiny shell; under all the unblinking stares in the room, he does not feel special, only very naked.

The huddled goat-men come forward when the king beckons them. They are tense and narrow eyed, their hands going to their knife hilts. One, braver or more impatient than the rest, stretches out a hand, ink settled into the vertical cracks and ridges of his fingernails, and touches the long hair that falls from Pedro's cheek. Pedro stands very still; and then they all come forward, their fear of him withering when he does not feed it. They touch him, every one of them, and point to bits of his body, murmuring together, nodding. They examine his ears and nose and navel; they spread his fingers and toes and turn over his hands and feet one after the other to peer at his palms and soles. One of them puts his big, porous nose just behind Pedro's ear and sniffs. The king-man watches, one half of his mouth curled up.

"Have you a name?" he says as one of the men nudges Pedro to turn around so that he can examine his back and buttocks.

"Pedro," Pedro says in a whisper.

The man cocks his head, smiling again with all his long white teeth. "Only Pedro? A prince must have more name than that."

Pedro has no family name; if Isabel knew it, she never told him what it was. Certainly, he is not a prince. Bare and shivering, he almost says so.

But he looks at the man, who stands very kingly, feet apart and elbows wide, as if to proclaim his right to more space than other men. If the man is mad, he seems to fully believe his own madness. How wonderful, to be able to turn king just by saying so.

But kings have family names. Dynasties. Pedro licks his lips, which are dry and flaking.

The man shifts his weight from one foot to the other. His eyes dull, just slightly, with impatience.

"Gonzales." Pedro forces the name out. Isabel's name, and Manuel's, too. He used to pluck finished beads from Isabel's workbasket, rolling them between his fingers; this feels somehow similar. "I am Pedro Gonzales."

"Pedro Gonzales," the king-man repeats, and then says it again, this time accompanied by other words in his own language, to the other men surrounding Pedro. They take up the name among them like congregants mumbling Latin prayers. His new name sounds handsome and proud, rolling off so many tongues. *Pedro Gonzales.*

He hopes, clench-fingered and aching, that—as with the beads—Isabel would not mind the borrowing.

THE DAYS FROM THAT point flow in and out like waves over the beach. The king takes great care of him—assigns him a chamber, all his own; and a *gouverneur*, a keeper just as his own children have, and the animals in the menagerie, too, someone to ensure their needs are seen to. His *gouverneur*, Monsieur de la Vacherie, speaks Spanish, though not so well as King Henri, and with the coins allotted from the king's coffers he buys Pedro clothing, toys. A fine jointed horse, a top that spins madly with the flick of his wrist. He is brusque, but kind enough, with a distant sort of kindness, though Pedro wonders whether the kindness is his own inclination, or if it is the king himself who requires it of him, the king who is so delighted by his wondrous hairy boy. The clothing Vacherie orders made for him is tailored to fit Pedro exactly; accustomed to wearing Manuel's old things, Pedro cannot stop marveling at a sleeve that stops just at his wrist, or a doublet fitted, glove-like, to his chest and belly. There is room for his toes to wiggle inside the soft shoes, but they are not so big that the heels flap.

The courtiers will want to see your teeth, Vacherie warns him. *They will want to touch your hair. Follow His Majesty's lead in this; he is fond of children, and fond of dogs, so I imagine he will be doubly fond of you, should you behave well.*

And fond he is. A stool is brought up beside the king's own chair. Pedro perches there, back straight and hands on his knees, mouth closed and gaze unfocused against all the covetous eyes of the court. Embarrassment, anger, fear, wonder all wash over him, again and again, turning him prickling-hot and shivery-cold in waves as the king shows him off to dignitaries; lets his mistress tie ribbons in Pedro's hair.

"You are the most interesting gift I have been given for my coronation," the king says, leaning close and whispering to Pedro, as if imparting a great secret. "Better even than the leopard." He grins, sets a warm hand on Pedro's shoulder. "It is very beautiful and very fierce; but it cannot speak."

Pedro can speak, though he is no longer supposed to speak his own language, but the language of his new country. Since he cannot, he says little. But His Majesty is patient; he points to objects around the room—a cup; a table; a sword—and names them in French. When Pedro repeats each word, the king applauds, as if for a tumbler's extraordinary feat.

WHEN HIS FORMAL EDUCATION begins, his keeper securing a tutor for him at King Henri's command, the man shakes his head when he sees Pedro; says that at ten years old he is too old to begin such rigorous study as His Majesty demands.

A little savage, learn? he says, distaste wrinkling his fishhook nose. *The other children are so far ahead of you they are but specks upon the horizon.*

But Pedro does learn; to please the king, whose rare smiles are as warming as fire, he learns and learns—first to speak French properly, then to read it in his hornbook, and to write, the letters small and looping and even. Then Latin, the language of the church, and Greek, and Italian. Manners; swordplay.

The more he studies, the less time he has, he finds, to *think*. To remember. To feel again the splash of salt water, the bruising grip of hands, the lock of the cage. His mind, he finds, is a depthless well; he can fill and fill it, and still there is room for more. The king's mistress, said to be the most beautiful woman in the world, likes to sit him by her side at feasts, that he might stand upon the bench at her request and declaim in Latin for the amusement of the entire court.

What a marvelous little beast he is. Such tricks he can perform!

Often, he imagines himself as one of the sea's empty shells; like a shell, he lets the waves bear him forward and back, day into night, again and again. And, like a shell, he is sometimes plucked up, turned over, wiped clean of grit, burnished. Admired; or discarded.

ONE DAY, HE SITS at the king's feet, on a little stool kept there for that purpose. His Majesty has been away, gone to the palace he keeps for his beautiful mistress, and Pedro has been left behind with the queen, who sometimes feeds him from her hand as if he is one of her dogs.

But King Henri is back now, returned for the birth of his newest child, Louis; and he is asking Pedro what he has been studying, his half-smile as he listens, nodding along, making Pedro's chest thrum with pleasure. It is February, the windowpanes frosted at their edges, the palace so cold that Pedro's breath goes before him like smoke. He hates the cold, finds himself wishing that his hair were a true and proper pelt; but there is a different sort of warmth in having the king back again.

"You have been diligent," His Majesty says.

"A noble beast, indeed," says the man directly beside the king. Older, with a white fluff of beard, he is someone the king looks to often whenever someone comes to him with a question; rarely does His Majesty seem to doubt this man's judgment.

But he does now, his lips suddenly frowning. "He is a man," he says, and the white-haired man bows his head in acquiescence and apology. "Or he will be, when he is grown. A wild man, now so tamed that he can speak in the language of scholars and the church." His smile returns when he looks back at Pedro.

"*Petrus Gonsalvus*," he says, casually returning Pedro's chosen surname to him in God's chosen language.

Pedro

It is on one of the first days of spring-like warmth, after months of such cold that Petrus's finger bones ache at the knuckles like an old man's, that he first speaks to Ludovico Gonzaga. Petrus's tutor, having thrown his hands up when Petrus peered longingly through the window at the sunshine for the tenth time in as many minutes, finally sends him outside with a grumbling, "Bah! Away with you—but practice your verbs while you are out."

Crossing the oval courtyard, he lifts his face to the weakly shining sun; he half-dances across the courtyard stones, and dares to splash through the meltwater puddled in their dips. He is alone in the courtyard but for the occasional harried servant, and he brought with him a little wooden horse, gifted to him by King Henri, cunningly jointed so that it could clop across the stones with a true horsey gait. Petrus plays a little; mumbles his verbs over in a desultory manner; gazes at his own face in gritty puddle water with something like fondness, the sunlight easing every sensation.

He is sitting alone in a patch of warmth when, from behind him, come the sounds of a door opening and quick running feet. A tumble of laughter. The back of his neck tightens; he stares fixedly at his blurred reflection and continues with his conjugations, though they hitch and stumble a little whenever the laughter behind him suddenly peaks.

After a few moments, he chances a furtive glance over his shoulder. It is as he thought: children everywhere, playing together in the thin sunshine. The court is filled with children now, and not only the king and queen's own steadily growing brood; noble families throughout Christendom send their young to the French court to be educated. Even Marie, the little Scottish queen, is here, trailed always by a gaggle of other Maries, companions and playmates, whom Petrus only distinguishes from one another by the bright and varied hues of their gowns.

As Petrus watches, a nurse blows bubbles for the children using a hollow reed. The smallest of them all, Princess Claude, turns in circles, arms outstretched and gap-toothed mouth open with delight.

He looks away again before anyone can see him watching, any wistfulness tamped down hard. He has learned that though there are no rocks thrown here at court, there are looks, and whispers, and laughter only half-hidden; and so he does not aspire to join the other children, only to be overlooked by them. There is only his head ducked low, shoulders drawn up near his ears, and the frantic whisper inside his head: *Just let me be. Please, please—just let me be.*

But footsteps break away from the throng, tripping across the stones of the courtyard. Petrus feels each one shudder up his spine. They stop; above his own breathing he can hear, as if from very far away, the muffled shouts of the others at play. Then:

"Are you a werewolf?"

Petrus swallows; turns slowly. A boy stands a few paces away from him, dressed vibrantly in red trunk hose and a deep blue, sleeveless doublet. He has the look of someone prepared to run away, if necessary, all his weight kept firm upon his back foot to keep him a little more removed from Petrus. Petrus licks his lips.

"Do you speak?" the boy says after a moment. "I thought they said that you can speak."

"I can speak."

A little of the tension leaves the other boy's shoulders. "Are you truly a werewolf?" he says, almost eagerly now. "That's what many call you, but that isn't the story I heard."

Werewolves serve the devil. They eat small children. If they are caught, they are burned until nothing of their evil is left. Petrus's teeth sink into the soft wet inside of his cheek. The story King Henri prefers, which the blue-eyed man told him while Petrus—still merely Pedro, then—crouched in his cage, and which Petrus never refuted, was not so horrifying; or at least, it horrified and fascinated listeners in a different way. He had been tamed; taken from his savage homeland and brought to France to be civilized and live among the French nobility, to learn their language and to love their God.

This last bit His Majesty kept in the story even after discovering to his surprise and delight, from Petrus himself, that his wild boy had been baptized as an infant. Even after they sat for the first time together at Mass and Petrus knew when to kneel and when to stand and how to take the holy communion.

"I am not a werewolf," he makes himself say now.

The boy nods. "I thought perhaps not, though they"—with a jerk of his head to indicate the other children—"say you are. You seem very calm. Not so frightening as a werewolf." He edges a little nearer; Petrus tries not to stiffen. "I am Ludovico Gonzaga," the boy says, and now he is smiling a little. "Well, Louis, here."

At once, Petrus recognizes the lilt to the boy's French; it is similar to the queen's. "I am Pierre," he says, which sounds less stiff than Petrus.

Ludovico tips his head, studying Petrus as a painter studies his subject. Then a peal of laughter from across the courtyard draws his attention away; he glances at the other children, a few of whom are staring openly at the odd sight of the two boys talking together; then back to Petrus.

"I think I am wanted," he says; hesitates, as if he would say more; and then hurries away. Petrus's belly cramps a little, and he presses his mouth tightly closed.

And then Ludovico turns back, dark eyes flying to Petrus, hesitating, as if pulled by strong cords in two opposing directions.

Petrus had no friend on Tenerife. It was only himself, and Isabel, and Manuel, a sturdy little three-legged stool. The other boys ignored or teased, drew back from or beat him. So now he holds his breath inside his puffed cheeks as something seems to tremble, just out of his reach, dappled, as if by sun through trees, so that he cannot entirely make it out. He only knows that it is *there* and he *wants* it. And then Ludovico stumbles a little toward Petrus where he stands, breathless, and shrugs as if to say, ah, well, fate. What can we do? And he turns his back upon the other children and returns to Petrus, mouth quirked up on one side.

"Want to come down to the pond and look at the fish?" he says.

There is a cracking, then, all along the length of Petrus's body. He is a conker, all sharp green husk, and this boy with curling dark hair and sheepish smile has split him open without even noticing the pricks of his spines. As if it were the most natural thing in the world, he has fished out the sweet nutty flesh inside the shell, so that Petrus feels himself naked and bewildered, following him at a run, the wind of his swiftness ruffling over his head and whistling in his ears.

Chosen, it sings. *Chosen, chosen, chosen!*

MANY MONTHS LATER, HE and Ludovico rest together on the ground. Their arms shield their eyes from the brightness of the late afternoon sun; their mouths release their hopes into the blue-white sky, into the ear of God.

"I will be one of His Majesty's gentlemen of the chamber." Petrus breathes in the summer scent of grass, of warmth, seeing himself splendidly dressed, one of King Henri's most trusted confidants, attending to him in the mornings when the king is still warm with sleep, hair rumpled, human.

Ludovico's voice breaks through the image. "And?"

Petrus shifts onto his elbow, looks at his friend, who chews on a blade of grass. "And?" Petrus repeats.

Ludovico keeps his eyes on the sun-hot heavens. "And what will you do, as one of the king's gentlemen of the chamber?"

Confusion. "Do?"

A sigh; a slight smile, with only one side of his mouth, the side without the dangling grass blade. A beard has only recently begun to grow above his top lip, in sparse patches around his mouth, the hairs delicate as spiders' legs. "What do you want to gain from the appointment?" A sideways canting of his eyes, squinting up at Petrus's face. "Or—is the appointment itself all you want?" Incredulity; disapproval. Those narrow eyebrows curving upward. "To help His Majesty dress? To hold his pot for him?"

Petrus wants to be in the king's company; to know himself needed, wanted, trusted. To have a position that will command such respect; to be useful, and not merely hairy. Anything beyond is—it is as if he is peering into the ocean, knowing there is life at the bottom, but too far away to see it.

"What would you do?" Petrus says.

"Oh, that's easy." Ludovico spits out the grass blade and sits up. "I'd help His Majesty keep his power—there are always, always people trying to take it, and a king cannot hold it alone. He needs advisors—even you, with your shoulders that hunch up to your ears whenever talk turns to politics—even you must see that advisors are nearly as powerful as the king himself."

Yes, of course Petrus knows this. The king has his favorites, men to whom he turns for counsel. And everyone knows about the troubles between the Catholics and the French followers of John Calvin, who call themselves Huguenots; whose manner of worship, the king has decreed, cannot be tolerated in France.

Ludovico grins. "I can never hope to be king—haven't the bloodline for it. But I can be powerful. I'm smart, I can puzzle my way out of nearly any corner. I understand"—with a sudden gravity to his words, his tone, which makes him seem a much older boy, a man even, those spider hairs that trail now across his cheeks grown in thick—"how to . . . influence. How to use what I know of people's heads to my own purposes. Like when Guillaume was taunting you last week? And all the others followed his lead? I told some of the other boys that Guillaume had been whispering poison in his father's ear, and his father dripping it into the ear of the king. That he was trying to keep them from getting top positions at court." Ludovico leans back upon his elbows, crossing his legs before him at the ankle. His grin is quick, like the flash of light upon a blackbird's wings, showing all the blues and greens hidden within the gleaming feathers. "Did they not turn on him instantly? Did he not stop bothering you?"

They did; he did. Petrus stares, dumb and silent. And then his own smile begins.

"Am I the king, then, in this story?" he says. And laughs long and loud when the red creeps up his friend's cheeks.

Pedro

He has been at court nearly seven years when the king calls for a sparring match.

It is a summer's day, so warm the very air is thick. Moisture beads upon the courtiers' brows and noses. Petrus is by now well accustomed to his place here, among these people, these fine things—accustomed to playing the lute for Queen Caterina and her ladies; accustomed to reciting upon command for the amusement of King Henri's guests. His muscles know the weight of a sword from years of practice in the sparring yard, first with the other children at court and later with guardsmen and other grown courtiers. And so he stands easily when the king commands; bows; waits patiently for His Majesty to gesture to some other courtier to take his place opposite Petrus.

But the king himself rises from his place on a blanket beside his mistress, a sly smile curling his long mouth.

"Let us see," he says, "how we two kings fare against one another." His tone all full of light, of easiness; and yet Petrus suddenly cannot bring enough of the summer-sodden air into his chest.

His Majesty calls for swords, and servants come to drag away blankets, to shift the platters of food that, in the heat, are mostly untouched. Courtiers rise, chattering together, everyone clearing a circle of trampled space for the impromptu bout. One servant divests King Henri of his doublet; another presses a sword into Petrus's sweating palm. Dimly, above the distracting thrum of his nerves, Petrus realizes that it is only a light practice sword, its tip softly rounded.

The king sees him looking at the sword and laughs aloud, the sort of unrestrained, lighthearted laughter which so seldom comes from his throat. "Don't look so nervous!" he says, and raises his own sword. "You're not going to kill me."

Petrus licks his lips, attempts a smile. The king shakes his head, fond amusement turning the harsh lines of his face into something soft and gentle. It is this look, the sort Petrus imagines a father might give a beloved son, which always makes him feel that he would do anything for this man, this king.

"Your Majesty has me at a disadvantage," he says, attempting to infuse his voice with a merriness to match King Henri's. "You've a few years of experience beyond my own."

King Henri raises one dark brow. "Do you call me *old*?" And before Petrus can respond, he adds, grinning, "Well, in that case, let us see which triumphs: civilized *maturity* or savage youth, hmm?" And with a flick of his sword, the bout is begun.

Petrus has little time to think; there is only the memory inscribed upon his muscles from countless hours of practice; the sweat trickling into his eyes, and down his chest, and dashing between the bones of his spine; the clang of blunted steel; the harshness of his breathing, and of the king's. His rushes, and thrusts, and parries, all on the strength of his training, forgetting, as his opponent swings and spins with a grunt of exertion, that his opponent is *His Majesty*. All thought is focused upon the ringing of their blades, the delicious ache of muscle and the hot air upon his face.

And then—the king stumbles. Only a little—only for a moment—but it is enough time to allow Petrus to touch his sword to the hollow of His Majesty's throat. There is silence, suddenly, but for his own ragged breaths and the faint echoes of their swords' final clashing. Petrus fixes his eyes upon the king's pulse, beating strongly beside the rounded tip of his blade, though nowhere near so quickly as Petrus's own suddenly bolting heart.

King Henri blinks. And then he lets out a roar of delight.

"Savage youth, indeed!" he says, grinning. "It is clear you are truly a man now. You have earned a man's position in my household, I think."

The king's household is huge and varied. His Majesty requires private secretaries to assist with his correspondence, cupbearers to bring him wine, gentlemen of the chamber to help him dress. These positions are filled by noblemen or artists, men whom the king wishes to have close to him. With such positions comes power—for they are only given to those whose requests His Majesty is prepared to entertain—as well as a salary from the crown's coffers.

For a moment, Petrus imagines himself slipping a doublet over the king's shoulders; writing out the king's thoughts in his most careful hand. And then he shakes his head as courtiers surround them both, showing their teeth in tight grins like a parody of His Majesty's honest joy. It is better to assume the king's words were idle praise, and that he had not meant them as promise.

WHEN PETRUS ENTERS THE palace kitchen for the first time, that vast space of heat and spices, the spit boy stares, forgetting for long moments to turn the meat so that the fat drips into the fire, making it sputter and hiss. A kitchen maid, reaching for a pot, burns her fingers red and shiny in her inattentiveness when she spies him.

"Rustics, the lot of them. Haven't seen anything to match you," one of the cooks says, snorting, and Petrus is for once too nervous, and too swollen with his own newfound importance, to care about the stares.

"New bread carrier, are you?" the cook says, and Petrus nods, small and tight, a smile pressing behind his lips, aching to burst forth. His Majesty had meant his words, after all.

The cook hands him two loaves and Petrus wraps them in a cloth as lovingly as he might wrap a child, placing them upon a plate of silver. Then he hurries from the kitchen, past a maid chopping spinach and another rolling pastry dough. His footsteps are as quick as he can make them without being so fast he risks stumbling. Corridor after corridor, from the humid kitchen to the chill of the upper floors, holding the loaves against his chest, both to feel their heat and to give them some of his own, that His Majesty might have warm bread for his breakfast.

HE HAS SEEN ENOUGH of bread bearers in his years at court to know the panting of their breath from the long rush up from the kitchens; to know the way they sometimes bend toward the king to murmur in his ear. He used to wonder, before the position was his, what he might have asked, his lips so near the royal ear, his body humbly bent. But when the time comes to take his place beside the king, to offer warmth and nourishment, to stand beside His Majesty's chair as he breaks his fast, Petrus finds he has nothing to ask for, too grateful for a position that pays in coin and respect alike. He has coin to spend—coin that he has *earned*—for the first time; and he has a place at court, a defined place, a place that shows all the world that Petrus Gonsalvus is more than his hair, more even than his ability to recite Latin. He is a favorite of the king, and he finds himself merely happy to be seen so, and to have others among the king's company step away, make space for him, that he might set the loaves upon His Majesty's table.

Pedro

For a time after coming to the court, a little hope grew, tender as a spring crop, inside Petrus's chest. So tender was this hope that he did not allow himself to put words to it; he experienced it in bursts of warmth, in quick images of himself on one of France's great ships. In the images he stood on the deck, King Henri beside him, one hand upon Petrus's shoulder and the other shading his eyes as together they scanned the horizon. And then the green height of Tenerife's hills came into view; and then suddenly the ship was near enough that Petrus—Pedro once more—could leap from it and splash joyously through the brisk salt water to the beach, where Isabel waited for him.

When he came to France, he was given all his fine new clothes and a little chamber entirely to himself. For months and months, alone in his room, he could not sleep. He lay in his bed and could not relax into its softness. His spine arched; his shoulders and neck were stones. He wanted to cry—his throat was full and prickling; the place where his jaw hinged ached with kept-back tears. But the tears would not come. Every night passed the same way—the room, *his* room, and silence.

When he could stand it no more, he would rise and pad to his window. When the moon was bright, he could see down into the courtyard. During the day, servants and couriers scurried back and forth across the courtyard from one wing of the palace to the other, but at night it was empty and silent, its rows of symmetrical arches from rooftop to ground making echoing shadows in the moonlight. Manuel would love the architecture; he would bore Pedro and Isabel to sleep with his explanation of the builders' genius. If only Manuel were here now, Pedro always thought, he could finally sleep. The thought made him smile; made him remember nights on Tenerife, when his own nighttime breath mingled with Isabel's and Manuel's in their single room.

During the day, he does not let himself think about *before*; he shakes off memories of Tenerife like a dog shaking off water. Sometimes from nowhere, even now after years, he feels the building of tears behind his temples; but amidst the rush and glitter of the days at court he can distract himself, keep them from falling.

But at night, *before* creeps in where sleep will not. It creeps in and fills him up, stuffs him to sickening with nevers.

Sea air he will never feel, hills he will never climb, a nook he has long since outgrown, lost to him forever. Ropy arms that will never again enfold him. Parents he will never find.

He stuffs a fist into his mouth.

Never, ever, ever. Never again.

Part Two

Marriage

CHÂTEAU DE FONTAINEBLEAU

1571

Pedro

It has been years and years since anyone called him La Bestia. Neither do they call him Pedro. Here in France he has been Petrus since that day in the *salle* when the late king proclaimed him a clever, a *thinking* human being, the name under which he was baptized cunningly altered to shake off its Spanish influence. A joke, at first; gentle enough from King Henri, but less so in the mouths of his courtiers. So funny, the little hairy boy lisping Latin verbs. But he likes to think its dignity suits him now.

Of course, sometimes he is not Petrus; he is Pierre. Pierre Sauvage. Another clever twist on Pedro, this one purely French.

And purely cruel, says Isabel inside his head, spitting each word. *Purely ignorant*. Usually, he is able to ignore her; but some days—like today—it is difficult.

He does not think of his old life very often anymore; the French court has beaten it out of him like dirt from a carpet, leaving in its place a different past, one woven of interlacing fibers of fact and figment. But he has woken this morning—his wedding morning—to a chest stuffed tight as if with flock and an ache for the woman who raised him.

Isabel, he thinks, lying in the near-dark. He so rarely thinks of her anymore that her sudden name is like a blanket thrown across his face; he sucks in air, just to prove that he still can. *Isabel*. Isabel, with her gruff patience and her grumbling. Isabel, whom he has not seen for almost twenty-five years; who will not be sitting in the chapel today, watching as he is wed. Whose name—Isabel—was not even truly hers, forced upon her by the Spanish who conquered her island. Isabel, who was old even when he was a boy, and who is probably long dead.

He remembers his toes in the sand the day he left her, in the surf. The warm lapping of the waves, like the tongues of friendly dogs. The trail of his footprints on the cool hardened shoreline. These are memories as clear as the tips of the waves themselves, caught in his mind like beetles under glass, every moment of that day on the beach there for him to examine, even from this great distance, whenever he closes his eyes. His footprints are still distinct as the blue-green rainbows of the pinned beetles' shells.

By contrast, so many of his memories seem removed and unreal as half-recalled dreams. In his worst moments, he thinks he imagined everything from *before:* that Isabel's hands, with their big rolling veins and their palms and fingertips all stained with dyes, never smoothed the hair back from his brow; never rubbed his back during thunderstorms. That he never walked barefooted upon the black gritty beach on Tenerife; never ran quick as a darting fish along twisting streets, the sun hot on his head and shoulders. He has told the false story of his life so many times that its falseness has been smoothed out and worn down, like the soles of shoes that have walked too far.

PETRUS RISES, NOW. HIS bare feet touch the skin rug spread across his chamber floor. It is made of several skins stitched together to form a larger whole, gray and brown and dun and white-spotted; they shield his feet from the chill but are too thin and worn to do much else, the sleek fur rubbed away in places to shiny patches by a quarter century of his footsteps. The court moves frequently, from palace to palace across the country, according to the king's whims or his need to be seen by his far-flung subjects, and Petrus's skin rug has always appeared in whatever chamber he is assigned. Like the queen mother's retinue of dwarfs, who travel with their own miniature everything, he has had his skins to make the French court more comfortable for him. More home-like.

He wonders what his wife will make of them.

You will have a beautiful wife. A fine new chamber. A soft new bed. Her Majesty made many promises when she told Petrus of his impending marriage; later today, servants will come to bring his things to some larger chamber, suitable for a man of the court and his new bride. Yesterday, he made certain that his best clothes were brushed, his finest ruff perfectly white. He bathed with fragrant Venetian soap, trimmed the hair at his chin and jaw so that it lies now like a short beard. Not so neat as King Henri's beard once was, but tamer than the drooping locks of his childhood, which grew from his cheeks in strands as long as the hairs on a girl's head. Whoever the poor woman is, he will not dishonor her by looking worse than he must.

Most days, he does not bother to look at himself in the small, round mirror hanging on his wall. There is no need. His fingers suffice to find snarls in his hair; his comb to smooth them. He keeps his clothing neat and in good repair; there is no reason to look at himself in it. Vanity, that's what mirrors are for; and he has little enough of that.

But this morning, he looks. Tentatively, like a man edging, belly-down, toward a cliff drop to peer over the edge. The dizzying sensation of being uncertain whether he wanted to see that long, jagged fall. The swooping beauty and danger of the world from such a height.

But there is no fall when his eyes meet their reflection in the mirror. There is only his face, slightly distorted by the warp of the glass. He touches his cheek, his temple, his brow—all thickly covered in hair—then looks down at his hand. The nails precisely trimmed so that not the smallest ledge grows beyond the boundary of his fingertips, the palm smooth. The back softly furred. He thinks, just for a moment, of his hands unlacing his bride's gown, then looks again into the mirror, where his eyes gaze back at him, blank and sheenless.

HE WALKS WITHOUT AIM for a time while the morning is still newborn and there is no one but sleepy-eyed servants and yawning guardsmen to see him. It is raining, the grounds of the palace churned and flattened by a thousand sharp droplets, the tall windows running with water, leaving the world outside a colorless smudge. Petrus's shoes sound too loud on the stone steps, and he pauses for a moment, waiting for the echo of them to fade, listening to his own harsh breathing. The stairs spiral like the shell of a hermit crab; standing as he is near the center of the delicate curve, he feels himself one of those reticent creatures. For the moment, safe.

Somewhere within this palace, beyond the shelter of this smooth stone wall and the sweep of these stairs, is his wife-to-be. *Catherine Raffelin*, the queen said, and the name repeats now through Petrus's skull as the only thing he knows about her, this woman who will be his wife; a reverberation of certainty attempting to out-clamor all the clamorous uncertainties. Assuming no terrible troubles on the roads, she will have arrived yesterday from Lyons, after enduring a journey of days in order to wed him. To wed *him*.

He remembers with sudden dread the wedding of two of Her Majesty's favorite dwarfs—a rowdy procession, the bride so draped in jewels she half-blinded onlookers in the winter sunlight; feasting and dancing that went on and on, a giddy whirlpool of wine and music. The new husband and wife dancing a galliard before the eyes of all the court, though he was clearly drunk and she well on her way. The rousing songs as they were effortlessly lifted, feet kicking in feigned foolishness, acting their part, and carried off to bed.

Let it not be like that, he thinks. Eyes closing briefly. It has been several years since he has been asked to play a part in one of the court's entertainments—mock battles, mock sieges, mockeries made of them all. Once, he was made to play a wolf-man attacking a castle. He was meant to pull a lady from a tower that had been built of wood, painted to look like stone, and rolled into the grand ballroom on wheels like a cart's. Though the lady must have known it was all an act—though she herself was part of the act—her face twisted with true panic when he appeared over the rampart; her scream was genuine. Petrus's entire body shuddered with shame as he pretended at ferality, face buried in the lady's neck as if he meant to tear her throat out, half-dressed in breeches and nothing else, the hair covering his arms and back, chest, belly, and calves exposed to all the court, gleaming in the brightness of all the fat candles. It was with relief that he relinquished the lady to her rescuers, allowed himself to be heaved from the tower by King Charles in his shining armor. The tower was not so tall that the fall truly hurt, and yet tears drew up from his lower lids like dew from dawn grass.

He begins walking again, his vision narrowed to a sliver just broad enough to let him move without falling, without blundering into walls or doorways. When he pauses at last, he is standing before a stone sculpture set into a wall: two women, nymphs perhaps, smooth-limbed, and rounded like jugs of wine, framing the head and torso of a curly-headed, curly-bearded man, with two horns jutting proud from his skull. Though his legs have not been sculpted, a goat head and two delicate hoofs have been hewn above him, as if to ensure that no one viewing the work might mistake him for anything too near to human. The nymphs' necks arch and turn, their gazes shifting away from the goat-man between them. Their hands clutch the gilded edges of the frames of paintings to either side of them; they hold themselves as far from the inhumanness of the satyr as they possibly can.

Petrus finds he cannot look away. *A beautiful wife*, he thinks again. *A beautiful wife. A fine new chamber. A soft new bed.* Looking at the wretched satyr now, and at the nymphs' desperate, clinging hands, the bow of their bodies toward the painting frames and away from the goat-man, his chest goes tight to the point of hurt. Oh, let his wife not be beautiful; let her be a plain woman, someone who can bear to look upon his face as the nymphs, who owe the sculpted perfection of their faces and bodies to the gods who sired them, cannot bear to look upon the satyr, for all that his parentage is no less prestigious than their own. A widow, perhaps, he thinks; a widow with years of laughter etched beside her eyes. Someone who would have little enough hope for a handsome husband, and might be easily reconciled to one as unnatural as he; and who might also find in all his education a source of respect. Someone who will not turn from him.

PETRUS WAS SEVENTEEN, BY the court physician's count, before he lay with a woman.

His friend Ludovico was not wed then, and so did not yet hold the title of Duke of Nevers. He liked to tease Petrus about his fear of women, though never seriously; he knew his friend's prickles, having spent the five years since he came to court observing the other children who were fostered at court by turns ignoring and taunting the strange, hairy boy whom King Henri had, inexplicably, thrown into their midst like a goat into a flock of starlings.

"The court is full of opportunities, even for someone like *you*," Ludovico liked to say, with no meanness, only his usual cheerful honesty. "The *courtisanes* would be mad for you, with all that hair; or at least, they'd do a fine job of pretending. Such, after all, is the art of love." He spoke with a casual knowing that rankled a little, being, as he was, two years Petrus's junior.

It was true enough that many of the women with whom Ludovico and the other young men of the court spent their time approached Petrus occasionally, curiosity in their eyes and avarice in their smiles. King Henri's favorite marvel, his very best gift, the boy on whom he lavished the same tutors who educated his own children; surely, that boy must have a few coins in his pocket aching to be spent. But he shook his head at them all, glad, for once, that his hairy cheeks made it impossible to read his blushes.

The woman with whom he finally lay had thin dark hair, lank with oil and smelling of her unwashed scalp. Her face was pinched, and a stain, purple as wine spilt across a linen cloth, dashed from the sharp corner of her jaw, across her throat, and down to the knob of her shoulder. The mattress to which she led him bristled with straw and rustled with other creatures. Ludovico remained behind, sipping sweet wine in the crowded main room of the tavern, with the lamps casting a greasy, smoky pall over the room. A smile twisted his mouth as Petrus sent a quick, desperate look over his shoulder before following her up the creaking stairs, and he raised his glass, as if to say, *You wished to be far from court for this, my friend.*

This tavern, in a narrow building on one of Paris's many twisting side streets, was as far from the luster of court as he could wish without actually resorting to a quick poke in the shadows out in the street itself, with the aroma of piss and refuse surrounding them like bed curtains. The woman took his coin and lay without flinching on the stained mattress linen. She did not flinch, either, when Petrus's face showed full in the light of the dripping candle stub, nor when he could not decide how best to go about their business together. She took him and led him where he needed to go, mumbling appreciative nothings about how virile he must be, to be so hairy. Her breath stank of rot, and her voice trailed off indifferently once he was hard enough to get where he must; but still, he fell asleep that night, back in his bed in the Château du Louvre, thinking about her hands fearlessly touching him, and dreamed, for the first time in years, of Tenerife.

HE HAD A PICTURE, once, of a woman like himself. A pamphlet, thrown at him by one of the noble boys fostered at court, and inside a rough woodcut of a girl. *Look*, the boy said. *A monstrous wife for a monstrous boy.*

Petrus kept the picture. He secreted it, crumpled in his fist, back to his chamber and looked at it from time to time. The girl was certainly not beautiful according to any of the usual definitions of beauty; but still, he looked and looked, the truth of her loosening something inside his chest. She was naked, her breasts small and round and hairy. Her legs long and hairy. He was old enough that the cushion of her thighs stirred him. For a foolish while that lasted years, he loved her.

FOR ANOTHER FOOLISH WHILE, he loved the Princess Claude, who was born the year he came to France; loved her for her twisted foot and the hump on her back. All her life she was teased out of range of any adults by other children, and he always looked away from her tight mouth and reddened eyes. Hid himself among the hedges, that they not turn upon him as well with stones in their voices.

Once, just once, he spoke, years after he'd had his first woman. The princess was herself then just budding toward womanhood. Petrus did not speak in the presence of her tormentors, under no illusions that she would welcome the wild man as her public *chevalier*. But he came upon her weeping, and saw the cluster of children in their bright doublets and swishing skirts just disappearing from view, and said, all in a tumble, "You do not deserve their cruelty."

A startled look, a straightening of her back as well as she could. A tilt of her head.

And then she rose and walked away without speaking, all dignity despite the unevenness of her steps, which set the width of her skirt to crookedly swaying. Leaving him to the splashing of the nearby fountain and the grainy rush of his own breath.

She was married to a duke later that same year.

Pedro

Ludovico finds him there, looking up at the nymphs, and at the satyr they refuse to see. Petrus sees him coming from the corner of his eye, marks his familiar easy gait, the brightness of his cap and hose. His friend often rises early to be with the king, who likes to get much of the day's business out of the way early, before he feels too unwell, falling into listlessness. Petrus would once have envied Ludovico his respected position, one of only a handful of courtiers thoroughly trusted as advisors by His Majesty; but this king is nothing like his father. This king is not someone in whose shadow Petrus longs to bask, as if it were sunshine.

Of course, Ludovico would no doubt remind him that the king's temperament is irrelevant; he is *king*, and that is reason enough to seek a place by his side.

When his friend stops beside him now, Petrus glances his way, smiles tight but does not speak. He cannot; all his feelings, the churn of them, the boil, are caught behind his breastbone, making his breath come short.

Ludovico stands beside Petrus for a short time without fidgeting, before giving over to his natural inability to be still.

"That fellow could be your twin, near enough, if you were unlucky enough to be horned," he says, nodding toward the satyr.

This is, of course, what Petrus himself has been thinking. But still he says, "He looks more like you, old friend," with a small sideways smile. It's true enough—Ludovico's hair and beard curl every bit as riotously as the goat-man's.

His friend chuckles. "I'd like to be a satyr. Wine, and dancing, and women—what more could a man want from life?" He grins in a parody of lechery, and Petrus laughs, the sound startled, half-choked, from his throat. Better, truly, to be a satyr than to be one of the other creatures to whom he himself has often been compared. Satyrs, at least, do not eat their victims, only ravish them.

Ludovico leans one elbow on the wall, upon one of the nymphs' smooth carved thighs. "I saw your wife."

Tightness in his chest again. "When? Where?"

"Yesterday. Around dusk. I was with—well." A little smirk. "It hardly matters who I was with."

Petrus's brows rise; Ludovico ignores the implied question.

"But we were out for a stroll, and we saw the coach arrive. I think it must have been her—she'd a fine trunk with her. And an old man."

"And?" Petrus curls his fingers into his palms, lets his short nails bite into the soft flesh there. "What is she like?"

His friend leans his cheek upon his hand, smiles sideways at Petrus, teasing. "Aren't you the curious one?"

Petrus merely looks at him; to give in to his teasing will only prolong it.

Ludovico sighs. "Very well. She is young and lovely." With his free hand, he makes a fluttering motion in the air. "Hair like gold, cheeks like roses. That sort of thing." He raises both brows. "You are a very lucky husband. Luckier than I—Henriette is unpolished silver compared to this girl."

Ludovico's wife remains in Paris with their children while her husband travels with the king, keeping his place, his influence.

Petrus's head shakes. "No—"

"No?" Ludovico laughs. "What 'no'? No, she is not young, beautiful? Or no, you do not wish her to be so?" When Petrus is silent, his friend's tone gentles. "Only you would complain of such a thing." He peers into Petrus's face. "The queen paid her dowry, did she not?"

"Yes." Linen, a little gold. Amethysts, purple as fresh bruises, to adorn his wife's ears, should he offer them to her; or to sell, should he not. All brought to him by a servant two days ago. "Her Majesty was most generous." His eyes wander, restless. "But she must be poor, to have no dowry of her own. To think that—" But he cannot expel the words; they sit, like bile, at the base of his throat. It is a small, private sort of horror, the thought of this marriage between a man, hairy as a wolf, and a girl with little choice.

Ludovico releases a strange, low laugh. "She will live out her life at court, surrounded by luxury—such a hardship!" Still his hand remains curled over the ball of Petrus's shoulder. "Do not . . . Do not demean yourself, old friend. You are not such an unworthy prize."

His eyes linger upon Petrus's face until it warms; he squeezes Petrus's shoulder, thumb pressing hard into the muscle before letting go. "She is a lucky wife, Pierre. And women—they are used to doing as they are told, no?" He steps back. "And now—how shall we pass the time until the wedding? A little drink, hmm, to settle your stomach?"

ONE CUP OF WINE becomes two, and would have become three, did Petrus not put his hand over the rim to stop Ludovico from pouring him more.

"I've had nothing to eat," he says, laughing, the wine he has drunk already making him warm, his fingertips tingling. "I do not want to disgrace myself by vomiting on the priest's shoes."

Ludovico sits. "You always were more temperate than I." A pause, his mouth curling above his beard. "Do you remember the night before my wedding? It is a wonder I was able to stand upright in church the next day."

Petrus remembers well, though nine years have since passed. His friend insisted that Petrus join him and several other young men as they wove their way from tavern to tavern. For Petrus, it was a night spent clinging to what shadows he could find, his head ducked that his face might remain hidden by the wide brim of his hat. Furtively watching as Ludovico grew drunker and drunker, toasting his intended's wealth, family, lands. Henriette was heiress to two duchies; it was a match that would benefit both, a political maneuvering that promised to push Ludovico into the waiting arms of power and influence.

"To my wife's purse!" Ludovico cried at last. "May it prove more pleasing than her face."

Petrus winced, but the other men laughed, a flock of merry blackbirds, at the lewd jest. Ludovico spoke this way only when he was with these men, courtiers all, jostling for better position near the king. Never when he and Petrus stood alone on the fringes of a room, waiting for the king to make an appearance; never when they spoke together, with no one else listening. *That* Ludovico, he believed, was the true Ludovico.

And yet—he remembers now, sitting alone with Ludovico in his room, wine warming his blood, how strong his pity was that night, the night before the marriage ceremony, for the woman Ludovico—his greatest friend, his only friend—was marrying.

But Henriette looked calm during the ceremony; Ludovico subdued. Petrus watched from his place among the lesser courtiers, subdued himself, even beyond his usual solemnity. A twist of guilt, for the gladness he should be feeling at his friend's good fortune, which was entirely absent. A sharp twinge in his chest at the sight of his friend leading a wife back out of the church, past Petrus, to yet another place to which Petrus assumed he would never follow.

King Henri used to say he would someday find Petrus a wife. But that was long ago.

A woman of learning, he said. *Someone who can equal you for wits, hmm?*

He spoke not a word of beauty, nor even of finding a woman whose appearance matched Petrus's hair for hair; only of matched interests, of minds as well suited to one another as a foot to a shoe made to fit it exactly.

He spoke as if his wild man was every bit as deserving of a bride as any other man, and Petrus allowed himself, on nights when he could not seem to move toward sleep, when the moon hung golden and suspended, edging, bright as sunlight, through the curtain gaps, to imagine that his king-found wife lay beside him, that her sleeping breaths were in his ears, that he could feel her heat, intimate, at his back. He and this woman would have been joined in one of the palace chapels, the king and his court watching.

But His Majesty died—borne hastily off the field after having his eye gored in a joust, and every warm and solid thing in Petrus's life borne away with him—died before he ever found Petrus his match; and his eldest son died only a year after inheriting the throne. Charles, who became king after his brother's death, has never shown any affection for his father's hairy marvel, or any inclination to think about Petrus's future. He is sickly, and often cross with it; and, too, he was made king when he was just a boy, practically womb-wet—Petrus has watched him grow from a peevish child into a peevish man. Born to privilege, on the one hand, in the most obvious of ways, and yet born, too, with lungs too weak for hunting, or fighting, or even, when he was a child, running with the other children as he so clearly longed to do.

King Henri and Queen Caterina tried for ten years to have children, but her womb remained empty; rumor had it, the king's advisors urged His Majesty to set the queen aside in favor of some other wife, one who could give him a child, an heir, someone to rule when he was gone. The queen, daughter of Lorenzo di Piero de' Medici, had been chosen for her family's wealth, though her dowry payments vanished as if by a sorcerer's trick when her uncle, the pope, died, and a new pope—from a different wealthy family—took his place. Petrus has little enough love for the queen mother, but he cannot think of her as she was—young, seemingly barren, and suddenly impoverished, a queen whose throne was crumbling beneath her—without a lurch of pity. A person whose worth is tied so completely to a small, nicked-out part of themselves—be it dowry, or beauty, the lines of their blood or the fullness of their hair—must feel precariously perched, always in danger of wavering toward penury, obscurity, earth. Bound for those ditches at the sides of the road, rolled there by capricious fortune.

But then, all at once, the royal couple must have learned some trick, for Her Majesty became with child, and the dauphin was born. And then, one after another, came nine more babes, snicking into the world like beads onto a string. Ten children in all, birthed during a narrow, twelve-year span; and if King Henri still did not seem enamored of his wife, he at least always made sure to leave his mistress's side to be with the queen when her time was upon her.

And yet, there was a frailty to many of the children they made together—the dauphin with his narrow sapling wrists; Princess Claude, with her crooked foot and little humped back; Alençon, whose spine twisted like a seaside tree warped by the wind. King Charles, of course, with his chest that never sounded clear, who had spent his life coughing. And three of the ten infants were gone, faded away, returned to God before they were old enough to speak. The most terrible thing for a mother, for a father, to lose a babe in arms—or the most terrible thing until it becomes necessary to bury a full-grown child, a man with a will and a shining soul. King Henri was spared this pain, for the dauphin died a year after he himself did; Her Majesty bore the unnatural force of it, her face all at once old and pouched after her eldest child's death.

AFTER KING HENRI'S DEATH, when Petrus's position shifted back to the shadows, the edges, he stopped imagining that the wife His Majesty had promised lay beside him at night. When he attended Ludovico's wedding ceremony, the sight of King Charles in his place of honor did not make him unhappy for the wedding he might have had, the bride he might have had, chosen for him by a man who, perhaps, loved him as an almost-father loved a foster son. That pale dream had faded further, and finally died; Her Majesty's choice to breed him at last has not resurrected it.

"Beautiful, you say?" he says now to Ludovico, who half-smiles in sympathy, lifts one shoulder in a lazy shrug, though his eyes are sharp upon Petrus's face. Petrus looks back into his glass.

"Ah, well," he murmurs, and thinks he might be sick after all.

Catherine

Catherine lingered too long in the kitchen in the days before her wedding, and now her fingertips smell of onions.

Their servant Marie scolded, sharp-voiced and anxious as a mother; told Catherine she should be attending to her packing, not dallying in the kitchen over tasks that were no longer hers to complete. But Catherine resisted, leaning into the solidity of the big kitchen table, letting the heat from the cooking fire curl the tips of her hair. "I have plenty of time," she said, and flicked a wrist at Marie's unhappy look. She turned her attention fully to her task, slicing the onions thin for the soup, breathing in their sharpness, and all the while feeling the sights and scents of the kitchen around her like a blanket tucked tight. Her shoulders hunched against the moment she would have to put her knife down and go heavy-footed to her chamber; when the blanket would fall away for good. Her eyes streamed.

Furtive, she raises her fingers again now and sniffs, and yes—onions. Unmistakable. Beyond the doorway of their sheltered alcove, the Château de Fontainebleau hums with sound, dizzies with its opulence. Catherine stands small and stiff and onion-fingered, and cannot concentrate on any of it. She misses Maman with such sudden sharpness in her chest that she thinks, just for a moment, that she is about to die.

Onions stay. Maman always said so, and here it is, the proof, dancing at the ends of Catherine's fingers. *Other smells need only a little soap,* Maman used to say, *but onions, raw and spicy, require thorough scrubbing; and even then, there is sometimes a ghost that remains days later.*

Maman would have scrubbed the cooking smells from Catherine's fingers; or better still, she would never have allowed Catherine near the kitchen in the days before her wedding. She would instead have spent those days readying Catherine for her wedding, bathing her with Venetian soap, brushing scented powder through her hair. She would have done everything that she could to ensure her daughter was in her very best looks, anxious that she not be disgraced before the entire court of France. She would have—

Catherine gives her head a sharp shake. Maman is not here; nor is Marie, with her motherly scolding. Only Papa stands beside her, fidgeting. He tugs at the hem of his doublet, rubs at his jaw through his beard as though it itches, twitchy as a child who has done something naughty and fears being caught. When he feels Catherine's eyes upon him, Papa's own eyes, watery blue and dearly familiar, meet hers for the briefest of instants and then slide away like secrets.

She tries to take in a breath, but it comes raggedly. All through the rattling journey from Lyons to Fontainebleau, she was too distracted by fear to realize that in all her preparations, she did not properly scrub the cooking smells from her fingers, and there is a stone inside her chest, now, heavy and grinding. It is her wedding day—nearly her wedding hour—and she cannot breathe, and her fingers stink—

"You look very beautiful," Papa says suddenly. His gaze still darts, avoiding hers, and he speaks softly. "I should have said so earlier. The gown suits you. Your mother . . . would be very pleased. Very—very proud."

Catherine puts her hand to her ribs; another to her hair. The gown he brought her is green, for love. An optimistic gown, the very color of the earliest, most tender leaves. She is like a painting, one that might be entitled *Allegory of Spring*. Where Papa found it—how he scrounged the funds to purchase it—she doesn't know, and did not ask. He said, once she agreed to the match, that he would provide a new gown—such a pathetic offering, in the face of all that he *should* be providing, and yet she could not bring herself to spurn it. But on her wedding day, her hair should be dressed with more than ribbons of yellow and green. She has arrived at court like a rustic wearing a fine gown for the first time, a rustic with no idea that the gown ought to be the beginning of a young woman's ornamentation, not the sum entire.

She is a softer variation of the countryside beyond Lyons, the fields green with dots of flower colors like splashes of paint, or gold and lush with wheat. All the things she had seen before only on the maps in Papa's office, painted by an artist's steady, diminishing hand.

And then, nearer to Fontainebleau, the rippling green of the forest, slashed with the black of bark. And then the palace, yellow stone walls and dusky roofs sprawled elegant, the broad staircase curling down to either side of the doors. A place that demanded the shine of gold, the flash of jewels. Her breath caught in her throat like a netted bird. Her hands going to her hair and its meager ribbons.

A little dizziness makes her sway, and she closes her eyes. She should have eaten more last night at the inn; should have eaten anything at all today.

"Will I please my husband?" she says when the world stops tilting; and she feels a jolt of surprise at the teeth in her voice.

Papa swallows, loudly. His fingers flutter. "How could you not?" he says. But then he falls silent, with a silence that feels final, the end of all their conversations.

WHEN SHE WAS SMALL, when Papa was home from one of his trips, he would drop his pack and leap down from his horse, dust puffing from his traveling cape, mud clinging to his boots. He'd hold out his arms and Catherine would barrel into them, hit his chest and knock the breath from it, feel herself lifted from the ground and spun, feet raised so she could imagine she was flying.

Later, after dinner, sitting before the fire, *Tell me a story, Papa.*

His hand, calloused from riding, cupping her cheek. His belly soft and comfortable against her back when he pulled her onto his lap. The creak of the chair as they settled into it together.

What sort of story, ma belle*?*

Any story.

A smile, half-hidden behind the cup of wine Maman poured him. *Well, that leaves us with a lot of ground to cover.*

Maman's token protest that it was late, that Catherine should be abed, and Papa's answering protest that their daughter had a tale or two in her. And Catherine always did; she ate Papa's stories up like warm bread. They sustained her between his long trips abroad, though her mind creaked with hunger by the time he finally returned, laden with gifts for her and for Maman. Gifts, and still more stories. He brought the world into their home, impossibly wide and smelling of river stink and road dust and spices.

He spoke of things both prosaic and astonishing: roads so riddled with holes they had to journey entirely over fields; a swindling spice seller. Twins born joined together at the waist, still living when Papa passed through their town and held aloft by the local priest as proof of their mother's heresy; already dead when he traveled back the same way.

A boy brought to court from a far-off, primitive country, the son of a savage king, a prince all covered in hair like a dog, head to toe, a marvelous brew of human and animal who was welcomed by the French king, and then educated, civilized, tamed.

UNTIL HER WEDDING, CATHERINE had never left Lyons. Fontainebleau was a small spot on one of Papa's maps. All her life, she had waved goodbye as her father ventured forth on his sturdy brown mare; had watched the plume in his hat disappear into the thronged city streets. And then, always, she had followed the trail of his intended route on his maps. Whispered the place names over to herself—*Paris, Genoa, Brussels, Basel*—as if they were spell words, and she a witch.

But she never managed to transport herself anywhere, except inside her own head.

Papa's newest clerk, Nicolas, had lately kissed her in furtive courtyard meetings. He professed to be just as ambitious as Papa, too ambitious to sit long behind a desk keeping tally of endless columns of numbers. Like Papa, he dreamed of ships, and fortune, and adventures one after the other like pearls on a string.

"I'll bring you with me, everywhere I go," he had murmured against the tender place behind Catherine's jaw, words humid as all the foreign places contained within them. And then the sweet stretch of muscle and sinew as she reached up to receive his kiss.

She was half with him, there in the courtyard with the kitchen cat folded watchful near the doorway and the forbidden sun hot upon her upturned face—so damaging to pale skin, Maman's remembered admonishments whispering through her mind, warning of early wrinkles, of little brown speckles. And she was half gone, a wagon jolting beneath her, jouncing over rocks and ruts, past the countryside she'd previously seen only on her father's maps, great tracts the greens of emeralds, of sage leaves. The sky unfurled, a bolt of blue silk overhead, and she and Nicolas smelling like Papa when he arrived home from a trip, their skin and clothing crusted with salt water and thick with road dust.

WHEN HER FATHER TOLD her of the lost ship—their fortune, and her own dowry, effectively pulled to the bottom of the sea along with it—he seemed a skeleton of the man she had always known. When he told her he had found a husband for her, despite their ruin, she thought at first, foolishly, of Nicolas. But no—

"Monsieur Gonsalvus," her father said. "He is a learned man. A member of the royal court. The queen mother thinks highly of him, and wishes him to take a wife. It is a good match—a great honor. The queen mother herself suggested you. And she herself will pay your dowry."

Catherine stared. Impossible—every word he spoke was entirely impossible. At last, she managed, "Why?"

"As thanks," Papa said, too quickly. "I have served the court for many years as draper; and, of course, I have never shied away from boasting about my lovely daughter. The queen wants a pretty, intelligent girl for Monsieur Gonsalvus. Who better than you?" He stepped forward, looked down at Catherine's lute, lying round-backed and silent on the chair opposite hers. "Monsieur Gonsalvus plays as well," he said, almost pleading. Her boastful, confident Papa, who never pleaded, whose gambles in business had never lost. Until now.

Catherine looked at the lute, too, looked at it until her eyes watered.

"It's this or a nunnery," Papa said then; and now his voice had a stretched and whimpering quality.

"Is that his name?" Catherine said at last. "Monsieur Gonsalvus?"

"Yes," he said, but his voice fractured. A pause, so long and heavy she could feel cloudbursts of terror at her temples and the nape of her neck. "Everything will be lost, you understand," he finally said, words dragged like enormous stones from a quarry. "Not just your dowry, but this house, my business—the clerks are gone, they have deserted us. I can sell our things, but they will not cover a quarter of the loss. I am so . . . so very sorry. I overreached myself." His big hands pressed briefly to his face.

She did understand, then, though all his words sounded faint and far away. It was an old, familiar story, one she had witnessed many times from a distance: the merchant who tied his fortune to the wrong vessel. The ship dashed apart on some far-off sea. Its cargo lost, silks ruined instantly in the salt water, spices floating upon the surface of the waves, dusting them crimson and yellow before sinking away. The merchant's reputation and fortune lost, too, and the lives of all those whose fortunes were knotted with his forever changed. Families with whom they used to dine suddenly vanished from the city, their big empty houses, all their beautiful things, abandoned to their creditors. She found, now, that she could almost hear the crack of the ship's mast and the screams of the men. Papa seemed to crack as well, a splintery snap of the bones of his spine until he could scarcely hold himself upright. Her head filled with a wailing cacophony of *no* so that she could scarcely hear Papa's next words.

"Her Majesty has been so very generous, ma belle*—offered to pay your dowry—and whatever debt is left once I have paid all I can from what we have—a good match—a good man—high in the queen's favor—"*

Catherine's hands pressed to her breasts; she could think only of Nicolas, his lips, his laughing eyes, his promises. Her father, after all, had also begun his manhood as a lowly clerk. Nicolas and Catherine were both young; they had time, he had murmured against her throat, for him to make his own fortune.

"Papa," she said, "I hoped—"

Her hope was shaped like Nicolas; and breathed his wine-scented breath; and had his empty purse.

When she looked at Papa again, his face was crossed with strange, uncertain lines—lines, perhaps, of pleading; lines, perhaps, of anger. Catherine breathed in, out; tried to blink away thoughts of the boy she thought she would marry. The boy who was vanished, now, without a word.

The clerks are gone, they have deserted us.

A daughter's duty is to obey her father. It is the first lesson instilled in girls by their mothers and fathers alike, by the priests at church. Catherine thought this, over and over; and she thought, too, of her mother, the daughter of a weaver, who would have been filled with joy to see her own only daughter wed to a member of the royal court.

It was this, even more than her father's desperation, which decided her. She nodded.

"Very well, Papa."

But he did not smile, as she expected; if anything, his expression grew more pinched. A hesitation; then he licked his lips and held out his palms. They showed damp in the candlelight.

"Do you remember," he said at last, so slowly that she knew he wished not to say the words at all, "the story I used to tell you, of the little hairy boy?"

A SERVANT COMES AT last to usher them to the chapel. Catherine's limbs are pendulous and uncontrolled as those of a string puppet. A glance at her father's face, and he finally meets her eyes. Wildly, for just a moment, Catherine thinks he is going to tell her he has thought of some other means to extract them from their misfortune—her lips part, her heart jumps—and then he says, "God bless you, my child."

She is entirely outside of herself now. Someone else controls her strings as she moves on Papa's arm down a corridor to the yawning chapel doors, passing people she does not quite see. And then inside, where the benches are only half filled but where it still feels as though the crowd presses, the air thick and full of eyes. Catherine takes in the chapel at a glance, all smooth sculptures and chinks of colored light.

She sucks in air, looks above the staring heads of the others to the priest in all his splendor at the end of the aisle. In her confusion, she does not take in the priest's age or features, only his presence beside the man who will be her husband.

He could have kept his back to her. She would have seen only the soft brown hair on his head then, until the moment she was beside him. But he does not choose to hide himself; he stands stiff and straight, chin raised a little above his white ruff, eyes raised above the heads of everyone assembled, including Catherine, whose feet carry her forward even as her mind struggles to assimilate all the incongruities of his face. From the edge of her vision, she sees Papa's face turn to hers, as if he cannot help it any more than she can help staring at the man waiting for her beside the priest; as if, like a sickness, he must know her reactions.

For her almost-husband bristles with hair—not only on his head and jaw, but all over his face. When she reaches him, he turns a little so that they are opposite one another and looks at her with steadiness. His eyes are entirely human, disorienting in what, at first glance, seems an animal face, and he is short enough that she has only to raise her own eyes a little distance in order to meet them. From outside herself, Catherine feels Papa's arm fall away from under her fingers, and hears the crashing of her own breath inside her ears.

Now that she is standing still, everything else begins to float. The priest's words, and the hairy man's, and her own, which stumble from her tongue. Then it is over, and the people rise again, seeming to hover at the edge of Catherine's vision, ill-defined even when she tries to make them out, a congregation of staring ghosts. She and her husband—oh dear God, dear God, *her husband*—retreat from the chapel to swelling murmurs, his arm inflexible under her palm.

Catherine

The wedding feast is a reeling nightmare of pressing eyes and whispering mouths that seems to go on and on. Catherine and her husband sit silently beside one another as trumpets announce the arrival of each course and musicians play unendingly upon their instruments. In darting glances, she takes him in—there, his hand, its nails brutally short, the candlelight gleaming upon its haired back; there, his face in profile, and it is a gargoyle's profile, a creature's. Only the nose, straight and long, pointed as an arrow at its tip, looks human from this angle.

Once, she catches him as he looks at her, and his eyes are as they were at the wedding, serious and dark. They drop to his plate when she meets them, and he takes up his fork, then puts it down again, his food untouched.

He can speak, Catherine thinks. He spoke at the ceremony, and Papa had assured her that her intended spoke French like a native. *He is a man. He can speak*. But she can think of nothing to say to him; nor, it seems, can he think of anything to say to her. A gathering of worms curls and uncurls inside her belly. She looks around again for Papa but does not see his familiar head, with its ruffle of graying dark hair, among all the others; does not hear his voice, so resonant, over the fluting tones of the courtiers. Catherine thinks, desperate, of how he always kissed her cheek in farewell whenever he left for one of his long trips. The dampness of his kiss; how his exuberance led him to lift her feet from the floor; the scratch of his beard. But now he has gone, leaving her alone amidst the strange, false-seeming gaiety of the court; and though she had not expected any of the old jauntiness from him, she thought he would have a kiss for her, at least.

Though it is large, the room is warm, filled with so many people.

The air smells of meat, of perfumed bodies, and of the ranker odors below the perfume. Of, faintly, the flowers laid at every table. Each table laid also with glazed plates and silver forks; with birds cooked and then redressed in their fine feathers; with spinach leaves cooked in cream, bright splashes of green. Everything further gilded by the shivering flames of candles, their winking reflections caught in the jewels worn by women and men alike, reverberating back and glinting off silver platters and all the broad, shallow glasses filled with wine gleaming purple and gold. Giddy laughter, the clink of forks upon plates, the careless sloshing of wine over the rims of cups and onto the long tablecloths. Even accustomed as she is to parties with fine people, fine food, music and dancing, it is all so *much*, so much of every possible thing, of food and gold and music and wine, all of it unfathomably endless, as if all the wealth and greatness in the world has settled upon this place, these people. There are paintings upon the walls, but Catherine is too dizzied to make them out; when she tips her head back, she sees that every bit of the ceiling is painted and gilded, molded with crescent moons and initials and intricate knots.

Tumblers perform for the king's pleasure, a whirl of limbs and ribbons, though King Charles at his table seems to take no pleasure in anything, sitting as silent as the newlywed couple, sometimes wetly coughing. The woman beside him, though—a fortress of black towering over a retinue of dwarfs—looks at Catherine and her husband, smiling a thin smile.

There is a moment in which Catherine's mind stutters and jumps; and then it catches upon understanding. The woman—who has already turned away, saying something to her son (who is the king, *the king*!)—is the queen mother. The woman who came to France when she was younger than Catherine is now to wed the king-to-be; who brought fine Italian manners to the French court. The woman her own mother revered.

Maman, she thinks, staring at the queen. Her mother used to speak of Catherine's wedding day, of the rich man her father would find for her; of the music, the dancing. All Maman's loving plans, rotted away like Maman's flesh, which was so fair in life.

We will serve ices, of course, she always said. *Just as Her Majesty, Queen Caterina de' Medici, served at her own wedding to King Henri.*

If her mother had lived, Catherine's wedding feast would have brought her such joy.

Maman loved the queen, who—just like she had—came to France from Florence to be wed. That Her Majesty was the daughter of one of the most powerful Florentine houses and Maman was the daughter of a weaver did not signify; she felt kinship between them.

Papa laughed at Maman's romantic notions about the queen.

Do not listen to her, ma petite belle, he would say to Catherine, gathering her onto his knee. *Her Majesty is no saint. I've seen her, don't forget.*

What does she look like, Papa?

Her teeth are sharp and pointed as those on a trap, he would answer. *Her eyes are black as her gowns, the pupils overtaking the irises. She has talons rather than fingernails.*

Maman always clucked her tongue at such blasphemy, and Papa always laughed; and Catherine was never certain whether his words were truth or jest.

Now, she can see that Her Majesty is an ordinary-looking woman, solid as a tree, with a chin that recedes a little into her jowls. She is too stout, now, to ride the horses she once loved so well, and she dresses all in black, mourning always for the long-dead husband who—according to the whispers—never wanted her.

Catherine's husband leans toward her suddenly, and she jerks her eyes away from the queen.

"You've got moon eyes," he murmurs, quietly enough that only she might hear him.

She stares at him—brown eyes, brown hair, mouth appearing from the great thatch of it and looking as if it is trying to smile. "What?" she says.

"'Swallow-the-moon eyes,'" he says. "That is what King Henri said of me in those early days, when I was just arrived at court." He takes a sip from his glass and looks out at the tumblers, juggling apples in an endless loop. Children, all but one.

His voice is an ordinary man's voice, neither very high nor very low. There is no growl in it, no animal threat. She tries to steady herself on the sound of it.

"I used to feel that this was all for me," he says, as if to himself, his eyes on the tumbling children.

His words, the wistfulness in them—she can almost see him as a boy, looking about him in wonder. Almost. Catherine opens her mouth; closes it again. Looks down at her plate, and feels her belly clench.

One of the queen's dwarfs, garbed in a monk's robe, clambers suddenly onto the table where Catherine and her new husband sit. His feet rumple the fine cloth and endanger the plates and glasses as he steps over them, the hem of his habit raised to show each weaving footfall. He stops directly before them and crouches, face near enough that Catherine can see the white threaded through the red of his beard and the fine bursting of broken vessel across his nose and cheeks. Leering, he says, "How *happy* a bride you seem, Madame Sauvage. And so beautiful—a fitting contrast to our wolf man, hmm?"

Her lips part; her cheeks prickle as if with sudden sunburn. The dwarf fixes his eye upon hers, raises his glass and cries, "*To Madame Sauvage!*"

His cry is taken up by others in the feasting hall, sluggishly at first then spreading until nearly the entire room is toasting them. To Catherine's spinning mind, it seems that not a single eye is not turned their way; even the king's lips quirk in faint amusement. Her husband sits stiff beside her, long after the dwarf monk has made Catherine a mocking bow and jumped down from the table; and she sits, too, utterly dumb. With sudden, crushing thoroughness, she thinks she understands how it will be, married to the wild man of the court.

THERE IS A SMALL round mirror on the wall of her new bedchamber, just beside the bed with its shadow-thick hangings. Catherine stares at it, a small, vicious part of her mind wondering why Monsieur Gonsalvus would have such a thing. And even as her mind reproaches her, her face in the glass remains as expressionless as if she were masked.

A dwarf readies her for the night. She is quietly efficient, with sharp dark eyes and nimble fingers. She brushes Catherine's hair, removing the green and yellow ribbons threaded through it one by one, leaving the heavy mass of it loose around her shoulder blades. Undresses Catherine one hook, one lace, one layer at a time. She lets the farthingale drop into itself, pooling on the floor around Catherine's feet, then takes Catherine's hand in her smaller one and says, "Step over it, please, Madame."

Madame. Catherine obeys, stepping out of the circle of hooped fabric, watching, shivering, as the dwarf crouches at her feet and taps her lightly on each ankle, removing shoes and stockings and leaving Catherine in nothing but her thin linen shift, her legs bare from the knee down. Her toes tense against the rug, which is woven in faded reds and blues.

Maman's lack of presence is like a slick river stone. There is the same falling sensation, the world slipping sideways, the ground that was once so solid now lurching out from underfoot. It should be Maman and Marie readying her now. Not this—unknown person.

She shivers as the dwarf smooths a cloth, scented with rosewater, over her arms, down her calves and between her toes. Her breath wheezes tight and fast. She closes her eyes against the sight of the dwarf's pity, and the unfamiliar room.

The dwarf touches her hip, turning her back toward the mirror. "Look," she says, sounding pleased with her work, and Catherine reluctantly does. Her own face looks back, calmer than she feels, paler than usual, her hectic heartbeat sending her blood anywhere, it seems, but into the gentle rounds of her cheeks. The dwarf has smoothed Catherine's hair back again, and the shape of her breasts and darker blush of her nipples shows through the shift's thin fabric.

"So pretty," the dwarf says, and she sounds so much like Maman that Catherine cups a hand over her own mouth to stifle the sudden sob. For the first time in her life, she does not want to be beautiful.

"You've nothing to fear," the dwarf says. She steps back from Catherine, and her smile is small and pitying. "You are so beautiful, Monsieur Sauvage cannot help but be delighted by you. And he is no monster."

Catherine looks down at her. She is actually rather pretty—perhaps fewer than ten years Catherine's senior, with dark eyes and a smooth pale brow, dressed richly as a queen in a gown that Catherine's merchant's-daughter's eyes recognize as costly Venetian velvet, jewels winking at the bodice. It is only her height that is unfortunate; the top of her head reaches no higher than Catherine's waist. Another sob, half-strangled. *Unfortunate* was Maman's word, the one she always murmured when they saw an unattractive woman. It was unfortunate that Madame du Parc had such a long, pointed face, marked so liberally with pox scars, and unfortunate that Madame LeBlanc's sweet-tempered daughter had inherited her father's nose, shaped like a lily bulb, and his pouchy cheeks. Unfortunate that Marie, their own servant, had uneven shoulders, one humped up much higher than the other. As if there could be no happiness without beauty.

Pedro

At the door to his new chamber, he pauses. In his mind are his young wife's cheeks, round and pink; the strong column of her throat, where her heartbeat showed staccato at the tender pulse points. Fear and fear and fear; that is what she felt as she wed him today.

Her Majesty has spared them, at least, the indignity of a rowdy bedding. He is alone outside her door. When at last he gathers the courage to tap upon the wood, there is no response; but he enters anyway, feeling foolish standing in the corridor in his nightclothes.

But he balks upon entering. He'd had some idea that his wife would be tucked up into bed; but she is standing before the hearth, clothed in nothing but her chemise, Agnes kneeling on the floor at her feet, her fingers at the chemise's hem. His wife's hair, unbound, the yellow-brown of autumn leaves, falling to her elbows, all the ribbons gone. The firelight behind her shows the outline of her body through the fine linen she wears and makes sparks of the fine pale hairs on her legs. A sort of magic, from which Petrus forces himself to wrest his eyes.

"I am sorry," he says, and both women look at him, his wife's eyes big, Agnes's laughing.

"Eager, are you, Sauvage?" Agnes says. "Well, you must wait a little longer."

His wife's entire face is red as if the blood moves not under the skin, but over it, and Petrus turns away.

This chamber is larger than his old one, the carved bed wider. It looms opposite the fire, a waiting, monstrous thing. Many of his things were brought here, as he expected—the mirror is his own; so is the wooden cross, and the small hideous painting of the Holy Mother and Child, which he has always hated, and which has followed him to each of his chambers in each of the royal palaces for as long as he can remember. But the rug on the floor, woven in faded reds and blues, is unfamiliar. The sewn-together skins are nowhere in sight.

He smiles a little at his flexing bare toes upon the swirls of red and blue.

Two narrow chairs are drawn up before the hearth, an elbow table between them; another table and two stools butt up against the far wall, where the only window shows the black of the sky and Petrus's reflection, a blur of brown and white. Just faintly, behind his own, are the smudges of his wife and Agnes. He watches the window as Agnes, still kneeling, lifts the hem of his wife's chemise and drops his eyes to the heavy dark wood of the sill when he realizes that she is cleaning between his wife's thighs.

Then Agnes rises, gathers up petticoats, partlet, and the sweet soft green of gown bodice and skirt. She puts them all neatly into an unfamiliar clothes chest, thick with carved scrollwork and blossoms. Petrus turns, watching; pretending he is not. His wife does not look at him, but she must sense his gaze for she shakes her hair forward so that it hangs like a cape over her breasts.

"Ah, God love you," Agnes says.

Inside Petrus's head, waves crash. The girl—his *wife*—looks at him as everyone does who is not accustomed to the sight. She looks as if she would run, half-naked and barefooted as she is, run through the gilded halls and past startled guards, into the grounds and then farther still—past the town, through fields growing brown at the tips as autumn approaches, crashing through forests where the underbrush would catch and tear at her shift like witches' fingernails and nettles would sting her ankles. Splashing through streams where her toes would sink into the silt. All to escape this moment, this life.

He turns away again, and now he does not even watch the images in the window glass. There is a little more bustle, the creak of the clothes chest once more. Footsteps, and the snick of the door opening. And then Agnes says, "The queen will want to see the linen," and closes the door softly behind her.

The waves crash, higher and higher, louder and louder, inside his ears. Dimly, he hears a pop from the fire, and he turns with ponderous slowness to face his wife, his limbs heavy as tree trunks. With one hand, he makes a gesture, half-aborted, toward the bed.

"Should we not pray?" she says, and then does not wait for his response, only kneels beside the bed and sketches the sign of the cross, then bows her head, hands clasped; a fire-lit ode to piety. Petrus stares openly before falling to his knees beside her. Of course she is a Catholic—Her Majesty would not have wanted a Huguenot, a heretic, as part of her son's court. Her lips move silently, fervently, and he watches from the corners of his slitted eyes, his own prayers dead dull things best suited to church and desperation; nothing he feels the need to air each night.

When at last she is finished, she rises clumsily to her feet. Looks at him, and then away.

Catherine

There are pamphlets that circulate widely, depicting woodcut images of all the monstrosities nature or God or the devil could produce. Catherine used to buy them without thought, eager for the thrill of the horrifying. Always, they seemed to confirm her father's most outlandish tales; they showed babes born to unlucky, impious, or indecent women, with two heads on a single body or with eyes on their kneecaps. Giants from the Americas, their heads bulbous, their bodies thickly hewn. Cows born with six legs or forked tails. The images of these creatures always sent thrills of wonder and revulsion through Catherine whenever she saw them; but she also often wondered whether they were faithful in their depictions of these unfortunates. She herself could conjure some horror in her own mind, sketch it—badly—and then take it to a printing house. She could distribute it as truth, and how would anyone know differently?

More thrilling and more horrifying than the monstrous creatures in the pamphlets were tales of werewolves ravaging the countryside, their teeth tearing into human flesh, their tongues lapping human blood. Papa told her of a man from Dole who was burned to death for the things he did in his canine form. He killed a small girl, ate the meat from her arms and thighs, then brought more of her back to his wife for her supper.

Maman would have chastised Papa for speaking of such gruesome things, were she still alive to hear them. But by the time the werewolf from Dole made his first kill, she had been laid in the ground for two long years, dead of a watery chest that settled in from nowhere; and it was only Papa and Catherine left in the house that felt too big now, and no one to mind when the stories he told grew too wild.

IT IS THE WEREWOLF Catherine cannot help thinking of tonight, standing beside the great wide bed, the smooth brocade coverlet. Its body half canine, half human, covered in coarse snarled hair but with limbs like a man's. Its lips pulled back from bloodstained teeth. The plume of its tail, lashing.

Her new husband looks just as she once imagined that monster must have looked, only neater. When he entered their chamber, stood by the window all burnished by firelight, he was utterly improbable; as unreal as a child's fever dream. She cannot think what to do with her hands, and so she keeps them knotted, tight as the balled roots of the apple trees Maman ordered for their courtyard garden.

"Well." Her husband's eyes list to one side. He, too, is dressed for sleep, and she averts her gaze from the terrible hairiness of his feet. Then, just as quickly, she looks back at them, her eyes drawn to his strangeness, devouring it as they once devoured the images and words in the pamphlets. He is moving onto the bed, and now she can see a reassuring flash of pink, human soles.

A breath. Two. After Nicolas kissed her for the first time, she found herself imagining the night of their wedding, even those few moments together having taught her that there was a physicality to love she had not understood before. She had little to fear from her wedding night, she felt, if it were to be with Nicolas.

"How old are you?" comes his voice from the bed. "Her Majesty never said, and I—should have thought to ask. But I did not."

It is almost the first thing he has said to her since the moment of their wedding.

Her throat is stuffed, as if with dry bread; she makes a terrible noise attempting to clear it. "Seventeen," she says at last; and her voice comes out a frog's. A croak. Mad laughter bubbles behind her breastbone; a gasp of crazed mirth bursts from her mouth. The wolf-faced man and the frog-voiced girl; what a pair they shall make. She presses the palm of one hand to her chest; presses her lips tight together.

He exhales. Catherine looks up hesitantly to find him gazing upward. Her eyes trail over his face, her mind trying to take in all the discordancy of his human features so utterly subsumed by hair. Without his ruff and the high collar of his doublet, she can see that the hair thins a little at his throat, so that what grows down from his cheeks and jaw and curves over his upper lip almost looks like a normal man's beard. But it grows too high on his cheeks for the illusion to hold, and grows upward over his forehead and back from there over the whole of his head. His eyebrows are delineated from the rest of the hair only as two slightly thicker tufts, which blend into the hair at his temples.

He has not moved, but his eyes slant sideways; Catherine can see the glint of them in the fire-and-candlelight.

"How . . . how old are you?" she says, because she, too, never asked, and it is impossible, in the shadowy light and the wilds of his face, to tell. Until her father told her the truth about her husband, she had told herself she was prepared for many things—old age, infirmity, even unkindness. She was unprepared for this.

"Thirty-four," he says, and pauses. "Or so."

Catherine's mind dashes in circles for something to say. In desperation, she finally bursts out with, "My father told me you play the lute."

Monsieur Gonsalvus runs a hand over his head. "I do," he says. "Though it has been some time since I practiced."

"Perhaps—you can play for me. Or we can play together—I play as well, you see."

A long look. "Do you wish me to play for you?"

No. "That would be lovely."

Another pause. Then: "Did you—" He coughs a little to clear his throat. "I want to know—were you a . . . willing bride?"

Catherine feels her eyes go round and moonlike once again. "Yes," she says in a whisper, and wonders whether he can hear the truth and lie knotted together in that single word. And then, with a tilt of her chin, other words burst forth with the rush and startle of bats at sundown. "Though it is rather late for that question, is it not?"

A spasm at the corner of his mouth, and his eyes blink slowly closed like a cat's; or like a man steeling himself. "Agnes was right," he says at last. "Her Majesty will want to see the linen."

"Agnes?" she says, and then, "Oh." The dwarf. Catherine had not even thought to ask her name, and her cheeks warm at the realization. Then, belatedly, the rest of his words nip at her, making her cheeks hotter. No one would have asked to see the bed linen if she were married to a clerk like Nicolas, or even to the great rich merchant Nicolas had hoped someday to be.

She flexes her fingers, her toes. Climbs onto the bed beside him. Joins him in staring up at the shadows above.

When he rolls over her at last, it is with a gusty sigh. This near, she can see that his eyelids are as hairless as her own, and that his nose, long and straight, is nearly so, the hair on its bridge shorter and finer that on the rest of his face. His lips emerge like any other man's from the bristle of his beard, but he hesitates before setting them against hers.

Instead, he turns his face to one side so that all she can see, so near, is the blur of his ear, the whorled shell of it, and the dark of hair before and behind. His hand reaches between them, brushing the insides of her thighs, and Catherine's eyes and fists squeeze against what is coming next. She thinks very hard about his feet, that their soles look as ordinary as her own, her heart beating frightened as a hare's, the sort of frantic pace that makes the hare's heart give out.

But she can hear his heart beating, too, beating near her ear in desperate counter time to her own. There is a brief moment of stunned realization—that he is, perhaps, as afraid as she—before the sharp breach.

FOR MANY NIGHTS AFTER that first, their relations happen thus:

May I? he always asks.

Always, she says yes, and then lies unmoving, thinking, too often, of Nicolas—sweet-faced, smooth-cheeked, curly-headed Nicolas—and the heat he brought to her belly with so little effort.

There is no sharp pinch after the first time, only a vague discomfort. She wishes that Maman had been more explicit when she told her what to expect; that she knew now, for certain, that this is how it is meant to be. The flitting beginnings of pleasure she felt when Nicolas kissed her were, she had assumed, only beginnings. Surely, surely there was more to come? Else, why did songs and stories and people themselves make so much of the act of love?

This does not feel like love. He is wordless after the request is made and granted, a pelted, sweltering form, near-silent but for grunts that make Catherine's entire body long to curl into itself; but she is trapped beneath him, and cannot curl or move or do anything at all without making her distaste for the whole endeavor known. With each drive of his body into hers, she thinks, *I—don't—want—this* in echoing rhythm.

Her husband always seems a little embarrassed at the conclusion, as if suddenly aware of the little sounds he has been making, and the mess, and the hideous faces. But the act clearly pleases him enough that he asks it of her again and again.

May I? May I? May I?

So many yeses, each one meaning the opposite.

Pedro

On their first morning together, he cannot seem to find any words for her. Last night, they pressed close together as a limpet to a rock; today, there is a broad space between them. He thinks of the rhythm of his body against hers, how he wished that she would touch him; thinks that they must do it again, and again, until he fills her belly to bursting. It is what the queen wants, after all; why she found a wife for him.

As he pulls stockings and trunk hose over his legs, hiding their great hairiness, he keeps himself half-turned from her where she stands beside her clothes chest. She is running her fingers over the carvings on its lid; Petrus imagines that she would gather them if she could, hold them to her nose like a bouquet of real flowers, breathe them in until the heady scent so overwhelmed her that there was no room for anything else. He thinks of her strange comment last night about playing the lute; the desperate way she spoke, as if scrabbling for purchase, for something solid. Her father, she had said, told her that he plays.

"Who is your father?" he says, lacing the neck of his shirt. Her hand jerks back from the chest's lid, her shoulders jump, and he winces. Abrupt; he was too abrupt.

"You mentioned him last night," he adds, when she merely looks sideways at him. "Her Majesty told me nothing of your family."

Something about her face seems suddenly creased; Petrus wonders, alarmed, whether she might weep. But she says only, "Anselme Raffelin. He is—he was—a merchant, and draper to the queen and her ladies."

"I am sorry," Petrus says. "How long since his death?"

Her eyes dull. "He is very much alive, Monsieur. You must have seen him at church—he gave me to you."

His brows meet above his nose, and she adds, "He is . . . disgraced.

A ship—a ship was lost at sea. Papa had debts, and not even all our fine things could pay them without that cargo."

It is the longest speech she has made since the moment of their bonding, and the effort seems to leave her rather breathless, a palm to her breastbone, fingers curled inward.

Disgraced. Petrus lets the word roll inside his head a moment. It calms him. The daughter of a disgraced man—no matter how beautiful she is—must have some gratitude for any man who would take her for a wife.

And the queen offered to pay her dowry, if she wed him. "Her Majesty must hold Monsieur Raffelin in great esteem."

His wife tucks her lips together and glances away.

They eat together, a meal delivered by servants who arch their necks to see the wild man's bride, who widen their eyes at one another when they see her sitting in one of the chairs before the hearth. She has dressed herself, in a bodice and skirt of stormy blue and a kirtle of gray silk, though her fingers fumbled so with the laces and hooks that, almost, Petrus offered to help her. Only the sight of his hands, the memory of her fright when he spoke earlier, her silence and tucked-in lips, stayed him. She has tugged stockings over her bare legs and feet, but her hair still hangs, a little tangled, down her back.

She is so beautiful that it feels like a jest, a mockery of the reflection Petrus knows he will see if he turns his head toward the small round mirror.

When the servants have left them, she slices neatly into a loaf of bread so fresh it still carries a little oven-warmth. Busies herself with serving them each slices of fig and melon, her eyes on her work, her knife's movements quick and efficient. She has done this before; she is not unaccustomed to kitchen work, to making even slices of fruit, of vegetables. To serving others. Even if her father was wealthy, as Petrus suspects, she still has not been raised to rely entirely upon servants.

Petrus touches the neat slice of bread she has given him, feels the crust and spring of it, the hollow pockets filled with nothing but air. Thinks of how quickly the servant who carried it must have walked to get it from the kitchen to their chamber, still warm.

The words come suddenly, then, in a tone of studied nonchalance. "I was a bread bearer under our king's father," he says. "King Henri. He made me so himself, when I was about your age. Daily, I brought loaves warm from the kitchens to his table."

His wife pauses, a bite of fig halfway to her mouth. He looks at the fruit—the red-purple pulp of it, studded with pale seeds—rather than at her face, her eyes, though he can feel them upon him now. Her confusion thickens the air between them. She does not understand. *Why*, he imagines her thinking, *is he telling me this?*

"It was a great honor," he says, and though they are utterly true, the words sound thin, pathetic. He chances a look at her face and sees only a blank politeness, a little groove between her pale brows, like a line drawn into the earth with a stick.

Catherine

At home, Catherine would have practiced the lute, or sewn, or helped Marie with the cooking. At home, she had Maman, until two years ago; Marie, always; Papa, when he was in Lyons. She had friends she had known since infancy, in whose homes she played while their mothers gossiped and planned the futures of their oblivious daughters.

But at court, her hands lay idle. She managed to save Maman's sewing kit from her father's creditors, tucking it, with its silk thread, its iron needle, its brass pins with their coiled heads, into her clothes chest to bring with her to Fontainebleau. But when she shakes loose a needle, it feels clumsy and unfamiliar as a sword in her hand. When she sets her mother's thimble—brought by Papa from Nuremberg and stamped at the bottom with a swirling pattern—over her finger, tears come fast and sudden, and she puts it away again.

She has no lute, and no energy for playing. The friends with whom she played and danced and whispered and dreamed are all far away; as the days pass, they begin to seem as insubstantial in her mind as the dried leaves she found folded among Maman's linens, herbs meant to sweeten them, to keep away the ravages of moths and the sourness of time; herbs that crumbled almost to powder when she shifted them aside, seeking her mother's scent below theirs. Her old friends must know, by now, of her marriage; the rustle of gossip would have reached them weeks ago. Catherine is glad that she cannot write, for even if she could form the letters to tell them of her new life, she could not form the words inside her head, or bear their strained responses.

Maman prepared her to keep a home; to help her cook prepare food for her family, and to manage the other servants. But here she has no household—no *house*. The days here rush forth like waves: bubbling at the surface with amusements, which hide the stronger, colder waters below. Catherine is plunged into the surge, and finds it easier to let herself be borne along than to fight the pull, however difficult it is to keep her nose and mouth out of the water.

Perhaps, she thinks, if her husband would talk more. But he is near-silent, and she does not know if he is merely disinterested in her, in her thoughts and her conversation, or if he feels, as she does, that his tongue has been hobbled. Does he, too, fear what he might say, if he were to be free and honest with his thoughts?

Catherine watches him, and sees that he does not speak much to anyone else, either. He is, she learns, the king's official reader, though His Majesty calls upon him but rarely. And even then, when he reads to the king, Catherine's husband speaks not a word of his own, but those written down by other men.

In the mornings, she catches glimpses of him when he dresses; she watches from the corners of her eyes as he neatens his hair, feeling with his fingers for knots on his head and arms and chest and attacking them with his little wooden comb. When one snags, he grimaces like any other man might; like Catherine does, herself, when her comb finds a tangle. The hair on his face does not obscure the subtle workings of his features; it is only that he seems careful to show his thoughts and feelings as little as possible.

THEY GO EACH DAY to the king's *salle*, his receiving room in which His Majesty's courtiers mingle, waiting upon his pleasure. The king is thin-faced, narrow-bearded, and only just past twenty, though his eyes are pouched like a much older man's—perhaps from the weight of having been thrust into kingship as a young boy, perhaps from the illness that plagues him despite his physicians' best efforts. Walking with Monsieur Gonsalvus that first day, through corridors where their footsteps lightly echoed, Catherine felt as if she were running through a dream from which she could not wake herself, all the ceilings too high, the corridors too broad. There must have been hundreds of rooms in the palace, a baffling maze, a gluttonous abundance of space. And everywhere they went, eyes followed them, and smirking mouths. They trailed whispers as a blown candle trails smoke.

In his *salle*, where footsteps are muffled by fine rugs, where long tables span the length of the room, their entire purpose to display dishes plated in gold, the king calls for wine that he does not drink; for food that he does not eat; for musicians who play a few notes upon their lutes and horns and violins before he waves them away with a heavily ringed hand. His eyes are ever-moving, his shoulders hunched, as if against an expected blow. He seems as disinterested in the bride of his resident savage as he seems in the savage himself, his gaze floating over them both as if they are no more worthy of notice than the benches and candlesticks. Only occasionally does His Majesty flick a finger in her husband's direction, and her husband always leaves Catherine's side instantly, murmuring to a servant who brings stiffly bound books, stacks them on a carved table set between his stool and the king's chair. Catherine moves as near to them as she dares, listens harder than the king does as her husband produces words from the pages of those books, rolling them off his tongue like drops of wine, fruit-sweet when he reads from books of philosophy, bitter when he reads from the histories that the king seems to prefer. A little life brightens His Majesty's thin cheeks, makes him sit straighter in his chair, when Catherine's husband reads with slow and measured words of the Spanish conquests in the new world across the sea, all the cannibals there subdued by the might of sword and the word of God, spitting the flesh of their enemies from their mouths, dribbling blood, bowing down before those who arrived to tame them, save them. The king twitches with interest, pauses the recitation to ask his reader whether his own people were so fierce as those described in the book he holds in his two hairy hands; whether he had been reared on human meat along with the milk of the beasts who suckled him. Catherine sees the flatness at the corner of her husband's mouth, the subtle tightening of his fingers, and moves away, cheeks hot for him and for herself.

She stands, then, alone and awkward, swallowing and swallowing to release the prickling pressure in her temples. Her husband, very grave, offered her amethysts for her ears on their first morning together; her only jewels, they pull so heavy at her lobes that she cups them from time to time to relieve the weight, though she is glad to have them, to feel as if she almost belongs here. Sunlight glints off the gold-plated dishes, off the gold and silver thread with which so many of the courtiers' gowns and jerkins are embroidered, off the gold and jewels in their ears, at their throats, weighing down their fingers and draped across their chests. She cups her amethysts and thinks of Maman's jewels, sold, gone, snatched away by her father's creditors.

The glances of other women drag like needles over her skin; they look at her, she thinks, as if she, too, is an oddity, the fur her husband bears having somehow tainted her. As if her own skin might sprout fur at any moment.

A very few women are curious; almost friendly, if friendliness it can be called when it smiles with such sharp teeth.

"I *must* know," one lady says, slipping up to her in the long wait of one late morning, with the king not yet arrived and all of them bored and drooping. She puts her mouth very close to Catherine's ear, as if she is about to whisper; but her voice is loud enough to carry down the whole shining length of the room. "Has he a *tail*, our Sauvage?"

Catherine's jaw hangs loose as a cupboard door off one hinge; the lady's laugh is like the twittering of birds. "I suppose that means he *has*," she says, and turns away before Catherine can protest, before she can gather a single syllable into her gaping mouth. When she drags her eyes around the room, they find her husband, standing alone, his face expressionless.

"HOW WILL YOU TAME him?" another woman asks one day; and again, Catherine can think of no witty response.

Later, lying beside him in bed, his snores in her ears, she thinks that she might have said, *He is a man. He has no need for taming.*

She lets the words run around and around her head like children chasing a hoop. *He is a man.*

He is a man when he lies with her as a man does, his face close to hers, his body a hutch around her own. He is a man when he falls asleep after, snoring. He is a man at meals, cutting his food so precisely.

If we have children—

But this thought she will not allow. She kicks its hoop so that it goes flying, and the thought after it.

THE QUEEN SUMMONS CATHERINE for the first time a fortnight after her wedding. Their chamber window shows a gray shelf of sky, and Catherine feels herself go just as gray when the servant at the door announces the summons.

She wears her wedding gown again, the amethysts in her ears. They were, her husband explained, part of Catherine's dowry from the queen—a portion of her worth.

She has seen little of the queen mother except at feasts, and she heard so many conflicting reports of her all her life, most of them from people who have never actually been to court. In the stories, the queen's astronomers work their calculations and watch the wheeling of the stars from their towers, reporting to Her Majesty when they discover anything of import. There are said to be secret compartments in the queen's chambers, where poison waits in glass bottles.

"What is she—what is Her Majesty—like?" Catherine says. She is pinning up her hair, panic in the closing of her throat, the short puffs of her breath. Her amethysts, swinging from her lobes, are too little, she thinks—too little richness for a formal meeting with a queen. Her chest is tight; she leans toward the glass, as if to see the glimmer and waver of her own reflection, but her eyes slide sideways, where her husband's face is visible over her shoulder, the dark of eyes, the slash of mouth, the hair, so carefully combed.

He is silent for a long moment. "I do not—I am not privileged to truly know her," he says at last, and Catherine feels herself about to sigh, or perhaps to scream. Her own hair is heavy, the pins too tight, and she can feel an ache starting at the base of her head, cupping, gripping her skull like talons. She closes her eyes.

But then he goes on, comes toward her, though he pauses before he is near enough to touch. His reflection grows larger in the mirror, and at the same time smaller, two-thirds of his face obscured by her own. "The queen mother is—she has always been good to me. In her way."

Catherine waits, looking at him in the glass.

"She is—generous with those she favors," he says at last. "But it is—"

But again, he stops. Catherine's teeth press together.

"I only want to know what I should do to please her," she says after a moment. "I only want to know—the truth of her."

The bit of his face that she can see reflected in the glass twists strangely, as if he tries to smile but cannot quite manage it. "If it is truth you seek," he says, "then court is the wrong place to be."

Catherine's chest tightens impossibly further; soon there will be no air left at all, everything squeezed out of her. Almost, she does not respond, for anything she might say at this moment, she will almost surely regret later. But—

"I assumed you understood," she finds herself saying, "that I would not be here at all had I any other choices available."

The words hit true, leaving her husband's face changed, slackened, stunned, as if she raised her hand and not merely her voice against him. A sudden tightness at the corners of her jaw, inside her ears.

"I did not—" she begins, but he holds up a hand, shakes his head. The slackness leaves his face. One side of his mouth curls up. His eyes trace elaborate patterns in the air in their efforts to avoid hers.

"Her Majesty is generous," he says again. "She is—very strong. And very private, except in her convictions. If you ever displease her, you will know it. Though if you please her, you will know that, too. She is . . ." He swallows, eyes still canted down and away from her. Catherine waits, turning away from the mirror to truly see the workings of his throat, the way he pulls at the fingers of his right hand with the fingers of his left. He releases air through his nose, long and slow. "She is a queen."

Catherine waits, presses her tongue into the curved, hollow space behind her teeth. But he is finished.

"I did not mean what I said," she says, as if in so claiming she might retract the blow she dealt him. She has the strangest urge to uncurl the corner of his mouth with her fingertip, to smooth away that false almost-smile.

But he shakes his head once more. "I am corrected," is all he says. "There is some honesty to be found at court, after all."

HE WALKS WITH HER to queen's quarters, and they are silent but for the soft slaps of his shoes against the floor and the shushing of her gown. When they reach an open antechamber where other courtiers are already waiting for an audience with the queen mother, he leads her to a bench set against one wall and, once she is seated, gives a little bow.

"I will see you later, Madame," he says.

Catherine's hand darts out but does not touch him. Her eyebrows press together. "Are you not staying?"

He hesitates. "Her Majesty has seen me nearly every day for twenty-five years," he says at last, lips curling up a little at their corners. "It is *you* about whom she is curious."

She holds his eyes with her own. His are the color of chestnuts, set deep in their sockets and thickly lidded.

"Do you wish me to wait for you?" he says very quietly, gaze averted.

No. Yes. No. "Yes," she says, before she can stop herself, not certain, even as the word stumbles from her tongue, why she would want such a thing. His presence so far has hardly been a comfort to her.

He says nothing, lips pressed. Something tightens in his face. But he stays. Catherine thinks of her earlier cruelty, and tries to find words to soften it that he will not dismiss. But her body thrums with nervousness, her mind jangles and will not settle. And, as he said, her words, however unkind, were truthful.

When at last her turn comes to enter the queen's receiving room, Catherine presses a hand to her belly, where her breakfast has begun to churn. She casts a single glance at Monsieur Gonsalvus, and he nods to her, solemn as a sermon.

She can take in nothing at all of Her Majesty's chamber when she enters, her eyes fixed so completely upon the queen herself. A female dwarf, the very image of the queen in perfect miniature, sits beside her in a chair just sized to suit her frame, and the queen's ladies surround her like dropped flowers, wearing all the colors Her Majesty, in her eternal grief for King Henri's death, denies herself. Catherine's breath shudders inside her throat, and she drops into a curtsy, holding it until Her Majesty gestures that she should rise.

"Well," the queen says, looking her over. Catherine exerts all her discipline over her hands, which twitch instinctively, anxious to smooth her hair, her gown. Then Her Majesty smiles, thin lips spreading wide. "Your father did not lie, child. You are as beautiful as he claimed. I would not usually take a merchant's word on faith, you understand, but Monsieur Raffelin and I have known each other for a very long time."

Catherine licks her lips. "I—thank you, Your Majesty. You are too kind."

The dwarf smirks a little.

"Come," the queen says. "Tell me something of yourself." Her face folds into lines of placid expectation.

Catherine says the very first thing that comes to her. "I am named for you, Your Majesty."

Her Majesty's brows and the corners of her mouth rise in unison, as if dancing. "I knew there was a reason I was so fond of your father beyond his exquisite taste in silks."

"I—it was my mother, actually, Your Majesty. She is—was—Florentine by birth, and a great admirer of Your Majesty."

Caterina, Maman says inside Catherine's head, her voice a hiss of embarrassment.

But the queen smiles even more widely. "A fellow countrywoman! Tell me—did your mother teach you *la lingua italiana?*"

"*Sì, certamente*," Catherine says, and then reverts hastily to French when the dwarf's smirk broadens. "She did, Your Majesty; but I fear I was a poor student." (Again, Maman's voice interjects, this time accompanied by thrown-up hands. *Atroce!* she cries. *Like a cat wailing!*)

The queen gestures toward a man Catherine had not noticed before. He stands back from the firelight, dark scholar's robes and woolly gray beard mingling with the shadows.

"Signore Ruggeri cast a chart for you and our wild man. He assures me yours will be a most *fruitful* union. A veritable pack of pups."

Catherine takes a quick backward step before recalling herself. A shard of ice has lodged itself in her chest; she cannot draw breath without a bright cold pain.

"Indeed, Madame Gonsalvus," the astrologer says. His voice is roughly accented. "And most all of your children will be as marvelous as their sire."

The queen's miniature lets out a hinny of a laugh, loud and startling as a donkey's bray.

EXITING THE CHAMBER, SHE cannot look her husband in the face. If he asked her what her impressions were, perhaps she might have found in him a confidant; but he does not say a word, merely offers her his arm.

In the following weeks, she holds her breath as he moves above her in bed, as if depriving herself of air might keep his seed from her womb. The ice shard in her chest expands outward, forming a cold crust around her. She watches from behind it as her husband moves through his days, days that often lack any sort of clear purpose. He lurks in the king's *salle* with the other courtiers; attends feasts and Mass and tennis matches; combs his hair and eats his meals and goes to bed, only to begin again the next day. Catherine holds a scream behind her teeth, the hinges of her jaw aching.

Pedro

He wakes after only a very short sleep, screams himself awake from a dream of tentacles dragging him down and down; of hands snatching at his hair in handfuls until he is speckled with bald patches like his old skin rug. Of Isabel, her voice gone from calling for him, her ears filled with water so that she cannot hear him calling out to her in return.

At first, he thinks the tentacles still cling to him; there is something clutching him, trapping his limbs, wrapping itself about his wrists. He thrashes, shouts, tears himself loose with a wrench that sends him staggering to his knees, a jar, a bruising thump. The sound of something tearing; a frightened cry that is not his own.

He opens his eyes. He is on the floor, curled over his thighs; when he looks up, he sees the bed curtains half-wrenched from their beam. In the bed, upright, is his wife, her eyes glinting catlike in the darkness, wide and frightened.

"You—what happened?" she says. She clutches the bedclothes to her breast. "You were up, moving about—I thought you had woken, but then you cried out—beating at the hangings."

He should say something—anything—to calm her. But the dream grips him, still; he shakes off the trailing edge of the curtain, a shudder rippling across his shoulders. His knee bones ache, and he is suddenly deeply tired. When he looks back at her, there is horror and wariness in her face as he moves, and she holds the bedclothes more tightly in her soft pale hands.

"I am sorry for waking you," he says, hoarse. Tentative, he climbs into bed again beside her, straightening the covers as best he can while she still holds her end so fast.

A silence, long enough that he hopes she will pretend it did not happen, will return to sleep. In the morning, a servant will mend the curtain, as they have in the past when these walking dreams took hold of him, when he stumbled in his terror into the table with his water pitcher, sending it cracking to the floor; when he tripped trying to escape from the sea monster and broke his tooth in his fall, dribbling blood on his skin rug.

But his wife speaks again, slowly, cautiously. "Are you . . . well?"

His shoulders curl with shame, embarrassment.

"I am," he says, tight.

"And what—why—"

In his head, he can still hear his own voice calling, pitched high as it was in childhood, and see Isabel walking away, heedless of his cries, the sea sloshing in the cavities of her ears and her own throat raw. But he cannot think how to tell her this, how to explain, not when her voice is edged so with fear, not when she shrinks away from him still.

She could not understand, he thinks; nor, probably, would she like to. He cannot imagine confiding in her about the dream, or about the things that led to it. How to communicate that which has scored his insides like the lashing stings of jellyfish; that which, like something he hopes one day to find again, he has buried as if it were a cask of treasure. His wife seems composed entirely of wide brown eyes and soft flesh, but he cannot find purchase anywhere about her; is not entirely certain he wants to, that he can trust the perfect slickness of her beauty not to send him sprawling on his backside, her laughter in his ears.

"I am tired," he says, and rolls onto his side, away from her.

IN THE FIRST DAYS after his wedding, the men at court congratulated Petrus on his good fortune. They were jovial, laughing, their heads shaking in amazement. *If only I had a hairier back; a thicker beard,* said one, his teeth showing bright in a grin. *Perhaps Her Majesty would pay me to wed a lovely young pauper, too.*

Petrus sees how they watch his wife; how their eyes trace the shape of her waist, her throat. Sometimes they approach her, one by one; sometimes two by two. Very fine in their stiff ruffs, with crosses like badges at their chests, they stand to either side of her, looking down with wide fox grins. Petrus looks on, sickness coating his throat, as she seems at once to lean toward and recoil from them. He wants, suddenly, to snatch her away, to wrap his hand around her wrist and pull hard enough to jerk the muscles of her arm until she is pressed to his side. He wants to scatter them with a feral scream like the wild creature some still believe him to be at his center; to loom above her, teeth bared, daring any man to touch her, to *speak* to her, this woman who is *his*.

And then he thinks of the fear in her eyes if he were to rush toward her, how she would likely press herself toward one of the other men instead, to keep herself safe from him. It is enough to keep him still and silent.

HE CANNOT FATHOM WHAT she thinks about. She cannot read, she cannot write. Growing up at court, among girls who learned Latin alongside him and penned passionate defenses of women's intellectual abilities, his wife's lack in this area leaves him bewildered. When he attempted to speak to her, just the once, of his studies—how his tutor thought him too old to begin learning like the sons of noblemen; how that same lemon-faced man offered grudging praise on the day Petrus presented him with a carefully penned translation of Aristotle's *Ethics* from the original Greek—she listened with bland courtesy.

And truly, the only thing she seems to think of, attend to, with any true interest is her appearance. Her mornings begin at the mirror, peering at her own reflection with narrowed eyes, as if it shows something she does not like, or as if she fears it might run away from her if she does not keep her eyes upon it. Her hair, plaited for the night, is unbound so that it falls, thick and waving, about her shoulders; and combed, a rhythmic combing that Petrus finds at once mesmeric and irritating. Sometimes she combs through the strands a scented powder that makes Petrus's nose wrinkle. She soaks her hands—to keep them soft, he assumes; checks her teeth in the glass, as if to make sure they are still white and strong; runs her hands over the front of her gowns, over her pinned hair, before leaving for Mass each morning, as if to ensure she is presentable for God. Petrus watches her, holding contempt between his teeth, itching for a wife to whom he might speak, who might see something in the world other than herself.

But another sort of restlessness comes over him when he lets himself look at her; when they lie together in the night, and she is all around him, sending bursts of sunlight off behind his eye sockets, all that soft flesh there for him alone. She does not touch him, but he never expected that she would. He pretends she cannot even see him, though the darkness is never so absolute that it might blind her; and so he closes his own eyes to hers as a child might in a game of seek, and he does not think of what their coupling might bring, some thorny brush inside his head defending against the imaginings of what they might create together. Sometimes he slides from her without conscious thought, removes himself at the last, that only the slightest dribbling might catch inside of her, not enough, surely, to make a difference, a change in her life, a life. He is rent between two desires: to be with her in this way, to move inside her body and glean the joy to be found there—she is summer, then, and her body offers pleasure like berries sun-warmed and sweet, for him to take as he wishes—and to keep away from her entirely, that no small soft creatures might emerge from her womb.

Catherine

Though he first made his fortune in Venetian silks, Catherine's father sold all sorts of things, buying when prices were low and storing them in his warehouses until such time as demand drove the price high enough for him to make a tidy profit. The one essential quality for a successful merchant, he always said, was instinct—and his had never failed him yet. He said it with unabashed pride, the sort for which Maman and God would both chide him.

Papa had been bringing Catherine with him to his warehouses since she was a very small girl. Showing her off, he said, grinning. He hoisted her up on a barrel of good French salt, where she would sit, swinging her legs so that her heels banged out a lively rhythm against the gray weathered wood, and they played at merchant and customer, pretending she was a fine lady, a member of the queen's retinue with a fat purse at her disposal. Then, as they waited for whomever Papa was doing business with that day to arrive, he brought merchandise forth for Catherine to examine. A scoop of saffron threads, bright and heady. Prunes, sweet smelling and soft, which he cut with his little knife, handing her a sliver to taste with solemn care. Paper from a mill right in Lyons; ribbons in every color that ran through Catherine's fingers as smoothly as streams of water; sweet wine; red leather; lace like spiders' weavings. She waved her hand when she wished him to take something away, wrinkled her nose in exaggerated displeasure until they were both laughing, Papa's laughter bursting from his chest in hearty bellows.

When his business associates arrived, he always introduced Catherine with great seriousness. The men smiled when she curtseyed very precisely, as Maman had taught her; they called her *charmante* and offered her sweets. While they conducted their business, she remained sitting on her barrel, sometimes listening, more often sucking on her sweet and looking about her at all the things from far away that Papa had amassed, and which he would distribute farther still by means of great sea ships and sleeker river vessels; guarded wagons along rutted roads and handshakes and clinking coins here in this very warehouse. She thought of the bob of a boat down the river—she loved it when her father brought her to see the boats, to watch the slap of the water against their sides and hear the creaking of their masts—and imagined working there with him when she was grown, the sun on the water and on her face until she was as creased and brown as Papa, a testament to how much of the world she had seen.

As she grew, the visits to the warehouse began to feel different; just as everything in life felt different, her childish fancies dissolving like sugar in water. Her thoughts were no longer so scattered; her focus no longer drifted from detail to detail in lazy contemplation. And she was far too old to sit upon a barrel.

Instead, she stood beside Papa, and the men who used to offer her sweets now bent low over her hand, their lips brushing the tendons that ran from fingers to wrist, their fingers hot upon hers. They still called her *charmante*, but there was a warmer undertone to the word now, one that shivered along Catherine's backbone and prickled over her scalp. They looked at her as if she were a painting or a sculpture, something to stand before and take in. Even when the men were old or their skin pitted from pox, when their breath offended or their manners—even when she felt no desire for them in return—she liked how she felt when they looked at her so. Powerful, able to command their attention with a flick of her eyes, as Maman had taught her to do.

PAPA THOUGHT HE CHOSE Maman; that he had plucked her, like a particularly fine bolt of cloth, from the house of her weaver feather and brought her home with him.

But Catherine knew the truth, knew that it was Maman who had chosen her husband.

"Though I was but fourteen," Maman told Catherine, "I could sense your father's interest immediately. I knew him as one of my father's best customers; I knew that he had a kind smile, and a jolly manner, and that he was rich beyond my ability to imagine. And I knew that he wanted me.

"You will know it, Caterina, when you feel it—a man's interest is unmistakable. But it is also like a fish—it darts here and there, rarely resting long enough to be caught. You, *piccola mia*, have a dowry that might keep that fish-brained interest a little longer. But I had almost no dowry, and certainly not one that would keep the interest of a rich man like your father.

"What I had in abundance, though, was beauty. I knew it; and I knew how to use my eyes to return his interest, how to flick a glance through my eyelashes, alive with desire, catching him like a fishhook right behind his ribs. I thrummed with power from my crown all the way to my toes."

Power, Catherine thought; wouldn't that be something to feel? She practiced that fishhook-look in the mirror even as a child but did not get it quite right until she had twelve summers behind her and made a delivery boy, bringing meat to kitchen door, stumble over his too-big shoes with the force of her glance. She felt, then, heady power rushing through her just as Maman had said she would; and she wanted to feel it again and again.

SHE RECALLS MAMAN'S LESSONS at court. The men here watch her, speak to her. Offer her cups of wine and sugared fruits. Laugh, when she has said nothing funny. Her chest fills with air when they circle her.

And then—a murmur in her ear, a suggestion, coupled with the stroke of a finger down the length of her arm, hidden from view by the angle of his body, and all feelings of power shrivel like dropped leaves. Another man makes a joke about rutting with beasts, asks whether her husband has ever bitten her. Their bodies walling around her, their words mirrors held up to her most secret skin. *No,* she thinks, *no and no and no,* but her mouth will not open.

It is the taint of her husband's hair that saves her here. Her husband's hair, and the monk-dwarf, who overhears one day and says, dry as kindling, as a field in the sun, that perhaps the good gentlemen would do better to turn their rudders elsewhere. "If she gets with pup," he says, "you wouldn't want to have to wonder if the thing is yours, eh?"

Catherine

There is one man who looks at her differently from the others.

In the king's *salle*, most of the men come together in knots, tight with their own importance. Standing at the periphery of the room, Catherine sometimes hears wisps of their conversations—they speak of politics, of Catholic might and Huguenot wiles, their voices low and intense, their eyes widening with meaning at the corners.

Catherine listens, though all their talk seems very far away from here, this court, this beautiful palace; even from her life in Lyons.

Catherine's husband does not take part in this talk. As far as she can discern, he is not asked to. He stands a little apart. Only country nobles, newly arrived at court, pause to speak with him. Some cock their heads, as if trying to determine whether there is some trickery—a wig, glue. Others ask him questions, then turn to one another and say, *How extraordinary!* when her husband does something so very ordinary as bow and greet them with politeness. Catherine's stomach sickens, watching him.

Only one person seems to seek him for himself. The Duke of Nevers, to whom Catherine was introduced on her first morning as a married woman, often comes to stand beside her husband, and they speak as old friends speak, every line of their bodies relaxed and easy. They even laugh, her husband's teeth—square and decidedly human, with one blackened molar and one front tooth a little chipped—showing as he grins.

The duke has a beard and dark curling hair. His eyes are large, his form elegant in its fine clothes. Sometimes, Catherine sees him watching her, curiously, she thinks, as if she is a puzzle. Whenever he realizes that she has noticed *his* notice of her, he smiles, gentle, with none of the hidden meanings contained within other men's smiles. His curious gaze is vastly preferable to the way the other men look at her, their eyes more like noses, practically sniffing; they see no puzzle at all in her, but think they understand her perfectly: penniless merchant's daughter, caught fast underneath her savage husband. Eager for the glide of something smooth.

The duke watches her in the king's *salle*. He nods to her on the grounds, where she walks alone through knotted hedges, always with a quick smile. Even when her husband walks beside him, it is the duke whose attention warms Catherine; his notice of her as someone, a person. Not a conquest, not Madame Sauvage. Her husband nods to her as well, but his gaze skitters away, nervous as mice across a kitchen floor. He has scarcely looked at her since the night of his dream—if that is what made him lurch upright from their bed, cry out as if something attacked him. Or was it something else—some innate wildness from his former life, some madness? When he tore the hangings from their bed, when he screamed, she thought, for a moment, that he had transformed, become the thing in truth that, already, he so nearly resembled. That he would eat her thighs, her belly, her liver, her heart.

LATER, THOUGH—HE HAD NOT seemed wild at all. He had seemed, if anything, childlike.

Catherine, lying very still beside him, feigning sleep, listened as his rapid breaths slowed. She thought he was sleeping, then, until the mattress shuddered lightly, and a pitiful sound, like a babe grizzling in the night, came from his side of the bed.

HER HUSBAND AND NEVERS spar sometimes in the wide rectangular courtyard, and Catherine watches them both, flinching at the swipe of their blades, the ferocity of their movements. They both have skill, even she can see that, though only the duke has used his in true battle. She watches, breathless, as they grunt and parry, hands over her mouth, her eyes, though for which man's tender flesh she cannot decide.

Today's match ends abruptly—her husband's sword hooking itself under Nevers's in such a way that the duke's sword flips from his grasp and falls, ringing, to the stones. They stand, breath smoking from their mouths in the late autumn chill.

Silence, just for a moment; and then someone calls "*Sauvage!*" eliciting cheers from the other observers. The king, wrapped in a heavy furred cloak, steps forward and flips a coin at Catherine's husband. To her relief, he catches it before it falls to the ground at his feet. Then His Majesty turns away to return to the warmth of his rooms, his fire.

"The wolf almost fights like a man," says one of the king's favorites to another as he follows His Majesty, and Catherine looks instantly to her husband to see whether he heard, her body hot. But no—as she watches, the duke puts a hand upon her husband's shoulder, his big fingers curling with tender familiarity.

"Thank you, old friend," he says. "I needed a good bout." Then his hand falls away and they gather up their scattered things, capes and jerkins and hats and doublets, all shed before the match. Her husband grins at something the duke says. If he heard the other man's remark, he gives no indication.

Nevers glances at her once, sees her watching. Catherine's cheeks warm, despite the cold-edged air, and he gives her a lively grin, one eye winking down.

He glances at her husband, who is fastening his doublet, and comes to her. "Madame," he says, still smiling. "I am afraid your husband bested me once again."

"You both fought well," Catherine says. Her voice wavers a little; her cheeks flush further.

"Ah—but was I holding back?" Nevers winks once more, then

adds, “Or was he? Could he have bested me more quickly than he did, do you think? He is a skilled swordsman, our Pierre; it is a shame he was never allowed to fight for his king.”

“Did he wish to?” Catherine says, startled.

A nod. “But of course. At least, when King Henri still lived. Now?” His lips pucker. “Now I cannot say. With so beautiful a wife warming his bed, what man would choose the discomfort of a march, a battlefield?”

She is silent, but she dares a hooking smile; thinks, by the lifting of his brow, that he feels it in his belly.

“And what of you, Madame?” he says. His posture shifts, shoulders settling back, legs thrown wide. “How do you find court? Marriage?”

He asks, she thinks, as if he truly wishes to know. She fumbles for a response that will seem at once refined and truthful, but before she can settle upon one another man is calling to him.

“Ah—I apologize, Madame,” he says, bows a quick farewell, and is off, the wind lifting his hair. He whistles a little as he walks, the sound lighter than the air, singing, Catherine feels, of a happiness that is complete.

SHE THINKS ABOUT HIM—HIS curling hair, his confident air, his smile. She thinks about him at night when she and her husband ready themselves for bed without speaking; the next day, when they walk silently together to Mass. When she combs her hair, she imagines the touch of his hand, smoothing her hair as Maman once did, but more slowly, lingering at the point where her neck and shoulder join. In the chapel, she cannot concentrate on the priest; her mind flies to where Nevers stands, she bites her lips to bring the blood to them, she wonders whether he will turn and look at her, whether he will smile at her again before all the court.

Whenever she can, she listens. Eagerly, to rumors of his valor in battle, his trusted place at the king's side; less so, when she hears of his wife in Paris, his children. And yet still, her head turns to impossibilities, to dreams—him as a minor country noble, not the son of a grand house in Mantua; a minor country noble with a sweep of land, an old, solid house for her to run, softened inside by rugs, candles, silver. She imagines sheep in broad meadows, geese herded by a sturdy young girl. Children—theirs together—learning their letters, scampering about the garden. Him, speaking to her, earnest. Telling her of himself, learning about her in turn. He would still have to come to court sometimes, she thinks, and perhaps she would join him, as long as she hadn't a child in her belly. They might stand together, looking about them, here; uncertain, but not alone.

She even ventures to ask her husband about him one night.

"How long have you known the Duke of Nevers?" she says. Her voice, she hopes, is disinterested, as if the question is merely a passing thought, easily dismissed.

He pauses, his comb in one fist, and looks at her. "Since we were boys," he says. "Nevers was fostered here at court." A slight smile, and he resumes his combing. "He never left."

"Is it true that he is a hero?" Catherine says then. "In battle, I mean."

This time, the comb continues raking through the thick hair on his chest. "Yes." Short, stiff.

"And a favorite of the king?"

A nod. Frustration builds behind her breastbone; she exhales to release it.

Pedro

"Too beastly to please your wife, Sauvage?"

The man who says this is a marquis. His stuffed doublet gives his chest and shoulders a breadth that looks almost comical paired with his legs, long and slim and knobble-kneed as a stork's. He speaks loudly enough to be heard above the music, the chatter, in the long, high-ceilinged hall; even the king, sunk a moment earlier with his cheek upon his fist, ennui covering his face like a mask, glances up at the sound. The queen mother as well, frowning. The marquis, who came up behind Petrus at his table in the feasting hall, gestures with his chin, and Petrus looks.

His wife, who rose from their table a little earlier without a word to him, stands against a wall. She is smiling, truly smiling—he thinks, with a jolt, that he has never seen her smile so before—and speaking to someone. She is too far away for him to hear her words. He shifts his gaze to her companion and experiences another jolt: it is Ludovico.

The pain that comes with the sight is strange, simmering. The upward arch of her neck, his friend's familiar half-smile. He has seen them speak before—quick snatches of conversation, witnessed between the bodies of his fellow courtiers, their words lost to the hum of gossip, of political chatter—but always briefly. This conversation seems a settled thing, a wall sunk gently into the earth. Her hands behind her back, lightly clasped; how she leans her shoulder blades against the wall. His sudden burst of laughter.

It is not an unusual thing, for married men, and even, sometimes, married women, to take lovers at court. Ludovico is circumspect, but Petrus has no doubt he is unfaithful to his wife.

But he would not—he would never—

He is taking her hand, now. Taking Petrus's wife's hand. His, of course, as smooth as hers. He is leading her toward a space beyond the feasting tables, the space cleared for dancing. Petrus watches, sick, the simmering moving outward like a flame from the center of a paper, as they join the ring of dancers, the music bright and cheering. They step side to side. The sway of their hips, the kick of their feet. The circle of dancers opens, spirals in upon itself like a shell. His wife's mouth open, laughing. She looks very young, lovely, free.

"What say you, Sauvage?" It is the king calling now, the king risen from his apathy. "Is this to be allowed? If that were *my* wife—"

A sharp chorus of laughter; the king's wife is well known to be a pious woman, reclusive from court. His mistress, seated to the side of him not occupied by his mother, smiles, though she stops when His Majesty's own laughter turns to wet coughing.

When he has regained his breath, the music is trailing away, the dance ending, and the dancers clearing the floor. He calls, "Madame! Madame Sauvage!" Petrus sees his wife's head go up like a hunted doe's, her hand fall away from Ludovico's. His friend frowns, glances at Petrus.

"You choose to dance with the man your husband bested only days ago in a fight?" he says. "You witnessed his triumph, I believe—did he not fight well?"

The quiet in the hall is such that Petrus can hear the harsh susurration of her breathing. "Very well, Your Majesty," she says, her voice small as a child's.

The queen mother shifts in her chair beside the king. "Surely," she says, "he deserves a better reward from his wife than such cold praise."

Muffled laughter. Petrus's wife looks at him, and to him she seems uncertain, all the loveliness of her face and figure eclipsed, all at once, by her obvious terror. "You fought so very well, Monsieur," she says, sounding as if she is trying to infuse the words with feeling, as herbs infuse vinegar with their flavor.

His own voice is very dull when he says, "Thank you, Madame."

"A kiss!" someone calls, and then other voices, laughing, wine sodden. "A kiss, a kiss!"

"Yes," says the king, smiling a crooked, sickly smile. "A kiss for our victor, from his lovely, *returned* bride."

Roots seem to have grown over Petrus's feet, twining, trapping them. When he does not move, his wife does, walking stiffly until she is standing before him. She looks up at him with her pale brown eyes, her pink mouth flattened at the corners, her cheeks rosy with humiliation.

And suddenly, the simmering reaches the edges of the paper and catches on something else, and something else, and something else, until the whole of him is aflame with anger, with a humiliation so bright it must eclipse hers as the sun eclipses the moon before dusk. Years upon years of humiliation. He rips his feet from the roots that hold him, steps forward, catches her arms in his two hands.

"May I?" he says, just as he does at night in their bed; but this time she hasn't the chance to say no, not with the king and queen watching them, and there is a terrible, shameful satisfaction in that. She nods once, clipped, eyes wide.

He bends to her. Her mouth is warm; he puts one arm about her waist and pulls her forward until their chests are touching. Her hands come up, tentative, to his shoulders; he thinks, just for a moment, of the woman with the wine-mark, how she touched him without fear or horror. Air passes between their mouths like wine from a shared cup; and then he presses harder, hard enough that she makes a startled sound and her hands fist in the fabric of his sleeves. He wants to nip, to lick, to devour; he feels her tongue suddenly against his and his arm tightens around her waist, a crook of root itself, ancient and immovable.

And then—

"*Sauvage!*" someone calls again, and he pulls away, her hands dropping from his shoulders, her lips folding in upon themselves, her chin red and abraded from his hair.

Catherine

That night in their chamber, their silence is weighted, heavy and crushing as the stones of a cathedral roof.

She can still feel his kiss, her skin raw where his beard rubbed it.

She sits upon the mattress, still dressed, while he stands before the hearth. She looks at the curl of his shoulders, his fisted hands at his sides. Her throat is tight. In her ears, calls of *Sauvage!* ring like war cries.

He is a performing bear, she thinks. And she has become part of the act. How has he endured such jeering, all the stares and the sneers?

"Why," he says suddenly; and though the word does not rise as a question ought, still Catherine knows he means it as one.

"I . . ." She shakes her head. How to tell him that the duke was pleasing, that his attentiveness was pleasing? That he spoke to her, and not merely when her questions required it.

He turns his head so that she can see his ear, his cheek, the arrow of his nose. "You are my *wife*," he says, and there is possession in his voice; and something else, something like the rawness of a half-healed wound. "I am your husband. Do you not think I *feel* when you carry on so with another man. With—with my *friend*?"

Now—he talks to her *now*, Catherine notes, as if from a distance. But all he seems to say is *mine, mine, mine*. Each *mine* crashes in her ears. Her back and shoulders tighten; her jaw is steel.

"And I am your *wife*," she says, her voice a sudden avalanche, rocks hurtling toward the earth. "You are *my* husband. But you will not—you will not let me know you. I do not know anyone here at court, I am alone, *alone*, and yet you do not *care*—"

He is motionless, his head still half-turned so that she cannot fully see his expression. The anger that fills her is almost frightening in its potency; for a moment, she thinks she might start screaming and not be able to stop, all the screams she's been stoppering since the day her father's fortune tumbled to the bottom of the sea. Why will he not *look at her*—

She swallows down the screaming urge, though it struggles all the distance down her throat. When at last it's sitting clod-like in her stomach and her voice has rolled itself up tight and controlled, she tries again to speak.

"The duke was kind to me," she says. "That is all." And then, when he remains stiff and still: "You have not said a word about Nevers and—and me," she says, for she knows, she *knows* how plain it must have been, how she sought Nevers out, started conversations, found things to say to make him linger. "Why?"

He turns, looks at her; and then his eyes are drawn to her left ear. No—to the amethyst hanging from her left ear. He stares at it, the wink of it in the firelight.

"We are—the same, you and I," he says, and ignores the sudden press of her brows above her nose, the twist of her mouth. "You were sold as surely as I was. I thought—I did not feel I'd the right to gainsay you, if you found something that . . ."

You were sold as surely as I was. The anger that rose inside her with such frightening ferocity seeps away, leaving her tired. She touches her amethysts. Her dowry. Her worth. Thinks of her father's debts, repaid. "Who sold you?" she whispers.

He shakes his head. "I—do not know his name."

So many questions. They clog her throat. But before she can choose one, he has turned away; she recognizes the closed look on his face, like a locked trunk, a closed tomb, and sighs.

He does not touch her that night. They lie beside each other for long minutes in the darkness before he says, "I wish—you would not. With Nevers. That is—"

He can speak. He can feel. He is a man.

"I won't," she says.

Pedro

Petrus draws his fingers over and over the wood of Ludovico's door, feeling the bump and scrape of the grain. He arrived here after leaving the clotted air of his own chamber, where his wife lies, finally sleeping.

At last he curls his knuckles to knock, and after a bit of shuffling from the other side of it the door twitches open. Ludovico looks out at him, hair a dark cloud around his head, face sleep-creased, and steps wordlessly aside; Petrus shoves past anyway, hard, as hard as if Ludovico had not made way for him, had tried to bar him from the room by force—the bump of bone and muscle, Ludovico's grunt when his spine thuds against the wall, his skull. And then Petrus is upon him, before he knows what he means to do—hands on his friend's arms, fingers biting hard as teeth, sinking deep into flesh, seeking the pressure that would bring bruises blooming red and purple to the surface of Ludovico's skin. He has never fought another man except through swordplay, and that is only sparring. But he wishes now that he did not clip his nails so short, that they might be long enough, sharp enough, to act as the claws people expect him to have.

"Why?" he says. "Why?"

Ludovico is taller than he, and broader of shoulder, but he does not push back, does not use his strength against Petrus. He only puts up his hands, as if to ward off blows that have not come, and says, "I have done nothing, friend."

Petrus pulls back but does not release him, his fingers tight as shackles around Ludovico's arms. His friend looks at him, tense, near enough that even in the dimness of fire and candlelight, Petrus can see all the individual hairs that make up his curving brows, the rougher skin at the end of his nose, the chapped lower lip. He is struck, as if by a physical force, a blow, by a sudden memory, and almost he reels away; but he holds on, though their posture—bodies close, hands clasping Ludovico's arms—is a mirror of his and his wife's in the feasting hall, a strange, dizzy simulacrum.

"You have done nothing—but dance, but flirt," he says. His friend watches him, for once silent. "But you could have—you would have—"

"Never," says Ludovico; and his teeth crush the word like sparrows' bones. Petrus startles back, releases his arms, flexes his own fingers, suddenly cramped. Ludovico moves past him; lights another candle from the fire; pours wine for each of them. Petrus finds himself seated across from his friend, the fire warm to one side, the bed, rumpled, the bedclothes askew, to the other. The crunching of hollow bones, Petrus thinks; all the ferocity he never sees in his friend, all the ferocity that must exist, must be reserved for the battlefield, for diplomacy, for all the places Petrus knows his hair will not allow him to go; all that ferocity focused now within that single, bitten-off word.

They sit together, cradling their cups before the fire, and despite it the air is night-chilled, all the curling dark hairs on Ludovico's legs shoved to attention by the stippling of his skin. After they have spent a few moments sipping and sitting—minutes in which Ludovico casts little prickling glances at Petrus from under the mad curls of his hair, puts a hand to the back of his head, rubbing where it hit the wall—he finally says again, "Never."

Petrus glances up at him. There is a strange calm pool inside of him where the fire existed earlier tonight, dampening it. "No?" he says.

Ludovico shakes his head, the corners of his mouth arching down. They are silent again, long minutes, longer than Ludovico is usually capable of silence, of stillness. And then he breaks it.

"So," he says. "Left your wife's warm embrace so soon? I thought you'd be there all night, after that display."

He says it without really looking at Petrus; says it and then gulps the last wine from his cup, a sloppy patter of droplets staining his white shirt purple-red. Immediately he rises and goes to the jug, pouring himself more. Then he returns to his chair, stretches his legs, long and thick, before him until his toes are near enough that Petrus could brush their tips with his own shod feet if he only unkinked his legs a little at the knees. Ludovico's feet are bare and pale, hairy at the toe knuckles and near the ankle, the bones long and standing out as the toes flex, showing pockets of shadow between.

Petrus fixes his eyes upon Ludovico until his friend looks up at last. "The *display* would not have happened had you not been—been—"

"I had no intention," Ludovico says, "of making a spectacle of her. Or you." A moment; a breath. "Of you, least of all."

His eyes are dark, with lashes that curl and brows that arch and jump more expressively than any Petrus has ever seen. He can convey any feeling with a single lift of one of those slim brows; he can pinion a man with a glance. He pinions Petrus now, so that Petrus feels held fast to his chair, helplessly stuck there by Ludovico, who knows his moods, his wishes, as no one else does.

Then Ludovico's eyes slide closed; he speaks without opening them. "She seemed very . . . Standing all on her own, day after day. And when I offered her a smile, a word, she was . . . ah, Pierre, she was so desperate for any kindness. If I did not know you, I'd have assumed cruelty was the cause."

Petrus stares into his glass.

"But then—she sought my company. It seemed . . . unkind to be cold to her. I know you, old friend, I know your . . . tendencies. And I have seen you with her—and you are as uncommunicative as a—as a silence-vowed monk. And then tonight—she said she longed to dance, that she had danced a great deal at the parties given by her parents, their friends, but had not had the opportunity at court." He opens his eyes now, raises a single, eloquent brow. Petrus grunts.

"I do not like to dance unless I am required to," he says.

Ludovico shakes his head. "And yet you do not want your wife to dance with anyone else."

Petrus merely looks at him, and at last Ludovico puts up his free hand, palm outward. "Very well. I am truly—truly—sorry to have distressed you."

Petrus nods, the movement slow and heavy, the weight of his head suddenly too much for his neck to hold. "Marriage," he says, "is not what I hoped it would be."

A snort. "When is marriage ever what we hope?" he says. "I know of no man who had much hope at all for marriage, beyond that it bring him sons. Or," he says, smiling a little, "do you speak of more . . . private things?"

Petrus huffs a laugh; rolls his eyes to the ceiling. A rosy warmth draws its way up from his chest. "I am not going to discuss this with you."

"Hmm. And here I thought my own years of matrimony might at last be of some use to someone."

Petrus could say something of the difference in their marriages—each one political in its own way, yes, but there the similarities end. Ludovico has a powerful family at home in Mantua to whom he might return with his wife and children, should the French court turn against him. Ludovico, who glories in all the things that Petrus tries to keep away from—skirmishes of words and swords between the powerful. Ludovico, who can slip away to court whenever he wishes; who needn't care overmuch whether he can converse with his wife. Who seems entirely capable of forgetting she exists at all, from one moment to the next.

But he does not say any of this. "The last advice I took from you, if I recall correctly," he says instead, "ended with my being consumed by flea bites, and God knows what else, contracted in a certain tavern, in the arms of a certain woman to whom you brought me. There is a reason"—with a studied sip from his cup—"that I have not taken advice from you in many years."

Ludovico's laughter drifts warm and lazy through the space between them. "If you remember," he says, "my *first* advice was that you take one of the *courtisanes'* offers. You'd have had a more comfortable experience." He tips his head to one side, mouth twisted. "But if I am not mistaken, you said it was a *wonderful* time; and so perhaps it is as well you did not take my advice. Fleas and other crawling things be damned."

Ludovico keeps those eyes upon him, staring over the rim of his cup; and they are the eyes of the boy who approached a werewolf and chose to keep him company. "I suppose," he says, scratching his curling beard and his chest through the open neck of his shirt, "I should be honored that you chose *my* companionship over hers at this time of night." And before Petrus can think of anything to say, Ludovico raises his cup. "To friendship."

THE NIGHT THAT PETRUS lay with the purple-stained woman and carried fleas home with him to the palace, he half-carried Ludovico home as well. He had descended the tavern stairs, returning to the smoky common room, to find Ludovico slouched at his table, looking up at him with so bleary an expression that Petrus, with a sigh, knew his friend to be very drunk. The tabletop was sticky with the sloshed wine and beer of countless drinkers; Ludovico's cup was empty, and Petrus wondered how many times he'd emptied it while Petrus was upstairs. As he watched, Ludovico settled his cheek upon his fist, lids drawing half-down, eyes settling, unfocused, upon the guttering flame of the candle stub at the center of the table. The candle's wax slid and folded like the flesh of a very old man; Petrus turned his own eyes away from it, seeing instead the woman upstairs, the dark purple stain upon her pale skin, which he could not feel at all when he traced it.

"Are you going to tell me how it was?" Ludovico said, and Petrus looked back at him. Ludovico raised his eyelids all the way, eyes rolling upward, too, so that they fixed upon Petrus with what seemed to be tremendous effort. Petrus smiled a little.

"No," he said, and rose from the table. "Or at least, not here." He held out a hand to lever Ludovico from his chair, and after a moment his friend grasped it and allowed himself to be levered, giving over much of his weight to Petrus's keeping. Ludovico was the taller by a head, and as they moved in a sideways stagger toward the door, he leaned his cheek upon the top of Petrus's head, the same cheek that, moments before, had rested upon his own knuckles.

Outside, stars had flung themselves through the darkness over Paris, and the streets were mostly deserted but for women like the one he left at the tavern, and beggars sleeping curled against the night air, and other men like Ludovico and himself, tottering from tavern to tavern or reeling hurriedly for home. Petrus gave a theatrical groan under Ludovico's weight, acting out again one of their boyhood games, when they would weave like wine-soaked courtiers through the halls of the palace, their arms about each other's shoulders, their voices raised in song and shattering with laughter.

Ludovico snorted into his hair; Petrus felt the hot huff of it, and the odd turn of his friend's head until the pointed tip of his nose was pressed to Petrus's head, too. "Now will you tell me?" he murmured, mouth so sunk in Petrus's hair that he lipped at the strands.

"It was," Petrus said, and paused, remembering the woman's vacant eyes; the decay he smelled inside her mouth. Her hands upon his shoulders, his back, his neck, everywhere touching him, her fingers buried in his hair like mice in tall grass. "Wonderful."

Ludovico was silent for a while; Petrus could feel the hard bump of his jaw, full of teeth, against his head with every jarring step along the unevenly cobbled street. It was just cool enough that their breath preceded them, except it was only his own breath he saw, gusting white and private, as if leading them back through the night to the palace; Ludovico breathed into the top of his head like a witch breathing life into spells.

Eventually, Ludovico said, "I am glad. I would not want to have wasted my coin."

At the Château du Louvre, they made their weaving way back to Ludovico's chamber. Petrus ducked out from under Ludovico's heavy arm when they opened his door, muffling his laughter against the back of his hand when Ludovico tipped with an oath against the wall. He righted himself with the careful dignity of the very drunk, and looked down at Petrus, frowning. A fire had been laid for him by one of his servants, and its light cast half of him in darkness; the frown looked strange and severe, for Ludovico was so often smiling. Petrus blinked, seeing in the sudden severity the part of Ludovico that he rarely saw, the part that had been to war for France, that had wielded his sword for its intended purpose, and not merely for sparring. Almost, he stepped back, away from the shadows that lay so heavily across Ludovico's face.

But then his friend's frown tipped upward, tugging with it his cheeks and eyebrows and his small, round ears, and Petrus found himself smiling in return. And then Ludovico sighed and bent, neck curving down and down in a graceful swoop like a hunting bird's; and he caught Petrus's lips against his own before Petrus knew what was happening. Petrus's eyes drifted closed, pressed so by the weight of an astonishment that was not entirely genuine; he leaned, just for a moment, into a warm dry mouth and felt the whisper of a long exhalation against his cheek; felt, too, the sudden heat of Ludovico's tongue against his own and the press of Ludovico's lust against his belly, startling in its firmness, making Petrus jerk back a little, wild-eyed.

When they parted, Ludovico smiled again, a little sadly, hand cupping Petrus's cheek, fingers tucked into the hair there with a casualness that loosened something at the nape of Petrus's neck, a wood-burl that had been there so long he had ceased to notice it until it was gone. And then Ludovico leaned his brow against Petrus's, bone to bone, a little too quickly so that it almost hurt, might bruise, leave a mark, a proof of what just happened; and he murmured, "I am glad that tonight was wonderful for you."

IT IS NEARLY DAWN when Petrus rises to leave. Ludovico brought out dice, and they tossed them for hours, a conversation of perfect nothings eddying between them as they gambled. Petrus rises, grinning, with a good deal more coin than he had when he arrived. He stretches, back arching, spine crackling; Ludovico watches, half-smiling, yawning, and gets up to walk with Petrus across the room to the door.

"Good night, my friend," he says. "Only for you would I willingly rise from so sound a sleep." A pause and then, "Listen to her," he adds abruptly. And when Petrus raises his brows, he smiles, wry and twisted. "I am glad enough that Henriette has little to say to me; but when she does speak, I know enough to listen. Your little wife is hungry for that. Feed her. That's my last marital advice."

He catches Petrus's wrist in the cradle of his palm; plays with the cuff of Petrus's shirt. His face is soft with tiredness, with wine, with wakening to a tapping at his door to find a friend there, with something else Petrus cannot decipher.

They have never spoken of what passed between them, so many years ago now that Petrus sometimes wonders whether he imagined it, whether the catch of the dry skin of his friend's mouth against his own was some strange dream from which he never entirely wakened. Soon after that night, Ludovico was gone again to war; and soon after that, married. And if their eyes catch against each other sometimes, just as perhaps their mouths did twenty years ago, nothing is ever said in words; and perhaps even the nonwords are entirely of Petrus's imagination.

It is a dangerous thing, to want the things that Ludovico seems to want—women, yes, but men, too. Or are the women merely a screen, held between the world and Ludovico's true, his only, desires? Do his flirtations with them never progress further than words, strolls in the moonlight, clasped hands?

Petrus has never had the courage to ask, though he has wondered. Has wondered, when he's seen Ludovico speaking with, dicing with, laughing with other men of the court. Has wondered, all the times that Ludovico has seemed so disinclined to return to his wife. But Ludovico would speak if he wished to; and after pulling away, after making it clear that his desires did not match his friend's, Petrus has not been able to bring himself to satisfy his wonderings, not when Ludovico has never trusted him with the words spoken aloud, has perhaps used his own drunkenness on that long-ago night as yet another screen. Not when speaking of such dangerous wantings, even softly, privately, feels almost like exposing his friend's tenderest places to peril.

Ludovico opens the door now, leans against it as Petrus takes his candle and steps into the darkened corridor beyond, watches as Petrus walks away, until Petrus looks over his own shoulder, raising a hand in farewell; and then Ludovico steps backward, closing the door behind him.

Catherine

The first child fills her belly soon enough, of course. No amount of breath-holding could prevent it.

Another visit to the queen's chamber verifies what Catherine suspected but has refused, until this moment, to consciously think about. She has not bled in more weeks than she has bothered to count. Behind a screen, at the bidding of a wispy-bearded physician, she empties her bladder into a pot, cheeks red with the loudness of the sound, the rustle and muffled laughter of the queen and her ladies in the room beyond the screen.

When she has finished, the physician takes up the pot. With a cup, he scoops some of the piss; from a flagon, he pours a measure of wine into the cup. Then he puts his face close to the cup, staring, nodding, muttering to himself. Catherine holds her hands together at her waist, where her bodice is laced more loosely than usual, as if she has been eating more than her share; breathes slow and deep to ease the rising panic. One of the queen's ladies—the dwarf who readied Catherine on her wedding night—gives her a twisted little smile, raising slim dark brows at the physician, whose nose is nearly inside the cup, wafting up the mingled scents of wine and urine. Her expression is so comical that it breaches the crust of ice Catherine has carried around her since the queen's astrologer predicted her many pups all those weeks ago. A thousand crackling fingers split the ice into wavering plates. Despite the panic, she finds herself smiling back.

And then the physician straightens, clears his throat. Her Majesty, who had been speaking to one of her ladies, turns.

The man inclines his head. "Without a doubt, Majesty, she is with child."

She sits after in her own chamber, empty but for her dull-eyed reflection in the mirror. Her husband is still with the king, who ignores him; it is only new-come courtiers who stare, and envoys from other lands who care to speak to him. Her hands go to the softness of her belly, a little thickened, yes, but not yet grown hard as the hull of a nut around the fruit within. But her body has been whispering to her all this time in changes slow and subtle. Twinges, only; sharp tugs that came from nowhere when she rolled over in bed, and then disappeared again. A prickling sensitivity to her breasts; a sudden darkness to her nipples, like figs. Some days, her eyelids have felt heavy as the weights Papa's clerks used to count his money, her bones seeming almost to creak; and *now* she knows—tears hot and frantic, running down her face like sudden snowmelt—that her bones have been shifting to make room for what her clever body recognized was coming.

NOW IT IS ONLY waiting. Waiting for the bloom of belly. Waiting for her husband to say something, to show he knows what, together, they have wrought.

Waiting for her slow-kindling fears to prove unnecessary; or true.

She begins to sew again, and to embroider, for the first time since coming to court taking an almost-pleasure in the familiar cadence of thread through needle, needle through cloth. A tiny coif to protect a tiny head; a blanket edged in flowers. *If I have a daughter, I will teach her these things, too,* she dares to think, remembering the hours with Maman, sometimes with friends as well, bent over small solitary projects or with a larger one stretched between them; and then shakes her head as a donkey shakes off flies, for to imagine such normalcy seems an invitation to the opposite.

She begins to attend Mass with more purpose and devotion than she ever has before. Kneeling and listening to the priest's intonations and the congregation's answering murmurs, her hands hold one another so tightly that her knuckles ache by the end of the service.

Their chamber holds a single painting, a small image of the Holy Mother and her newborn infant. Catherine has paid it almost no attention before now—the artistry is nothing compared to all the wondrous works the palace holds, the Virgin's features oddly crooked—but she spends hours now staring at it, at the figures' faint golden halos and the fat, hairless child. She fixes all of her attention on the holy infant's smooth, dimpled flesh, her mind full of wordless, thrumming prayers.

In stark reversal of her earlier attempts to draw him out, Catherine now stops looking at her husband. If he speaks to her, she focuses just above his shoulder. Otherwise, she keeps him always at the edges of her vision, closing her eyes quickly whenever she catches an accidental glimpse of soft, abundant hair.

If she does not look at him, or think about his hairiness, there is less danger that her thoughts will influence her child's appearance. She remembers Papa's story of the joined-up twins, and stories from the wild pamphlets she used to love to read, where women startled by hares gave birth to children with great splits in their mouths, like the lips of the hares themselves; where women who slept under bearskins birthed babes covered with hair as thick as that of a bear.

It is her responsibility to keep her mind pious and clear of thoughts of wolves and animals and monsters. Away from the devil's clever influence. Her child must be kept safe.

It is like a miracle, the day she wakes one morning to a little humped roundness, more solid than her belly's usual sloping softness. She puts her hand against it, palm cupped to follow the shallow curve, and feels in her chest a suspended, creeping joy. And when, not long after, the first faltering moth wings begin to beat inside her, she closes her eyes and thinks of hairless things—stones rolled by the river, pearls built up and made glossy inside the oyster's mouth—and imagines her child undulating so inside her, built up from nothing, rolled to perfect smoothness.

THE LETTER COMES SOON after her child's first turnings. It is delivered to her by a palace servant, delivered negligently, hurriedly, as if it were a scrap of nothing, a paper of no importance whatsoever. Catherine stands holding it, looking down at the dark ink, scratches like some ancient witchcraft, symbols that meant something if you'd the magic key inside your mind to decipher them. She does not, and no amount of staring will change that.

She finds her husband with the Duke of Nevers, dicing in the king's *salle*. The king is nowhere in evidence, but his courtiers sit waiting, talking, drinking, amusing themselves until he appears in order to be amused by them. The duke sees her arrival; his dark eyes follow her as she walks the length of the room to reach them. There is nothing in them of expectation, or even of greeting; only of observation. Gone is the friendliness, the encouragement; and oh, how she burns to imagine what he must think of her. But he looks at her now with a mild raised brow, as if to say, here now, what is this? And then he nudges her husband's knees with the back of his hand, nodding toward her with his pointed chin.

Her husband sees her and blinks.

"Wife." He rises, eyes flicking to the paper she thrust toward him. Catherine turns her eyes hastily away from him, thinks a prayer inside her head.

Then she says, "It is—I think it is from my father. Would you—"

He takes it. Though she does not look at him, she hears the whisper of his breath as he reads. Then: "Come," he says, "let's—" and nods toward the door leading to the corridor. To Nevers, he says, "I'll return in a moment, Ludovico. Don't think I haven't forgotten you owe me for this last round."

A half-smile from Nevers in return, and then she finds herself moving back through the sprawl of the king's receiving room, hot with the movement of bodies and gossip, to the cooler, darker corridor beyond.

He draws her a little farther down, away from the guards who are pretending not to watch them, and says, "Would you like me to read it out to you? Or just tell you what it says?"

A sudden fear cuts through her then. She sees her father, her big, bull-shouldered, round-bellied father, felled like a tree. Some skirmish, perhaps, between the Huguenots and the king's men, and him caught, as so many people are, between? Or an illness? An accident on the road? He has always been so unaccountably fortunate. In all the years he traveled he never had worse luck than a lamed horse. Never had he fallen; never had he been injured by bandits on the road. The ships he took down churning rivers and across stretches of sea never sank; even the weather did not seem to trouble him, his chest remaining clear even after days in the rain, his spirit undaunted by the wet and cold.

"Does he live? Is it in his hand, or written by another?"

In her sudden urgency, she grasped her husband's arm, crumpled the sleeve of his doublet. He glances down at her fingers, and then at her face, his own very still. "I—yes, it bears his signature," he says. "He lives."

Catherine releases his sleeve, too relieved even to worry that she has touched him, looked up at him; presses a hand to her breast, where her heart had begun to beat once more, and another to her belly, where the babe is turning. "Please read it out," she says.

He clears his throat, and reads:

"My daughter,

I have returned to Lyons and found myself among true friends. Not all have turned from me, despite our misfortune; and the queen's generosity in assisting with my debts has gone a long way toward allowing me to regain my standing here. It is with happy expectations that I write you now, and with affection that I think of you always. I hope that you are well, my little beauty, and that you are happy in your new life.

May God grant that we meet again soon,
Your Papa."

He folds the letter and hands it back to her. A brush of fingers. Catherine pinches the paper's edges, swallowing and swallowing, a burning behind her eye sockets. There is a terrible flash of something inside her head, a whip of lightning across a black sky, showing all the storm carnage the darkness had concealed. Her mouth tastes, suddenly, of sickness, of vomit.

"He is well, then," she says at last. The paper in her hand crushed suddenly in the curl of her fingers.

Her husband says, "Yes," and shifts from one foot to the other. Another moment, and then he says, "Is there more that you need?" And then, "Are you . . . well?"

His inflection, she thinks, is all impatience, discomfort, wishing to be gone.

"I am well," she says. "I do not need anything else." And then, as he turns to go, "Thank you."

He pauses; she can feel him looking at her. "If you would like," he says, "I could write a response for you."

Catherine feels the offer like a palm over her heart, gentle, slowing the frantic beats. Almost, she says yes.

But that twisting, flashing thing inside her head is coming again, and again, an angry lash. She has nothing, as yet, to say to her father.

"No," she says, and again, "thank you."

He nods a slow nod. Turns once more.

And then he turns back, perhaps to say something else, in time to see her hand come up to cup her mouth, to hold inside the scream that has tunneled its way up from her belly. He becomes motionless, frozen in a moment of splayed fingers and open mouth, and Catherine knows what he must be seeing, the roaring creature who lives inside her, the rage she has kept bound up since her father told her of his ruin. She can feel the twist of her features, the contortions of anger and grief, knows the ugliness that he must see in her face now, the blotches of red and white, but she cannot care.

Papa is well, Papa is well, and that should be the only thing that matters now. The man who held her to his chest, who told her stories in the night, who knew she would not make a happy nun—the man who left her here, who brought her through a chapel to wed a wild man and then walked away without a word of farewell. He is well—thriving, it sounds!—well, thriving, on his way to becoming rich once more. His life undisturbed, her marriage buying his return to it. And she left here, with this man who stares at her now, who knows not what to say, who is alarmed by the raging creature she is trying to hold inside, stuffing it back with her palm, only a tearing snarl of a sob emerging.

Pedro

The court will move to Paris for the summer. The queen mother has made a match for her daughter, the Princess Marguerite, a match that sends whispers, hot as flames, through the court. The princess's intended is a Huguenot prince, and the rumors claim that Her Majesty means for her daughter's marriage to be balm that heals the country's wounds, knitting Catholic and Protestant flesh together, neighbor to neighbor, husband to wife. But the pope himself has refused to grant the couple a dispensation and how healing, go the whispers, can an unsanctioned union be? Unease makes snakes of Petrus's insides, and when he tries to catch Ludovico, who seems always to be with the king, to ask his opinion of the queen's plan, his friend has nothing to say that lessens the sensation of coiling, of hissing.

"All will be well," Ludovico says, smiling with one side of his mouth and neither of his eyes.

There is always a great upheaval when the court moves from one palace to another. Like an army—an entire town—a great, thousand-headed beast, with so many bits of itself to bring along it seems a miracle that so few are ever forgotten. The royal family, of course, and all their attendants, and all the courtiers who must or care to come. Servants, guardsmen, musicians, priests. Physicians and astronomers; cooks and tailors. Spit boys, their hands scabbed from fire sparks. Dwarfs, in their miniature coaches. Foreign dignitaries, who follow the king like beggars hoping for a scrap of his time.

And all the carts—full of furnishings, rugs, tapestries. Pots for cooking; glazed bowls and plates for eating; glasses for drinking. Casks of wine and sacks of provisions. Trunks of furs and silks and velvets. Hunting dogs and falcons. Weapons for the soldiers and the guardsmen; needles and thread for the ladies. A hundred other details Petrus is grateful not to have to know.

His wife is big with their child, and pale with it, the brightness disappeared from her cheeks like the landscape when the sun drifts beyond the horizon and drags all color away with it. He cannot think how to speak to her, even more so now than when they were first wed; she is remote as a sculpture, her eyes always cast down or up or otherwise away from him, her mouth chewing over prayers like a nun's or a madwoman's. She says nothing at all about their coming travels, though something bright as a candle flame flares in her eyes when he speaks of it. But the flare is not for him—her eyes still avoid his—and he does not understand her well enough to know the reason for its short existence.

Sometimes he finds himself wondering whether she might be a little witless, for of late she mumbles her prayers and little else; and then he remembers her question the first time they lay together, when he asked her whether she had been willing: *It is rather late for that question, is it not?* There is something sharp under her softness, her prayers.

At night they lie beside one another, and he listens to her sleeping sounds, and wonders if she ever dreams.

Ludovico will ride with them most of the way, then break off for his townhouse, where his neglected wife, two daughters, and infant son await him. He shakes his head when Petrus speaks of his own wife's impenetrability, all of her—expressions, mind, soul—enclosed behind a bricked-up fortress, too thickly guarded for him to enter. Amusement creases the skin beside his eyes.

"I haven't the smallest notion what Henriette thinks most of the time," he says. "I believe we both prefer it that way. She has her small intrigues and the children to keep her busy; no doubt your Catherine will be just as contented when she has a babe in arms and not merely in the belly. Henriette is always a misery when she is breeding."

Petrus kicks at a stone. "It does seem . . . a burden."

Ludovico shrugs. "It is a man's misfortune that we risk death in war. To bear children is a woman's risk and misfortune." He squints at the sky, where a hunting bird circles above the distant trees. "You might show her a bit of this magnificent palace before we leave it, if you'd like to shake her from her misery."

The feasting hall; His Majesty's *salle*; the tennis courts. The chapel, daily. Of the entire palace, hundreds upon hundreds of rooms, this is what his wife has seen. Petrus glances at the sky, where the sun burns white and threatens to slip, any moment, into a bed of clouds.

HE LEAVES LUDOVICO TO return to their chamber. His wife is dozing when he finds her at last. Her head lolls; her work—a very small white gown, embroidered all about the hem, which makes his heart stutter in his chest—is a tumble in her lap, the skirt drifting over the disconcerting round of her abdomen.

He was far too young, on Tenerife, to give any real thought to his own future. If pressed, he'd have said that he would live with Isabel and Manuel forever. And here at court—well. What does he know of marriage, or children, except those strange examples set by the people around him? Wives left on country estates while their husbands travel to Paris to curry favor with the king; mistresses given their own fine palaces, their children raised high. He thinks of the hairy girl from the pamphlet, her proud stance, her tilted chin, and thinks of how much easier it would have been had the queen mother found her for him to marry instead.

Years upon years of *let me be*, of never approaching unless approached, has left him without words. Almost, he backs from the room again before his wife wakes. But he forces himself to remain, leaning a little forward on the balls of his feet, rooting himself through them into the floor.

She comes awake all at once, as if his thoughts clanged through her own head. Her eyes blink away sleep and then fix upon him—

widen—hasten away. He sees her tongue come out to wet her lips, and those lips move soundlessly for a moment before she rises, setting aside her work and facing him without actually raising her eyes again to his.

"Husband," she says; no more. Question and statement at once.

Anger behind his breastbone, like the stirring of embers. Her hands cupping the mound of her belly; her eyes carefully keeping away from the sight of him. The smooth loveliness of her cheeks. He swallows to dampen the embers, forces himself to say, "We leave so soon for Paris and I—well, it only just occurred to me that I have been rather remiss—that is to say, you've seen very little of this place, and that seems a shame, for there is so much to see—"

Several expressions ripple over her face as the words fall helplessly from his tongue, a cataract of stupidity. He cannot guess at any of them. Another swallow, and then he says, "A tour, I thought—and if the weather holds, we could explore the grounds."

"If you like," she says.

THEIR FOOTSTEPS MAKE HOLLOW echoes in the corridors. The servants and guardsmen they pass offer curious glances, but nothing more. Catherine's right hand rests light as a petal upon his elbow, her left under the heavy globe of her belly, as if holding it up, and Petrus tries to keep his pace slow to match hers.

The gallery, which was the work of King Henri's father, should dazzle, should *honor* anyone lucky enough to see it. His wife looks at the frescos and sculptures and gleaming woodwork with the late king's salamander emblem without expression.

"This king was a great supporter of art and modern learning," Petrus says. "He was a patron of Leonardo da Vinci himself—King Henri told me that his father was with the great artist upon his death."

She makes a small humming sound that might be an acknowledgment of his words. His teeth clamp together.

Into the great ballroom—where they have sat small among the rest of the court during feasts and entertainments, but which she has never seen empty and echoing, without all the noise and movement of courtiers and servants to detract from the mythological stories that cover the walls and the glory of the coffered ceiling. The room gleams warm, all oak and gold and the colors of the frescos, and Petrus loves it as much as he has ever loved any place.

"King Henri commissioned this room," he says; and now he is speaking more to himself than to the mute woman on his arm. "When I was a child, I thought I had seen all the wonders that man can create—until this was built, and I was certain I had entered Heaven itself."

"It is very splendid," says his wife, and he looks down at her, surprised. Her eyes are fixed upon the crescent moons in the ornate ceiling, a line between her pale brows. He looks away again from the brown-gold of her hair, the stretch of her throat above her gown's high collar.

Unexpectedly she says, all on her own, "My father covered the walls of our dining room with tapestries showing classical Greek stories. My favorite was the simplest—only the three Fates, holding the thread of some poor person between their fingers, woven all in blues." She turns a little, carefully not looking at Petrus, her eyes roaming over the walls. "These remind me a little of home."

It occurs to him, like a tap in the center of his brow, that he has no idea what sort of home she lived in before their marriage. He clears his throat, says, cautious as a man trying to catch a skittish horse, "Was it very grand, then, your father's house?"

"Oh," she says. "Not so grand, I think. It was a merchant's house—my father's offices on the ground floor, and the kitchen, too; then upstairs the receiving room and the room where we dined. Our bedrooms above that, and then the attic, where our servants slept."

"It sounds a great deal grander than where I spent my earliest years," Petrus says; and now her eyes fly to his face, sticking there for long moments before she wrenches them away, whispering words to herself that his ears cannot snatch. His chest fills with a quivering sensation, too tentative to be identified.

"Was it—did you have a house, then? Where you came from?"

The quivering lessens a little. "Yes," he says; but the word comes out all wrong, too sharply, a claw slice. He sees the flinch that ripples over her features and draws in air.

"You thought, perhaps," he says after a pause—more careful now, but with an underlying bitterness he cannot mask—"that it was as the stories say? That my hairiness comes from being reared in a cave, suckled by—what, by bears, by wolves?"

There is wariness in the line of her shoulders. "I—I don't know."

He says, "That *is* what you heard, though?"

She turns her face away from him entirely so that all he can see is her ear, from which one of the amethysts dangles, and the strong line of her neck. "Yes. Or—not precisely, but—"

Anger is irrational. It is what everyone thinks, for he has never renounced the tale. King Henri introduced him so to anyone new who came to court. *This is our savage prince,* he would say, glance bright and affectionate. *See how tame?*

"Come," Petrus says now. "You have not seen the grotto."

She comes along, eyes cast down upon the sway of her skirt over its frame as she walks.

SHE WOULD RATHER BE anywhere than here with him. He suspected, when the queen informed him of his betrothal, that it would be so; but he had not fully understood how deeply his wife longed to be away from him until this moment, with her eyes canted sideways, her body turned a little so the breadth of her belly is in no danger of touching him accidentally. They step into the gardens, and though there are of course no mirrors here, he sees his own face reflected in the eyes of everyone they pass. These reflections show nothing of his personhood, only his strangeness to them all. And beside him his wife, who refuses to look at all.

Anger, again: a vivid, chilling flare. And then it melts abruptly to a muckish pool. She follows him, to all appearances as tame as he has ever been; but he remembers again her question the night of their wedding, and the wild panic in her eyes as they stood in the ballroom, closed in by eyes and mouths and the room's high walls, their two bodies brushing as he asked permission to kiss her. Her *yes* in his mind now seems to echo every one of his own to the people who inquired as to the veracity of the stories they'd heard of him. *Yes* his father was king of a primitive people. *Yes* he grew up clothed in nothing but his own hair. *Yes* he loves the lions in the menagerie, for they remind him of home, and of the lioness who fed him with her own sweet, hot milk.

Birdsong drifts over and between them as they walk, footsteps crunching over the cool pathways. The gardens are bright and tousled, and Petrus feels a little foolish, leading her briskly through them, not stopping, as he supposes he should, to give her time to take in their splendor. Into a small cobbled courtyard he takes her, surrounded by a stand of high maritime pines, whose trunks bend and curve, the needles a happy cluster at their crowns. The green here making the shadows deeper and the chinks of sunlight that pass through the top branches all the more golden by contrast. He slows his steps as they near the structure across the courtyard; and now he hears the quick gusting of her breath, though she does not complain aloud, only puts one hand to her back and another once more to cup the heavy curve that goes everywhere before her.

The nights upon nights that led to this broadening. His tongue goes dry. In the rustling of her breath, he hears his own whistling too fast between the oiled bars of his cage.

He hears her steps slow further as they draw nearer to the structure, though he does not look at her, his eyes, as ever, caught fast. Though it was clearly built by men, made of gray blocks of stone, with three narrow archways leading to a dim interior, the thing looks as natural as a hole in a mountain; a place at once elemental and sinister, where anything might lurk. When he was a boy, he imagined the malevolent spirits Isabel described lying here in wait for him.

There are male figures to either side of each archway, hewn from the stone like primitive people conjured by some ancient god. They are naked, their thighs and bellies muscled, their arms and feet not fully formed so that it looks as if they have been caught and hardened in the act of emerging from the stones behind them. Their heads and faces are thickly haired and bearded; though not so thickly as his own.

His wife makes a small sound, and Petrus pulls his gaze, with a great effort, away from the grotto and to her. She stands like a woman turned to stone herself, eyes huge, one foot frozen in a forward step—toward whatever her imagination has conjured in response to this place, to him. A bed of skins, a fire circle, a smear of blood on stone in a vaguely recognizable shape, perhaps; the ancient equivalent of all the paintings and frescos that adorn the palace walls.

"It was built before I came to court," Petrus says. "Ten years before, perhaps? I am not entirely certain."

At the sound of his voice her eyes dart to him and then away; her lips press, as if she is angry with herself. But then she looks back at the thing before them and says, "I thought—it seems much older, somehow."

He shrugs, though she does not look at him so she cannot see the gesture. "Yes, I think so, too. I suspect that was the intention."

Still, she stares.

"King Henri—he told me once that had his father not already created this place, he'd have made something very like it for me."

Her eyes close, squeezing at the corners.

"He meant it kindly," Petrus says, a lance in his voice; he is thinking of the king's smile, usually so reticent, but which he gave so generously to his wild boy. And then, when Petrus showed himself capable of learning—showed his strong appetite for proving his brain was as thoughtful as anyone else's—His Majesty's teeth showed white above his dark beard. *You were better suited to a palace than to a cave.*

"I need to sit down," his wife says now, the words like a frayed thread, and Petrus lurches instinctively forward, fingers curling around her upper arm to steady her. He releases her when he hears her teeth click together, only touching her elbow to guide her to the bench, a half-circle of cool stone, within the bower of pines. There she sits gracelessly, hands clutching the edge of the bench to either side of her lap, neck bent.

Petrus stands before her, arms hanging loose and empty at his sides. Inside his head, guilt and defiance clash together, scraping and grinding like two swords. This young woman, curled over the being they made together, is not his enemy. He is hurting her—unwittingly, perhaps. Or perhaps not; for the urge to make her *see* him fills him, the force of it like to split him open. He has been turned entirely inside out, every instinct that has kept him biddable and silent—shoulders hunched against jeers, palms poised to cover his ears against hisses of witchcraft and devilry—tumbling, without his skin to hold it in, out from between his ribs. In its place this new instinct sits screaming: *Look at me*, look *at me!*

But his wife's knuckles merely tighten over the edge of the bench seat, and when she raises her eyes at last, they are vague and unseeing.

Catherine

The journey is strange and straggling, groups leaving in untidy lines from Fontainebleau. Her husband rides beside Nevers before their paths diverge, but Catherine is bundled into a coach, with cushions for her back. She sits for what feels like a very long time before they actually depart, dozing lightly, listening, when she is awake, to the snorting of the horses, the calls of harried servants, the creak of harness leather.

When the coach door opens, she startles, then stares as the small woman who undressed her for her wedding night climbs inside and settles on the seat opposite.

"I hate these trips," the dwarf says cheerfully, smoothing her skirt. "I think I'd have done better as a wife to some peasant who at least was rooted to the earth." She tips her head, eyes assessing. "You're nearing your time?"

Catherine licks her lips. "I've a few weeks yet, I hope."

"Don't want to whelp in this coach?" The dwarf laughs. "I do not blame you at all." She must have seen Catherine flinch, for she sighs with mock-frustration. "My dear, you really must grow a heavier skin if you are to survive at court. Or heavier *pelt*, as your husband has done."

Catherine looks down at the round of her belly and says nothing.

Another sigh. "Well. We are to be together here for a good long while—you mustn't blame me for seeking gossip." She leans forward. "How *is* marriage suiting you? You were like an aspen on your wedding night, you trembled so—I hope Monsieur Sauvage no longer frightens you, at least."

Catherine's eyes flick to the window of the coach, where the curtains are parted just enough to show a seam of sunlight.

"I've known him since I was a child, you know," the dwarf continues, undaunted by Catherine's silence, "but I confess I never imagined him wed." A long pause, during which Catherine stares at the line of light until her eyesight blurs with it. "Ah," the dwarf murmurs then. "But he is happy about the child, yes?"

"I—do not know his mind," Catherine says to the curtains.

"Ah, men. Who can know their minds?"

The coach lurches to a slow roll then, and they both settle back, Catherine wincing with every jolt over the pitted roads.

Much later, she is forced at last to knock upon the roof of the coach so that it might stop long enough for her to scramble down to relieve her bladder behind a tree. The dwarf—Agnes, Catherine recalls belatedly—crouches beside her, raising her skirts without shame. Catherine looks away, wonders whether she has ever done so before the entire court, recalling one memorable feast during which another dwarf made water upon request, prompting uproarious laughter throughout the hall.

The road is lined to either side by trees that stretch out and out, deepening shadows between them, blackish moss and the rustle of underbrush. Behind them, Fontainebleau; before them Paris. She closes her eyes, pictures Papa's maps, sees the long blue snake of the Seine. Remembers the dance of Papa's plume as his horse trotted away from them. So much to see. To smell, to taste. To hear. Music and languages. Spices and wines. Until she came to court, Catherine had never seen a dwarf, or a giant, or a man like her husband, except in rough woodcuts. It is a giddy thought, how much more there must be.

For a moment, she forgets the heaviness of her belly, the ache of her back, and feels instead only the urge to walk, move, stride out over the land like the old men in one of Papa's stories. The stretch and burn of muscle, the road firm and dusty under her shoes, the world spreading out before and behind and to either side of her, everywhere a newness, a discovery; over each horizon something more.

They just stood up and walked away, and explored the great wide together by sea and soil.

Back in the coach, resettled against the cushions, she draws the curtain over the window to shut out the sky and the road and the ache she cannot satisfy, and says, not caring if the question is rude, "Why does the queen keep so many dwarfs?"

Agnes stares at her long enough that Catherine can feel it; only when she meets the other woman's eyes does Agnes respond.

"We're magical, you know," she says, with a funny, quick raising-and-lowering of her brows. "We offer Her Majesty protection. We are *very* valuable."

For a moment, Catherine cannot decide whether she is serious or jesting. And then Agnes rolls her eyes to the coach's low roof, and Catherine smothers a startled laugh behind her palm.

A little later: "He is . . . indifferent to me, I think."

Her voice is low; she ought not speak of her husband so, and particularly not to a near-stranger. But she has suddenly remembered Agnes's laughing face when the physician examined the cup with Catherine's urine, and after her own almost-laughter now, the words come fast and slippery as salmon through a narrow neck of river.

"He hardly speaks, except to tell me the most—the smallest, barest details of himself. He has not mentioned the child, though he must of course know of it." She gestures to indicate the swelling in her lap. "I have no idea what he cares for. *If* he cares for anything at all. He is—not cold, not cruel, but . . . indifferent."

Agnes screws up her mouth. Catherine looks at her, and then away, already regretting her words.

"Monsieur Sauvage does not care to mingle with the rest of us oddities," Agnes says after a time. "Not Her Majesty's dwarfs, not the giants who guard the gates. He holds himself quite apart from us all."

Catherine's brows come together above her nose.

"He came to me today," Agnes goes on. "Braved our chambers to speak with me—because he thought I was kind to you on your wedding day. I've spoken to him only a few times in all the years we've been at this court together, and I suspect he was happy to keep it that way. But he saw you were unhappy, and thought you could use a little kindness. A *friend*, I believe was his word."

Catherine realizes, quite suddenly, that she is staring; and that her nose is dripping. And her eyes as well. She wipes her nose with the back of her hand, and Agnes lets out a sound halfway between laughter and disgust.

"Ah, you pathetic thing," she says, and Catherine would be offended, but there is no tinge of malice to the words at all, only great swathes of understanding.

THE CHÂTEAU DU LOUVRE rises high, pale and imposing. Catherine and her husband are assigned a chamber furnished exactly as their chamber was at Fontainebleau—the same rug upon the floor, the same wooden cross and ugly painting and round mirror upon the walls. At night, as the babe rolls within her, Catherine listens to her husband sleeping, his sounds at once soft and rumbling, childlike and bestial. In the dark, refusing to look at him, Catherine can pretend, if she wishes, that an entirely different husband lies beside her, one she can look upon without worry that doing so will harm their child, one who speaks more than a few words to her at a time. One who does not come with a false story attached to him, whose history is true, and as comprehensible as her own.

He sent Agnes to me, she thinks, guilt stilling her thoughts. Something almost too tender to prod blooms behind her breastbone. Without conscious thought, her hand goes to the basin between her hips. Beside her, her husband murmurs in his sleep.

FOR HER CONFINEMENT, THE period before the babe decides to come, their chamber is hers alone, her husband banished to some other part of the palace. The room is turned dark and airless—a womb, the servants call it, as they tack a heavy tapestry over the precious window. *A tomb*, Catherine thinks, balking, frantic. She presses her hands together to stop herself from tearing the tapestry down again. Feels the imagined burn of muscles working at the tug of the heavy fabric, the glare of sunlight gilding her. As all the light disappears from the room, she sucks in a great gasp of air; and then it is as if she holds that single breath fast inside her mouth.

She thinks, then, of her mother's visard, the black velvet mask she wore whenever she was forced to be in the sun for any length of time. When she was a small girl, whenever she saw her mother wearing the mask, Catherine's breath grew cold and short, as if the faceless, voiceless devil before her were freezing the air on its way to her lungs. Maman, slipping the visard off to show her own pale face behind it, had chided Catherine for a silly thing; but still the fear remained.

As she neared womanhood, to keep her from venturing too often into their courtyard when the sun was high, her mother used to threaten her with a visard of her own.

"You will have to wear one someday," she would say. "If you don't want that day to be today, come inside at once." Her white hand just barely venturing beyond the shadow of the doorway, beckoning.

She died before she ever dispatched her threat.

After Maman died, Catherine put the visard for the first time to her own face. Her heartbeat quickened and she sucked in a great breath of air before taking the bead—which dangled on a short length of ribbon from the mouth of the mask—between her lips. She worked the bead behind her teeth to hold the mask firmly in place, and dropped her hands.

With the bead in her mouth, she was voiceless; in the mask, featureless. Her nose was compressed against the leather, making it difficult to draw air in through her nostrils. She had a sudden feeling, panic flaring, that if she kept it on for even a moment longer, she would suffocate entirely.

Standing now in the airless room—womb—*tomb*—the breath she held feels solid as the bead of Maman's visard. Both breath and bead prevent her from screaming as she is closed away.

DAYS EDGE INTO A week, and then two, the weight of the child beginning to feel like a stone holding her underwater. She cannot breathe fully, cannot find a position in which to lie that does not make her hips ache, or her spine, or numb her legs all the way down to her toes. Except for Agnes's visits—kept brief, for, as the small woman says, the air in the room is too thick for two people to comfortably breathe it for long—she is mostly on her own, but for the servants who bring her meals and lay her fire and take away her pot. She lies and stares at the Virgin and her child, and hopes and *hopes*, though she dares not give words to her hope, even inside her own head.

But the heaviness of the child, the thickness of the room's air, the twin pressings of fear and hope—even these cannot occupy all her time, and boredom creeps in through the chinks. Boredom, and something else, a restlessness that is not entirely to do with being shut away like a gown in a trunk. Catherine paces the length and width of the room, pauses before the window, aching to tear away the concealing tapestry, not merely to feel the sun upon her face, upon the too-white skin of her hands, but to see what she can of Paris through the glass. All her life she has imagined coming to this place, this city; hungered for it as a beggar hungers for bread. Now she is here, but she has seen almost nothing of it—she could be anywhere, this room could be *anywhere*, she might be buried in a tomb in the bowels of a church. She imagines her fists battering against the wall at the outer edge of the room, the stones there crumbling under their assault, chunks falling to whatever lies below, outside, until there is a hole large enough for her to stand in, to perch upon, to look through, to hear the things Papa used to hear when he came here. For it is to this palace that Papa often journeyed, bringing with him bolts of bright cloth, spools of thread to match. Fabrics so fine that when she was small, he would only allow Catherine to touch them with the tip of one finger, scrupulously cleaned beforehand, before he wrapped them up safe for their journey to the queen and her ladies in Paris.

She stands before the wall, before the tapestry covering the window, her hands fisted. And then, all at once, her fingers unclench, make their way to the heavy slope of her belly, holding it as gently as her father once held his bolts of velvet and silk.

"When you arrive," she whispers, the first words she has spoken directly to the person who swims inside her, "we will see Paris together."

THE DAY OF THE Princess Marguerite's wedding, Agnes comes to see Catherine early. The smaller woman is roped with pearls; they coil through her dark hair, wrap themselves about her throat to trail over her chest to the dip of her waist. She finds Catherine in her chemise, the bloat of her belly lifting the hem higher at the front, showing her legs to the tops of her knees. The room is hot, for it is August; outside, the city smells of excrement.

"I never thought I would say this, but you're lucky to be shut away right now," Agnes says, wrinkling her nose. "It's a foul day for a wedding." She swings her legs, feet dangling more than a handspan above the floor, fanning herself against the closeness of the air. "Is Sauvage entirely barred from this room, then?" she says.

Catherine, feeling peevish, all the more so at the thought of the royal wedding she is going to miss, all the things Maman would have gloried in seeing, says, "Why must everyone call him that?"

"What? Sauvage?"

"Yes."

A pause. A faint laugh. "Well—it is what he is, no? We are all called what we are. The queen is the queen; I am petite. Your husband is *sauvage*—or looks it, which is near enough to satisfy almost anyone." Agnes taps her fingers on her knees. "And you? Did your family have no pet names for you?"

Ma belle, Papa called her. Catherine blinks him away—his plump smile, the affection in his voice. Her jaw tightens. She has let few thoughts of him into her head since he left her at Fontainebleau; she will not, *will not* let him in now.

But her thoughts, instead, edge toward her husband. The rumpled look to his face when he turns to her. His sudden smile when he was briefly cheered after he bested Nevers at swordplay.

Catherine's breast hums with fear. "How do you bear it?" she says, low.

Agnes hops down, landing with a surprising thud upon the carpet.

"I know nothing else; except hunger, that is, in my parents' home, they were so poor. When they sold me, my stomach was full for the first time I could remember. And then when I came here—" She snorts. "It is no small thing, to have food in your belly, a warm bed."

Catherine says, "If this—if it—"

But she cannot—will not—speak the words, lest speaking make them true. Instead, she puts her hands on either side of her belly.

"If it *is*," Agnes says, "then Monsieur Sauvage will know best how *it* feels."

LATER THAT MORNING, WHILE the Catholic princess marries her Huguenot prince at Notre Dame Cathedral, the midwife arrives in Catherine's room and sets herself up immediately to stay. Three servants lead her into the stifling chamber, bearing between them a bundle of fresh linen, a chair with a sloping back and a half-moon carved out of the seat, and a pallet to lay for the midwife at the foot of Catherine's bed.

The midwife is a round woman with a chip-toothed smile and sturdy forearms that prove, when she pushes up her sleeves, to be covered with hair almost as dark and thick as a man's. Catherine cannot stop staring at the woman's arms as her belly is pressed like dough, the midwife grunting a little in satisfaction when she feels a foot where it ought to be, a head down near the curling hair between Catherine's thighs.

"The babe is hearty," she says. "And in a good position. Won't be long now."

Catherine swallows. She knows that she is staring, and she knows that to stare so is rude; but there is something about the midwife's hairy arms that mesmerizes.

And then she heaves her eyes away, horrified. Her eyes pinch closed and she promises herself and the painting beside her bed that they will never again stray to the woman's hairy arms.

Pedro

For a moment, under the high arches of the cathedral, watching the princess and her intended standing before the cardinal, Petrus thinks that perhaps the queen mother's plan might not be mad, after all. Princess Marguerite is gowned in blue and fur and jewels; the prince holds his head like a man pleased to be doing his duty. If the staunchly Catholic queen mother is willing to so compromise about the faith of her daughter's husband, what other miracles might take place? In a show of magnanimity all the strongest and most important among the noble Huguenot leaders have been invited to Paris for the wedding festivities, though they, and the Huguenot prince, were forced to remain outside the cathedral for the Mass.

During the celebration that follows the wedding, Petrus stands on the fringes of the dancing. Though he has been at court for more than twenty years, the spectacle of this wedding feast fills him with something like his old astonishment. There is more glitter, more gilding even than usual, so much that he nearly misses the sharp, metallic tinge to the merriment, the faint tension that vibrates down the length of the feasting hall. He watches as the princess and her new husband dance the pavane, their bodies stiff as corpses. He drags his eyes away from the gold-plated dishes, the peacock dressed in all its feathers, jewels winking in its eye sockets, and finally sees the odd rigidity to the way the Catholic courtiers hold themselves, as if they are armored under their fine doublets.

He seeks out Ludovico, who is dancing and flirting as usual. But despite his apparent liveliness, Ludovico's dark eyes flick, sharp, about the room, and when he spies Petrus watching him, he does not quite smile. A trickle of cold makes its way down Petrus's spine then, all the warmth he felt this morning shivering away as he realizes that this marriage, which was meant to solidify the peace between Catholics and Huguenots, has only emphasized its weakness.

HE RETIRES LATE THAT night, so late that the sky is brightening at the horizon. He pauses at the junction between the corridor to his bedchamber and his wife's. She danced about the edges of his mind all night, young and moon-eyed, and he thinks, for a moment, of going to her, tapping on her door, sitting with her for a time and telling her all about the marriage ceremony and the merriment afterward. That is how he would say it—*merriment*—he would make no mention of the strange atmosphere in the feasting hall, the air, under the smells of food and perfume, bristling as if with lightning. He would amuse her, as a husband ought, with stories of the guests' drunken foolishness, the Fool's antics. He would describe faithfully the princess's gown.

He hesitates, imagining this. The two of them, side by side. Her smile, welcoming. His words, entertaining.

He turns toward his own room.

A FEW DAYS LATER, he wakes to find the city of Paris in uproar.

The news is enough to cut holes in his chest: one of the Huguenots' most popular leaders, a man invited to attend the wedding, narrowly survived assassination in the night. When Petrus ventures out of his chamber, the air inside the Château du Louvre is thickened, milk churned to cream. Ludovico is closeted with King Charles and his advisors; the princess and her new-wed husband are locked in their chamber; the queen mother passes through the king's *salle* with a sharp smile until she, too, disappears into seclusion with her son and his most trusted men.

Petrus finds himself standing with a group of Her Majesty's dwarfs, who have been shut out of whatever is happening just like the rest of the court and who, just like the rest of the court, are carefully pretending at normalcy. But this is not normal; he usually takes such care to stand apart from these people, as if their status as oddities of nature might draw further attention to his own. But today he stands beside them, near enough to hear them breathe, to imagine he hears the thumping of their hearts. Agnes glances at him, smiles tight and small.

PETRUS GOES TO SLEEP and wakes, drowning, early on the morning of Saint Bartholomew's feast day, caught in a net, roped and grabbed and gulping in salt-thickened waves. The things holding him are shouting, his ears are filled with screams. He flounders up and up, gasping, and when his eyes open at last it is to his narrow chamber, the walls and furniture rendered grotesque as sea serpents in the darkness. He lies still on his back, chest heaving, trying to breathe away the nightmare.

And then he hears them again—the screams—and his entire body goes rigid as driftwood. He strains to listen, and hears them once more, animal in their terror. Outside Petrus's dreaming mind, they seem utterly senseless, and yet—

A bell tolls somewhere in the city, deep and resonant, raising gooseflesh all along his arms and shoulders. The danger might yet be nameless, formless, but his body recognizes it. Another cry, tearing roughly as a knife through the fabric of the night, and Petrus finds his limbs working of their own accord, finds himself out of his bed and standing barefooted on the floor, feeling heat in all the soft and vulnerable places where he might be pierced. His belly, his sides, his throat; the soft cupped pulse-points at elbows and behind knees; the flesh of his heel, where he might be sliced to the tendon, cut down like Achilles.

But he is no Achilles, glorying in battle. Men's shouts, the ring of swords, and Petrus finds himself backing up, away from the door, seeking shelter behind the bulk of the bed. His heart knocking against the bone of his chest, water that tastes of the sea sliding into the corners of his mouth.

Catherine

The midwife wakes Catherine, shaking her roughly, and then, when the mists of sleep refuse to part easily, shouts into her ear to *get up, Madame, get up, they will kill us all, for the love of God, rise*!

The woman has her by the arm before Catherine understands what is happening, is tugging her, stumbling, from the bed. Her hip bumps a table, the midwife's fingers dig bruises into her flesh, and Catherine says, all baffled, "What? What?"

The midwife's other hand comes up, cupping itself over Catherine's mouth. "*Hush*, Madame," she says, and even in the darkness, Catherine can see that the other woman's eyes are wide, fear showing in all the white. They are silent for a moment, Catherine breathing in the sweat of the midwife's palm, lipping as she gasps at the mound under the thumb. And then she hears it—the tolling of bells, the shouting of men, cries like those pigs make when they are butchered. Thought disappears from Catherine's head; she clutches at the midwife, heedless, now, of the other woman's hairy arms. The midwife takes her hand away from Catherine's mouth.

"Who—what—?" Catherine whispers, and the midwife shakes her head.

"It's got to be the Huguenots, no? They say the king should never have opened the city gates to them. He invited our doom right into this place."

"Oh, God," Catherine moans, and tucks her arms around herself, around the babe who is turning merrily within her. Her throat tastes suddenly sour, as if she has already been sick. *Oh, God—*

"They know nothing of God," the midwife says, and Catherine sees a silver flash, a knife from the woman's kit. "Heretics, heretics—"

They are going to die. Another scream rends its way down the corridor, and the sound of thudding. Behind Catherine, the midwife has dropped to her knees, prayers spilling from her mouth like vomit, the slim silver knife caught between her fervent palms. "*Our Father, Who art in Heaven . . .*"

Her prayers sound like nothing, nothing; for the first time in her life, Catherine cannot feel the weight of the familiar holy words. Instead, she feels the walls threatening to collapse around her; feels each shout from beyond the closed door like a blow to her own body; feels her child, *her child*, the weight of it, pressing down, grinding inside her pelvis, a foot or a fist pushing upward into her ribs as if trying to punch its way to safety. She will never see her child's face, she thinks with sudden, terrible certainty, a hollowness under her breasts, a fullness inside her throat. This babe, whose welfare she has tried so hard to protect, sheltering it within her own body, doing her best to keep her thoughts pure—it has all been for nothing.

"*. . . forgive us our trespasses . . .*"

Another shout, furious, murderous, and Catherine flinches, tears stinging the outside corners of her eyes.

"*. . . deliver us from evil . . .*"

"No," Catherine says, the word coming from her belly. Her child speaking through her. "*No.*" She turns this way, that way, seeking something to do, and her eyes alight upon the trunk pushed up against the wall near the covered-over window, across the room from the vulnerable door. She is bending toward it before the thought is fully formed, her belly changing shape as the babe sloshes forward, a sharp pinching at the base of her spine as she begins to shove. An animal growl coming up from her throat as she heaves the heavy trunk across the floor.

Pedro

Petrus's sword has come into his hand somehow, and prayers have come into his mouth, though he could not say to whom he is praying, only that he is. There is a rush and thud of footsteps in the corridor outside, voices much nearer than those that have been screaming. Someone cries, "To me!"

Petrus huddles back against the wall, clutching his sword. He has never used it in any real sense, only for spectacle's sake; never has he wielded it with the intension of carving through skin and muscle, catching on bone. His back is sweating, his breath coming in frantic gusts, terror rattling his ribs. He has not felt the like since the hands, and the ship, and the selling of him. He knows that he should push himself away from the wall, out from behind the bed, and seek out the screamers to defend them, whomever they are. But his muscles have hardened and will not move except to hunch his shoulders around his ears, to rock his body back and forth as he prays, the tip of his sword scraping the floor in time to his movements. There will be scratches there in the aftermath, like claw marks, as if a beast were trapped and terrified in this room, trying with no success to pare away fear with its scrabbling, to leave the clean lines of rational thought in its place.

Is it the Huguenots attacking, as some of the courtiers feared they would? There was meant to be peace in Paris for this wedding, a cessation of bloodshed, but no matter who is responsible for whatever is happening beyond his chamber door, it is clear the fragile peace is ended, torn to ribbons, stomped upon.

Scratch, scratch, scratch goes his sword point.

Another scream, this one high, a sound like a fox. A woman's voice. And all at once, Petrus's head fills with shoving, clamorous thoughts. Isabel's family, slashed, felled, stolen. The bars of the cage, immovable as he shook them. His wife, grown big because of him.

The fox's cry comes again, more weakly now. The sword scrapes the floor again, this time as Petrus rises, gathering the flayed strips of his courage about him, feet taking him to the door, and then out—*out*—

The corridors are full of shadows, thickets of torchlight jouncing somewhere ahead of him. Petrus clings to the wall, his sword arm trembling, his heart a hammer in his throat. The familiar palace corridors are turned unfamiliar by the sounds echoing along them. War cries, that is the only word for them, carrying so strangely that they seem to be coming from every direction at once, closing in upon him. The shadows flicker and dance and fall away, leaving him in near-darkness.

He knows the way to his wife's room. It is not so far—just down here, only his bare toes touching the floors as he moves, and then around this corner—a quick look finds only more darkness.

There is something up ahead, a shape, darker than the darkness. Petrus approaches, toes now curling painfully. One step, two, three—

It is a man, not one he knows by sight. Slouched nearly to the floor, his legs spread and crooked. In the dark, all Petrus can make out are the eyes, half-lidded. The man is still, with a stillness that makes Petrus's skin curl in more tightly around his muscles. He lets out a short huff of breath and does not stop, for he is nearly there, nearly to his wife's door, though the corridor seems to shift around him, stones rearranging themselves, making him doubt his own recollection of the distance from his chamber to hers. He is moving faster now, running, each foot scarcely making contact with the floor before it is off again, moving up and forward.

When he reaches the door, he still does not stop moving, hurtles himself against it, a shock of pain along his arm and neck and shoulder. He hears a cry from inside, and all he knows is relief—she is there, she is alive—and he shoves again, but the door moves only a fraction, the tiniest of spaces appearing between it and the wall. He pants, peering in through the narrow cleft, and finds an eye peering back, as near to his own as if they lay in their wide bed together, whispering secrets in the night.

"It is I," he says, and through the crack hears a sound that might be a sob or a laugh.

"The trunk," his wife says a moment later. "I moved the trunk, and now I cannot shift it. Here—quick"—this to someone else, someone inside the room with her—"help me, help me—!"

Petrus pushes from his side, and they tug from theirs, and the door inches open, bit by bit, until there is a gap wide enough for him to slip through. He half-trips over the trunk when he is in, and drops his sword, turning immediately to close the door behind him, pushing hard so that the trunk slides back into place against it. His body is made of water, and when he turns she is looking at him—and then away, as is her usual habit—and then back, quick flitting glances, and he wonders if she can see the puddling of his flesh on the floor beneath him, every once-solid bit of him melting with each noise from beyond the barred door, each flash of memory, the too-still man huddled in the corridor, the torchlight dancing away from him as if with a terrible joy.

Catherine

They sit together on the floor behind the bed, and though Catherine's eyes still slide off of him like shoes over the slickness of ice, she lets their sides press. "What is happening?" she asks him, but he shakes his head.

The midwife is on her knees, endlessly praying, and Catherine cannot even make out the words now, ears filled with her own heartbeat. Her husband is silent. He is dressed only in his shirt, open at the throat, his legs bare. His sword rests across his lap, the tip angled away from Catherine's body; she fixes her eyes on the point of it and thinks of the day he bested Nevers, his sword hooking itself around the other man's, the swift end to their bout.

They wait and they wait. It must, she thinks, be after dawn by now, this endless night at an end—but the tapestry is still spread wide across the window, and none of them move to take it down, as if fearful of what they might find outside. At some point Catherine looks down and is mildly surprised to see that her fingers have entangled themselves with his, tree roots clutching, keeping one another upright on the earth. His hold is so tight that the tips of her fingers are bloodless.

Despite the creak of fear, she eventually sleeps, drifting uneasily, eyes opening now and again to find that the midwife has gone silent, her lips pressed closed.

Pedro

It is Ludovico who comes to them, though it is so long before he does that Petrus has tried twice to leave the room only to have Catherine clutch at his hand. After hours of stillness, of clenched muscles and waiting for the worst, for the door to be battered down, the trunk shoved away, his swordsmanship put to the test to defend his family—his *family*! Despite the fear-sweat that still dampens his armpits, the trembling of his fingers, he feels the need to move.

The palace has grown quiet, but now there are noises from outside; it sounds as if the city of Paris is pulling itself apart. His wife, again awake, is biting her lip, a little blood running under the edge of her tooth. In his hand, hers has grown damp and limp, but she has not released him.

The knocking at the door makes all three people in the room sit tall, their heartbeats rapping a half beat faster. Petrus drags himself upward, ignoring the silent, frantic shaking of his wife's head. He holds his sword and steps to the door, places his palm against the wood as if he might somehow, in that way, discern the identity and intent of the person on the other side.

"Friend," comes a familiar voice, and Petrus sags. He drops his sword upon the floor with a sound like a struck bell, and pushes at the trunk to move it. Then his hand is on the door latch, and the door is open, and Ludovico is standing there, half-smiling. There is a crust of red across his cheekbone, a spray of blood.

"I looked for you in your chamber, but I should have known to seek you here," he says. Looking over Petrus's shoulder, he says to Catherine, "I am glad you are unharmed, Madame."

Petrus's wife, in her chemise and nothing else, nods stiffly, even as she edges away, looking for a wrap.

"What is happening?" Petrus says, and Ludovico looks back at him. He shifts, beckoning Petrus into the corridor; Petrus follows after telling his wife he will return in a moment. Her face is pale as snow as he closes the door.

"It was . . . an attack. On the Huguenot leaders. Coligny is dead," Ludovico says, naming the Protestant leader who, only days earlier, survived the assassination attempt. "So are most of the others."

Petrus is silent, stones filling his belly one by one and leaving no room for anything else.

"They would have attacked *us*," Ludovico says, strangely fierce. "Do you not see that? They blamed us for the attempt on their leader's life."

The stones pile higher, threatening his heart. "And so we forestalled them by . . . completing the thing at which we—at which someone—failed before." *We*, he says without thought, though once spoken the word has the feeling of rough cloth. Of untruth.

But it seems to calm whatever excited Ludovico a moment ago. "They are not a danger now."

Almost, he asks who gave the order that set this butchery in motion. His mind fills with the image of the still man in the darkened corridor. Instead, he says, "But—what is happening?" For he has heard the sounds from the city, loud enough to carry through stone, through the tapestry slung over his wife's window.

Now Ludovico swallows, his eyes flitting. "Ah, well. There has been—that is to say, men will sometimes take matters into their own hands, and this *has* been brewing for many years. The, ah, fury with the Huguenots has spread beyond even their leaders. The city is . . ." He shakes his head, and Petrus feels his throat closing off, stones stuffing it so fully that he could not ask his friend what his part was in this even if he was sure he wished to know the answer.

HE RETURNS TO HIS own chamber, dresses swiftly. It is the work of a few moments to discover that the dead are mostly Protestant. To his surprise, the Huguenot prince who wed the Princess Marguerite survived, though his men did not. Already, the court runs with rumors: the princess shielded her husband with her own body when the assassins came; the prince has sworn he will convert to Catholicism. An official call ordering the end of the bloodshed has been issued; but still, the city seethes. The Huguenot leaders might have been the first to be killed, drawn to their doom by the lure of the wedding, of one of their own being joined to the royal family. But after the leaders fell, the Catholics' eyes turned to other Huguenots, pillaging their homes, their shops. Unspeakable things done to the people within, with no care given for whether they were young men or old, or not men at all but women—old women, young women, *breeding* women—or children.

Petrus watches from his window, stomach sickening, as servants scrub the stones of the palace courtyard clean of blood. He thinks of his wife, her distended belly slit open to reveal the ropes of her insides, the tiny being curled within. Outside the palace, the rumors say, so many bodies have been tossed into the Seine that the river runs red.

When he returns to his wife's chamber, it is with a lie on his tongue, his thoughts with the swelling of her body, the understanding that further disquiet might harm the babe she harbors. All is well, he tells her. A scuffle, only, between the Catholics and Huguenots. But all is now well.

Even as he speaks, the butchery spreads outward in rings. Thousands of souls will ultimately be lost in Paris, most of them Protestant, their only crime worshiping God in the wrong way. And in the days that follow, Petrus's lips move with near-fervency at Mass, that he might not be mistaken for a heretic. During those days, he cannot look into the faces of the people around him for fear he will see the truth of their involvement in the slaughter. During those days, he hardly sleeps, hardly breathes, waiting for the torch, the shouts, the stones to turn upon him.

Catherine

In the week after that terrible night, Catherine waits and waits for something worse to happen; but it does not. She remains padded inside her room. And yet, when twinges spark along the sides of her belly, across the meat of her lower back, she finds herself pausing where she stands, saying, "*No!*" with such firmness that the nips of pain subside. She must wait, she thinks, until she is certain it is safe before she brings this child into the world.

At night, she finds herself thinking of her husband. How he came to her, nearly naked, only a shirt for armor. How she woke from her doze to her cheek pressed against the hard knob of his shoulder. She shakes her head to stop these thoughts, as if in doing so she might shake off the influence of his hairy-handed touch; but still they return, shuffling in like rueful children who know they are doing something naughty. When she finally sleeps, the midwife snoring on the floor beyond her bed curtains, Catherine dreams of the queen.

Her Majesty is hunched and weeping, her black gown and veil painted all the colors of the bright glass windows of the chapel. In life, she is so formidable a figure that it is strange to see her so diminished, her spine bending into the shrimp-like curl of old age.

Catherine approaches this dream-queen hesitantly. She can see only in chinks, the edges of her vision dark, as if something sits there, blocking them. Her footsteps make no sound upon the stone church floor, and the air is humid with patient anticipation. Only when she draws close to the queen does she realize that someone sits beside her, someone round and sturdy who cradles a swaddled child in the thick, hair-covered arms that the queen herself chose to deliver Catherine's babe.

Catherine stumbles back and tries to cry out, but her voice will not come. And she realizes she holds in her mouth a small, round bead, attached by a short span of ribbon to the mask that keeps the sun from her face and the air from her lungs. Something squeezes her, starting slow but steadily gripping tighter until Catherine's knees buckle.

Her Majesty turns, smiling through her tears. "Saturn will rule you during the birth," she says; and now her smile is a frozen thing, as if she set it down upon her face and forgot it there.

No, Catherine tries to say; but something is crushing her, and the bead is in her mouth and she cannot spit it out, however she tries.

SHE WAKES TO THE midwife's brisk and gentle hands, swimming up from the depths of her dream and into wakefulness, gasping like a drowned woman brought to the surface. But no—she cannot be awake—whatever was crushing her is still there. When she tries to wriggle away from it, it squeezes impossibly tighter until Catherine thinks her spine might snap.

Catherine

It was Maman's beauty that bought her a wealthy merchant husband, and she guarded it as carefully as if it were a pirate's trove.

Pride is a sin, however, and Maman was a pious woman. Catherine saw how her mother peered at herself in her hand mirror, touching the faint creases running from nostrils to mouth, examining the little lines about her eyes, delicate as the prints birds' toes make in mud; and then how she shook her head, as if chiding herself for looking, and set the mirror aside. But she never wavered in her daily rituals, which seemed like magic to Catherine when she was a child, but which, to her mother, were necessities. Her hair—lustrous as the silk her father once wove and as thick plaited as her own forearm—she kept silken and strong with a wash of herbs, then hid the kitchen-garden smell of the wash with hair powder scented with roses, cloves, and nutmeg. Her hands and face were white and soft as a noblewoman's, cleansed daily in the green-tinged water of boiled nettles, and hidden, always, from the terrible effects of the sun. She kept her gums pink and her teeth healthy by taking daily a little wine in which pomegranate flowers had been immersed, and kept her skin sweet-smelling by using only fine Venetian soap stamped with flower petals. She preserved her looks as best she could, as a peasant preserves food against the coming months of winter want.

But there was something different to the way Maman noticed Catherine's appearance. Something prideful. Each evening, while she brushed her daughter's hair until it crackled, Maman hummed prayers into the strands. Healthy hair is indicative of healthy insides, she said, and so she hummed for strength and thickness, and gave thanks that God gave Catherine such fair hair that it needed little lightening.

Maman tried to hide her pride in Catherine's beauty, but it was there for anyone to see, though she always attempted a modest smile when anyone complimented her daughter—just the smallest, pleased upturning of her lips, her eyes cast down; but not before Catherine saw the flash of delight in them.

Such long eyelashes! one of her mother's friends might say, peering at Catherine. *Just look at them!*

And such a lovely smile, from another. *She will be a great beauty, like her mother.*

Inside her chest, Catherine often felt a small, pleasurable eruption when she heard these things, and when she saw her mother's pride and love for the lovely creature she bore. She was pleased to have pleased Maman, pleased to be pleasing to others, their admiration rolling benevolently as bathwater down her spine and over her limbs.

If she sometimes heard insidious, devilish whispers inside her head—Would her mother's eyes hold such warmth had Catherine not been born beautiful? If her eyelashes were not so long and did not frame eyes that were so large? If her hair was too dark for fashion, or her teeth askew in her mouth? What if she were too scrawny for beauty, or too fat? Would her mother love her as much then?—she thought they must be God's punishment for her own vanity.

AT THE FIRST SIGHT of her daughter, Catherine's heart drops, swift as a stone from a cliff. The midwife holds her up, says, "A girl," and smacks her, sucking the fluids from her mouth until she gives a hoarse, startled shriek. Catherine, slumped in the birthing chair, thighs trembling, can only stare, her mind swiped clean of rational thought as her heart plummets away from her. Even plastered down with wet from the womb and daubed with red and white, the hair that covers the infant's entire body is unmistakable.

The midwife wraps the babe up warm and sets her, without a word, on Catherine's chest. Catherine's arms rise on instinct to cradle her, and she lets out another lusty cry, fists jerking.

The midwife watches. "You've a good strong little one, there," she says, seemingly unruffled by the baby's strange appearance. The queen, likely hoping for this very outcome when she bred her wild man, must have forewarned her. Catherine's throat fills with bile. "We'll get you both cleaned up and into bed once your body's all finished with its work."

Catherine jerks; whispers, "There's more?"

The midwife's cheeks, ruddy in the warm room, look like apples when she smiles. "The afterbirth," she says. Catherine nods, dazed, not quite understanding.

But soon enough, her body expels something large and fleshy that looks like uncooked meat. The midwife inspects it, declares it healthy and intact—"A good thing for you Madame," she says. "It's bits of this stuck fast in the womb that cause stinking sickness in too many mothers"—and severs the birth cord, tying it off neatly at the infant's abdomen. She throws both afterbirth and birth cord into the fire, poking to make sure they catch fully. Then she takes the child from Catherine's arms, gently rubbing her clean; clouts and swaddles her; and holds her easily in the crook of one elbow as she uses her other sturdy arm to help Catherine stand and totter to the big soft bed, where she has laid folded linen to catch the blood still trickling from between Catherine's legs. Catherine holds on to her, thumb brushing the dark strands of hair on her forearm, and thinks rather wildly that it does not matter if she looks at it now.

Her daughter is returned to her arms. Catherine looks down, feeling addled, weak, away from herself. Her entire body has begun shaking.

"That'll be the shock of the birth," the midwife says. "Takes women so, sometimes. I'll send for some good hot bread and broth; that'll set you right."

Catherine says nothing. The infant's eyes are squeezed closed so that she cannot see their color. All of her—every bit, it seems—is covered in generous wisps of pale hair. She is like the monsters from the pamphlets, Catherine thinks from a very great distance. Too strange to be true; too perfect to be real. Her features are the sweet features of an infant, the face round with eyelids that tilt a little up at the corners like Catherine's own and a nose that seems impossibly small, with two flawlessly hewn nostrils. Her red mouth, minuscule and puckered, emerges from the surrounding hair, incongruous as a rose in the forest.

With one fingertip, Catherine touches the hair and finds it soft. The child turns her head without opening her eyes, mewling and nosing, some instinct moving her toward Catherine's breast.

"And the wet nurse," the midwife says, chuckling. "Seems Her Majesty's generous enough with her coin to have found one willing to suckle a little monkey."

Her words fall on Catherine like a sudden rain shower, turning her skin icy. Every terror she held at bay throughout the last months shrieks now from the midwife's gently smiling mouth. Her fingers tighten around the child, who, oblivious, roots in earnest, her mewling turning to insistent cries.

"I'm going to suckle her myself," Catherine says. The words hover in the air between her and the midwife for a moment, then fall to the floor in a patter like breaking glass.

"Well, now," the midwife says. Her eyes dart to the door. "That would be—very unusual, for a wellborn woman like yourself."

"I'm not wellborn," Catherine says. Her voice is high and unfamiliar, with a frantic, keening edge. "My father is a merchant. My mother's father was a silk weaver."

"Well, and still—you'll not want your milk to keep you from having another babe in your arms before next year."

Catherine's limbs are still shaking. There is a soreness between her legs that puts the soreness she felt after her wedding night into harsh perspective. She can almost feel the ghost of each pain, squeezing without mercy. "I am *not*," she says, "doing that ever again."

The midwife's head rolls back and she shouts her laughter, until tears run over her apple cheeks. "Oh, Madame," she says, wiping her eyes. "All women say that."

The child's cries are growing louder; they scour Catherine's skin with sand. It is impossible to think of anything but quieting her. "Show me," she says, baring a breast. "Show me what to do."

And when the midwife hesitates, she says, "*Show me*," once more; and this time the words are a growl.

WHILE THE BABE IS at suck, the midwife and several servants clean away the aftermath of the birth, dragging the birthing chair away, bundling the stained linen off to the laundry. Catherine has eaten a little bread and broth and taken a little wine, and watches them from a distance, as if they are performers in a play that has nothing to do with her. When the child released her breast with a painful pull of hard gums on tender flesh, Catherine glances down to find her eyes open. They are the deep, dark blue of the sea on Papa's map of the world.

Something bubbles up inside of Catherine, then, sweet and heady and unexpected, making her laugh with sudden lightness. Ignoring the startled glances of the others in the room, she bends low over her daughter's serious, puzzled face and babbles in her own mother's voice. "Oh, *cara mia*, just *look* at you, you are so beautiful—*oh*, just so *beautiful*—"

And then she is sobbing, a gasping rush of sound and waterfall, something, having patiently worked itself loose inside her chest, finally giving way entirely. Her tears drop onto her daughter's soft cheeks, and she rocks forward and back, howling.

The servants and midwife exchange a look, and the midwife says, "Hush, now, Madame—your husband will want you smiling and rosy." And when Catherine's sobs only grow louder, she tucks an arm around Catherine's shoulders and sighs. "There, Madame. Let it out, let it out now," and holds her arm there, allowing Catherine to rock and wail until the rush has passed.

Pedro

When a servant fetches him to meet his child, Petrus cannot at first understand her, her words soft and unreal against the cacophony of a court still reeling from the fear and bloodshed of the last weeks.

"A girl," she says, and then, with a flick of her eyes that seems to Petrus like the sketching of a cross over her breast, "Very—like you."

His own breastbone aches suddenly, as if from a physical blow. Petrus is dressed all in black, severe as a Spaniard. He follows the narrow sweep of the servant's woolen skirt down a network of corridors until he arrives at his own door—or what was his own door, until his wife's confinement transformed it into something else entirely. A place for women's secrets, which he was glad enough to let them keep, until the night of the massacre. He thinks of his wife's hand, grasping his of its own volition, and his stomach clenches.

He taps at the door with one knuckle, lightly enough that he is not certain he even wants her to hear. His ears are filled with a rushing song, at once familiar and strange; it is several moments before he recognizes it from long ago as the voice of the sea, as he used to hear it on Tenerife: echoing faintly through the streets on stormy nights; in the spiraling bellies of the shells he liked to hold to his ears.

"Enter," he hears, muffled, through the wood. After a moment, he does.

The room is shadowed and overwarm. His wife sits up in bed, surrounded by pillows. Her elbows are propped against two fat cushions, to support her arms as they cradle something small and tightly swaddled. Petrus's hands curl around the edge of the door.

"Are you well?" he says, and her face turns toward him, creased and smudged.

"Very well," she says, with something that approaches, but does not quite become, a smile. "Thanks be to God."

He takes a step into the room. "I heard—it is a girl."

"Yes."

"And"—his voice rends—"that she bears me strong resemblance."

A laugh that sounds like water from a fountain; like rain. "Yes."

"Ah," he says, more sigh than word, and stands limp as a flag when the wind stops blowing. "I am sorry."

A log shifts; the fire snaps. She looks down at their child. "Petrus," she says. "Come here. Meet your daughter."

His lips close at her use of his name, which sounds like earth, like sage leaves, from her mouth. He comes forward very slowly, each footstep weighted. When he passes the mirror, he sees himself accidentally and falters—his reflection looks untamed, his hair standing up wildly from his scalp, as if he spent the walk to this room tearing at it with his fingers.

A step or two from the bed, he stops, hands hanging at his sides. His wife moves the child's swaddle aside so that he can see her unobstructed: the curl of ear, the curve of cheek, her little mushroom nose. The closed eyes and diligently working mouth. Petrus's heart stutters oddly in his chest at the sight—of her hair, fine as clouds, covering every bit of her that he can see; of her miniature hand, so softly furred, splayed against her mother's breastbone. Of his wife's breast, unashamedly bare, threaded with startling blue like a river's tributaries spread across a map. He has felt the weight of her breasts, but until now has seen them only in gray, moonlit flashes. He glances away, full-throated and hot, to where the child rests on the still-rounded shelf of his wife's belly.

"Come closer," his wife says, still not looking at him, and he does, the command tugging him like a lead rope. He leans over a little and has the dizzying sensation that he is looking at his past self. When his wife's eyes find his, Petrus sees his every fear and joy reflected in her face.

Then she yawns, long and wide as a whirlpool sucking down a ship. He starts backward.

"I should leave you to rest," he says; but his eyes stray once again to their child.

Her hand reaches out. "No—" she says. "Please—stay. I have . . . I have been almost entirely on my own ever since . . ."

He pauses.

"Please," she says again; and she looks at him—*at* him—until he finds himself shifting forward, perching with tentative care on the bed beside her. For an excruciatingly long moment, there is no sound in the room but that of their child's determined swallows.

"I would have thought," he says at last, "that Her Majesty would provide a nurse." Nevers's wife has engaged a nurse for all three of their children; the ladies at court all do, as far as he knows.

"She did." A pause; he hears the scrape of his wife's top teeth against the bottom. "But the midwife—she said—" She looks down at the baby, then up at him, just for a moment, before her eyes dash sideways. "It does not matter what she said. It was clear the nurse—was not suitable."

Then she laughs a little, softly. At his inquiring look, she flushes; and then tilts her head to a defiant angle. "Her tongue," she says. "I can feel it. It tickles."

The babe chooses that moment to come away from her mother's breast, mouth slack and dribbling. Her eyes are closed, her head thrown back over Catherine's arm. His wife, face flushed, rearranges her chemise as best she can one-handed.

"We will need a name for her," she says. She smooths the hair on the child's brow. One corner of her mouth curls; her face is tender as new grass. She glances sideways at Petrus, and her smile drops just a little.

"She is perfect, is she not, Monsieur?" she says; and now, in terrible contrast to her tenderness, there is a sudden hardness to her voice, like a shield thrust out between him and the child. As if he might wield a sword. Petrus leans a little back.

"You called me Petrus, only a few minutes ago."

Everything soft has left her face, as if the sword she thinks he wields has sliced it off. "You have not answered my question." And then, when he cannot speak, only makes a drifting, helpless motion with both hands, she says, "I did not think you—anyone—*you*—could look at her and not see—"

His eyes are drawn again, of their own accord, to their child. The slow rise and fall of her chest. The toothless mouth, half-opened. The ache in his own chest presses, more insistent; he can feel his wife's eyes fixed upon him, and after months of her eyes resting everywhere except on him, her stare now is ferocious.

"She is—" He reaches out, and then lets his hand drop to the coverlet. How to say that until this moment, the babe she carried had not seemed entirely real to him? That he observed the swelling of her week by week as if through church glass, the colors distorting, making everything appear unreal.

This, though, is real. The scents of herbs are sharp in Petrus's nostrils; and underneath is another smell, somehow earthier than the herbs, and less pleasing. The smell of birth, he suspects; though it smells disconcertingly like death. He has the sensation that his wife, in giving birth, has become someone like one of the queen's astronomers—a person who can decipher meaning in curls of smoke; a scattering of stones; a crooked angle in the stars. Someone who has brushed the mysteries of the universe with her finger ends.

When he looks at her, though, he sees not an astronomer but a young woman with a creased and crumpled face, clutching a child who looks like him. And it is that clutching that loosens something that has, for much of his life, been drawn tight and painful inside him; for this woman, his wife, has no intention of giving up their child to anyone.

One thought slipped free from his mind's fierce grip as he followed the servant who fetched him to the birthing chamber. A reluctant half-formed image, and the accompanying squalling noise. His child—his daughter—lying naked and alone, her mother's eyes pulled away from her inexorably as a compass needle pulls north.

He has imagined the scene so many times—how he was placed on the steps of the church—but he could never decide whether his mother, his father, would have felt any reluctance as they set him down, as they released him from their arms, their care. Whether his mother might have turned back to see him one last time before hurrying away; whether Pedro's cries might have echoed in his father's ears. All he knows is how hard Manuel said he was screaming when Manuel came upon him, when he was too small to do anything but scream, too small to know why he was screaming.

That scream, he thinks sometimes, has been lodged inside of him all his life.

"She is beautiful," Petrus says at last, his voice catching on the last word. His wife's eyes jump; her brow loosens, just a little. Mouth thin, she nods, short and emphatic.

"She is."

They sit in silence. She has not offered the babe to him, and he does not yet feel that he can ask; is not even confident that he can hold her without somehow causing her injury.

His fingers curl into his palms, lest he reach for her anyway.

And then Catherine yawns again. But before Petrus can try to excuse himself again so she might rest, she says, "Tell me a story."

He blinks. "A story?"

Another yawn, so wide her eyes close helplessly. "Your story," she says when it has passed. "Your true story." Very gently, she strokes a finger down the soft slope of their daughter's nose. "I want to know where this little one comes from."

"I—"

"The caves are false, no? They are not where you lived?" Her eyes pluck at his, one brow raised.

"They—no," he says, and then, "that is, they are real. But they were not where I lived."

Her second brow joins the first. And then questions come from her mouth in such a scramble, he understands that they have been waiting there all this time, unspoken. "Where *are* you from?" she says. "Was this all very strange to you, when you came here? France—the court—the church—?"

Petrus shakes his head. "I was baptized as an infant," he says. "I've been attending church all my life, even before I came here." Her face shows astonishment, all the more so when he allows a little harshness into his voice. "The Spanish conquered my island—Tenerife—a few dozen years before I was born, and brought Catholicism with them to the poor rude natives."

She gapes. And then she astonishes him in turn. "Tenerife," she murmurs, and closes her eyes, as if trying to recall something. When she opens them again, she says, "Near Africa?" and tucks her lips together, as if trying to keep back a grin.

He stares. "How did you—?"

"My father was a merchant, Husband," she says, tart. "He traveled widely. We owned maps. *Many* maps. My father let me look at them as much as I wanted, and endured all my questions with good humor." She softens a little when she says again, "Please—will you tell me everything?"

He swallows, loudly enough to hear, then pushes himself back so that he is sitting beside her, back against the great carved bedstead. He folds his hands over his stomach. And then, haltingly, he begins.

Part Three

Family

CAPODIMONTE, ITALY
1618

Catherine

The rhythm of her days is all wrong with Petrus gone, as if her life's song, highs and lows alike, have been played until now by a musician whose fingers never fumbled a note. But his death startled the musician from her playing, and now the song wavers, the notes jar. Catherine finds herself often standing still, staring at nothing, her head empty.

Strangely—or perhaps not strangely—she misses Agnes now nearly as much as she misses Petrus, though she has not seen her old friend for so many years. But though others stop to speak with her when she walks through the village—though her goddaughters and godsons, all eleven of them, are brought by their various parents to visit with her in the days after the funeral, bearing fruits and sweets, as if to tempt a sulking child back into the world—she finds herself longing for Agnes's pragmatism and gruff kindness. Her eyes, which showed her every feeling. Her laughter, which she shared so generously.

Catherine stuffs her own forearm into her mouth and bites down—gently at first, and then hard—*harder.* When she takes her arm from her mouth, her teeth have left two half-circles of crooked little indentations.

HER DAUGHTER MADELEINE LIVES with her husband near the outskirts of the town. Catherine walks there, feeling the jolt of each footstep over the uneven streets, and the deep stretch of her thigh muscles. Though she nods to those she passes, she keeps moving quickly in the hopes that none will attempt to stop and speak.

She has walked this way countless times since they came to Capodimonte; knows which of her neighbors will be at the market square, which will be spying through their front windows upon those who pass. She knows that the black-speckled nanny goat with the twisted horn has wandered away from her home and will shortly be followed by little Nardo, who will scamper after her on his bare feet, arms outstretched, that his ferocious mother mightn't notice the goat's disappearance and hide him for his carelessness; knows that Signore Telani, the blind wizened father of a fisherman, will turn his empty eye sockets upon her as she approaches the little bench upon which he sits outside their house enjoying the press of the sun, and unerringly greet her by name. She knows the toll of the church bell, which makes her chest vibrate like a plucked lute string; the playful screams of boys swimming at the edge of the lake; the calls of their mothers, urging them home.

She knows every bit of this place, where she and Petrus made their home for so many years. The first place that felt, truly, like theirs, their house all their own, even more so than Rome, for here there was no expectation that they would open its doors to anyone unless they wished to. But this familiar space, which they occupied for so long together, is ill-fitting when she is alone within it.

She finds Madeleine sewing, and Madeleine's daughter Paola with a pot at her elbow as if she might expel sickness at any moment. Madeleine rises to her feet instantly to greet her; but there is something wrong about her face, and she wraps Catherine in strong arms, burying her nose in Catherine's shoulder.

When she pulls away, Madeleine scrubs at her eyes like a child. "I am sorry, Maman," she says. "I think I still expect Papa to come with you."

Catherine smiles, very small. "I understand." She turns to Paola, whose expectations are impossible yet to see, her bodice still laced tightly, and kisses both her cheeks. "You are looking well, *cara mia*, though I am sorry you don't feel it." She nods to the waiting pot.

Paola has inherited both her father's pale eyes and his hairless flesh. When she smiles, she shows her dimples, like divots in cream. Her elder sister Caterina—Catherine's namesake—resembles their mother.

"I am happy enough to make up for the illness," she says.

Madeleine shakes her head now, and rubs her tear-damp palms briskly on the edges of her skirt. "Well. Are you hungry, Maman? I did not expect to see you today."

"No," Catherine says. "I'm not hungry. I could help with dinner though, if you would let me?"

THEY SPEAK BUT LITTLE as they work, Madeleine rolling thin pastry for a pie; Catherine cutting meat into cubes and chopping herbs to fill it. Paola rouses herself from her chair to help, fetching more wood from the back courtyard to build up the cooking fire. Her husband, one of the guardsmen at the Rocca Farnese, the great octagonal fortress overlooking the town, will join them for supper. Caterina is in Rome at the Palazzo Farnese, summoned by the duke to meet with some foreign visitors, to charm them with her hairy face and talent for the violin.

"I worry for her," Madeleine says of Caterina. Her eyes are unfocused; she has stopped rolling, her hands idle. "She thinks because she is as she is, the rules of womanhood do not apply to her. That her music will gain her entry to some other royal court—she's all eager to see the world."

"Would the duke consent to her leaving?" Catherine says. A lumpen thing has appeared abruptly inside her belly, sick-making and heavy. Inside her head, a small figure hurtles toward her, sobbing; two arms close around her neck.

"I don't know. If there is someone he wishes to flatter with a gift, perhaps." She glances at Catherine, and then away. "He has done so before, after all."

The arms squeeze tighter about Catherine's neck, nearly cutting off her ability to breathe. For a moment, she is certain they are there, truly—the weight and pull of a small body hanging by those arms from her shoulders; the dimpling of her flesh under the press of fingertips the size and shape of ladybirds. The hard touch of a brow bone to her collarbone; the pucker of a mouth. So real, for an instant, that her eyes close and her arms come up to hold the little body close, to bear all of its weight.

And then the sensation passes. The weight does not fall from her shoulders the way it would had a child suddenly released her grip and dropped away to the ground; no, it lessens gradually, the way warmth in a room will slowly abate as the fire turns to embers and the embers cool. When the weight is gone, and the clutching with it, Catherine opens her eyes again to find Madeleine watching her; and she looks back, and carefully does not allow herself to remember, for more than a blink, how her youngest daughter, long ago, once made a game of hiding herself in corners. Keeps her neck straight, though it longs to turn, to carry her eyes from corner to corner to corner of the room, searching out the shape of Antoinette in the shadows.

(Palms over her eyes, cheeks stretched in a smile. A quiver of anticipation, for the moment someone might find her.)

If she stretched out her hand, Catherine imagines she might feel a smaller hand, its back soft as mullein leaves, its fingers curling around her palm.

(Don't look. Don't look.)

Perhaps she is going mad.

"There aren't so many hairy marvels available to summon to his court, now that he would so easily give one away," Catherine says when she feels she can speak, though her voice lacks conviction. "There were several of you, but with so many of your brother's children gone—and Paola so unremarkable in appearance—"

Of Catherine's four children, three bore their father's hair. Of those three, two live still under the protection of the Duke of Parma. Both Madeleine and Henri have had hairy children of their own, but only one—Madeleine's Caterina—has lived past infancy. Her children are like coins—Catherine imagines them stacked and shining, like the coins in her father's office. And then depleted, slowly, until there are no longer enough left that the duke who owns them can afford to spend them freely.

But Madeleine lets out a fretful sound. "Giovan does not know how to talk to Caterina, either; how to make her settle."

Catherine folds her lips together. It is best to avoid discussions of Madeleine's husband, unless she is willing to have nothing but chafing between herself and her daughter. As stubborn as her own father once was, Madeleine has always refused to hear the sly insults in her husband's words, or to notice when he is too often in his cups. When their son Henri spoke privately to Petrus and Catherine against the marriage when the duke arranged it, Catherine knew there was no use in trying to dissuade Madeleine from accepting. Her daughter had thought, since she was a small girl, that she would never marry; when the chance was offered, she chose not to understand the artful joke behind the match.

But Catherine easily recalls Henri's outraged voice. *A kennel master!* He scowled through the wedding ceremony and refused for weeks to visit Madeleine at her new house, near the Farnese kennels. *It stinks of dog*, he said; though really it was only Giovan who did, a distinctive canine musk clinging to his fingers and clothes until he had washed and changed.

Paola comes back in now, sets down her armful of wood, and steals a bit of dough like the child Catherine remembers her being, not so long ago, her fat cheeks forever stuffed with pilfered almonds and pinches of dough. Catherine's heart constricts in an alarming way, just briefly, and she closes her eyes, sending up a prayer to God that her granddaughter's child might be as ordinary in appearance as Paola herself; that the extraordinary chain forged with Petrus as its first link might be broken now.

The next moment she opens her eyes and gives her head a violent shake.

When the pie is assembled, Catherine settles into a chair near the window, tiredness coming over her all at once until she feels pressed into the seat. Madeleine and Paola murmur together, guessing what Caterina might be doing at this moment in Rome; whether she will extend her visit, or whether she will miss them enough to come back again.

When Caterina and Paola were small, Madeleine confessed to Catherine once that though she loved them both, she loved Caterina, with her round soft face, best.

"She needs my love most," she said simply; and it was the first time in many, many years that Catherine had heard her acknowledge, even obliquely, the difficulties her appearance has caused her. Her mouth tight as a flower bud; her eyes dark and serious as they were when she was an infant.

WHEN SHE FOUND HERSELF with child for the first time, Madeleine did not pray, as Catherine had, for smoothness. She behaved as if her expectations were no different from any other woman's, and Catherine watched her, wondering; and felt ashamed, a little, of her wondering. When Catherine asked whether Giovan worried about the child's appearance, her daughter turned her wide brown eyes upon her and said, "You mean—does he wish she were more like him? Less like me?"

"I—yes. I suppose so."

A small shrug, and words that fell like sugar from her mouth. "Why should he? He married me, after all. And my appearance has done well for us, has it not?" A gesture that encompassed their comfortable house, paid for by the duke, and all the lovely things in it, bought with the stipend the duke paid for his Hairy Maddalena's continued existence at his court. "His wages alone would not have bought him all this."

Only once, near her time, did Madeleine voice any fears. "How did you feel when I was born?" she said. "And all the others?"

She had never asked such a thing before. None of Catherine's children had. Catherine paused, and as she paused, saw her daughter's fingers grow tight upon the stem of her glass.

"You were yourself," she said; and it was a simple truth. And, too, one that was not simple at all; but Madeleine would, of course, know this better even than Catherine herself.

CHÂTEAU DU LOUVRE
1572

Pedro

His story is many hours in the telling. It is interrupted when his wife drifts to sleep, or when servants come with laden trays. When Catherine relieves herself for the first time with the help of the brawny midwife, she moves gingerly, as if she has been wounded. Petrus almost does not notice the red-stained linen, many times folded, where she had been lying, for Catherine shifted their child into his arms before rising from the bed. The babe is heavier than he anticipated—there is true solidity to her. She is not a dream-child, but a soul made flesh—and bone and muscle, too. Though she sleeps, her sleep is restless, and he stares as her small face contorts suddenly, brow furrowing, mouth opening as if she would cry. Then her brow smooths itself and her mouth, impossibly, curves upward in a smile.

He leans a little closer. She looks—sweet. Familiar and strange. She looks like him, poor thing.

Months and months of praying—to whom, he couldn't have said—ever since his wife's body began to change; and she is the result. She is enough to at once buttress and crumble his disbelief in a god.

Catherine listens hard to him while she is awake, the line sharp between her brows, her lips folded tight. She does not look away from him except to adjust their child in her arms. She seems another woman entirely from the one who entered this chamber alone, but he cannot decide which is more likely: that a true transformation occurred within these walls, some alchemy of new motherhood; or that he simply did not recognize his wife before now.

When his mouth becomes too dry to speak, he falls silent for a time.

Catherine looks at the thread-fine strip of sunlight visible around the edges of the tapestry that hangs over the window.

"It looks warm," she says, starvation in her voice. "The sun."

"It is—though it is nearly autumn, I'm afraid."

"I was too delicate, in those final weeks, to risk too much light. My eyes, you know." She rolls them a little, smiling; a true smile, face lined with humor, and Petrus finds his mouth feels dry now for a different reason entirely.

"Are your eyes still in danger?" he manages to ask, though his tongue is clumsy in his mouth.

She shrugs, smile going one-sided. "No one has said."

Shadows lie thick as piled rugs upon the floor; stretch themselves out toward the corners of the room. She has been kept in here for weeks. Petrus pushes himself off the bed and strides to the window. He is too short to reach the nails that pin the tapestry to the wall, so he drags a chair over to stand upon, the chair's legs bumping unevenly over the rug and teetering like a child just learning to stand when he steps up onto the seat. The tapestry falls at last into his arms, heavy enough to make him stagger precariously upon the chair, and with a puff of dust that leaves him sneezing. But the window pours forth a veritable waterfall of sunlight. His wife's laughter, delighted and helpless, makes him smile.

He helps her rise, and together with their daughter they stand at the narrow window. Their view shows a slice of the palace, a swathe of bright sky. Though the babe sleeps, Catherine holds her up a little, as if to show her, letting the light bathe her face like the waters of baptism.

"SHE STILL MUST BE named," Catherine says a little later.

"Catherine . . . would be appropriate, would it not?" he says. For the child's mother, of course; and in honor of the queen.

But she looks at him sharply. "*No*," she says, so loudly that the babe startles in her sleep and begins to wail, eyes squeezed shut.

Catherine closes her own eyes, as if the noise pains her, shifting their daughter to her other breast. Then, more temperately, she says, "I do not . . . I had another name in mind."

Petrus sits on the edge of the bed by her feet. "Yes?"

She flicks her eyes at him, looking almost shy. "Isabelle."

She says it the French way; and yet still it slices. He flinches, and sees her flinch in turn. "No," he says, and poppy flowers bloom over her face, patches of pallor between them.

She looks away, to the corner of the room where her clothes chest sits. "Why—why not?"

Petrus looks at her—the bunching of muscles at the corner of her jaw, the blotch of angry flowers over her skin. There is no sensible explanation for it, and she meant the suggestion kindly—honorably—she meant to honor Isabel and their daughter at once. He knows this. And yet, something says *no,* shouts it. The something bears Isabel's lined face, speaks with her voice, reaches toward him with her dye-stained hands. Opens its mouth to say something else but speaks too quietly for Petrus to make out the word. As if there is danger in the speaking of it.

"That wasn't even her true name," he says at last.

THEY SETTLE FINALLY UPON Madeleine. Petrus thinks at first that Catherine suggests it for no reason but that she likes the sound it makes; the feel of it in her mouth. But then she says, "The Magdalene is sometimes shown as hairy, is she not? And holy, in her hairiness?"

She says this looking not at him, but at their daughter, who lies in a little square of sunlight, the hair on her limbs and torso almost white in the brightness. Like the follower of Christ who so eschewed worldly concerns that her robe and veil fell all to tatters, until her hair grew to cover her body, to preserve her modesty, to keep her safe.

For all that the saints seem as distant to him as the stars, gratitude, like some thick sweet draught, closes Petrus's throat to whatever words he might otherwise have formed.

"I THOUGHT THE QUEEN would want to inspect her immediately," Catherine says the next morning. Her eyes are ringed with tiredness, but she eats her morning meal with gusto while Petrus holds Madeleine against his shoulder. The servant who brought their breakfast looked incredulous at the sight, but Petrus remembers how King Henri cradled his own babes, even laughing once when Charles spewed something white down the back of his fine velvet doublet.

"I think under other circumstances, she already would have," he says. "But I think she has been preoccupied, what with the Huguenot killings."

A swift inhalation. "The—what?"

Petrus squeezes his eyes. "The . . . they have continued," he says. "First in Paris, and now there are reports that they have spread throughout the country." The king himself has assumed responsibility for the earliest portion of the massacre, claiming that the Huguenots conspired against him.

Catherine shakes her head. "But..." A swallow. "What news of Lyons?" she says, and Petrus curses himself for a fool.

"I believe—the city has not been spared," he says after a moment. And then he hastens to add, "But your father—he is a good Catholic, no? I am sure he is in no danger."

His wife looks at him silently.

WHEN SHE DOES AT last send for her wild man and his family, the queen mother is enraptured. She presses one soft palm against the other in an attitude of prayer, then scoops Madeleine from Catherine's arms. "What a perfect, perfect creature," she says, tracing with one finger the child's nose, her chin; lifting one hand and inspecting each knuckle. She pushes aside the swaddling blanket Catherine had embroidered and lifts the hem of Madeleine's gown, a confection of pearls and blue velvet, which Catherine said, wincingly, she hoped their daughter would not soil, at least not in front of Queen Caterina. When Her Majesty finds Madeleine's legs and arms, chest and belly as hairy as her face, she gives a strange little cry of joy.

"You clever, clever woman," she says to Catherine when at last she relinquishes the babe. "You shall have a rope of pearls for your service."

Catherine

Her early days with Madeleine are a blur of pure sensation. The newness of everything, tender and easily bruised as leaf buds. The grating noise of a fresh child's hungry cries. The quick tightening and warm release of her milk letting down. The lines of her husband's face, once so startling, becoming, slowly, familiar.

No one told her she would be unmade in those hours of birthing, torn to pieces and poorly sewn together again. But there is something fierce and elemental about being thrust into motherhood—into womanhood. She feels the teeth inside her head, the nails on her fingers; and feels as if she could use them, as they are tools given to her to protect this mewling mass of humanity she holds. It is a bestial sensation—she is become the animal others see in her husband and child—and she wonders whether all women feel this way, if her own mother felt this way, or if it is only the howling fear of others' reactions to Madeleine's appearance that has turned her, between birth pang and the release into the world of her child, into a wolf woman.

PETRUS TELLS HER OF King Henri's death, how the queen dreamed a prophetic dream to which he paid no heed. Catherine's own dreams have never been weighty things, but she begins paying them more attention after that tale, amusing herself, in the broken hours before dawn when her daughter's hunger pulls her from sleep, by trying to find meaning in them. These are the good nights, when Petrus, sleeping again beside her, looks gentle in the moonlight, and her daughter's suckling causes warm bright starbursts of both gladness and fear for her behind Catherine's eye sockets.

There are good days, too; when she can feel the small, stiff unbendings that began after the birth continuing, care for one another unspooling between herself and Petrus like one of the silk ribbons at Papa's warehouse. When her husband looks at her with something that might have been wonder as she smooths Madeleine's soft hair; when she feels, in his there-and-gone smile, the passing of some shared feeling.

Other nights, and even days, are not so good. On these, she weeps, fear winning out over gladness and exhaustion dragging at her until her very hands shake with it. On these nights and days, she misses her mother with a pain like a gut wound, and rocks back and forth with Madeleine, grief that her mother never met her baby granddaughter warring with the grief that her mother might not have loved Madeleine as Catherine does.

Of Papa, she tries not to think at all, though this would be easier if he had sent word that he was well. The Huguenot killings have moved outward through the countryside in a great, butchering wave, and all she can do is pray that he had the wit—and the money—to defend their home against the madness that has seized the country.

"SHALL I WRITE TO your father for you?" Petrus asks one day. His voice is low, and he puts a hand upon her shoulder; a small intimacy, which draws both smiles and raised brows from the others attending the queen mother that afternoon.

They are sitting in the cloud-covered gardens, feasting on fruits and listening idly to a flautist whose notes hang, melancholy, in the air. The court has become a strange place, the courtiers almost frenzied in their jollity, as if trying to make up for the king's melancholy, his new fits of disquiet. All around, courtiers whisper to each other, and pretend not to. *Madness*, they mutter. *He hears the cries of blackbirds and imagines them the dying screams of Huguenots.*

Even his mother calls him mad. Some servant or other heard her shrieking, gossiped of it, and now the entire palace knows and pretends not to.

Papa has not written again since that first letter, and she has never asked Petrus to respond for her, all the words she might have said tipped and dangerous as arrows in her mouth. Though her father had written of his enduring success, all his prospects bright as sunlight, she knows, too, the false flash of his teeth when her mother would ask about a venture's likely profits, the jollity of his voice when he tried to make something sound more certain than it was. Though his debts have been paid, the rest of his letter lacked specifics—had his clerks returned to him? Had he managed to scrape funds enough to invest in another ship?

Or is he perhaps a pauper, one of the many sour-smelling people on the streets of Lyons, their clothing hole riddled and ragged, their flesh wasted and greasy? The thought of Papa so—Papa, who always looked so fine in his black cape for travel and the white feather in his deep blue hat—bores a deep hole in her belly. His strong arms, which used to swing her so high above his head, grown thin from lack of nourishment. His eyes pouched, rheumy.

She imagines a messenger riding to him at last, bearing a note in her husband's hand. Then the long wait for his reply, if he were to send one. And she cannot decide whether her reticence is to do with the fear that he is not doing well, or the feeling—gray-tinged and grimy as old rags—that she might hate him if he is.

But no. Papa was always saying how opportunity existed for any man with the courage to seize it. Surely he would not have allowed himself to sink. Surely, he would have men to defend against the slaughter that moved through his city. And her other thoughts, other feelings, can be set aside, can they not? She can fold them away like a child's clothes, outgrown.

"Perhaps," she says to Petrus. She looks across at Madeleine, held firmly on the queen's lap.

A man has the right to know of his granddaughter's existence, does he not?

"Yes," she says at last, watching the queen dandle her daughter, whose big dark eyes are wide and watchful, fixed upon the branches of a nearby chestnut tree, its leaves making a whispering symphony above their heads.

AGNES AND THE OTHER female dwarfs—those who have not been married off to other dwarfs at the queen's pleasure—share a set of rooms near Her Majesty's chamber. The first time Catherine enters, cradling Madeleine in the crook of one arm, the other women present stop their chatter and simply look, as if some strange storied creature has come into their room, and not a smudge-eyed new mother, otherwise unremarkable in her dark gown and flat cap. Catherine stands so still she scarcely breathes, all their incredulous eyes looking up at her, and knows, just for an instant and in a very small way, what her husband must have endured all his life; what her daughter will endure in hers.

And then Agnes, bent over a small desk with legs carved like serpents, says without looking around, "Come in, then! Don't let the guards listen to our gossip—it'd make their ears fall off."

A few of the other women laugh, and one, who is older than all the rest, her hair gray as snow clouds, says, "Sit, Madame Sauvage," gesturing to one of the chairs in their little circle. She laughs as uproariously as the rest when Catherine, after a brief hesitation, sits, her knees jutting up nearly to her chest, in the chair that is sized for a much shorter person. But the laughter sings of merriment only, without the sting of unkindness, and after a moment, Catherine laughs, too.

"Let us see the babe, then," someone says, and suddenly Madeleine is scooped from Catherine's arms and passed about, a small, sleepy bundle. The women crowd over her with murmurs and soft exclamations; but their mouths smile, and when Madeleine is returned to Catherine's arms, she seems to feel a shift in the way they look at her—a speculation in their eyes, a light of recognition, as if perhaps she could belong among them after all.

JEANNE, THE ELDEST OF the female dwarfs and the one who has been with Her Majesty the longest, holds her feet out to the fire with a hum of satisfaction. Catherine knows by now that she is the one affectionately known as *l'oiseau chanteur*—the songbird—because she was brought to court in a covered cage as a gift to the queen.

"Before removing the cloth," she tells Catherine, "Her Majesty was told that a parrot sat inside the cage—a parrot who could speak six languages. I chirped out a few phrases in French, English, Italian, Spanish, Dutch, and German, and then the cover was whisked away." She folds her little hands together and smiles a pleased-with-herself smile. "The queen was delighted."

Catherine smiles, too. And then she looks down at Madeleine, whose eyes are open, gazing up at the tall ceiling of the dwarfs' chamber, and thinks of a child named Pedro, naked and trembling in his cage; and the smile drops from her face.

Catherine

That night, she says, "Why do you avoid the other . . . oddities here at court?"

Madeleine stirs briefly in her cradle, and Catherine reaches out a hand to rock her gently. A slow and gentle clunking of the cradle's curved base. A pulling of the muscles in her arm, her shoulder, from leaning so far over. Slow and careful, as if haste might spring a trap, she draws back her hand and turns to Petrus.

His eyes, set deep in their sockets, are lost to the room's dimness. "Oddities?" he says, voice so low it is little more than a vibration at the base of her spine; and she does not yet know it well enough to know whether he is insulted, whether her choice of word will prove to be a brick in a new wall between them.

"I mean," she begins, more loudly than she meant to. She pauses, but Madeleine sleeps on. "The dwarfs. Monsieur Petit"—the giant, more than half again the height of the tallest man at court, who stands sentry at the gate and comes to feasts for the courtiers' mock-sieges, where he sometimes acts as a giant guarding the king, sometimes as a fortress to be besieged—"and Madame Impaire"—the mute woman without arms who sits smiling vacantly during court ceremonies, and who can pluck out a simple tune upon the lute with her flexible toes. "I would have thought you would . . . find a home among them."

"Well. As to Madame Impaire—she does not speak, and so would make fairly poor conversational company. And as to the rest—" He shrugs, the motion just perceptible in the dark. "I . . . suppose it is because I was kept very separate from them when I was younger. I was educated like the king's own children."

Catherine bites the inside of her cheek to keep herself from speaking further. And then the words slide sideways from her mouth anyway.

"But you—you do not associate with many of the noblemen either, except Nevers. And not all the dwarfs are uneducated—Jeanne told me today that she speaks six languages! And Agnes writes—I know not what, but she is always scribbling something. Her family was poor, she told me so; she must have learned to read and write here at court, no?"

Petrus is silent for so long that she begins to regret her questions. Then he says, "Jeanne does not *speak* six languages, if by speak you mean to imply fluency. She can say a few things, but I hope you understand the difference between that and true scholarship."

The muscles of Catherine's neck and shoulders go hard as tree branches; her face hot. Since Madeleine's birth, she has felt as though they were, perhaps, accomplishing a slow, quiet settling into one another. They no longer stand apart during court functions, but as a unit, their daughter a rope tying them together. Sometimes, as when he asked whether he might write to her father, he even speaks to her in front of the others.

"I defer," she says, "to your superior knowledge, of course. Husband."

He makes a small, startled motion with one hand.

"As I cannot read or write at all," she adds, "I should not have spoken of something about which I know nothing."

The silence from his side of the bed is wary. And then he exhales.

"Ludovico, I think, is the only person I have known since coming to court who treats me just as he would any other man."

He says nothing else, and Catherine crosses her arms over her rib cage, as if to hold her anger in place, to keep it from flying out between the bars of her ribs.

Another motion, this one frustrated. "I do not—like to look foolish," he says.

Several retorts dart upon her tongue, but she swallows all of them, thinking again of Jeanne chirping in her covered cage, and a small hairy boy trembling in his. She wants to reach for Madeleine, to assure herself that her child lies beside her in her cradle; that she has not been penned and taken somewhere else.

I do not like to look foolish. As if he is nothing like the others; as if a dead king's affection is proof against his own physicality, his fine clothes and pride in his learning armor against the opinions of the rest of humanity.

And then comes a sudden, drenching rush of understanding, and she unclenches her arms. Looks at him across the bed—the line of his nose, the hair of his face combed smooth before he tucked himself under the coverlet. The stiffness, which had seemed so innate a part of him until recently, until Madeleine, is back, his jaw tight as a trap, his body perfectly straight, though his arms are crossed, the humps of his shoulders up around his ears. He has, Catherine thinks, been hunched against the world for most of his life.

She wants to ask whether he is ashamed of what he is—what their daughter is. But instead she reaches across the narrow space between their two bodies, and finds his hand there. His palm is warm; when she curls her fingers around it, the hair that grows over the back of his hand rasps pleasantly against the tender pads. There is another small movement in the air; then he clasps her hand in return, his grip strangely fierce.

SHE REALIZES THAT ALTHOUGH he had asked to touch her nearly every night before he put Madeleine in her belly, since their daughter's birth he has not asked once, not even when Catherine's birth-blood stopped flowing. Her belly has by now resumed something like its former shape and size, though her bosom swells huge with her milk. But even this does not seem to stir him. She finds herself watching him from the corners of her eyes when their daughter suckles; when she dresses in the mornings, lacing herself tightly so that her breasts push up, soft and threaded with blue, over the necklines of her chemise and stays, before she laces her partlet over them. But he seems oblivious, even turning away sometimes, as if the sight of her unclothed, even just a little, embarrasses him.

By contrast, his affection for Madeleine is visible to anyone who sees them together. He cannot hold her without smiling; never relinquishes her to anyone but the queen without first dotting her little face with kisses. On the day of her baptism, he flinched at her thin cry when the holy water touched her. Though Madeleine has begun to nap well in her cradle, he insists still on holding her whenever he can, even as she grows big enough to squirm, to protest with lisped words and demand to be set down. And unlike many fathers, he is only rarely required elsewhere.

Catherine thinks sometimes of his awkward kisses early in their marriage, as stiff and self-contained as the rest of him. Oddly, the thought makes her smile; a small, secret thing.

1574

Pedro

The king of France dies raving and angry, his lungs and then his mouth filled with blood. Like kings the world over, his death is not a private affair, but witnessed, and then whispered about.

His death was not unexpected, precisely. And yet when it is announced, Petrus reels. He stands among the other courtiers, all of whom were waiting for news of the king's condition, and has to put out a hand to steady himself against the wall. As if he were drunk, or ill himself. This king who never cared for him, who seemed mostly indifferent to his presence among his courtiers, his death sets everything adrift. Just as his elder brother's did nearly fifteen years ago. Just as his father's did the year before that.

The king's elder brother had died, only a year after being crowned, of an infected ear. Also not entirely unexpected, for he had been sickly all his life. But terrible nonetheless, that entire year since King Henri's death like the gray days of winter; and then his son stumbling into the afterward so quickly behind him. And terrifying, every solid edifice of Petrus's life since he came to France suddenly full of fissures that spider-webbed up and up and out and out until it seemed there was no possible way they would not all come plummeting down.

The dead king's younger brother will no doubt be recalled from Poland, where he has been king for scarcely a year. Petrus thinks of him as he was as a child—the favorite of his mother, spoiled, petulant, merry with spite. Though neither of his elder brothers had developed their father's affection for the hairy court oddity, they had at least generally ignored him; King Charles had even used Petrus's mind to his advantage, making him official reader to the king for the rare occasions that His

Majesty's mind turned to history, philosophy, poetry. But this new king, as a child, was like the boys on Tenerife, poking at Petrus with words and sometimes with his sword, the tip of it tapping lightly against the front of Petrus's doublet. *Where are you going, Werewolf? Don't you know we burn your kind in France?* It mattered not that Petrus was near manhood when the little prince was born; princes have nothing to fear, and no reason for humility.

THE NEWS SHAKES CATHERINE hard. "What will we do?" she says. She picks bits from the roll and makes soft doughy balls of them between her thumb and forefinger.

"Do?" He shifts Madeleine's weight.

"Will the new king want us here?"

Oh. He smiles. "I have been here through the rise and fall of three kings; and the queen mother values us. This new king is her favorite son; I cannot imagine he will not want us here, especially now we've produced such a marvel as this *petite belle*."

But Catherine does not look reassured. She frowns, dropping bits of roll onto her plate; and for all that they have been shifting nearer and nearer to one another since their daughter's birth a year and a half ago, he finds that he does not understand her mind well enough to know what she is thinking.

THE NEW KING IS crowned at Reims. Petrus thought Catherine—never before privy to a king's formal entry into a city—might be overwhelmed by the pomp of it all, with the crowds pressing on all sides and the absurdity of young girls clothed like ancients, symbolic of Concord and Peace, their hands trembling as they handed the new king the city's keys, as if the trading of one king for another might mean a true end to the bloodshed among the Catholics and Huguenots. But Catherine merely frowns, eyes watchful.

The court, with the new-wed king and queen, travels then to Lyons, the city of Catherine's birth, of her whole life before coming to court; and it is here that his wife goes quiet. Usually so patient, she snaps at Madeleine, who, now two years old, is wild with sudden strength and energy; but after the snapping, Catherine presses her hands to her face, shuddering. Petrus chews his lip, words eluding him; at last, he touches a hand to her back, feeling the jut of one shoulder blade through the fabric of her gown like a broken wing.

She smiles dutifully for the actual entry into the city, a city Petrus has not seen since the last king's own entry here during the years-long tour he and his mother embarked upon when he was still just a boy-king, not even half-grown. It is not quite spring, but the red roofs of the buildings glow, reflecting their warmth onto the gray waters of the Saône.

As is often the case when the court goes on progress, the best rooms in noble households and inns get snatched up, first by the royal family and then by their favorites, leaving the dregs for everyone else. Their chamber is cramped and smells strongly of vinegar from the common room below; but at least they are not relegated to sleeping rough in the countryside beyond the city. With Madeleine clutched tight in her arms, Catherine looks around the room, taking in the window, sludged with countless other sleepers' fingerprints and nose prints, and the bedstead, which sags toward the middle, as if someone too heavy for the frame slept upon it last. The linen is frayed and rumpled, either hastily laid over the mattress or else not disturbed since the last sleeper left.

"No doubt there are fleas," she says. Her voice is strange and high, as if it might break to pieces at any moment. Madeleine squirms on her hip, trying to get to down, but Catherine only holds her more firmly.

The common room downstairs was nearly deserted when they arrived, but it will likely be overfull by dinnertime. "Are you hungry?" Petrus says. "We might do well to eat early, before the crowds descend."

She shakes her head, a short, staccato burst. "I want to—" she says, and then stops, jaw working hard, as if chewing over tough meat. "Can we—venture out?" she says at last, and gestures vaguely toward the street.

His brows come together; his own jaw tightens. He thinks of the stares; the jeers. The dead rat that was hurled at him once in the streets of Paris, with a cry of *Loup-garou!*—werewolf—from the hurler's mouth. He looks at Madeleine, her soft improbable face peering out eagerly from under her white coif, and imagines her snatched from his very arms, taken aboard a ship, sold at a market. His knees tremble, his arms burn with imagined emptiness.

"Please?" Catherine says. She is not looking at him now, but at the smeary view from the window. "I thought—my home. I could show Madeleine—"

He thinks of that long-ago letter from her father. He knows that she keeps it in a leather pouch in her trunk; he has seen her, once or twice, take it out, tracing the words she cannot read with one finger, before folding it with tender care and putting it away again. Her father never wrote back after Petrus finally penned a letter that Catherine dictated, informing him of his grandchild's birth, asking how he had fared during the massacres. He thinks of his own yearning, long ago locked away, for the beaches and mountains of his boyhood; for the chance, just for a moment, to look upon Isabel and Manuel once more. A bruise blooms under the skin of his chest, and he breathes out.

"Of course," he says. "Yes."

SHE KNOWS THE WAY. This surprises him, though he supposes it should not. He had imagined her caught like a butterfly under a glass before she came to court, waiting to be released into matrimony. But her feet move unerringly down one street and then another, faster than he has ever seen her walk. He carries Madeleine, whose mouth hangs open over her teeth, and tries to ignore the startled looks of passersby.

He is unused to so much teeming humanity, for it has been years since he ventured into the streets of Paris with Nevers and some of the other court foster-sons, in search of women and drink; and he did so then only reluctantly, and after dark, when the thick pooled shadows helped to disguise his appearance. People here jostle one another as they walk. Carts pulled by horses and donkeys push their way through the narrow cobbled streets. He remembers running all on his own through the streets of Garachico; how he grew used to ignoring the looks and calls of other people. Court life has softened him; being around so many people who are accustomed to the presence of human marvels has made him forgetful. He braces himself for stones, cupping his hand around the back of Madeleine's head, though she bucks and struggles against him.

"Papa's largest warehouse is on this street," Catherine says, pointing up ahead. Her breath comes quickly, and her eyes are everywhere at once, as if they cannot possibly see enough; as if they fear they will never see these things again. They linger on the anchored ships with their tall masts, where sailors call to one another as they unload their cargo and the water slaps softly against the hulls. But when they reach the building that she says ought to house her father's warehouse, it bears another man's name and symbol.

She stops, staring up at the sign, swinging lightly in the wind, the chains creaking. And then, without a word, she walks on. It is not until they have put some distance between the warehouse and themselves that she says, too brightly, "You should see the city on market days. It's an unimaginable crush at the Place du Change—but so exciting. If we ever have the chance, we should come back for the fairs; Madeleine's eyes will be as big as mine were when I came to court." And she offers him a small smile, touching their daughter's cheek, pressing her palm there as if to anchor herself.

At last, they reach a street with fine tall houses pressed wall to wall, the illusion of their stern and elegant facades a little broken by their painted brightness, each building splashed with yellow or pink. Catherine wets her lips, her breast rising and falling. Then she points with her chin.

"This way."

Petrus follows, keeping his face averted from those they pass and Madeleine turned so that only the back of her coifed head is visible. Catherine's footsteps are halting now until at last they drag to a stop in the middle of the square before a house with a high arched doorway and great mullioned windows. He tips his head back, looking up and up, eyes widening at the sight of so much expensive glass.

After she has knocked, Catherine's fingers tighten around his arm. They wait for one breath; two; and then one of the double doors is opened by a narrow, hump-shouldered woman wearing a limp white apron over her brown skirt. Her eyes, gray as the skies above, widen and fill when they fix upon Catherine, and her arms spread to either side, readying for an embrace.

And then she spies Petrus, and her mouth sticks halfway between open and closed, her arms still lifted, as if the sight of him has turned her to stone.

"Marie! Oh, Marie!" Catherine says, either oblivious to the other woman's fright or trying to shove past it. She releases Petrus's arm while he concentrates on breathing evenly, on keeping his expression unthreatening and open, and throws herself upon the shorter woman, arms wrapped tight around her thin shoulders. "I was so afraid you would not be here," she whispers.

The servant's eyes are still fixed, wide and astonished, upon Petrus, but she says, "Yes, *ma petite*, I am still here, thanks be to God. But—" She draws back a little, though her hands still hold fast to Catherine's upper arms. Her eyes hold a question.

"We are here for the new king's *entrée* to the city," Catherine says, and then looks over her shoulder; and her smile is so wide and guileless,

Petrus's temples ache with it. "Marie—this is my husband, Monsieur Gonsalvus. And this is our daughter. Petrus—Marie is—well, she is our cook, but she has looked after me all my life, and after Maman died—" She smiles still, but tears wet her cheeks. "I have missed you so," she says, pulling the other woman toward her once more.

Marie takes her eyes from Petrus just long enough to close them; and her face, too, is wet. When she opens them again, she looks only at Catherine.

"Are you well?" she says, an intensity to her tone that belies the ordinary words.

"Yes—yes," Catherine says. "And you? Are you well?" But there is a sudden uncertainty to her tone, and she steps back, just a little, and catches her tears with her palms, swiping them from her cheeks.

The servant glances quickly at Petrus, and then away. She takes her apron into her hands, twisting the fabric between her fingers.

"Marie?" Catherine says. She leans a little to one side, peering over the other woman's shoulder to the darkened entrance to the house. "May we—may we not come inside for a moment?"

Marie shakes her head, and the lines of her face draw down and down. "This is not . . . you don't know then?" she says.

Catherine takes another step back, quicker this time. Her ankle rolls as her foot lands sideways in the shallow trough of the cobbled gutter. Petrus grasps her arm to steady her, and then keeps his hand in place when she leans against him, something seeping, like a runnel of water, slow and gentle between their two sides.

"What do I not know?" she says, voice steadier than her feet.

"Your father—does not live here anymore. He . . ." Marie holds up her hands. Calluses from her work stripe her palms; a dab of creamy sauce is hardening to a crust beside the knob of her wristbone. "A Monsieur du Roux bought the house for his family, and let me stay on. Monsieur Raffelin was kind enough to tell him I am a good cook, a good worker."

His wife puts a hand to her lips, as if to hold some ugly sound inside. "Where is Papa?" she asks around her palm.

Another head shake. "I do not know. I have heard nothing of him since he sold the house. I have hopes that he has found a new—a new venture. But I do not think he remained in Lyons."

Catherine's gaze is vague and fixed upon the shadowed entranceway to the house. Marie hesitates, then comes forward, putting a hand on Catherine's arm, peering up into her face.

"I must return to my work—Madame du Roux is very particular about mealtimes. I am so sorry—*ma petite*, I am so sorry I cannot ask you to come inside. I wish—"

But she shakes her head.

Catherine swallows loudly enough that Petrus hears; she puts a hand over Marie's on her arm, and squeezes the servant's fingers. Then she glances at Madeleine, and at him; he tries to return her look with steadiness, though he is acutely aware of the other people coming toward them down the street, who might see him, and of Marie, who has pricked him with a half-dozen furtive glances.

"We'll leave you be," Catherine says, releasing the servant's hand and shifting just enough that Marie's own hand drops away. When Marie cringes away at the cut of her voice, Catherine says, "No—I am so glad to have seen you—so glad you are well. I lo . . ." She rubs the back of her hand over her mouth. "Thank you, Marie. I will miss you terribly. What is served at the king's table is nothing to your fine cooking."

Marie hugs herself hard and stands watching them as they retrace their footsteps up the street. When they round the corner, he and Catherine both glance back; Marie raises a hand and then lets it fall, limp as defeat, back to her side.

CATHERINE IS QUIET ALL the way back to the inn, and eats little of the stew the innkeeper sets before her, though it has been hours since their last meal and the stew smells richly of herbs, and it leaves Petrus's lips slicked with meat juices.

He chews slowly, watching her between bites. Uncertainty niggles, bothersome as the strings of tough stew meat that catch between his teeth. Her home was much grander than he had expected, even knowing that her father was draper to the queen. For all that he has only ever seen her in palaces until today, he cannot imagine her there—cannot imagine her life. The surety with which she strode through the streets of Lyons. The way she looked up at the sky, squinted against the sun, followed the flight line of the seabirds. She was entirely unfamiliar to him; a person with a history. Not the silent young woman who refused to look upon him; not the mother of his child. Someone else.

He thinks of the letter, so long ago now, that came from her father, and wishes he had seen the lie tangled up within its words. There had been nothing solid, no particulars—only vague assurances of his well-being, his *happy expectations*. Even its brevity should have made it obvious that there was no good news to tell.

In their room, she sinks upon the mattress—thick with lumps and likely riddled with crawling things—as if her legs cannot hold her any longer. Madeleine, tired out from a long day of wide-eyed watchfulness, is half-sleeping already; she snugs against Catherine's side, eyelids closing.

Petrus lights a candle with the stub given him by the innkeeper. The light flickers, as if from a draft, casting shadows on the dingy walls that dash and menace. He settles beside Catherine in his clothes—they roll tipsily together from the cant of the mattress, though she only shifts Madeleine into the circle of her arm and slumps a little farther down—and watches the shadows dance, thinking vaguely of devils or Isabel's girlhood spirits.

He is halfway toward sleep, uncomfortable as the bed is, when she speaks.

"Our marriage was meant to save him."

He opens his eyes. "What?"

"It was meant to save Papa from ruin. I thought—I thought with my dowry paid, and his debts cleared, he might . . ." One hand goes to her brow, pinching. "But I see now that I was very stupid. For people have long memories; of course it would not be so easy to start again. Of course he would need to sell my—to sell his home—in order to start again."

Petrus is silent.

"It is why I agreed to it. At least—partly. He would be saved. But I was the only one saved."

His voice comes out rustily. "Saved from what?"

"The convent. Or . . . no, there is nothing else. Without a dowry, who would have me? Even peasants must have dowries; and the men who might have married me before were not peasants."

She goes quiet, and Petrus swallows down a sudden bitterness, like stems of parsley.

Then her voice comes again. "She did not even want to know Madeleine."

"What do you mean?"

"Marie." In the thin, shifting light, she is washed of all color. "She hardly looked at her. I told her—I told her Madeleine was our daughter, yet she hardly looked at her."

Tiredness sinks upon him then, mires him where he lies. Even his chest moves only faintly with his breath, as if his lungs cannot be bothered to expand fully. "It must have been a shock," he says, though all he wants to do is close his eyes and let this exhaustion pull him swift away; to be a twig like those he dropped from bridges into rivers as a child, rushed off by the water so quickly that he sometimes could not spot them again when he raced to the bridge's other side. Unable to—and not expected to—steer his own way.

A restless movement of her hand. "I told her—she *knew*. She knew who I was going to marry." A sound that is caught in the filaments between a laugh and a sob. "I told her."

He would sigh, were he not so tired. "There is knowing," he says, "and there is seeing."

She shakes her head, hard enough that the bedstead judders. "But—"

Impatience rises, displacing a little of the tiredness. "You would not look at *me*," he says, voice rising like his feelings. His head snaps to face her; his hands become fists without his intending them to. "As much as I could tell, you pretended I did not *exist*—"

In the candlelight, her tears look obscene. They crumple her face like cast-off paper, and glisten all down the creases. "I didn't—"

"You *did*."

Catherine covers her eyes, as if she cannot abide the sight of him; and then she yanks her hand back down. "It was not—I thought I could make her *ordinary*, I thought—"

He cannot tell what his feelings are—disgust or shame, pity or fury—but they are tearing him to bits. He pulls at his hair until it hurts.

She is weeping now, great ugly, gulping cries that the residents of the other rooms cannot help but hear. Madeleine stirs between them, and Petrus raises himself onto his elbow, rubbing her chest and belly, his gaze fixed on his wife's shuddering form even when their daughter moans in her sleep.

With a clear effort, Catherine calms herself, pressing her palm to her nose and mouth until she is sucking in breath more slowly. When at last her hand falls away, she looks across to him; eyes steady, mouth pinched.

"I had the keeping of her, you understand," she says. Her hand goes to her empty belly. "If she did not come out . . . like other infants . . . *I* would be blamed. Not least of all by myself."

He eases himself back down; lies quietly for a time with the bruising of her words.

"And now?" he says at last.

She lies flat as well, and takes one of their daughter's hands lightly in her own. Madeleine's is limp with sleep, the fingers curled in toward the palm. "Now," she says, "I hate anyone who does not look at her. Even the woman who stood in for my mother after her death."

Her eyes flick, gleaming, to his. He takes Madeleine's other hand, and they lie there for a time, atop linen that smells of some other traveler's sweat, listening to the hum of voices from the tavern room below.

Then he says, "Tell me about your father."

The sound she makes hurts him, just under the jut of his left ribs. "I cannot talk about Papa right now. Someday—soon—but not now. I cannot . . ."

With his thumb, he feels the pin-size scoops in the soft flesh of Madeleine's hands, just at the base of each of her knuckles. The hair on her hands is much sparser than his own.

"Then tell me . . . about Marie." And when she is silent, chewing at her cheek, he says, "Or your house. Tell me about your house. It looked very fine."

Her smile is a tremulous thing. "It was. It is. I—" She shifts a little toward him. "Oh, I shall miss it. I do miss it. The ceiling in the dining room—all painted in blues and golds—not so fine as anything at Fontainebleau, of course, but . . ."

He smiles a little, though the candle is guttering and he is not certain she can see it.

Soft, he says, "Tell me more."

Catherine

In her dreams that night, Catherine goes home again.

Finding the dream-house entirely empty except for her, all four storeys echoing with the sound of her footsteps and the rustle of her skirt, she begins a slow tour. Her palms caress the thick rope rails as she descends the staircases one by one, beginning at the top where Marie slept under the sloping eaves, ending at the bottom floor where Marie reigned over the kitchen by day and Papa held court in his office. Her feet are bare of shoes and stockings, and she feels the cool of tile and the plush of rug with the acute attention of an infant learning the texture and give of each new step.

In every room, she pauses to say goodbye.

She kneels upon the brilliant blue rug, imported from Persia, which softened so many childish tumbles. She bids farewell to each of the figures in the Brussels tapestry behind the dining table, at which she used to stare during the long dinners with Papa's merchant friends, when the discussions of business seemed endless. She stands on the table—bare feet on the embroidered tablecloth, a devilish delight at doing something so naughty dancing wildly in her breast—the better to make out all of the details of the chandelier from Basel, with its fish-tailed woman and splendid elk's antlers.

Then she climbs down from the table and crawls underneath it on her hands and knees. Carved of walnut wood, with the tablecloth falling to either side, the space under the table was her favorite childish hideaway and the place where so many of her solitary games played out. Her own little cave.

She no longer fits so well, even in a dream; in her eagerness to tuck herself away, she misjudges the distance between her head and the underside of the table. But she strokes one of the table's feet, fingers bumping down the clawed toes, before crawling reluctantly out again.

SHE FINDS HERSELF, ABRUPTLY, a child again, bare toes small as wild berries, gown, still tailored for her grown-up self, trailing behind her, just as her mother's used to do when she tried them on. In her dream, she bunches her skirt in her two hands and navigates the stairs to the ground floor by feeling for the edges with her toe-tips. At the foot of the staircase, she could turn left, toward the kitchen where she spent so many happy hours helping her mother and Marie, taking nibbles of the bitter parsley or sweet figs left sitting on the big table, waiting to be used. When they prepared tagliatelle in broth, they always gave her the first taste. Her mother took the recipes of her Florentine childhood with her when she came to France as a young girl—just, she liked to say, as Caterina de' Medici brought Italian refinement to the brutish French court—and she taught them to Marie. Her mother's table was complimented by all lucky enough to be invited to dine there.

But the cold hearth, now, does not feel welcoming, and so she turns right instead, pushing open the half-ajar door to her father's office to find, to her startlement, her father standing there, just as if neither of them had ever left.

He stands beside his desk. His clerks are gone, the candles unlit, and the room washed in shades of gray. The scales for money-weighing sit idle; the ledger books are stacked and closed.

Her father turns at the sound of her too-long gown swoosh-swooshing over the tiled floor. He smiles, tiredly.

"Tell me a story, Papa," she says as she nears him.

His eyes wet, though his lips still tilt upward. "I've no stories left, *ma belle*."

She stops directly before him. This near, she can smell the faint, unwashed odor of his skin and clothing. His doublet hangs open; his stockings sag. His hair is mussed, standing up strangely around his ears.

"But," he says, and reaches down to scoop her up—for his sake she stoically endures the vinegary smell of him, the rushing stink of his breath—"I will show you where I am going."

She clings to his neck. A merchant's family is forever waiting, and a merchant's child learns patience through necessity. He carries her easily in an unhurried circle of the room, pausing before each and every one of the maps that cover the walls like tapestries. These maps show lands he had been to, himself, and lands to which he sent his ships, and lands so far away their names are like whispers. She used to study them with a dedication that, to her mother's dismay, she brought to nothing else. She kept her hands knotted behind her back so they would not be tempted to reach out and touch, smudging oils from her skin onto the surface. She stood quietly, wonderingly, her eyes following her father on his travels. Surrounded by the world but not allowed to touch any of it.

She looks at them all again now. Her father's arm holding her steady on his hip, her legs dangling; and as with all the things upstairs, she whispers goodbye to each one. Florence, Maman's city of birth, all golden buildings and lush green hills, with naked painted women frolicking in a river. Paris, viewed from above just as God must see it, the city like a cracked wheel cleaved by the curve of the Seine, its houses sketched in tipsy rows, their roofs painted blue and red, a city all of fruit. And the Château du Louvre, one of the royal family's many palaces, sprawling near the river's bank. A place her father had visited many times, but which she had never expected to enter.

Her father pauses longest before her favorite map, which shows all the known world stretched out like a table linen, with great brown humps of mountains and broad swathes of forest and all the seas rippling in between. Sea monsters, if the cartographer is to be believed, fill the oceans as deer fill the forests. They gaze at this map, this world, awhile, and then her father says, "It's an age of adventurers, *ma belle.* Of men with restless feet."

She knows this. He used to tell with relish the story of a group of friends who gathered for a drink at a tavern, and, emboldened by wine and each other's enthusiasm, decided to set out then and there to see the world.

"They were gone for years, hopelessly consumed by the need to wander," he would say. "Just stood up and walked away, and explored the great wide world together by sea and soil."

"Their poor wives," her mother would say every time, dry, head bent over her embroidery to hide the humor in her face.

He would offer a self-deprecating smile. "Yes, well. As always, I suppose, the wives were long-suffering. Very long-suffering, for these men were gone wandering for years and years, and not all of them lived to return."

Waiting by the window, Catherine would feel a clutching sort of fear sometimes, that perhaps her father would prove to be one of those men who took years and years to return home; or who never did.

Now, he rests his cheek on her hair, and points. "There," he says, his finger circling like a gull over a stretch of sea so deep and mysterious the mapmaker painted it a blue that is nearly black. "I am going there."

A sea monster, purple-scaled and serpentine, menaces this part of the sea. Three mermaids cluster on a great rock nearby, sunning their breasts. When she seeks France on the map, it seems impossibly far from the place her father is going.

"How long will you be gone?" she says.

A shrug; a smile. "Who knows? As always, a journey takes as long as it must."

In her dream, in her head, just as they always did in life when her father spoke of journeys, her soles itch, and she wriggles her toes.

Catherine

The new King Henri is not so fond of sport as his brother had been; and he seems a great deal more serious, despite the almost absurd richness of his clothing, so stiff with gold embroidery, with pearls and jewels, that it might have stood at attention when he was not inside it. Some of the courtiers—Petrus included—have known him for much of his life; but Catherine, who has only heard of him until now, finds herself shrinking back whenever there is a court function she must attend. His brother Charles, the last king, had largely ignored her—and Petrus, too—but this king seems a man of contradictions. Serious enough to rise early each day and spend the entire morning writing letters and attending to the more tedious aspects of the affairs of state; so committed to his faith that, according to rumors, he goes so far as to mortify his own flesh. A soldier who fought the Huguenots; a man of learning and charity, who offers food to the poor in return for honest work.

But he is also foppish—ridiculous—and has garnered a reputation for debauchery, for all that he sleeps in his wife's bed each night rather than his own. His *mignons*, the group of young men with whom he surrounds himself, gather riches and titles even beyond the usual largesse bestowed upon a monarch's favorites. His tongue is full of poison, his humor smart and cruel. Petrus has said little about him, but Catherine sees the way he holds his shoulders, as if expecting a blow.

THE TREES' CANOPIES ARE threaded with fire when the king calls for a hunt. Catherine stands with Agnes and the other ladies who are not planning to join, watching the hunters and servants readying themselves, patting the necks of their eager horses, whose breath steams in the cool misty air. Dogs, tails waving, are a seethe of furred bodies around the horses' and hunters' knees.

The Duke of Nevers, returned to court with the new king, mounts the horse beside Petrus's, and leans over to say something. Petrus grins, unselfconscious and easy as he only ever seems to be when speaking with his oldest—his only—friend. Something lashes at Catherine's breast, then, like the burning sting of nettles, and she flinches, shifting Madeleine higher in her arms.

"Ah, good, Barbet!" calls one of the king's *mignons*. "You can lead the pack."

Rolling laughter, sounding good-natured enough, and Catherine's husband chuckles, too, as easily as if the joke were not at his expense, as if being called a dog before the king and all the court were nothing at all to him. Then he bends over, as if to check his horse's bridle, his face turned away from the others, and Catherine, whose entire body had flushed with mortification for him, feels a little cooling needle of sadness. Beside her, Agnes stirs; leans a little against Catherine's hip.

The king, seated upon a fine dappled creature, has been gazing into the distant trees, as if he can already see the stag they mean to kill; as if he circles like a hawk over its prey. But he looks over his shoulder at his fellow's gibe, half-smiling.

Something sparks inside Catherine then—something foolish, and frightening in its potency. She presses Madeleine into Agnes's arms and marches up to Petrus's horse, which stamps and snorts.

"Husband," she says.

She can feel the curious eyes of others; but it is Petrus's eyes upon which she fixes her own. They look down at her from under the hoods of his lids with something like the old hateful dispassion from early in their marriage; and for a moment she almost falters.

"Come here, if you please," she says.

He hesitates, gaze flicking to Nevers, whose eyes are dark stones;

and then he swings his leg over the horse's back, and leaps down with a thump.

"Yes—Wife?" Drafty, his look, one brow raised; but she sees the tip of his tongue wet his lips, and how his fingers clench upon the horse's bridle.

"I forgot to wish you luck in your hunt," she says, and then, before her fast-beating heart stops altogether, sets her hands upon his shoulders and pushes up with her toes to reach his mouth with her own.

It is like and unlike their kiss in the feasting hall. A fence of eyes again surrounds them, and Catherine can feel the pricks of all of them, like spear tips. A king watches. But this time, this time she has chosen this course.

A startled sound from the back of his throat; and then his hands wrap around her wrists, tugging her gently forward, and his mouth opens against hers. Just long enough for her to feel a confused rush of something almost-familiar; and then he pulls back far enough to look at her. Over his shoulder, she is dimly aware of Nevers, turning his horse, turning away.

"With such a token as that, luck will no doubt be on my side," Petrus says. One side of his mouth tips up; his eyes warm, as if by candlelight.

"SUCH A SPECTACLE," AGNES says, after.

Catherine tips her head back, gazing up at the sky to hide her smile. "I was provoked."

Agnes laughs. But she says, "Her Majesty is impatient for another of your miraculous babes, you know. This one is far too old to be without a sibling."

Catherine takes Madeleine back from her and they stand, watching as the horses and hounds and booted servants disappear into the wood, trees closing around them like curtains.

"If you do not get to work soon, she'll likely send someone in to observe you. To make sure you have not forgotten the knack of the act."

A horrified look. She waits, though, until the rest of the ladies have trailed back into the palace, to warmth and gossip, and then she says, "*Observe?* Truly? Hasn't"—a glance around, but they are quite alone—"hasn't Her Majesty other things to concern herself with?" The country is poised on its toes, if the murmurs are to be believed, waiting to see how it ought to react to the new king.

Agnes snorts. "Of course she has. Which makes distraction from serious matters all the more necessary. Even a queen must have her amusements."

They begin to walk, pace leisurely, Madeleine straining between them clutching a forefinger in each of her fists, tugging to make them move more quickly. The wood beckons, smelling of autumn, the ground a tumble of acorns and crisping leaves; but they turn instead toward the courtyard.

"Her Majesty endured such scrutiny many times during her marriage," Agnes says, voice still pitched so quietly that Catherine has to lean down to hear her. "I was not here then, of course; but I've heard of it. There is no privacy at all, the higher you rise; everything must be seen as it happens, lest someone claim it did not happen at all." A pause; she looks up at a sudden rush of wings overhead, and crouches a little to point upward, that Madeleine might follow the flock of wild geese as well until they are mere dots upon the horizon. When she stands, she looks at Catherine with great seriousness. "You know she's married some of us to one another over the years." A gesture that encompasses her small stature. "Well, not a single marriage has proved fruitful, to her disappointment. And though her own trouble conceiving in the first years of her marriage makes her . . . more kindly disposed toward those with similar troubles, one still does not want to be a disappointment to a queen."

"No," Catherine says, faint. She allows Madeleine to tug free; watches her squat to look at a crack in the courtyard stones.

"It's a pity," Agnes says after a moment, "that a woman cannot rule France. Her Majesty is formidable enough."

"Hmm? Oh, yes." Catherine shrugs. "Very stupid."

Agnes smiles a little. "But Her Majesty managed to . . . shall we say . . . circumvent that problem quite well for more than a decade."

Startled, Catherine glances back at her. Agnes returns her look with a mouth that is pressed pointedly closed.

It is true, then, Catherine thinks, and the horror comes in a slow seep. True, what the rumors say—that it was the queen mother's doing, and not the late king's; that the very earth trembles with fear, waiting for the next inevitable war, because of her. That when the slaughter of Huguenots moved inexorably from Paris out through the countryside, it was she who sent it? That night in Paris—that night which went on and on, the longest night in the world. Pressed against Petrus, their hands clutching, the midwife moaning and praying beside them. She missed witnessing the full horror of it, confined as she was, but she heard, after.

Her father's jests echo in her mind, now—*Teeth sharp and pointed as those on a trap; fingernails like talons.*

But Her Majesty is a woman—just a woman. A woman whose desire for little hairy children saved Catherine from the nunnery, or worse. Whose desire led Catherine to Petrus, to Madeleine. Catherine tries now to feel the usual, uncomfortable gratitude that rises inside her whenever she sees the queen, filling her until her insides cramp.

But Her Majesty is also a woman with the power to crook her finger and make anyone at whom she glances come hurrying to her side, eager to please. To welcome Catherine's child onto her lap and stroke her as she might a pup. To order massacres.

No, Catherine thinks, wrapping her arms about her middle. One does not want to be a disappointment to a queen.

SHE WAITS FOR HIM that night inside their chamber. Madeleine sleeps in her cradle, mouth pulled down in a dreaming frown. Catherine's legs ache to move, to stretch; her hands pluck uselessly at things—her mending, abandoned on a chair, the thread a hopeless tangle; one of Petrus's shirts, draped over his clothes chest rather than folded neatly inside. Something rises inside of her, heady and warming as fumes from a cup of strong wine, and she shifts her feet against the rug, her hips against the mattress. She thinks of Petrus's eyes before he mounted his horse, and her own eyes close.

They fly open with the door to the chamber, and she smiles as Petrus enters, closing the door softly behind him. He nods to her but goes immediately to Madeleine's cradle, leaning over it, gazing down at her for a time with his hands clasped behind his back, as if otherwise he might reach for her, snatch her up, heedless of the hours that would then be needed to make her sleep again. Catherine stares at his hands, the palms as smooth as her own, the tops so delicately haired.

"Will you not come to bed?" she says at last, softly. His shoulders tense and release, a flexing and bunching of muscle, and he turns to face her with ponderous slowness.

"Of course," he says. "If you wish."

But he undresses as slowly as he turned. Catherine, still seated on the edge of the bed, puckers the coverlet in her hands, squeezes the crumpled fabric. Almost, she looks away from him as he disrobes, for he keeps his eyes meticulously away from her, as if he wishes himself alone in the room. But he does not attempt to hide, and so she looks on from under half-drawn lids as stockings and trunk hose peel away to reveal his limbs; as he unfastens his doublet, flings it away from his arms like binding ropes that have been cut. And then he stands in his shirt, legs bare below the middle of his thighs, head canted to one side, as if listening to the minute vibrations of her attention.

"Petrus?" she says; and then cannot think of what to say next. She wants to reach forward, to touch his sleeve, his hand; to cup the back of his neck and pull him toward her. And, too, she wants to keep things as they have been these last years, gentle, easy, the tentative warmth between them, the occasional clasping of hands, the smiles, the murmured secrets, fragile as spring ice.

He looks over his shoulder, not quite at her, his gaze directed just to her right. "I need to know," he says, and his voice is strained, frayed rope, all the depth gone, something of the boy he must have been revealed. "Why did you"—a pause, a darted look, as if he expects mockery—"before the hunt?"

Her breath catches. "I—I wanted to," she says. And when he says nothing, merely continues to look at her, "I wanted to. They were"—a swallow, a tightening of her fists around the covers—"they were calling you a dog. I—wanted them to see you as a man."

His eyes briefly close. Open again. "And now?"

"Now—" She rises from the bed, releases the covers so that they fall behind her. Stands before him, their toes aligned. Their daughter turns on her pallet, and oh, how foolish to be able to hear such thundering in her ears, to feel it in her chest, when they have made a child, when they have coupled so many times, when they have been married for so long already. She raises her voice, that she might hear herself above the thundering.

"Now," she says, "I should very much like to kiss you again."

For a moment, he is utterly still, and heat beats in her cheeks, scorches her neck. But then he leans forward, ducks his head down the short distance between them, and his mouth meets hers with frantic force, teeth clicking against hers, hands cradling her jaw, bearing her back and back, down and down, his body warm and heavy, bones and muscle and flesh and hair, and her body splays to welcome his, the familiar slide and give suddenly made unfamiliar for her flesh's wanting it, for the sparks of it that had never been there before. The awkwardness is not gone from his kisses, the hesitation; but she is able to open her mouth, *wants* to open her mouth, to show him how two tongues might meet, how teeth might deliberately nip, raising gooseflesh and pleasure together. Wants to draw her legs up, is startled by the primitive urge to do so, to tuck them tight against his sides and invite him farther inside her. The noise he makes when she clutches him so with her thighs, when she draws her fingers through the hair on his head and presses her brow to his, is not just one of pleasure. It hums between them, sobs between them, an elemental sound that makes her want to draw him closer and closer, in and in and in and in.

IN THE MONTHS FOLLOWING the hunt-kiss, Catherine and Petrus learn each other by touch, by sight, by smell and taste and by the rhythm of one another's words and breathing. Catherine searches out Petrus's shape under his hair; the structure of his face. Looks with her eyes, and feels with her fingers, learning the bones of him. His cheeks more sunken than hers, the cheekbones lower; his chin more pronounced, a solid point under the tuft of his beard. Beneath the give of hair and flesh, she explores the perimeter of eye sockets, the line of jaw, the high curve of brow.

And then she lifts her fingers so they rest lightly atop his hair rather than seeking what lies beneath.

It is nearly as soft as Madeleine's, though much denser, like the hair on Catherine's own head. Where it thins near the bridge of his nose, it rasps gently under her fingers. Where it grows thick over his shoulders and chest, she draws her fingers through it as she once drew them through the ribbons at her father's warehouse. Petrus closes his eyes, presses a little upward with his body, as if seeking more and more of her touch. Being together so is a sudden joy, so different from their early stiff couplings.

He looks at her, all of her, as he has not before. Raises her chemise over her head, hem first, and then takes his fingers over the dips in her collarbones, the strong arching bones of her ribs, the folds of her belly. She lets him look, lets him touch and taste and breathe her in, without shame. She has the idea that their clothing, all the layers of it, linen and silk, velvet and boning, obscures their humanity—their animality. It disguises them. When they shed it and lay together in their nakedness, when he explores her body and she his, she feels as if her skin is no less absurd than his hair. When they clutch one another, fingers digging into shoulders and thighs—when they cry out down one another's throats—she sometimes has the sensation that they are seeking whatever it is that lies even below the further obscuring disguises of their bodies; that if they could, they would find the seeds of themselves there.

1575

Pedro

Aristotle claimed women were a sort of deformity; almost like men, but incomplete, as if some fundamental limb had been left off in their making. They were not, Petrus had understood from this, as human as men were. Memories of Isabel sometimes broke through while he was a boy and studying, reading Aristotle's words in the Greek, whispering them to himself. Her eyes warm but rolling with scorn for what he was studying at the great palace, from his learned teachers with their long beards and scholars' robes. It was easy enough, though, to see her as something different, someone different—a person apart, a mother-figure, not like all the others. Entirely herself, and not *woman*.

And so there is something almost startling in the understanding that Catherine has a breastbone, just as he does; and toenails; and breath that sours overnight. That she can find a pleasure in their coupling that rivals his own; that despite her lack of education, her mind often leaps, quick as a frog into a pond, from thought to thought.

"WHAT DO YOU PREFER to be called?" she says one night. "I have been calling you Petrus because that is the name my father told me; but you have had more than one name, have you not?" She turns over, speaks each name into the world with careful solemnity. "Pedro," she says, and, "Pierre. Petrus."

It is a question no one—not even Ludovico—has ever asked, and Petrus stills, all of him, every bit: his hand, which had been arcing toward her across the bed; his breath, which had been coming in slow, unhurried drafts through his mouth; even his mind, if only for an instant.

"I—" he begins, and then stops.

Pedro—a boy from the town of Garachico on the island of Tenerife, who collected shells and gathered mussels, who loved the sand under the soles of his feet and the saltwater wind in his face, who was stolen away from the beach and the people he loved. In *Pedro* he hears the reverberations of uncertainty, of danger. A beetle, scrambling through layers of leaf litter, of fungi, of bracken, feeling at once the ground thrumming under the feet of small, curious children. Helpless to determine whether it would be scooped up, or stomped upon; left unnoticed, or placed, careless, in a lidded pot.

Pierre—a French name for a boy in France, a name held in the mouths of kings and courtiers, and nearly always coupled with the surname Sauvage, at least in speech if not in writing. There is shame in this name, shame with roots that twist and twine firmly together deep within him, wrapping around his insides, wringing them. Sauvage. A glance at Madeleine's cradle. He might have little power to keep that name from her head, but he can, at least, not *choose* it.

Petrus—A name for a scholarly young man, a young man whose dedication to his studies earned him the respect of a king.

But, also, a witticism. A cause for muffled laughter among those who used it.

(But also, bestowed upon him by King Henri. Kindly meant. An honor.)

"Petrus," he says at last, feeling it on his tongue, one moment sweet as a sugar lump, the next crumbled and dry as earth all used up.

Words intrude as he sinks toward sleep, snag at him like a rough-woven net and pull him out of the warm roiled depths of dreams and into the chilled night air of their chamber. *Not even yours*, are the words, and he listens as they echo inside his skull, listens until he understands that the voice in which they are spoken is his own.

THEY LIE TOGETHER, HIP to hip, and she tells him at last of her father, the wanderer. How he was so often gone, and how entirely he filled a room when he was there. How her mother spent hours readying herself when they thought he might return, wearing the jewels he had bought for her on previous trips so that her earlobes and throat shone, and her fingers twinkled starlike. How Catherine crept into his office to visit his maps.

"I wanted to follow him," she whispers into Petrus's shoulder. He feels the warmth, the moisture of her breath, stirring the hairs that grow thickly down his shoulder's slope, delving beneath them to reach his skin. He feels the press of her toes against his ankle, the canting of her breasts and belly toward him when she turns a little onto her side. He hears her words, and he hears the wistfulness behind them like the lingering of a note of music after the player's fingers have stilled.

"Where did he go, that you would follow?" he asks, his voice dropping low—that he mightn't wake Madeleine, that he mightn't disturb the dreamlike quality of this moment, this place, with this woman, his wife, beside him, her breath warming him down to the skin, her toes curling against his ankle bone. "Where did you want to go?"

And she tells him, the names like wishes released into the air until the room feels swollen with possibility, a brimming cup, into which one more word will set the contents to sloshing over. *London. Brussels. Paris. Genoa. Venice. Amsterdam. Basel.*

He hums, strokes a hand over the round of her hip. Imagines her on a horse, a feathered cap upon her bright head, a cape pooling over the horse's hindquarters. Her body springing up, down to the rhythm of the horse's gait. Her smile as big as the world she is off to see.

He feels himself stir, and would turn to tell her so, not with words but with a press of himself into the giving flesh of her belly; but she is leaning up on her elbow, putting her lips to his ear, warm over the lobe.

"*Tenerife*," she breathes, sending the cup to overflowing.

Pedro

Though it is several years before it happens, their second child is conceived in joy.

He tells her, when she is heavy with the babe, and fearful of what is to come, what Ludovico told him before Madeleine's birth—that men's battles are in war, and women's in childbed.

"Both are equally valiant," he says, clasping her hands in his own.

She looks at him, both eyebrows raised as high as they could go. "And how many wars have *you* fought, Monsieur?"

HE IS WITH HER in the birthing chamber this time, and feels the shame of his words then as his wife fights her battle alone. The midwife tries to keep him from her, but he remembers when King Henri lived and how, though his heart belonged to his mistress and not to the queen, he was certain to be with his wife during the births of their ten children. The midwife closes her mouth when he tells her this, though he can see mutiny behind her eyes, if only she could find a way to free it without seeming to be someone who would criticize a king.

Their son comes rumple-faced and peevish from her womb, as hairy as his sister. Catherine seemed sanguine during the months before the birth, blithely accepting of the notion that this child would likely be hairy, too. She takes him from the midwife, kisses his brow, his cheek, his small waving fist. They name him Henri, which pleases both the new king—the third Henri to rule France—and Queen Caterina, though, of course, his and Catherine's Henri is named not for the man now on the throne but for the man who welcomed Petrus to his court; who looked at him without fear and declared he belonged.

THE YEARS ROLL, NOW, in a way they have not since Petrus was a small boy. Season upon season of unexpected sweetness. Although the court feels very different under this new king—the air full of mistrustful humming, courtiers' belts bristling with daggers, and many wearing breastplates under their capes—and although the country, by all accounts, seems to be tearing itself along its seams, the danger feels far removed, their family a small, warm world unto itself.

But it is impossible to entirely ignore the rest of the world. These sweet years are filled, too, with political prisoners escaping from windows; with the king's younger brother turning against him and joining forces with the Huguenots, forcing the king's hand. His Majesty signs a peace accord, allows space and freedom to the Huguenots to worship as they please; but within months, Catholic nobles have formed a league against the accord, against the king himself, and the peace breaks apart until there is nothing left of it but jagged splinters.

The king has not appeared in his *salle* today, and the courtiers make Petrus think of fishing boats, bobbing all unmanned in ruffled waters. Ludovico is missing, too—with His Majesty, perhaps, for the time being included among the king's favorites—and Petrus wishes he himself could slip away. Instead, he does as he has done for all his life in France—stands at the edges of the room, cradles a glass from which he only occasionally sips. Listens—or tries not to. Is generally ignored.

But today, someone notices him. A country noble, spring-green, clusters of red spots all along his cheeks, his whisper-whiskered jaw. He steps toward Petrus with his eyes held wide, his hands spread wide, too, the fingers splayed, as if he means to snatch at Petrus, if Petrus were to try and run. Inside his head, Petrus sighs.

"What is this?" the nobleman says in a voice that is pitched soft, the syllables drawn out soothingly. As if, Petrus thinks, he himself is a horse, skittish, likely to bolt, to bite, to kick. In need of calming words and slow movements and open palms. "What manner of wondrous creature graces the palace today?"

Petrus feels his mouth pull into a tight and tacked-on smile. "Petrus Gonsalvus, at your service," he says.

At these words, the young courtier's eyes blow impossibly wider; his spread hands rise, delighted, to frame his face.

"Oh, Monsieur! You must tell me of yourself."

And so Petrus finds himself reciting the familiar tale. Much of its fabric is threadbare, worn out from so many recitations, but he has taken, in recent years, to strengthening it by adding new threads, new embellishments he creates from the air, from the bones of the story King Henri was told when he was given the gift of a small, caged boy. He tells this arrogant nobleman, this barely-more-than-boy, of his bold and fearless father, king of the heathen Guanche. His mother, so beautiful the Spanish conquerors found themselves falling, enraptured, at her feet, incapable of cutting her down as they had her husband. His own astonishing good luck at having been brought to the golden civilization of the French court.

The young courtier exclaims his amazement.

"And what," he says at last, "do you think, Prince of Tenerife, of the treachery of His Majesty's brother? To think that he would use the king's troubles with the Huguenots for his own political gain!"

Petrus swallows. "I am always saddened to hear of any rifts in the affection that one brother holds for another, kings or no. But *this* family, which has been so good to me—"

It is his usual mode of deflection, whenever such questions are put to him. Show that he is loyal to those who feed, clothe, house him. Who educated him; who gave him a wife. Be slavishly grateful for all the things most men take for granted.

And never speak the language of politics—pretend it is a language whose syllables his primitive tongue cannot manage—for to lean into the political would be to lean over the edge of the cliff; to dance along the palace roofline. One sharp push would send him flying, to land sprawled and splattered on the stones far below. Better to not allow the intrigues of court to touch him, to touch his family. Better to make it clear that Petrus Gonsalvus is loyal to those he serves, but that he has no troublesome political feelings that would, if necessary, prevent him and his family joining another court someday, should the need arise. That he will do his duty to the crown—no matter whose head it might rest upon—by showing his hair gladly, eagerly.

But this stripling cocks his head at Petrus's measured words. "You cannot have no opinion on so grave a matter, surely," he says. "The world is all in turmoil, and yet you bleat about *brotherly affection*. What of the king's compromises with the Huguenots? Would they have created peace in the end, do you think, had the Catholic League not formed so strong an opposition?"

"To that, I cannot speak," Petrus says; and he feels a withering inside himself, a curling up. All those years of education, of learning to *think*, to use his mind, negated in this moment by those five words. But it is safer to let his pride wilt a little than to let it be the thing that prevents his family from keeping safe. The king's treacherous brother is next in line for the throne, unless the king produces a son. And after him, the Princess Marguerite's husband, a Huguenot leader, a man nearly murdered during the massacre that followed his own wedding, a man forced to Catholic conversion, who only lately escaped his palatial prison to become a military leader of the Huguenots. A man like that cannot hold any love for the household of his former captors, however extraordinary their appearance. A man like that might choose to keep the marvels of the former court caged, might pen them up in the menagerie where their nearest neighbors would be the dromedary, the lions; unless he thinks they are harmless, political eunuchs, no more capable than kittens of seditious thoughts. Petrus's chest hurts; his throat closes itself off from air until he feels like gasping.

Inside him, Isabel's admonition—*Be stone, be stone*—thumps like a drumbeat, like a second heartbeat.

WHEN HE MEETS LUDOVICO later for dice and wine, Petrus cannot banish the country courtier from his mind—his voice, at first quieting, then demanding. The arrogant tilt to his spotty chin. His insistence that Petrus produce an opinion, nudging him toward the cliff's edge—it broke apart the warm and happy oneness, apartness, of him and Catherine and their children, thrust all the things Petrus always tries not to think about into his thoughts.

Usually, though he is so politically minded himself, Ludovico is good for conversation that does not center exclusively upon the king and his movements. But tonight he is irritable and spends much of the evening complaining that the king refuses to listen to his courtiers.

"He fears poison," Ludovico says, "and so now all his meals are closed affairs. Even his *lever* is turned private."

This last said with something like despair. Petrus understands why—a private *lever* means that the host of courtiers who would usually attend His Majesty during his morning rituals of dressing and drinking broth are now kept away, only a few favorites, chosen for companionship rather than counsel, allowed into his chamber. And yet it is too much—after the earlier breaching of his life's walls, his sense of security, Petrus does not wish to hear about threats of poison or the king closing himself off to good advice, and, exasperated, he finally says, "Can you speak of nothing else, man?"

Ludovico turns cool. "I know that *you* prefer to ignore affairs of state," he says, raising a brow, "but some of us haven't the privilege of ignorance. We do not all have such fine hair upon which to recline."

Petrus's mouth opens on a retort; then closes. *Privilege,* he thinks, testing the word, the heft of it, like a bag of coins tossed, all unexpected, into his hand. *Privilege.*

CHÂTEAU DU LOUVRE

1583

Catherine

The first time that she was painted, Catherine was sixteen years old, mere weeks away from her seventeenth birthday and months away from her father's ruin. She sat upon a dusty velvet-topped stool in her father's office, with his map of the world behind her. She can remember, still, the awkwardness of posing; how the artist fussed for a time for the perfect composition, asking her to angle herself a little this way, lift her chin a touch higher, hold her hands in a more natural manner. Catherine tried, she did, but she was like a horse upon which flies insisted on landing, and no matter how often she twitched within her skin, they returned.

She felt them, those flies—those eyes—the eyes of all the men inside the room. Different men, as time passed, the square of sunlight on the worn black-and-white tiles at her feet shifting slowly through the hours as her back began to ache, her toes to cramp. The *fuff-fuff-fuff* of the painter's brush seemed overloud as one of her father's clerks left the room on some business, pausing—so briefly that Catherine almost could not think he paused at all—to take in the tableau she presented. His eyes, with their wine-reddened whites, *lingering* even as he himself moved toward the door. Another merchant, broad-bellied and wind-chapped, entered to speak with her father, and from the edges of her vision Catherine saw his slow smile as he observed her, as if she herself were a painting.

"A lovely gown, Mademoiselle," he said, head nodding in an almost-bow, forcing her to look at him. He smiled again, and she felt she must smile in return. Then he glanced back at her father, who stood now beside his other clerk—Nicolas, who had kissed her; Nicolas, whose name she whispered over to herself in the night—reading, over Nicolas's shoulder, whatever it was he was writing. "Venetian velvet, eh, Raffelin?"

Papa raised his brows. "It wouldn't do for my daughter to be seen in anything less, would it? I've a reputation of a certain *quality* to maintain. And her mother—God rest her soul—would never forgive me if Catherine were immortalized in something common."

Catherine's chest began to ache dully. Maman would have wanted her in silk, silk as fine as the silk her own father once wove. Her fingers began to trace a pattern through the softness of her yellow velvet sleeve; only when the painter darted her with a quelling look did she still.

"Ha!" said the other merchant. "True enough. Me, I'm a bit stingier with my girls. But then, I haven't quite the reputation you have, either."

"You do well enough to half-bleed me in negotiations," Papa said, drily, and the other merchant laughed again.

"That's where *my* reputation lies," he said, tapping his nose. He nodded again to Catherine, more deeply this time. "A lovely gown for a lovely girl," he said, and again her lips curled up like puppets to which he held the strings.

Nicolas caught her eyes, then; and with Papa standing behind him, he smiled his own all-knowing smile, a smile that was at once tender and said he had learned the secrets that lay inside Catherine's breast and inside the warm hollow of her mouth.

Abruptly, she was too aware of herself—of her body, newly tender, under the weight of her clothes; of the painter's eyes looking at her so dispassionately, and then of his hands creating her again with brushstrokes as delicate as sighs. Her eyes moved like evening moths trying to find somewhere safe to rest. Her neck ached, and her back, and she thought of the strain of her neck and shoulders from reaching up on her toes to meet Nicolas's mouth, so much higher than her own. A flush. Would the painter see it? Would her memory of her first kiss be forever captured in circles of red on her painted cheeks? She glanced again at Nicolas, who tucked his lips between his teeth to prevent a grin; she looked away again quickly to prevent her own.

UNTIL TODAY, NO OTHER artist has captured her image. It is a different experience, she finds, as a matron of several years' standing, with two children loose in the world and another tucked tight and secret in her belly. She does not wear velvet this time, but soft black wool, unornamented but for a high ruffled collar. Her hair is not dressed with flowers, as it was when she was a maiden, but smoothed back until it scarcely shows, tucked away under a flat-brimmed bongrace.

And it is not a painting the artist creates this time, but a mere sketch. Catherine sits in three-quarters profile, looking ahead of her with what she hopes, according to the artist's directions, is a look of serenity. The sketch is the work of minutes; when he is finished he shows it to her, and Catherine hates it instantly for the dullness of her expression.

He takes a great deal more time and care when he sketches Petrus, Madeleine, and Henri. Catherine suspects he only took her likeness because she has borne two such marvelous specimens as her daughter and small son. The artist had heard of them, he says; their fine hair is being spoken of across Christendom, and he knew he must take their likeness.

"Kings the world over will pay handsomely for portraits of you and your children," he says to Petrus, one palm cupped, as if already anticipating the heft of coins. "Other artists, too, will be eager to copy your likenesses."

Petrus and the children are dressed more finely than Catherine, in their best court attire, Madeleine's gown sewn with pearls and rubies, which are echoed by the jewels in her headdress; Henri in a robe that closes all down the front from neck to hem and a cap that adds inches to his small height. Madeleine, nearly eleven years old now and long accustomed to stillness, fares better than Henri, who at just two cannot yet lisp more than a few words, his energies concentrated wholly upon motion. Catherine has to stand beside him, to touch his shoulder when he begins to wriggle; but the artist seems nevertheless charmed.

He shows the finished sketches to Petrus and Catherine, and her eyes linger upon her husband's face, transferred with uncanny truth to the page. There is his nose, its bone so straight; there is his small mouth. His eyes, dark and serious, cradled deep within their sockets, looking, grave and weary, out upon the viewer. Madeleine's face is serious; Henri's small and round and so sweet Catherine aches with it; she longs to take the pages from the artist and hold them to her breast; to hang them in their rooms. It is said that the queen mother ordered portraits painted of her children whenever she was away from them for long. These portraits were sent to her wherever she happened to be. Catherine understands this impulse now, though it had seemed so immoderate when she first heard of it, before she herself became a mother. But when he moves to take them back, she releases them without a word, though she hates to let them go.

AFTER SITTING FOR THE artist's sketch, Catherine finds herself paying closer attention to the wealth of art that adorned the palace walls. So much of it is of women—young women, lovely women. She looks at the impossible shapes of their bodies, their imperfections, if they had any, softened by clever pigment. After two babes, and another sprouting, her own body is forever altered, the flesh no longer unmarked as cream but streaked and dimpled. Her breasts stretched and drooping. She has the shameful urge to unlace her gown and cry, *Paint these!*

Men still look at her sometimes with hunger; she has not entirely lost her power. But she cannot expect it, now; their attention is no longer her due. And this has not bothered her so very much, not since Madeleine—and Petrus, the whole of him—came into her life. But for some reason, just now there is a shortness to her breath. She has let her mother's beauty rituals go of late, releasing them from her life as a child releases dandelion seeds into the air; and, of course, she was never terribly faithful to them in the first place. Not as Maman was, and wished her to be.

But now she has a strange urge to strike out for the kitchens, wherever they were, somewhere in the bowels of this place. Petrus would know, of course; he used to go to the kitchens several times every day to fetch the king's bread. But she cannot ask him, cannot face the disdain he would surely feel if he knew she wanted nettle water for her hands, herbs for her hair.

She can almost smell them, those herbs.

When the children's lessons, delayed today by the artist's request to sketch them, are finally through for the afternoon, Madeleine comes forward, says she is hungry, twines her arms about Catherine's neck. She is smiling. The artist made a comment as he sketched her, casual as a sip from a cup, that if her face were not so hairy, Madeleine would actually be quite lovely.

Shame is a worm inside Catherine, now. And wriggling beside it, that old, old fear, the one she has not named for years. *What shall I teach her? What do I possibly have to offer her; to ready her for this world?* Maman readied Catherine the best way she knew, by teaching her to keep her hair thick, her teeth bright, her skin smooth and pale.

I cannot even give her that, she thinks; and now despair joins the fear and the shame; wraps itself around them, strangling vines around a tree, until they are subsumed. For Henri, perhaps it matters less; she had never imagined she would be the one to armor her sons against everything that would be hurled at them during their lifetimes. But her girl. She curls over herself, as she used to in the tub that Marie would set up before the wide kitchen hearth. She would inhale deeply as she washed her hair, smelling her mother all around even after Maman was gone. But the thought that lustrous hair might save her daughter—it is like a cruel joke. And nettle water would only make her hands, with their soft hairy covering, smell like grass, growth, wildness.

Catherine

Henri and Madeleine sit on stools at the queen mother's knee. Madeleine wears a gown of yellow, her toes, in round embroidered shoes, peeking from under the hem, Henri a belted white doublet and blue trunk hose, both, against the queen's black skirts, bright as spring flowers nestled in the dark, damp roots of a tree. Each sits straight and still, Henri sucking on a lump of sugar offered to him by one of the queen's ladies.

Antoinette sits on Her Majesty's lap. She was the bud rooted inside Catherine when the artist sketched them all. Born with her eyes open, wide and wet, as if she were all eager to see as much of the world as she could as quickly as possible, she has not changed in the two years since. She sits like a little bird, the hair that covers her from head to feet soft as down feathers, eyes bright, inquisitive, alive with questions she does not yet have the language to ask. Her hair is plaited with ribbons; she is as fine as one of the springtime festive trees about which Papa told Catherine long ago, their trunks trailing ribbons colorful as rainbows.

When Antoinette was born, Her Majesty was delighted by her. *Three!* she exclaimed at Antoinette's baptism, where she held the child to her own stout bosom and examined every strand of hair. To Catherine, she gave a gold ring set with a ruby; to Petrus, a fat purse.

Petrus stands beside the queen today; the men to whom she has granted an audience have been sent from Spain. He speaks to them in their own language, though even Catherine, unschooled in Spanish, can tell that his tongue stumbles a little over syllables it has not spoken in many years. She stands to the back, rather like a servant, unnoticed by anyone, but there if the children need her.

The men seem awed by Petrus, which was surely the queen's intention, scarcely listening to what he says, instead gazing at his face, and at the children, as if they are dream and nightmare at once. When the queen speaks, their eyes snap to her like trained dogs, but Catherine knows in her chest that their eyes long to drift, that they hold them still and attentive to Her Majesty only by a great force of will. The queen smiles a mild smile, her hand reaching out to stroke Henri's head.

Only when their business has been conducted do the Spaniards give rein to their desires, kneeling, with Her Majesty's permission, to look more closely at the children. Madeleine returns their looks with a bland stare of her own, but Henri tries to shrink back, recalling himself only when Catherine steps forward to tap him—*behave!*—in the center of his back.

"They speak French, Your Majesty?" one man asks.

"Like natives," the queen says, smiling more widely.

"Will they say something if I ask? Would that be a presumption, Your Majesty?"

A tap upon Henri's head from the queen's forefinger. "Henri, *ma petite*. Say something to the ambassador."

Henri gives a grave nod. His voice, like piper's music: "*Je m'appelle Henri. C'est un plaisir de faire votre connaissance, Monsieur.*"

The delighted widening of the men's eyes. The admiration in their voices.

"Remarkable! Like hearing a lion sing. May we touch it?"

The queen nods, and the men hold their fingers out to the children, as if for them to sniff. The room feels suddenly very close; the high ceilings look as if they are dropping. Catherine touches the space between her ribs, under her heart, where something inside feels tight and desperate.

Sometimes in the afternoons, she asks her elder children to read to her from their hornbooks while she sews. They are not so well educated as Petrus, but they can read and write in French and Italian, the language of the queen's birth and, still, of her heart, and when they read Catherine finds herself swaying to the rocky rhythm of their words, as if they are singing hymns. When she catches a glimpse of her face in the mirror, it is smiling, her eyes shining like coins with pride for them.

Impossible, she thinks now, when the queen has bred her and husband so true—when she dresses them in finery, when she educates even the girls—to protest now what she does with their progeny. As Catherine watches, the men pet her children, murmuring together, fingers drawing back between their brows and over their skulls, as if they are cats. And though Madeleine and Henri both remain carefully still throughout, Antoinette smiles, and, like a cat, seems almost to purr.

When Catherine flicks her eyes to Petrus's, she finds him already watching her; finds an echo of her own impotent distress at seeing their children so diminished painted across his own face. She feels the press of his eyes like the cupping of his hands around hers, warm and steadying. When he tries to smile, she does, too.

OF ALL CATHERINE'S CHILDREN, Agnes loves Antoinette best of all. "What a sweet," she cried upon seeing Antoinette's newborn, sleeping face, so round and covered with such lovely, silky hair. "What an absolute, perfect love." Agnes's face alight with some passion Catherine had never before seen there. Agnes is kind to all of Catherine's children, but with an indifferent sort of kindness—the kindness a good person would show to any small, vulnerable creature, whether she loved it or not. But it is, from the first, different with Antoinette; a perfect, inexplicable, immediate love.

She spent much time in Catherine's chambers after Antoinette's birth. "I'll hold her," she would say, "so that the little mother can rest." And she paced the chamber, all patience, even when Antoinette turned fractious, giving her a finger to suck, crooning bawdy songs gleaned from God-knew-where. Petrus was mildly horrified, but Catherine shook her head at him, struck by the way Agnes's head bent to their babe's, the tender curve of her neck.

"Have you never wanted a child of your own?" she said one day, and Agnes gave a laugh so lacking in humor it sounded like a cry.

"Never," she said, short and pointed, and Catherine knew better than to ask anything more.

WHEN CATHERINE COMES TO the dwarfs' chamber, Antoinette in her arms, Agnes consents to turn from her writing. She never lets anyone know what it is she writes—or at least, she never lets Catherine—and the other dwarfs, who tease her occasionally about her mysterious scribblings, seem obviously in ignorance of their contents as well.

Even Catherine, so untutored, can see that Agnes writes a crabbed and desperate hand, her thoughts flying from the pen, the ink blotting the page. Sitting at her small table, Agnes hunches over the words, a mother bird above her nestlings, fingers stained and cramped, etching a deeper and deeper line between her dark brows. Reflexively, Catherine longs to smooth that line away with her thumb, to keep Agnes's brow smooth and pretty, as her mother used to do for her when she frowned. And then she loathes herself, just a little, for the impulse.

But when Antoinette is in the room, Agnes leaves her table to sit with Catherine by the fire. Jeanne might join them, too, with the infant on her embroidered blanket on the floor before them, kicking her feet and crowing. The line between Agnes's brows smooths then, of its own accord, and her fingers uncurl.

SOMETIMES SHE AND AGNES go out together into Paris.

Once—only once—does she say to Petrus that she would like to take Madeleine with them, and perhaps Henri as well, though he is likely to scamper away, to twist his wrist in her grip and dart, careless, into the path of a horse. But they both would love the city; she can see in her mind the fierce wonder on each small face, the way her son would stand up on his toes to peer at the goods on display at each stall; the way her daughter would inhale the reeking city smells, smiling.

But, "No," Petrus says, without looking up from the small book he is reading.

The word is so softly spoken that Catherine thinks that perhaps she has misheard, or imagined it. She sets Antoinette on the floor, away from the fire, and leans closer to him, repeating her intentions.

His hands curl in a spasm about the book edges before he flexes and releases them. "No," he says, louder. His face closed as a walnut's green husk. Catherine takes a step back.

"But—" she begins.

"*No*, I said." The book thumping against the table; his teeth clicking together as he sets his jaw.

"Petrus," she says. Her hands turn outward, her voice drops. "Do you not think they would enjoy being outside the palace grounds? Seeing the rest of the world?"

He turns back to his book, stares at its binding, the leather dark as wine; his hands go into the hair at the crown of his head, fisting it, twisting it. "The palace," he says, each word precise and clipped, dignity like a pike prodding her away, "is hardly a prison."

She is glad, then, that Madeleine and Henri are at their lessons; she can feel her next words rising inside her throat, clawing their way out. "They go *nowhere*," she says. "Nowhere, but from one palace to another! Don't you think they would like to see something of the *true* world—"

He stands so quickly that his chair of heavy oak tipped and crashed, the noise of it reverberating in Catherine's ears and setting Antoinette to screaming. Catherine scoops her daughter up, lets the shoulder of her gown absorb her tears, and stares at Petrus. Here, all at once, is a man she has never before seen, a man as wild in appearance as any caged creature: his fists come away from his hair, leaving it stiff and bristling as the hair on a boar's back; his lips draw back from his teeth; his eyes stare back at her, but sightlessly, as if they are seeing something else entirely.

"*This*," he says, breathing as if winded, "this is *our* world." He gestures with both hands, taking in the wide soft bed, the children's truckle beds tucked away, the fire in the grate, the cool panes of the windows, which overlook all the bright and green of the palace grounds. He makes a fist of one hand and pounds it once against the wall behind him, hard enough that he winces, hard enough that the frame of the Virgin's ugly picture tap-taps against the plaster. But in spite of the wince, the rattle, he continues without stopping, ignoring Antoinette's renewed crying at the ripping sound of his voice.

"What's out in the wider world for them? *You*—you can come and go, you've nothing to fear in the markets, the streets. You've your skin to hide behind."

He says this with his teeth still bared; with a sneer in his voice. As if, Catherine thinks, she is separate, apart from all the rest of them. From the children she has carried, fed, rocked in the night; from the man who has been inside her body, who has planted their children within her.

Apart, she thinks. *Apart*—

"But for *her*," Petrus says, pointing to their smallest child, who is gulping in too much air against Catherine's neck, "for Madeleine and Henri? Beyond the court is—nothing. There is nothing for them. Have you no sense? Do you not remember what happened to me—because of *this*?" And his hands go again to his hair, fingers dragging through it as if he would tear it out, like weeds, at the roots. In his face, Catherine sees the terror of a boy in the arms of a sea monster, stolen away, lost.

"I—I am not trying to send them out into a life without us—

without the court's protection," she says. "I only wished for them to see—" He begins shaking his head, slowly at first and then faster, faster. "In Lyons," she says, voice pitched too high in her confusion, "we took Madeleine out in Lyons. We walked to my house—we spoke to Marie—we passed so many people—"

"It was to see your father," he says. "And it was poorly done. Madeleine could have been snatched from us—"

"But she wasn't! Nothing happened! Agnes comes out with me—"

"And how do people speak to her?" Petrus says; his voice is a hammer, and she the nail, relentlessly driven. She wants to throw up her arms to stop the blows. "Are they kind? Do they jeer?" He does not wait for her answer, only steps forward, jabbing with words and a single, accusing finger. "Even if you are so—so naive, so careless, as to ignore the danger to our children, do you truly want them exposed to the world's cruelty?"

"They are exposed *here*," Catherine says, her voice rising to a cry. "They are exposed here! You know that—you must know that. You've experienced it yourself, I have *seen* it. There is cruelty everywhere. Madeleine and Henri are exposed to others' stupid remarks, their cutting ignorances, every single day."

Only the day before, Madeleine stabbed at her needlework with such force that Catherine asked her, half-laughing, whose face she was imagining when she stuck the needle into the linen. And then her daughter's face crumpled, as if it were linen itself, and the whole sorry story—a ring of servant children, who turned the spits and swept the ashes, carried slop bowls to the pigs and mucked out the horses' stalls, suddenly around her; their voices, a low, chanting taunt. *Devil girl, devil girl, devil girl, devil girl. Your father's mother lay with the devil*, cried one. *Your mother is the whore of a devil*, shrieked another. A clod of earth, a handful of pebbles; Madeleine's hands over her eyes, her shoulders curling down, her mouth stuffed with curses she didn't dare utter.

"They usually ignore me, or just whisper things as I walk past," she said, weeping into Catherine's lap; and Catherine stroked her head and wished she were a witch in truth, with the devil at her beck and call, that with a glance she might smite those foul children with warts and boils that grew and grew, bubbling upon the surface of their cheeks, their arms, their fingers, until no smooth flesh could be seen between them; rashes that stung and itched and disfigured.

But Petrus's mouth turns down; and his breathing still whooshes through his nostrils like storm winds. "They are not going," he says, and rights his chair as Catherine watches, opening his book once more with a pointed deliberation that makes her jaw ache. It is only the trembling of his fingers as he turns a page that keeps her from arguing further.

LATER, ALONE, SHE DUCKS her head against her knees, wraps her arms tight to shield her brow. She listens to the murmur of her breath, the skittering and scratching of mice in the walls, the beating of her heart in her ears. There is a point of pain inside her belly, hot as metal heated to glowing brightness within the fire of a forge.

His words are like a shirt too long worn, the patches that held the fraying fabric together no longer enough to keep the holes from showing. It is passing strange to realize this—that those exposed holes, those words, were there all along, barely held back. For years—since their meeting, probably, and even before. Does he hate her—resent her—just a little, for her ordinary skin? Will her children, someday? She thinks of all the nights she has lain awake, fear for them moving through her mind like a burrowing insect. Of all the days and nights of terror before Madeleine's birth, when she could not look at Petrus for fear of what might come of the looking.

Then she looks down at the backs of her hands; reaches up to prod the flesh of her cheeks. Feels ashamed of the smoothness she finds there, and then angry about the shame. Her throat tastes of curdled milk.

SHE AND AGNES GO out the following day, one of the manservants who serves the queen's dwarfs following at a sullen distance. They pass into the city proper and both let out their breath in a rush of giddiness, hands clasped tight together. Catherine breathes in again, dirt and horse droppings and sweat and sunlight and release, and decides to ignore the pricking thought: Madeleine and Henri should be here. Free.

Though all the people within the vastness of the city of Paris must feel the fearful vibrations under their soles, just as Catherine does, of the country at war with itself, they do not behave as if they do. She and Agnes stroll among the market stalls outside the Palais de la Cité, examining gloves lined warm with the fur of hares and hats in red velvet, jaunty with feathers. Sellers call their wares with cheerfulness or aggression; buyers step up eagerly to touch and sniff and see, rolling coins between their fingers. The women who sit at the stalls mostly ignore Catherine and Agnes unless they turn to them with clear intention to buy, coins clinking in their purses; the sellers' eyes are upon the noblemen, and the wealthy students from the university, who might be tempted into a bauble for their wives or sweethearts.

Agnes stands for a long time, however, at a stall of quills while Catherine enjoys the bustle, so like that of Lyons and her girlhood. She watches as, with a timid finger, Agnes brushes the plumes; as, with a critical eye, she examines the nibs.

"I really could use a new quill," she says to Catherine; but her hand does not move to her purse.

"Do you—not have the coin for it?" Catherine asks softly, but Agnes shakes her head.

"Oh, I do. But . . ." A shrug of one shoulder. "It all feels rather . . . futile at times. Do you not think?"

"I—" Catherine swallows, suddenly prickling with strange, frightened heat. "I suppose yes, at times. But it would be—I imagine it would be a great shame if you did not—that is—"

But Agnes takes her hand, which is colder than the rest of her. "I am not about to do myself a *harm*, dear Catherine," she says, smiling with half her mouth. "But no one shall ever read anything I pen; it seems . . . a waste of time, though I confess I've no idea what I would do with all that sudden excess."

Catherine curls her fingers around Agnes's palm, pulling her a little aside that the other shoppers mightn't jostle them. "Why do you write?"

"It—oh, I suppose it keeps my head clear, and my humor high. It's a . . . an *itch* almost, but inside my very skull where my fingernails can't reach. I have thoughts, and they must come out or forever pester me, like fleas."

"What sort of thoughts?"

Agnes's cheeks go pink. "All of them, really. Songs, sometimes; very poor ones, I am sure. I wrote—well, I wrote to my mother and father recently, a very long letter of *great* eloquence, the contents of which I will not bore you with. Of course, I couldn't anyway; I burned it to finest ash once it was written. They cannot read in any case, even if they are still living. But I like to imagine the smoke of it reaching them, wherever they are."

She moves back to the quill stall, brushing a goose feather with two fingers. Glances over her shoulder at Catherine with a sly look. "If I ever write a song about *la bête* and his beautiful bride, I promise not to burn it. Perhaps someone shall find it long after we are both gone and know the story of your great love."

Part Four

Flight

CAPODIMONTE, ITALY

1618

Catherine

She wakes from a drowse to the din of Madeleine cooking.

Living as they now do in a village rather than a palace, their meals no longer appear like toothsome bursts of magic upon the table. She had to remember the art of cooking; had to teach her eldest girl. Madeleine comes over often, and they prepare large meals all together, sometimes with Henri's wife, as well. The joy of a hot fragrant kitchen, of feminine hands working side by side and feminine voices all raised, talking around and above one another, chattering like starlings. She'd forgotten it until they came to Capodimonte. It leaves a bittersweet taste at the back of her throat, like wine at once dry and bursting with fruit. She is an old woman, but in those moments, she misses Marie and her mother with all the desperation of a bewildered child.

Petrus used to make himself scarce while they cooked, claiming the patter of their voices overwhelmed his own thoughts; but he loved the meals they produced together, pulled from Catherine's memories of cooking with Maman: rolls stuffed fat with rucola; cabbage salads, dressed with sweet vinegar and olive oil; soups of peas and mushrooms; spring tortas, flavored with parsley, mint, and sage, made rich with butter and cheese, and sprinkled when finished with sugar and rose water. His favorite was pasta in a broth made from chicken bones, turned thick and golden with egg yolks, and flavored with vinegar, saffron, cinnamon, and nutmeg.

Catherine watches for a moment as Madeleine, who has always been noisy in the kitchen, beats eggs in a bowl as if they have wronged her, all the frustrations she keeps inside herself much of the time emerging here. *Ah,* Catherine thinks, her belly stirring in anticipation. They will eat omelettes today. With rosemary, perhaps, cooked in plenty of butter. She lets her eyes drift closed again, listening to her daughter's noisiness.

But she should not be napping now. There is always something to do. She had forgotten this, too, somewhere along the path of her new life, leaving busyness behind her as she settled into a period of obscure luxury at court. She'd forgotten about carpets that needed beating, and meal after endless meal that needed preparing. Floors and steps that must be swept and scrubbed. Dishes to be scoured, clothing and bed linen to be cleansed of their dirt and sweat and other fluids, mattresses to be turned according to the seasons. She had forgotten about bottling herbs in vinegar; preserving fruits; keeping careful count of how much olive oil and flour they had to hand. About keeping the mice *out* of the flour. Though she has Elisabetta, a young woman from the village, to help—paid for from the duke's generous allowance—she is not the idle creature she once was. Such was the price of their decision to leave Rome, and the palace of the Farnese.

Sniffing the air, now heavy with frying butter, Catherine cannot regret their choice.

HER MOOD SPOILS A little after the meal is eaten and the dishes cleaned and put away. The omelette has settled warm and heavy in her belly, and she thinks, as she has so often since they left France, of Agnes and her hungry childhood. It seems clear that Petrus's parents abandoned him as an infant, and Catherine cannot dampen the hatred this makes her feel. But Agnes, with her tale of poverty and starvation; of fields where nothing would grow, and hens who first stopped laying, and then slumped dead themselves, and goat's milk drying in the teat—well, perhaps her mother and father truly did do what they thought best for their child when they sold her to the traveling troupe.

Or perhaps, she thinks sometimes, in the secret part of her mind that insists on voicing terrible thoughts, perhaps they stupidly believed that Agnes was the cause of their misfortune. That her form was evidence of some great evil; that a witch had cursed them while the babe was still in her mother's belly, the curse spreading to the goat and the hens, and then to the land itself, turning rich soil to crumbled dead earth where no plant but those riddled with poison would take root. Get rid of her, they might have thought. Let her wrongness spread to some other place. Let our fields become fertile again; and so too shall we. We can have another child; and one this time that is born in the perfect image of God.

She shakes her head now; but the thought clings, tenacious as some slimy thing growing upon damp-slicked walls. Papa's face appears in her head, too; Papa as he was when she loved him, with his beard thick and soft and his eyes full of smiles. And then Antoinette—always Antoinette—Antoinette as Catherine last saw her, dressed in a gown of blue, with a heavy jeweled cross hanging upon her narrow breast and tears making pools of her eye sockets.

Catherine puts a hand to her mouth, the omelette threatening all at once to dislodge itself from her stomach. *Dear God,* she prays, *do not let Antoinette think of me as I have thought of Agnes's parents. Let her understand. Let her forgive—*

But here, her stomach clenches, and she rushes for the back door. Falls to her hands, palms scraping on the stones, and to her knees, which thud and bruise. Retches into the bucket beside the door, oblivious to the exclamations of her neighbors who witness her sudden sickness. Madeleine, with a cry, follows her outside, puts a hand between her shoulder blades, says, "Maman, Maman!" over and over, as if repeating Catherine's role in her life aloud, a word of magic spoken with pure intent, might chase away whatever malady has caused this. But Catherine shakes her head, hard and then harder, scrubbing her sour mouth with the back of her hand, *Maman* an accusation in her ears.

CHÂTEAU DE BLOIS

1589

Pedro

News that the king has murdered two of his greatest enemies at Blois whips like a storm through the palace, so loud and ferocious that Petrus cannot stopper his ears against it, cannot deny its stormy force. The two men murdered were brothers; though Catholic like the king, they wanted to take his throne for themselves. Petrus stands beside Catherine, listening to the rumbling voices of the other courtiers, and reminds himself to breathe in and out, to keep standing, though panic scrabbles at his rib bones with its terrible claws. The queen's astronomer walks about looking grave and portentous but stays clear of the clusters of courtiers who murmur together, plot, plan. As if he knows that he has nothing to say to them that any will wish to hear; or as if he has never had anything of consequence to say at all.

"A mistake," he hears one man murmur to another. "His Majesty has made a terrible mistake."

"Two fewer enemies," the other man disagrees. "That can only be a good thing, no?"

But a third man shakes his head, the cant of his brows etching a fierce V above his nose. "Impulsive," he mutters. "A man with so many enemies as the king cannot afford to act so. This will be the ruin of him. With the Huguenots rising, how could he do it—how *could* he strike a blow against good Catholics?"

"But these Catholics would have dethroned him, if they could," the second man objects. "His Majesty faces traitors both within and without our faith—"

Such talk would have seemed impossibly disloyal even a few months earlier. But now, though they keep their voices low, these men speak their minds, hands curled around the hilts of their daggers. Petrus has sidled nearer to them against his own will, drawn, desperate, by the juddering fear of what effect His Majesty's actions will have on the court, all these lives that have tied themselves to the king's fortunes. The king's younger brother died some years ago, and now there is no heir but the Huguenot who married His Majesty's sister, who Petrus imagines will scour the court of all Valois influence. He looks down to find that his hands are shaking, trembling in the air like aspen leaves.

The murmuring men take no more notice of him than they might of a piece of furniture that happened to be situated near them.

A THUNDERING AT THEIR chamber door wakes Petrus from his sleep that night. He pushes himself upright, blinking through the shadowed room, still dream-caught. Catherine stirs beside him, unbending from the sheltering curl she formed around Antoinette in the night. When she hears the frantic knocking, her breathing hitches; when Petrus swings his legs out from under the bedclothes, she tries to catch his sleeve.

"*Wait*—" she hisses, whites glinting all around her irises. But Petrus reaches for his sword, removes it from its scabbard with a scraping of steel, the warlike noise of it out of place in this room. It wakes his older children, makes them sit up on their pallets, questions in their yawning mouths. Petrus makes a slashing motion in the air with his free hand—*Silence!*—and creeps toward the door, where the pounding has begun anew, echoed now in the frantic beating of his heart. He puts his mouth very near the door, almost kissing it, and says through the stout wood, through the noise of the battering fist on the other side, "Who is there?"

When Agnes's voice comes, muffled, Petrus folds over with relief, half collapsing against the door. "I have news," she says. "Sauvage—please let me in—"

He opens the door at once and Agnes hurries through, shutting it again immediately behind her. Catherine has climbed out of bed and lights a candle from the embers of the fire. In its wavering light, Petrus can see that Agnes is not dressed in her nightclothes like the rest of them, despite the late hour, but in the same fine gown she wore that day. Her hair, though, is unbound and disheveled, as if she has been pulling at it.

"What is it?" Catherine says, coming toward her friend. She stops, however, beside Petrus and leans just slightly into him, the flesh of her upper arm warm against his own. He shifts his weight so that their arms press together more firmly.

Agnes glances at the children, as if wondering whether she ought to speak before them, then shakes her head. "Queen Caterina," she says. "She was—she has been so angry, *furious* with the king. She has been ranting . . ." A gulp of air. "She has been unwell for some time, as you know."

They nod; despite her best efforts, news of the queen's weakness, the gasping of her breath when she exerted herself, was impossible to keep secret.

"But tonight, she has become worse, much worse. She complains of a pain in her chest, like a knife stab. Her body burns with fever, but she shakes as if with cold. She breathes with the greatest difficulty." Agnes presses her hands to her face, fingers spread across her brows. "The doctor is grave, and will not tell us anything, but I think—" Her shoulders shake.

Catherine leaves Petrus's side and folds Agnes into her arms. Petrus feels a heaviness, a weight at the end of his arm, and looks down, dazed, to see that he still holds his sword, the tip of which drags lightly against the floor. He looks at his wife and her friend, their embrace tight as ropes, their faces both an agony of fear. He looks at his children, two of whom stare up at him in bewilderment from their pallets at the foot of the bed, the other of whom has continued, in the miraculous way of small children, to sleep through the commotion. They exist because the queen willed it so. They exist because she bought Catherine for him. It is this thought that rises above all the rest in his head, which smooths out and brushes away the decades of bitterness he has felt toward the queen. She wanted them, and so they are here. She wanted them—but she is almost certainly dying. He must put his palms against the wall, brace all his weight upon them, and gasp heavy through his open mouth.

Catherine draws away from Agnes and looks between her friend and Petrus. "What are we going to do?" she says, but Petrus has no answer.

"We're all of us awake, if you'd like to wait with us for news," Agnes says. Catherine agrees, and Petrus nods as well, and they both, without having to discuss it, reach for their children, Catherine drawing Henri and Madeleine by the hands to follow her and Agnes down the corridor, Petrus scooping Antoinette up from the bed and cradling her against his chest, her head lolling upon his shoulder. They could leave them in the room, let them sleep; but any separation just now feels too risky with the queen's life thread floating gossamer just out of reach of the waiting sheers, as if anything might happen, the very worst things their minds could conjure.

They go together to the female dwarfs' chamber, the first time he has entered it since he knocked upon the door when Madeleine was still curled tight inside her mother and asked Agnes to ride to Paris with his wife. The dwarfs are all there, men and women both. The monk and the gray-headed songbird pass a wineskin back and forth—wet smacks of their lips and overloud gulpings of their throats—but all the rest sit very still, tight with the same fear that wraps around Petrus.

Agnes takes Antoinette from Petrus's arms. The other children press together to form a hillock of arms and legs and great, staring eyes, not certain what is happening but alert to the terrible tension. "Will you stay with the court? If the queen—" Catherine says, but Agnes makes a shushing sound.

"Hush, you," she says, as if she had not just wept her terror into Catherine's shoulder. "Don't you know better than to speak of such things aloud? Besides"—rubbing her nose to Antoinette's, who sneezes; Agnes grins, just for a moment—"it is you I am more concerned about. I don't know that His Majesty has much care for your protection. But we'll be taken care of." She nods to the other dwarfs, still sitting wooden about the room; and she clears her throat, clutching at it above her ruff, as if it is closing itself. "We must. We *will*. Her Majesty—well, she has assured us all that we are to be provided for in—in any eventuality.

"But you." And now she looks at Petrus; a look that makes his skin tighten, and his heart pound within his breast. "*You* must provide for yourselves, I fear."

Then she takes the wineskin from the monk and takes a hefty gulp.

They wait together, all that long night, for news—for life, for death. When Antoinette wakes, she looks around and says, "Where is the queen?" An odd question, given that Her Majesty has never joined them in the dwarfs' rooms, given the night-blackness that fills the room, only a little softened by candles. Antoinette is accustomed to being called to sit with the queen almost daily; accustomed to the sugared fruits, tough as leather, that the queen's ladies slip her to keep her still and quiet during Her Majesty's audiences with important visitors. But despite Catherine and Agnes both shushing her, murmuring reassurance, telling her it is time to sleep, not time to visit with Her Majesty, Antoinette's voice rises higher and higher.

"Where is the queen, where is the queen?" she says, over and over, voice rising toward a screech until Catherine gathers her up and holds her close, her face a closed and stoppered jar of feeling. Petrus looks about the room and thinks he sees his own feelings reflected in the faces of all the dwarfs, Antoinette's frantic keening giving voice to all his—all their—fears.

He must fall into a doze, for he wakes to more keening, a terrible moaning that seems, in his sleep-drugged state, to come from everywhere, above and below and all around them, as if the very walls and floor are grieving, and he knows at once that the queen is dead.

The dwarfs cling to one another, to Catherine, to Madeleine and Henri and Antoinette. Petrus curls into a corner alone and weeps without shame, great eddies that wet down the hair of his cheeks and jaw. But then come Catherine's arms about his middle, her head resting on his thigh. Her fingers shake, and she clenches them around the hem of his shirt. Her tears wet through to his skin. He bends over her, making a bower of his body. He hasn't the words to tell her that he weeps not merely for the terror of their circumstances, but also for the woman who once taught him to use a fork and who—whatever her motives—kept her husband's long-ago promise to find a wife for his wild man.

Catherine

The weeks after the queen's death are fogged, as if Catherine cannot see clearly. She and Petrus keep to their chamber with the children as much as they can, though Catherine ventures once or twice to the dwarfs' rooms to gather news, like a mouse gathering crumbs. What she brings back with her is scanty, and terrible—soon after the queen was cold, the court physicians cut her corpse open to find all her insides rotten. The thought of it—Her Majesty's body brutally sliced from breastbone to pelvis and stinking of rot—makes Catherine's stomach roil, makes her heart clench with something like anger, something like sorrow.

The queen has loomed large over them all for so long that Catherine cannot entirely believe that she is forever gone. Her Majesty was like some sculpture in a church, distant, remote, meant to instill both love and fear at once. They hardly ever spoke to her, except when she bid Petrus and the children entertain newcomers to court with shows of great hairiness and surprising intelligence. She seemed to bear some true love for her dwarfs, whether she truly believed they were mystical tokens of luck or not. But she took no pains to truly know the hairy marvels she had bred, and it is so very strange to think how she affected everything—how she had determined the course of both Catherine's life and Petrus's—and yet knew them not at all.

PETRUS SPENDS THOSE FEW days in a panic that he will not admit to, though Catherine tries to draw his thoughts from him.

After the night of her death, he does not speak of the queen at all. Instead, he speaks of King Henri, father of their current king, a man who, by Petrus's account, was more saint than ruler.

"He told me I was a better gift even than the leopard," he says, warmth and wryness tangled together in his voice.

Catherine wraps her arms tight around Madeleine, who has perched upon her lap for the first time in ages. She envisions her arms as a shield, a barrier against her child ever thinking that such words—even from the mouth of a king—were worthy of her. When she manages to reply to Petrus, her own voice is hard.

"Better even than a leopard. Imagine that," she says.

"You judge him?" Petrus says, as if surprised. In that surprise, in the sudden slackness to his features, Catherine has the oddest sensation, as if she is watching the joy he once felt to hear the king call him a wondrous gift fading away, like color leeching from a fallen leaf, all the brightness gone and only a curled crumple of its memory remaining.

He has so few happy memories that Catherine's chest hurts at the thought that she might unwittingly have taken one away from him. She tries to say something that will comfort him, but all she can think of is their own children and what their memories of the queen will be; whether they will think with fondness about the sweets her ladies gave them, the stroking of her palms over their heads, the times she told them how glad she was to have them as adornments in her court.

But Petrus surprises her by continuing to speak of the late King Henri, small memories, some of which he has shared with her before. It is as if he cannot help himself, as if he is purging himself, the queen's death having cracked him open like an egg. And so she listens.

Pedro

His Majesty told me the tale, once, of his own captivity by the Spanish, when he was just a boy. Slouched in his chair, informal before me, as if he were tired of holding himself kingly. His father traded both his sons to the Spanish in return for his own freedom, promising to free them as soon as he possibly could. The princes were given a dwarf to keep them company. His Majesty said the little man could clown better than any other dwarf he met before or after, that he made their confinement that much brighter. Petit Georges was his name, and King Henri claimed his elder brother would have succumbed to misery, those first months, were it not for his antics." Petrus licks his lips. "But after a time, the Spanish took the dwarf away."

"What happened to him?" Catherine asks, and Petrus looks at her with something like gratitude.

"I asked His Majesty the same thing," he says, and now his voice is breaking all to pieces in his throat. "He . . . squinted. As if he were trying to remember something. And then he shrugged and told me he could not recall what happened to Petit Georges; said that perhaps he never knew."

Catherine makes a sound of disgust.

"After that, His Majesty said the Spaniards kept them in conditions that became less and less congenial. Wet walls, black with mold; water that dripped all day and night until they thought they'd go mad. They forbade the princes to speak their own tongue." A pause. "And the king told me that he never thought he would willingly speak theirs again. Until I appeared in his receiving room."

Catherine is silent. When Petrus speaks again after a moment, his voice is dreamlike, moonlight on water.

"I always used to think of this memory with gladness," he says. "It was evidence that King Henri was a captive like I myself once was; that we had something in common with one another, something large. But now—" He swallows. "Now, I cannot stop thinking of myself, of my cage; how he did not at once release me, though he spoke so bitterly of his own captivity. I saw him in myself, and myself in him, but I do not think he ever truly saw himself in me."

He falls quiet, thoughts pressing outward against his skull, too many of them, all of them at once eager and afraid of what their release might bring. They have left the children in their chamber and come out into the hush of the night-chilled gardens, the dew a clutching dampness, creeping up the hem of Catherine's gown and darkening the seams of Petrus's shoes. Sculptures and hedges cast deep shadows over the ground, for the moon above is round and bright, hanging low and heavy as the belly of a breeding woman who is near her time.

Years ago, when Madeleine was small, Petrus used to bring Catherine outside when the swell of black sky winked with a thousand pinpricks of light. He would point to star clusters, naming them, reciting the stories of the swan, and the dragon, and the twisting, sinuous form of the many-headed Hydra, finally bested by Hercules. He traces with his finger in the air the twins, Castor and Pollux, so devoted to one another that when the one died the other begged for death as well, until Zeus placed them, forever together, in the sky. The bright points of their joined hands, the dancing angle of their legs.

He looks up at them now, but it is as if the heavens have shifted, and he cannot recognize anything he sees. The constellations tell different stories than those he learned from his tutors. He squints. There—a cluster of young men, very fine in their smooth leather jerkins, caught in the act of kicking a workbasket, sending a scattering of beads, turned to a trail of stars, rolling all down the sky's broad street. There, crouched, is Isabel, those five stars her outstretched fingers as she scrabbles to retrieve her work, her livelihood. There are no stars for her eyes, which are flat as stones, as empty sky. And there, beside her, Manuel, a cracking fury in the sharp line of his shoulders. *Guanche*, hiss the boys, as if the word is a curse.

Petrus staggers a little, suddenly dizzy.

It was not until he was grown and gone from her that he understood the deep basin of anger that must have existed beneath Isabel's stony surface, hot and ever present, sending fissures up and up. She had seen her father killed, unarmed; her brothers chained; her mother taken for a slave. She was saved from her mother's fate by catching the eye of a soldier, a soldier who had not touched her family but who must have torn to tatters dozens, hundreds, of others. After such things, she sometimes said, attempting to smother Manuel's rages, what are little nicks here and there?

Isabel, with her private prayers to her god who was meant to be dead; killed by good Catholics. His wife still prays nightly on her knees, though Petrus long ago gave up the pretense, and he does not miss the ache in his knee bones, the sense that even in his own chamber, with the door closed firmly against the prying eyes of the court, he must still be something he is not. Beyond a look at him over her folded hands on the first night that he climbed into bed without kneeling beside her, Catherine has never said a word, and when he thinks of this, of her quiet acceptance, his stomach swoops like a giddy bird with something like gratitude, like wonder.

But when he sits in church, he tries to feel whatever it is that Catherine feels, the mysteries upon mysteries toward which she leans, yearning. There is great danger in stepping even a toe-end outside the narrow circle of the Church's proscriptions. Huguenot worship has been condemned, the bodies of its followers mutilated; and how much worse for someone who cannot find God in any church, Catholic or Protestant; whose entire being, so thickly haired, so wolfish, raises thoughts of witchcraft, easy as a necromancer raising the dead?

Since he came to France, witches and werewolves have been burned by the thousands. Yet at court, the queen mother keeps her portentous dreams, keeps her dwarfs for their magic, consults the stars rather than the church. Sent her son's Catholic soldiers to kill Huguenots, as if it were the only natural thing to do.

"All I could think of, while the massacre was happening that day in Paris," he says now, speaking in a whisper, "and after, when I saw the true horror of it all—the abandoned bodies, men, women, *children*—all I could think of was Isabel. The slaughter of her family, so many people she knew. She never even taught me the old ways, so great was her fear that I might be killed for them. Killed by the very people beside whom we sat each Sunday for Mass. And I cannot—I cannot separate—it is all entangled, Isabel and her people, the Huguenots worshiping secretly in barns, in hidden rooms—"

Catherine lifts up on her toes and kisses him. Pulls back and looks at him, long and silent, then drops her head back to rest upon his chest.

He says, "King Henri . . . he continued—he *expanded* his father's edicts against heretical worship." He shakes his head. "When I had been at court for only a year, the king himself watched the burnings of seven heretics. You must have heard of the burning chamber, no? That is what the people came to call his court for the trying of heretics. I loved him . . ." A swallow, his throat working desperately. And then, "I loved him—and he did terrible things. But I did not . . . I was not witness to those things, and so it was easy to pretend—to ignore—"

Petrus presses his eyes closed. He knows, all at once, why he has felt this compulsion to comb through his memories. He needed to unsnarl them, and his feelings about them; and now that they are laid out in the open air, flung bright across the sky, he can at last release them.

He opens his eyes, tilts his head back, exhales up, up, up, toward mysteries upon mysteries. Exhales his breath, his memories, his Isabel; imagines them hanging between the twins and the bear, suspended and bright and forever.

Then he takes Catherine by the shoulders, looks at her face.

"We cannot remain in France," he says. "I am going to speak to Ludovico."

Pedro

The king has shut himself farther away since his mother's death, and much of his court has deserted him, slipping away over the frost-hardened roads to their country homes or tall Paris houses. The air is taut with waiting.

The urge to snatch up his family and run snaps at Petrus's soles like a pack of starving hunters. At any moment the dogs will be upon him, upon them all—lips pulled snarling back from the knives of their teeth, hot tendrils of saliva hanging. Waiting for them to lunge, to sink those teeth through the layers of his cape and doublet and shirt, Petrus feels his lungs squeeze and squeeze within his rib cage, and he blows the air out of his mouth, then sucks it back in, again and again, draw and release, gasp and suck; and yet still he feels as if he is suffocating, some invisible force plugging his chest with straw like a poor man's mattress, stuffing it so tight that there is no room for anything else.

Before leaving the room, he had taken his coins from their box to count them. Though they were a reward for a lifetime as this court's resident wild man, they clinked pitifully, as if they knew how few they were, and were ashamed. Petrus felt shame, too, felt it rushing up from his soles to draw like a coverlet over his head. Paltry, he thought—oh, so paltry, so utterly *useless*. Though he was sitting, though his feet pressed against the floor, he seemed to be falling, down and down; and though he leaned forward, he could not seem to will himself to find the bottom of this fall, it just went on and on, air rushing past, the sickening impact never coming but the waiting for it almost worse. His hair has kept him and his family fed and housed, but now they are losing their home, and he has no idea of how far their few coins will stretch. How much does it cost to hire a coach, horses? How much for a night at an inn?

Catherine looked at the coins, and her mouth folded up tight at the corners. Petrus recalled how she strode through the streets of Lyons, so sure of her way; recalled, too, her merchant's-daughter stories, how she understood the reasons for the changing price of grain, why silk from one country was considered less valuable than silk from another. He used to think her uneducated, but in truth she knows so much that he does not. She would know where to inquire about a coach, what to pack for the journey, whether a merchant meant to swindle them. She would go out into the city, if he asked it of her, to take care of all these practical matters.

But neither she nor Petrus knows where they can go. He has been a scholar, a curiosity, a bearer of bread, a reader; he does not know where to turn, where any of these skills might be wanted. And the city is dry kindling now, just waiting for the flame. He cannot send his wife into that.

And so he goes in search of Ludovico. He has not seen his friend in days upon days; as ever, Ludovico has been with the king, and Petrus with his own family. But Ludovico has been lurking about the edges of Petrus's mind, dark head bent near the king's, mouthing plots, battle plans, intrigues, wading into all those boggy places Petrus always avoids. The thought of it makes Petrus's belly ache. He imagines Ludovico sinking entirely away, the suck of his plans at his feet, his knees, until, with a last breath, he disappears entirely into their soft, chancy depths.

Late as it is, Ludovico is awake; he opens the door, leans against the doorframe with a shade of his old grin, beckons Petrus inside as if they might toss some dice, drink some wine, talk and laugh and pretend to have forgotten that long-ago night when they were hardly more than boys, and their mouths touched.

But once inside, the wood of the door shutting out the rest of the palace, Ludovico slumps in his chair. A single candle burns, new-lit, the wick scarcely singed; but even by its faint light, Petrus can see the tired way his friend's face lies, slack as melted wax itself.

If he had to, he'd planned to crumple himself at Ludovico's feet, to clutch beggarly at his knees. To ask, though he already knows the answer, whether there is any hope that the king might think of them. And then to ask for help, ignoring the deep-dug part of himself that hates the necessity of asking. But now he discards his question about the king entirely, discards it as a child's question, the wondering of someone too innocent, too self-involved, too thoroughly naive to comprehend that when the king of France is in danger of losing his throne, his life, he will not spare a whisper of a thought for the hairy family that has lived so long at his court. He will run, or fight, or hide; but he will not think of Petrus and Catherine and their children; they will have already been forgotten now, though they still sleep under the same roof as he.

"We must leave," Petrus says instead. "Mustn't we?"

The nut in Ludovico's throat moves up and down with his swallow. Petrus has the strange urge to reach out and touch the ridge of it, to feel it move under his fingertips.

"Yes," Ludovico says. Swallows again. "You truly must."

Petrus feels his own throat bob and constrict. "And you—will remain here?"

His friend nods, slow as a horse pulling a cart far too heavy for its strength. "What would I do elsewhere?"

"Live!" Petrus says, an explosion, a war cry. His skull might come apart from the release of the built-up pressure. "You would live! And Henriette and the children, too."

Ludovico's smile is gentle. "I've worked for this for *years*, my friend—for this moment, for this fearful moment, when the enemy is surrounding us. I've been a part of . . . of great and terrible things. But I can see glory on the other side of it, if I am only clever enough to reach it."

In his eyes, in his stance—suddenly so eager, so energetic, where only a moment ago he was bent with exhaustion—Petrus knows, very suddenly, with a thud as if he has finally fallen, finally found the bottom he sought earlier: the rumors he ignored for so long must be true. Ludovico was one of the minds behind the Huguenot massacre of Saint Bartholomew's feast day; behind the screams of women; the weeping voices of children, suddenly silenced. He stares at his friend, and thinks, just as he has always done whenever Ludovico's name was knotted with such terror, *No, it is impossible*. But even as his mind forms the words, it is a reflex, only; he knows the truth now, and cannot unknow it. He remembers lying together as boys, planning their futures, the fervency with which Ludovico spoke. The lust he felt for power.

All his years of scheming, of ingratiating himself with others, has purchased for Ludovico a rich and titled wife, a big Parisian house, a place at court where all men pause to listen when he speaks, his voice calm and confident as his swordplay. Sickness rises from Petrus's belly to his throat, and he swallows and swallows to force it back down. Sickness at the thought of his friend's calm and confident voice suggesting to the king that the Princess Marguerite's wedding would be the perfect way to lure the most important Huguenots in the country to Paris. Sickness at the twist of envy in his chest, for the foolish thought that if he had been more like Ludovico—if he had stepped, just once in the last thirty years, from the corners to which he'd relegated himself—then his only means of action now would not be this, this reaching out of his hand, this begging of someone else to unhook his cage latch, to toss him a little bread, a little water. Perhaps he'd have no need of a murderer's help.

He staggers back a step, the thought too brutal, too raw. And if Ludovico was the orchestrater of such atrocities as occurred that long-ago night, was he not also the boy who chose Petrus above the other children? Could a person be reduced to a single act, to the best or the worst of themselves? He thinks of what he said to Catherine about King Henri—*I loved him, and he did terrible things*—and forces himself to look up, to meet his friend's eyes, which are dark and long-lashed and patient. His heart clenches in his chest, threatens to burst itself with too much feeling.

"I . . . need help," he says. "I need your help. If I'm to take them away—but I do not know where to go. What to do."

Ludovico nods slowly. "Of course," he says. "Old friend." And he clasps Petrus's shoulders in both hands, the gesture bittersweet, aching, for its familiarity.

Catherine

Catherine begins packing the moment Petrus leaves the room. She is too taut for sleep, and so she tucks her children, all three, together in the large bed, and in her stocking feet moves about the room as they find their dreams. She picks and chooses from among their fine clothes, for they will not, most likely, be able to bring very much with them in the coach. She flings skirts and chemises, petticoats and doublets aside; tries not to think too long or too deeply about which things she keeps and which she chooses to leave behind. They are things, only, though they felt so important to her before, so weighty, anchoring her and her family to this life of richness, of safety. Their sturdiest shoes she sets out, one pair beside the next, each set of shoes smaller than the one before it. They await the start of their journey, which *must* be soon, Catherine thinks, a flutter in her chest, a tightness in her belly. The very stones of this palace seem to creak with tension, with the danger the king has brought upon himself, upon them all, and she feels that they might crumble soon, might bury all who have not yet escaped. Fanatical Catholic or bitter Huguenot—who knows which will come for them first? Catherine intends to be far away before the danger reaches this place.

When all the clothes are folded away, she goes to the box where she and Petrus keep their few coins, along with the gifts Queen Caterina gave to them upon the births of each hairy child, and Catherine's dowry amethysts. The coins will not last long, not with the cost of travel, of feeding five people and finding safe places to sleep each night. And who knows how far they might need to go? Who among the French nobility would take them in? The jewels, at least, might be sold; she told Petrus, before he left in search of Nevers, to offer him some in trade for whatever miracles he is able to perform.

Everything is ready now; they might leave at any moment. Catherine's body thrums, as if with the forward motion of a coach and horses. Surely Nevers will help them. Surely.

She sits on a stool, her very skin vibrating, so she knows she will not sleep, and looks at her children. They, at least, are sleeping, all in a tumble across the bed. Henri's mouth is a little open; he snores little hitching snores that would make Catherine smile at any other time. Now she sees only the vulnerable length of his throat, his head thrown back; in her ears are all the noises of the butchery in Paris in the days before his elder sister's birth. The remembered noises rise in pitch until she stuffs her fingers into her ears, as if that might block out death's clamor.

When the door opens, she nearly screams. As it is, she topples the stool by standing too quickly, whirling to face the person silhouetted in the doorway. And then, relief—*Petrus, thank God*—and his familiar hands around hers. He rights the stool and they sit together before the fire, and speak in whispers.

"Ludovico will help," he says, and Catherine nods, still too fear-bound to feel relief. "He said to give him the morning to make arrangements." A pause. "He wants to send us to Rome."

Her lips part, but no sound emerges, for her tongue has turned to stone. *So far.* Petrus waits a moment, then adds, "He knows a duke there, a good man, he says, who would be glad if we joined his household at the Palazzo Farnese."

Again, Catherine nods, not trusting her voice to keep steady. How long will it take to travel to Rome from Blois; how many leagues will they put between themselves and whatever is to come here? It seems impossible that the king will survive this, and if he does not, his Huguenot brother by law will take the throne. Catherine cannot imagine he will feel kindly toward any of the old king's household, toward anyone who keeps Catholic prayers waiting inside their throats. The thought of all that distance is too impossible for her mind to contain.

She tries to picture one of her father's maps, and cannot, *cannot*, not with the formless threats they faced lurking like monsters in a children's story at the edges of her vision. There is a wrongness to this feeling, to this fear of the wider world; she cannot make herself think about it too closely just now, but it is there, at the core of her, as if her very self has begun to unravel.

After a time, Petrus falls into a doze, his head lolling against the wall. Catherine watches him, glances at the window, where the cold gray light of a January dawn shows around the shutters. She flexes her toes against the floor. She cannot stay here, waiting. Her nerves sing a terrible, off-key song. She must do something, anything, to pass the time. But she already did everything that needed doing while Petrus went to Nevers.

And then, like a shock of lightning—*Agnes*. She must go to Agnes.

This time, she eases her way off the stool, stepping over Petrus's feet, skirts held high, bunched in her fists, that the fabric mightn't brush against him. He needs his sleep. She opens the door slowly, cautiously, glancing behind her to make sure her family has not wakened. When she sees that they sleep on, she steps into the corridor, closing the door softly behind her.

AGNES AND THE OTHER female dwarfs are awake as well, though it is so early. And they are readying themselves to leave with a furious energy, holding open one another's trunk lids, stuffing pearl-studded bodices and jeweled headdresses inside as if they are no finer than sacking. Catherine stands in the doorway, arrested by the sight of Agnes gathering paper and ink and quills, muttering to herself.

"Are you all leaving, then?" Catherine says, and all the other women look at her as one. It is Agnes, though, who drops what she is holding and crosses the room, clasping one of Catherine's hands in hers.

"We are," she says, closing the door behind Catherine. "We've been offered a place in the Catholic Netherlands."

"All of you? Together?"

Agnes nods, almost smiling. "Yes, all of us."

"What fortune!"

"Dwarfs are always wanted," she says, shrugging. "But if France has a new king"—her voice lowering to a whisper at the treasonous words, though it is only she and Catherine and the other female dwarfs in the room—"we fear he will not be inclined to be merciful to anyone from the Valois household. Our queen and her sons were not terribly merciful to him, after all."

"Yes," Catherine says. "That is our fear, too. I came here to—say farewell."

Agnes's fingers tighten around hers, nails pinching. "Oh, thanks be to God—where do you go?"

"Rome," she says, the word strange in her mouth.

Agnes swallows, nods. "We'll be very far apart, then. But I am so glad you and Sauvage have somewhere to go."

"Write to me," Catherine says. "Please. Petrus will read it to me. Write to me at the Palazzo Farnese."

Agnes nods again. "I will, when we are settled."

Jeanne, the dead queen's songbird, approaches, presses a packet of sugared fruits into Catherine's free hand. "For the little ones," she says. "I know how they enjoy them."

Catherine blinks against the pricking of tears. "Thank you."

Agnes glances at her trunk, only half-filled; bites her lip. "I should—" she says, reluctance drawing out the syllables. "But . . . oh, how I wish I could kiss those babes of yours one more time!"

"I will kiss them for you," Catherine says, speaking around the sudden choking in her throat. "Antoinette, twice."

Agnes's face twists and crumples like paper. She drops Catherine's hand and swipes at her own eyes. “I will miss you, Madame Sauvage,” she says when she has again composed herself, and there is the shadow of her old mischievousness in the teasing use of this name, which she knows Catherine hates. Catherine manages a damp laugh; manages to smile in the doorway, to blow a kiss to her friend, to raise the packet of sweets in thanks to Jeanne. But after the door closes behind her, she only manages a few steps down the corridor before the world becomes so tear-muddled that she cannot see at all and must lean against the wall, helplessly sobbing, hand stuffed into her mouth to quiet the sound.

Pedro

They leave in a coach, all crammed together except Petrus, who rides a horse gifted by Ludovico. The coach is a gift as well, and the horses who pull it, and the man who drives it, a sword and dagger at his waist; or rather, they are a loan, for Ludovico claims he will come for them in Rome, when things in France have settled.

They have few enough possessions that, looking at their meager baggage, Petrus understands, with a sharp ache, exactly how little he owns; how fully others have owned him. They have not even left without receiving permission, albeit through Ludovico, who went to the king in his chamber and suggested that His Majesty send Monsieur Sauvage and his family to Rome, to his ally the Duke of Parma, who will no doubt appreciate the gift in return for his service.

"What did His Majesty say?" Petrus asks, and Ludovico shrugs, waves a hand—an uncanny imitation of the king's irritated manner when he does not wish to be bothered with trivial matters. Petrus might laugh or cry—or both together—at any moment.

When he presses the ruby ring Her Majesty gave Catherine after Antoinette's birth into his friend's hand, Ludovico jerks his own hand away, as if the gold stung him.

"Absolutely not," he says. "I do this for friendship, not for coin." There is a tightness to his bearded jaw, a hurt to his eyes, that make Petrus nod and fold his pride, and the ring, away.

"You have the letter?" Ludovico says after a moment, and Petrus nods, patting the front of his doublet. In Rome, they are meant to throw themselves upon the mercy of the Duke of Parma, who spied Henri and Madeleine once on a trip to Paris, sitting at the feet of the queen. Ludovico, ever shrewd about forming friendships that might be beneficial, either then or in the future, had cultivated one with him.

"They will have you, I am certain of it," Ludovico says. "His Excellency will be overjoyed. And he is loyal to our king."

Loyalty seems to Petrus a rare and precious trait, and one as slippery as eels. But he thumps Ludovico's shoulder hard in gratitude.

"I can never thank you enough, my friend," he says, and Ludovico shakes his head, hard and then harder, his dark curls, silver-streaked now, flying.

"You can thank me by keeping safe," he says, and there is a tightness now to his voice, as well. He blinks into Petrus's face, gazes at him for a moment as if memorizing his features, and Petrus does likewise, drinks in the sight of his friend in thirsty gulps. He does not think, now, of what role Ludovico might have taken in the massacre at Paris; he thinks only of his friend, and all the good that lies tucked safe under his breastbone; feels only the stiffness of the paper tucked safe inside his own doublet, against his own breastbone, closed with the Duke of Nevers's seal.

When they embrace—Ludovico's arms sudden and tight around Petrus's shoulder blades, so tight that his breath leaves him on a sigh—Petrus cannot speak.

BASEL, SWITZERLAND

1589

Pedro

They rest awhile in Basel. Little Antoinette has a cold and a wet cough that will not shift. With the political climate so dangerous, they have been forced to take a roundabout route to Rome, Madeleine becoming ill with the rocking of the coach, Henri chafing against so much enforced stillness, whinging unceasingly. And, too, it has been raining for days with only the briefest breaks, and the roads are a danger; the fields no better. Muddy ruts suck at the wheels, and the rain is a misery, a terrible drumming against the coach's roof and sides, the brim of Petrus's hat, the shoulders of his cape, grown heavy with water. The world is a blur of wet; even during the rain's short pauses, the air is thick and damp, the tree branches dripping, the streams so swollen they seem heavy and quick as rivers. If their coach does not get caught in the mire, they might get swept away at the next true river crossing. Better to find an inn.

The inn they find is pitched above a tavern that is clearly popular, the tables mostly full. Petrus goes ahead to inquire about the room and tries not to be ashamed of himself for wishing he could hide his face as long as possible; but he is very tired. His body aches, not merely from the hours of riding but also from the particular pain of keeping his muscles tense and his sense alert as a prey animal's. All along the road these endless weeks, he has expected disaster—in the form of a cracked wheel, a lamed horse, or an attack from either side in the endless war between the faiths—but until now, they have been lucky.

A week ago, they learned from a man driving a cart filled with hay that the king was dead—stabbed through the belly by a Jacobean monk while he sat on his pot. The news must have raced past them on riders while they were on the road; or perhaps it was merely Petrus's appearance that put the gossips off whenever they stopped for food or rest. The man peered with eyes touched with milk, his mouth hanging open over the yellowed stumps of his teeth. He could not possibly see clearly through the thin white film, and in the instant of understanding this, Petrus felt his very skeleton shift and settle, shoulder bones sloping down after days upon days of holding themselves tense.

When he understood they did not already know of the king's death, the carter whistled. "How?" he said. "The news has been flying—the very birds singing of it!" But they were a ready audience for a story that must already have grown frayed in the telling, so he offered the children some tangy cheese from his sack and sat down in the yellow grass to relay the entire, gory business. Petrus listened with half his mind; with the other, he watched his children as they moved swift as falcons across the field, the girls raising their skirts so that they might run with nearly as much freedom as Henri; and eventually he let the hum of insects drown out the carter's words altogether. When he tipped his head back, letting the sun warm his face, he caught Catherine's eye. She smiled, small and discreet; then tilted her own face up as well.

ONCE THEIR ROOM IS paid for, the lot of them go dashing across the inn yard, even Antoinette, who is so tired of being wet that she ignores the lure of the puddles. Inside, their clothes steam gently, for the room is humid with bodies, well lit by fat-dripping candles and by a great hearth, generously laid. Catherine immediately draws Antoinette over to the fire, rubbing her arms to warm her; Petrus looks about for an unoccupied table, furtive under the brim of his hat, though Henri—brazenly hatless, his hair wetted down to his head and face as if he'd just come from the bath—has already drawn the attention of half the room. All about them, the chatter at tables goes abruptly silent.

There comes the scraping of a chair against the floor. "My good monsieur," says a man, suddenly close at hand. He gives a deep nod in greeting, though his eyes flick from one hairy child to the next, excitement bringing spots of red to his narrow cheeks. Petrus's heart batters his chest, but he nods in return.

"Will you not join me at my table? You mean to dine, yes? Let the little ones dry, fill their stomachs with good hot soup." He spreads his arms, smiling. "I am all on my own, you see, and would welcome the company."

His French is thick; his beard but a feathery circle of hair about his lips and over the point of his chin. Almost, Petrus refuses; he cannot trust the man's eagerness, the brightness of his eye, the open palm with which he attempts to guide them to his table. But a glance about the room reminds him that every other table is full, that his children are hungry and damp and cold. So he nods, gruff, half-expecting the man's open palm to reach out and stroke the hair of his or his children's faces without permission.

But the man merely leads them to the table; conjures more chairs by speaking to the innkeeper; orders soup for them all, the broth thickened with bread and rich with cabbage, turnips, and parsley.

"Nourishing," the man says, smiling at them all. Then his eyes widen. "Oh! Please forgive me—my manners have fled! I am Felix Platter. A physician here in Basel. And you? Are you passing through? Staying?"

His expression has a hopeful cast, open as a child's. Petrus pauses for long enough that Catherine, face pinking and eyes darting Petrus with a fierce glance, hastens to say, "I am Catherine Gonsalvus, Monsieur. This is my husband, Petrus—and our children, Madeleine, Henri, and Antoinette."

"A beautiful family," Platter says. He nudges a loaf of bread, the dark grain flecked with herbs, toward Antoinette, who snatches a slice and nibbles at it like a mouse. Platter smiles.

Petrus clears his throat. "We are—on our way to Rome, Monsieur. We had been part of the court in France, but . . ." He waves a hand, grimacing.

The other man's expression turns grave. "Ah, yes." He pauses. "I think—I believe I have heard of you, Monsieur Gonsalvus; and your children, too. But I never dreamed I might have the opportunity to meet you, to . . ." His fingers flutter; his face flushes. "I am a physician, you see; and a scholar of—unusual, ah, manifestations of . . . well . . . of humanity." He puts a hand over his narrow chest. "I would be honored if your family would visit me while you are in Basel—it is only me, and I have a garden in which the smaller children might enjoy playing. My cook makes the most delightful almond tart."

Petrus forces his fingers to remain splayed upon the tabletop, though they long to tense and curl. "Monsieur, that is . . . most generous of you, but we mean to stay for only one night—"

But a look from Catherine quiets him. "Antoinette would benefit from a rest," she says. "We all could, I think. And unless the sun is unusually hot, the roads will not be much better tomorrow, even if the rain were to cease this very minute."

The din of the tavern has lessened since they were noticed; even now, several minutes later, people speak in low voices, and Petrus can feel their gazes like probes within the torn flesh of a wound. But he slants a glance at their youngest daughter, who made quick work of her bread and dozes now in her mother's arms. Her breath clatters in her chest upon each inhalation. Platter watches, too, frowning.

"I could make the child an electuary," he says. "You needn't make her endure a coach ride to my home—keep her here, tucked up warm, and you—or Madame—could bring it back to her. Though she is welcome to come, too, of course, if you wish."

"That is very kind of you," Catherine says, glancing at Petrus, "but we would not want to put you to any trouble—"

"Nonsense! It is no trouble at all. Sickness, and the healing of it, is my business, after all."

"Well—that would be most welcome, Monsieur. Thank you." Catherine tucks Antoinette's head more securely into the cradle of her elbow, though Petrus knows her arms must ache already from holding their daughter in the coach. Antoinette has grown large enough that her weight is not insubstantial.

Platter's eyes roll a bit from side to side. He licks his lips. Petrus sets down his spoon, waiting.

"I . . . I hope this does not sound presumptuous," Platter begins. His fingers tap the table edge; his own bowl, empty, rattles a little as the table rocks with the motion upon the uneven floor. "But I—well, as I said, I am—rather a scholar—of plants, and of the human body, in all its marvelous incarnations. I have a—well, rather a collection."

"Of human bodies?" Henri says, speaking for the first time around a mouthful of bread, ignoring Catherine as she hisses at him.

But Platter laughs. "Oh dear me, no. Of *plants*. Pressed plants, but also live plants, in my garden. Of human bodies, I've only my sketches, and my notes. I am a teacher at the university as well—the medical school. I always tell my students that observation is the *most* vital of skills in any physician. I'm writing a treatise and . . . forgive me, but your family would be a deeply important addition to my work. If you would permit me to make notes—to learn more about your . . . unusual condition—"

Petrus's breath has become hutched behind his breastbone, and so it is Catherine, after a long moment, who answers for them both. Under the table, her shoe presses his. He concentrates upon the knob of her ankle, at once sharp and settling.

"That does sound like—most important work, Monsieur Platter," she says, smooth as butter spread upon hot bread. "We would be honored to contribute."

THEY PASS A RESTLESS night. The inn is a good one; but still mice scrabble under the thatch, and the chimney in their room smokes badly, the wall above it is stained the gray of linen long unwashed. The bed is large enough that he and Catherine can fit comfortably with Antoinette snuffling between them, and the innkeeper offered blankets—wool as scratchy as a man's whiskers, and smelling faintly of horse—that the other children might make nests for themselves upon the floor. The noise from the tavern room below only grows more intrusive as the hour grows later, and Petrus's mind refuses to still. Danger, it whispers; though the little physician seemed sincere, and sincerely kind. But still—

"Why?" he whispers to Catherine in the night, when she rolls a little, her breathing changing from the evenness of sleep to something wakeful.

She tilts her chin, that she might look at him as well as possible through the darkness. Leans closer until their faces are very near, their daughter still curled between their two chests.

"Scholarship," she says in his ear, her lower lip catching upon the lobe. "My love, you might be in one of those books you hold in such esteem."

Petrus loves her then, in the same way he loved her when she sat with their first child in her arms and proclaimed her perfect. But he knows, too, he will not go into the physician's house, no matter how good and earnest the man appears; nor will he force his children, do they not wish to go. Even now, so many seasons later, he can still remember a nose behind his ear, sniffing; hands comparing the texture of hair on his shoulders to that on his buttocks.

Careful of Antoinette between them, he reaches across to shift the hair that has straggled from Catherine's sleeping plait away from her face, and lets his thumb linger upon the ropelike weave of the plait itself. Her hair, softer even than his own.

(*It's the herbs*, she told him once, years ago, when he had insisted she unbind the whole of it, let it spill over them both. She climbed atop him that the pale curtain of her hair might fall down around them, the tips undulating across his chest, his shoulders, over his ribs. *It's the herbs that make it so soft.* With his fingers in her hair and hers trailing through his beard, along his arms, his hips, firm and unflinching through his own hair, leaving gasping prickles in their wake, he had no idea what she meant, only knew that it was soft, and sweet-smelling, and that he would stay there always if he could, hidden behind it, safe even from the eyes of God.)

His thumb drifts now under the neckline of her chemise, finding the hollow of her chest, that shallow dent between her tired breasts where he can feel the strength of her breastbone. He rubs small gentle circles there until she returns to sleep. Eventually, he follows.

WHEN MORNING COMES, PETRUS'S eyes are crusted nearly together, and his cheekbones feel as if thumbs are pressing upon them. Perhaps he has caught Antoinette's cold. He lies still for a moment, feeling the dull ache beginning at his temples, and sighs.

But then he remembers—today Catherine is going to Monsieur Platter, and bringing the children with her, all but Madeleine, who does not wish to go, who crossed her arms over her chest and shook her head and said, "I do not *want* to be studied by that odd little man." Madeleine, so petted at court, so beloved of the court ladies, saying now that she hated to have others' hands upon her, that she would not let that physician look at her body, her face, her hair. Petrus imagines, for a moment, remaining here at the inn, eating a hearty meal in their room with his eldest child, resting and cosseting himself so that, perhaps, the cold will not root itself so deeply inside him.

And then, just as suddenly, he has a flash—his body splashed with cold seawater, the creaking and damp of a ship's hold, the burn of rope at his wrists. And then: a market selling people, the checking of teeth, the pinching of sides, the feeling for swellings in the glands of necks and in the hollows under arms. The air stagnant and acidic with human fear. His own good fortune—and how odd to think of it so—to be so covered in hair, to be so miraculously strange in his makeup, that he was bought to impress a king, and not for the strength of his back or the power of his shoulders. That he was not, like so many of Isabel's people—his mother's people, *his* people—consigned to spend a few years with fields of sugarcane around and above him, twice as tall as he, all their tasseled heads rustling above in a wind that was choked off down below, the sky blotted out by green. Only to die at twenty, all the life labored out of him, muscles shredded, back bent and twisted as an old man's.

No, he thinks. He hears stockinged footsteps in the room; feels Catherine's absence from the bed without having to look. Murmured, argumentative voices. Petrus opens his eyes, cracking the crust at the corners, and sees Catherine, already up and mostly dressed; Madeleine and Henri awake but yawning, sleep-rumpled, folding the blankets upon which they had slept and squabbling quietly, Madeleine's voice peevish and sounding much younger than her sixteen years. His wife is ignoring them, her hair, unplaited, hanging loose down her back, her fingers on the laces at the front of her bodice. Hearing the rustle of shifting coverlets as Petrus folds them back—trying not to disturb Antoinette, who sleeps on, a little open-mouthed curl of child in the center of the mattress—she looks over her shoulder, smiles a tired smile. Her own eyes are smudged underneath, as if with soot, and her hair is lank with travel, darker than usual with her own unwashed oils. But there is something soft in her expression, which he longs to touch. He rises and comes toward her, cups her face, feeling the bones of her jaw under the give of flesh; kisses her mouth and the tip of her nose. Remembers when she would not look at his face but spent long hours at the mirror, combing her hair, scenting it, smoothing her skin, as if it were something to be preserved, like the furs and skins of mounted stags' and boars' heads, stretched tight over their false insides and kept as they were in life.

She looks at him now, though, looks with a smile and a hand to his cheek; and she does not smell of hair powder, but of her own skin and sweat, and of the weeks they've spent together on the pockmarked, dusty roads.

"I will come with you," he says softly.

Her smile broadens, and he hastens to add, "Not into the house. Madeleine does not wish to be examined by the physician, and neither do I. But I want to be sure that you are safe—we will go, all together, as long as Antoinette is well enough." She looks better now, in sleep, her breathing a little easier, her dreams untroubled by fever. Well enough to sit in a garden, at least, rather than in this drab little room. Through the window, the fast-rising sun is pinking the sky, all signs of yesterday's rain eased away.

If there is more than one entrance to the physician's house, Petrus thinks, he can watch one, and the driver the other.

Catherine's shoulders jump, and she steps away from him. "Do you truly believe the man is dangerous?" she says, a jittering quality to her voice as she twists up her hair, pinning it tight under her cap. Madeleine and Henri, kneeling beside the hearth, both turn to look up at their parents, the game of knucklebones they had only just begun forgotten between them. Petrus frowns at them without meaning to, his fingers fumbling on the lacings of his shirt.

"No," he says, for he does not. And yet, the splash of seawater remains, wetting his memory limbs and chilling his blood. "But I would rather be careful, in any case."

Catherine

Monsieur Platter's house lies on a branching street not far from the university. Catherine nearly regrets her agreement to visit him, Petrus's nervousness bleeding over into her own chest, making her turn over every word the physician said the day before for hints that he might not be the scholar he appeared to be. She knows what Petrus fears, knows it is a fear that riddles his insides, his bones, like wormholes in wood. It is a fear that she does not want to hold inside her own body, that she refuses to hold inside her body. And yet.

Petrus sits beside the driver of the coach, and inside, Antoinette snugs against Catherine's side while Madeleine and Henri gaze through the windows at the passing city, Henri's head nearly outside the coach itself as he strains to see everything at once. Catherine herself is no less fascinated, despite the misgivings thrumming through her breast. As they drive, her eyes turn inward, that she might revisit the map of Basel that once hung directly behind her father's desk. She can see the walls that surrounded the city, with their neat towers set at intervals; and the wide swoop of the Rhein. Beyond the city walls lay square fields like a madly, charmingly patched shirt; and within, little white, red-roofed buildings.

"The university is near the river," she says now. "Perhaps we can walk down to it after this visit. There might be river birds upon the water."

The university is a jumble of sunset-colored buildings, but Monsieur Platter's home is white as a clean apron, its shutters painted a good-humored blue. They are shown, Catherine clutching Henri and Antoinette by the hands, into the courtyard garden, where the physician awaits them, surrounded by climbing vines of yellow and green. He wears a doublet and hose of fathomless black and a smile that makes sweet wrinkles of the skin beside his eyes and mouth.

"Madame!" he says, rising from a stone bench, hands clasped before him. "I am so happy you have come—and of course you," and he stoops before the children, hands upon his knees, so that he is the same height as Henri. "Now, let me see if I remember correctly—you are Henri, correct? And you are Antoinette? Ah, good," grinning as they nod.

"Your husband could not join us?" he says, straightening and looking at Catherine.

"Ah—no. He sends his regrets, Monsieur."

"I am sorry to hear it." He smiles down at the children then. "As I recall from my boyhood—a very long time ago, of course—growing young ones tend to have a ferocious hunger. My cook has prepared her renowned almond tart for your arrival—would you like a slice?"

Henri, and then Antoinette, nod again, more eagerly this time, and he gestures to a servant, who carries out fat slices of tart for them all on glazed plates painted in blue and gold.

"I hope you will forgive my eagerness, Madame, but may I ask you some questions about your remarkable children? I have readied my things—" He bends to retrieve a little book, bound in brown leather, along with quill and ink. The ink he sets upon the bench beside him; the book he opens to a fresh page.

"Would you—prefer to go where you might write more comfortably?" Catherine says, but Platter chuckles.

"Oh, no, I am well able to make my observations wheresoever I happen to be. Now, Madame Gonsalvus, do tell me—how old are your children?"

"My eldest, Madeleine, is sixteen," she says. "Henri is nearly nine; Antoinette, six."

His pen scratches something out. "And how long did your husband reside in France?"

The story comes out in bursts—Petrus's time at court; their marriage; their children's births. Platter's quill moves with great industriousness as she speaks, his neck arched, nose nearly to the page.

"And your husband's origins?" he says at last. "He comes from a savage country? I have heard that there are men and women both in such places whose appearance is very like your husband's and your children's."

Catherine hesitates and glances at the children in question. Henri and Antoinette have devised a game of chase around a lush rosemary bed, Antoinette's cold improved enough by last night's warm, dry sleep that she runs now without coughing. She thinks of Papa's map of the world; the island of Petrus's birth so small and so distant from everything she knows. A speck upon the sea. As unlikely as Petrus himself.

In the end, she does not tell him the old, conjured story. She does not elevate her children to the level of princes. But neither does she give Platter all the details of the truth, for those are Petrus's to do with as he wishes. She says, halting a little, only that Petrus was a gift to the second King Henri; and that he never knew the identity of the man who gave him away.

After, Platter brings her and the children inside. Catherine helps Henri and Antoinette to undress just enough that the physician might gain an impression of the extent of their hairiness. He never touches without first telling the children what he is doing, the skin between his brows tight as he concentrates, noting, perhaps, the thickness of the hair around Antoinette's spine bones; the sparseness at Henri's throat. He makes his notes swiftly, muttering to himself.

"WILL YOU READ IT to me?" she says when he is through. The children, once more laced and coifed, have run out to the garden again. Platter, scratching at the side of his nose, his eyes flying from word to word upon the page he only just filled, startles a little at her question.

"I cannot read, you see," she adds. "And I do not mean to . . . impose . . . but I should like to know how you see them."

"Of course," he says after a moment, then laughs, ruffling the hair at the back of his head. "I confess to a little nervousness; I have not shown these books of mine to many others." He flips the page back, and begins.

A boy and girl—

—exceedingly hairy in the face—

—dorsal region along the vertebra of her spine—

—father, his whole body reported to be covered in hair—

—the hair on the forehead so long he must pull it up to see—

—even her palms are not hairless—

And then he clears his throat, and reads, "After all, since we have hair in each pore of the body, it's no wonder that in some people, as in many animals, their hair is longer and continuously grows, like fingernails."

He closes the book gently; folds his hands and looks at her, brow a little creased.

Catherine's jaw seems almost to creak as it works. There is nothing of horror in his words; nothing of wrongness. There is *rightness*, in fact, a rightness that settles upon her like a cape, secure against the worst kind of weather. He speaks the language of a man seeking to understand; puts forth her children as people in his book of observations.

If only Petrus had come inside.

"Thank you," she says at last. "That was—perfectly said, Monsieur Platter." She cannot even look into his face for fear she will weep. "Perfect."

Pedro

He had watched his wife and children knock upon the physician's door, Catherine straightening Antoinette's cap, stilling Henri's shuffling feet with a tap on the shoulder; watched as they were led inside by a servant, disappearing into the house, out of his sight. Now he and Madeleine sit in the coach, waiting. The driver has gone for a drink nearby, there being only one door that leads to the road, and Madeleine is sullen, temple resting upon the coach's wall, mouth small and crinkled. Everything seems to scrape her these days, to annoy her. Her family are all gnats, she swats and snarls at them, she stalks away, she spends most of the day looking as if she holds a scream at the back of her throat. It is terrible, sometimes, to be around her, and more terrible to realize that this disquiet is prelude to something else—the splitting of her childhood skin, the shedding of her family like an outgrown shell, Madeleine readying herself to move through the world without them.

Petrus remembers feeling so, in that strange, in-between time when childhood had ended but manhood not yet quite begun. He remembers the itch inside his head, the irritation that curled around his skull, how nothing could please him. But he never let this feeling show outwardly; with no family to tolerate his ill humor—with nowhere to go—he would never do anything to show himself less than wholly contented in his life at court.

He sits across from Madeleine now, and his daughter glances at him, rolls her eyes, breath huffing through her nostrils. Glares through the coach's window.

"I wonder what they are doing in there," Petrus says.

"I don't."

He tucks his lips together to hide his smile.

"I wanted to stay at the inn," she says after a moment. "I thought I might sleep a little. It's hard to sleep on the road."

"Everything is . . . unsettled," he says.

She looks at him. "Yes." A pause. "Why did you not want to visit with the physician, Papa?"

His anger from the day before has melted, leaving him only tired. He leans his head back against the coach's high seat back, looks up at the ceiling, where the leather is cracking, and thinks again of old men sniffing him, touching him, trying to decide whether he was human or animal or something in between.

He does not want to speak of these things, these humiliations, to his daughter, his lovely girl who was accepted at court from the first as herself, who never had to be dragged naked before the king, that he might assess her humanity. She has worn fine gowns all her life; has eaten the best foods; has played with toys paid for by the king's treasury. And though she has surely known little cuts, little unkindnesses, they cannot, he thinks, be anything to the cage; the nakedness.

And so he says only, lightly, gently, "I did not feel like being prodded."

She looks at him, long, with those eyes like her mother's in the face so like his. She nods, once.

"No," she says. "Neither did I."

He thinks he can see, then, how she will grow away from him—solid and rooted and twining-trunked as a yew, and with a yew's mystery, its complexity of roots and melding trunks and overlapping branches. She will show one face to him now, and then another; and still another to the other people they meet, to those who might marvel at her furred exterior and miss all that is inside. In her complexity, he thinks, she will survive.

CATHERINE, HENRI, AND ANTOINETTE emerge from the physician's house, the children nudging one another, bickering and smiling at once, his wife clutching a parcel of herbs to make a poultice for

Antoinette's chest and a stoppered bottle with a liquid inside, the very green-brown of pond water, which Catherine tells him is a tincture.

"Monsieur Platters says it ought to help her lungs within a dose or two," she says.

It takes both of them to force each dose down Antoinette's sputtering throat back at the inn, but she does not protest when Catherine puts the poultice on her chest and wraps her tight in bed between herself and Petrus. The poultice gives off a smell of growing things that makes Petrus think of childhood and lying on the ground beside Ludovico, watching the scuttling of the ants and breathing in the sharp damp earth.

When Petrus asked him, over dinner, what happened at the physician's house, Henri shrugged and licked grease from his lips and said, "Not very much. He wrote things down." Chewing, swallowing. "We had cake."

Now, with Henri and Madeleine sleeping on their pallets and Antoinette snoring softly between them, Petrus whispers to Catherine, "How was it?"

She is quiet for long enough that he thinks she has not heard him, or that she is asleep. Then he sees the glint of her eyes as she turns them to him; the brief, ghostly white of her smile.

But when she speaks, it is in measured tones.

"Monsieur Platter was respectful," she says. "He is a serious man of science, I think, not a—a seeker of wonders."

"As you hoped," Petrus says.

Another smile, smaller, almost private. "Yes," she says. "As I hoped."

A lull. And then: "I think," she says softly, and touches the very center of his palm, "that you would not have been sorry, had you come."

Catherine

The day they quit Basel, Catherine watches as Petrus—hat brim pulled low, head ducked—leaves the tavern to help their driver load their trunks onto the coach. Beside her, Madeleine has turned herself a little away from the few people in the room, facing the grimy window, and Catherine swallows, seeing, for a moment, what her daughter wants others to see—the curve of her back in its gray traveling gown, the knot of hair at the nape of her neck. Her hands, buried in her lap, are hidden from view, her face angled so sharply away from the tavern room that no one is in danger of seeing her clearly.

Raising her eyes to the window, she sees Petrus, shoulders humped like an old man's to avoid notice.

For a moment, Catherine's anger with the world could swallow her whole, like a whale gulping down a fish.

And then Antoinette—entirely better now, the tincture prepared by Platter having worked its subtle magic—kneels up upon her chair, nose nearly to the window glass, voice an eager piping. "Maman, Maman! There's a cat! May I pet it?"

Catherine breathes out through her nose in two warm, calming streams. Leans over to peer through the glass at the right angle to see the cat, a sleek spotted thing curled in a patch of sunlight in the inn yard. A cat grown fat and happy on the inn's steady diet of mice and rats.

At court, Antoinette was forever patting the heads, scratching the backs, rubbing the bellies of the dogs who slept at the court ladies' feet and the hunters who wheeled about their masters on the lawn, tails like mad pendulums. She chased the kitchen cats, who were reticent creatures, tempting them with stolen scraps until they finally came to her, purring, rubbing at her ankle bones. If the animals' keepers were not there to stop her, she would no doubt have wriggled her way into the lions' den, dragging a stolen haunch of venison, a headless plucked goose, through the dirt to lay like an offering at their great, clawed feet.

No, Catherine almost says then. *We must stay here and wait for Papa.*

But the sun is shining today, hot enough for the cat to stretch luxuriously, toes spreading, head rubbing against the ground. It streams through the dirty windowpanes, highlighting the smudges and streaks, showing bright the twirling dust motes over their table. And she can feel the curiosity and disgust of the eyes of the maidservant wiping down the tables from last night's merriment. The cat is in a sheltered alcove; surely that would be better than sitting here, bearing that girl's stare, forcing her beautiful children to bear it. Even Petrus, with his terror of the world, must think so.

So, "Of course," she says, and rises to gather their few things: her purse, Henri's cape, Antoinette's doll. Henri leaps eagerly down from his chair, ignoring or oblivious of the servant girl's startled backward step. As if, Catherine thinks, the anger rising up again, as if her narrow-shouldered son, her high-spirited boy, might knock her over like a rolling barrel. As if he might be a danger to her.

She gives the servant her mother's best disdainful glance—the one that said *unfortunate* as clearly as words—as she sweeps past her after her children, out the tavern door, and into the sunlight to pet a cat.

Pedro

He looks up to see his wife and children leaving the tavern, curling in a single, sinuous line toward the inn's inner courtyard. Anxiety leaps in his belly, and he drops whatever he was holding, to the startlement of the coach driver, and hurries after them, his boot thuds echoing his pulse.

But they have not gone far; he stops when he sees them, Antoinette crouched, hand poised to stroke the inn's cat, its white coat speckled with orange. He looks at Catherine, who watches their youngest child with a faint smile, hands at her hips; Henri, who gives the cat a perfunctory scratch behind its ears; Madeleine, who turns her face up to the sun, hands extended behind her, fingers splayed, as if in rapture.

He is smiling himself when he turns away, back to the coach.

Catherine

The innkeeper's wife finds them there, and Catherine knows that though the woman's features will fade from her memory, her kindness never will. For without blinking, she crouches down beside Antoinette, smiling into her face; says in halting French, "My husband doesn't like us to name the cats—says it makes them lazier. But my son named this one, anyway." She touches the cat's head. "Pox," she says, with a wrinkle of her nose. "For his spots." And when Antoinette turns an outraged face upon her, she laughs, slapping her thighs.

"I know!" she says. "Isn't it just terrible?" She leans closer, as if she and Catherine's daughter are friends, conspirators. "I won't tell him if you want to give this boy a new name."

Antoinette smiles, showing the gap where her bottom two teeth have recently gone missing. "Pierre!" she says. "Like my papa."

The woman nods. "Pierre he is, then." She stands, smiling as Antoinette sits right down in the dusty yard, the better to fondle Pierre's great, soft ears. Then she turns to Catherine.

"My son is in school," she says; and there is pride in her voice. She nods toward Henri, scuffing at the dirt with the toe of his shoe. "Yours, too, I imagine?"

Catherine nods, even as she reaches out to steady herself against the rough brick wall of the inn. Not a word from this woman about her children's strange looks; not a whiff of nervousness or discomfort. She has the urge to reach for the hands of the innkeeper's wife, calloused and reddened and beautiful in a way that makes Catherine's chest hurt; to wrap her own hands around them and feel the other woman's heartbeat at her pulse point, the tendons in her wrists.

"My daughters, too," she says, half-choked. "They read and write and figure as well as their brother."

"My, what a thing." The woman wipes her hands on her skirt. "I can get you some extra cheese, some bread, for your journey if you'd like. Your boy looks just my son's age, and he eats every meal as if we starved him."

"Why—thank you," Catherine says, and the woman nods, smiles, and holds up one finger, vanishing through the inn's kitchen door.

Catherine turns back to say something to Antoinette—about Pierre the cat, about the woman's kindness, about how sad it is that they must coop themselves back up in a coach on such a lovely day. She turns, smiling, all these words and more bubbling at her lips, happiness rising in her like water from the center of a fountain, all because the innkeeper's wife looked at her children, and saw children and nothing more.

She turns, intending to crouch with her daughter, to put her fingers into the cat's thick sun-hot fur, to kiss her daughter's own warm head, to ask whether Antoinette would like a little of the inn's cheese at the start of their journey, or if she would rather wait.

She turns, a smile on her mouth, such lightness in her body that she is like a seed caught in the wind, carried up and up into the blue.

She turns—

But both the cat and Antoinette are gone.

A QUICK, CIRCULAR TURNING, in case Antoinette is hiding nearby. The inn's courtyard is a narrow rectangle, almost entirely enclosed by the pale red brick of the inn's walls and the weathered gray wood of the stable's; only an opening, high and wide enough for a coach to pass through, leading out to the street, breaks the enclosure. Their coach stands there, Petrus and the coachman with it, checking harnesses, talking together about the unevenly worn coach wheels, Catherine's husband nodding seriously, as if coach wheels were something he has considered every day of his life. Henri and Madeleine have wandered over, watching their father.

The yard is dirt, mostly dried out from the other day's terrible rains, only a few darker spots in the dips and divots of the narrow space serving as a reminder that the ground here was a great churn of mud not so long ago.

There is nowhere for a small girl to easily hide; all is open. Only inside the coach—

Catherine hurries over in a rustle of skirts and breath—jerks open the coach door, ignoring the men's confusion—half-climbs inside, peering into the shadows, as if Antoinette might have melted into them. But she is not there.

Pedro

Antoinette is gone," Catherine says. She comes down out of the coach, her voice calmer than her face, her hands touching Petrus's sleeve, plucking at it. "I do not know—I cannot—"

Petrus's head swings around, searching the inn yard; but the only other living creature, other than Henri and Madeleine, is a draggle-feathered chicken pecking forlornly at the dirt. "The cat," he says, "the cat is gone, too, she must have—"

"Yes," Catherine says, as their elder children come up to them, questions in their eyes. But she says, "Your sister is missing—have you seen her?" And when they shake their heads, "You must stay here with the coach. Do *not* move," this to Henri, nearly shouted, as their son opened his mouth to protest; and then, to Madeleine, "Watch him. Stay here. I cannot have either of you disappearing, too."

"She is probably inside the tavern," Petrus says, half-believing it, though a peculiar sort of panic is rushing through his veins as hotly as blood. It is the panic of foreknowledge, he thinks; the panic Queen Caterina must have felt when she woke from the dream that foretold her husband's death. "Or the kitchen, if the cat went inside—"

"The innkeeper's wife was wrapping us some food." Catherine nods to the coachman. "Go to the kitchen—see if Antoinette is there. Petrus, check the tavern, the other inn rooms—see if perhaps she went back up to our room. I will—" She gestures toward the yawning entranceway leading to the street, through which the din of city life murmurs.

Almost, Petrus says he will go, instead—but he sees his wife's bright, hard glance, the one that says she knows his fear of the wider world, and honors it; and, too, that they haven't time to indulge it. She will go. He will check the inn. They will find Antoinette very soon, almost certainly curled around the inn's fat cat in some hidden corner.

A nod, a press of hands, and they part ways.

Catherine

Which way, which way? This is what dashes through her head, over and over, again and again, the terrible drone of it leaving no room for rational thought to intrude. Standing in the sunlight, squinting up the street and down, uncertain of everything except that her child is not here, there is no flash of blue dress, no soft little face, no thrum of her shoes coming nearer. A dog snuffles around Catherine's feet, and she nearly kicks out at it. An old man nods to her as he passes, and she rushes up to him, nearly clutches his arm, stopping herself only at the last moment and holding tight to her skirts instead. *Have you seen a little girl?* she asks, and when he shakes his head, she turns without thanking him, without returning his greeting, and hurries down the street where it curves out of sight. Everyone she passes, she says, *Have you seen? Have you seen?* All give the same answer: no, they are sorry, but no.

She passes a woman selling cheeses—a man selling gloves. She lets her skirts drag through a puddle, heedless of the streaks of dirt and wet. Heedless of everything but one thought—*If Petrus was right—if she let their daughter outside and the worst happened—*

If, if, if—

No, no, no—

Pedro

She is not in their room, where the bed is still unmade, the hearth unswept, the stub of the candle they burned down last night still stuck in its holder with streams of wax. There is nowhere to hide here, either, and so Petrus does not linger; he is thudding down the corridor, down the stairs, calling his daughter's name. Through the tavern once more, ignoring the maid's staring, the jump of fear in her eyes as he approaches her at a gallop, leans his hands on the table she had been scrubbing and says, "Have you seen my daughter?"

"N-no, sir," the maid says, staring at his face as if she were staring into the face of the devil himself; but for once, Petrus does not care.

OUTSIDE ONCE AGAIN, WHERE the driver says Antoinette was not in the kitchen, and the innkeeper's wife, a parcel of food clutched to her bosom, says she will look, too, she will check the cellar, the attics, all the secret places a child might like to hide—

Petrus nods to her, thanks her, even as he is moving away. Toward the busyness of the road, all fears disappeared as suddenly as paper in a hot blaze, all save one.

Catherine

She has chosen the wrong direction. No one has seen Antoinette—even when she stopped asking whether they had seen a little girl and began asking whether they had seen a hairy girl, the answer remained, firmly, *no*.

Turning back, skirts bunched in her hands, shoes beating the cobbles. Pins loosening, hair tumbling down from under her cap. Heart beating in her throat hard enough to hammer its way through the thin skin.

Pedro

He passes merchants with their carts, boys with deliveries, an old woman leading a donkey on a rope. All of them whirling about him as he runs.

For a gasping moment, he sees not the tumult in the street around him, but a different street entirely, one that wound its way near to the blue crash of sea, to where the fishing boats docked, where poor children gathered shellfish to fill the bellies of their families. Down that street runs a woman, her cloud-white hair snarling in the wind of her swiftness, one hand pressed to her narrow chest, as if to keep her heart from beating through the bone. All the way down to the beach she runs, her feet sinking into the black sand where, sometime earlier, the footprints of a boy were swept away by the same tide that swept him away from her forever in a pirate ship. She calls his name, hands cupped around her mouth so the sound will carry. She calls until her voice is hoarse, her throat aching. Up and down the beach, stopping the fishermen as they return for the night, nets filled. Begging for news.

She spies a pair of shoes and caves into herself there, her knees giving out. She sits, awkward, upon the rock into which the boy used to tuck himself, where he listened to the calling seabirds and the rhythm of the water. She finds the bag beside him, the bag she wove with her own cramped fingers. Inside, she finds shells, just perfect for stringing into necklaces, for a moment lying white and black and iridescent against the lines of her palm until she flings them from her with a wild, torn cry. They patter into the sea, return to the water, as water washes the woman's face, as she keens her grief in a forbidden tongue.

Petrus's chest cracks and he lets out a desperate sound of his own. And then—he sees her, Antoinette—and for a moment it is as if he is viewing a painting. A woman, perhaps a little younger than he, bending toward his child; Antoinette looking up into the woman's face, her own face tear-wet. The woman's fingers around Antoinette's wrist, the gentle tugging of them, and his daughter following, docile and trusting as a pony on a lead.

Petrus is barreling through the street toward them before he knew he meant to move, running with the swift urgency of a dog on a scent, his body recognizing the danger in the moment before his head had managed to catch on. He has grabbed Antoinette about her middle before either she or the woman holding her wrist had noticed him coming, half-lifting her from her feet so that she yelps. Then she looks back, sees that it is her Papa holding her, and twists so that she can catch Petrus around his neck with her free hand, wildly sobbing, fingers scrabbling to find purchase.

Petrus, bent in half, clutches her, and he looks up at the woman, who still holds his daughter's wrist, who is looking back at him as if he is one of her nightmares come to life. For once, he is grateful to be seen as a wild man—a single low, throbbing growl of his voice, and she has dropped Antoinette, has backed away, has begun to run.

And his daughter wraps her other arm now around his neck, buries her face in the hollow between his neck and shoulder, wets his collar with her tears. "I want Pierre, where is Pierre?" she cries, and he says, "I am here, my littlest love, I am here."

Catherine

She sees them coming through the inn yard. She'd returned, panting, asking the driver, the innkeeper's wife, for news; but neither had any. Her husband had gone out, they said, and when Catherine stared, asked, *Which way did he go?* they pointed in the direction she had not taken.

She sees them, and her breath stops as if stabbed. Antoinette in Petrus's arms, her arms about his neck, and he is holding her with both hands splayed over her narrow back. Just a moment, half a breath, and then Catherine finds herself running; she can hear Henri and Madeleine pattering behind her, but she—heavier, slower, more encumbered by her clothing—still reaches Petrus and Antoinette first. She is prying Antoinette's fingers from her father's hair, lifting her from his arms, and Petrus lets her, pressing a hand to his own chest.

"Oh, *cara mia*, thanks be to God," Catherine says, over and over, touching her daughter's hair, her dress, her face.

Antoinette says, "Maman, Maman, I could not find Pierre!"

"He will return, little one, he will come back," Catherine says, and Antoinette looks up at her, clearly disbelieving, tears pulling her lashes into spikes sharp as thorns.

"What happened? Where was she?" Catherine says, looking up at her husband.

And he tells her, stripping off his gloves. Tells her of the woman, her grip on Antoinette's wrist. Her fear of him he describes with something like pride, though he says, "She might only have been trying to help—but I could not think, I only took her away—" A slap of his gloves against the side of his leg, punctuating every other word.

"And thank God you did," Catherine says, and then stops, for at the same time Antoinette says, "She *was* trying to help, Papa, she said she would take me to her coach, that you and Maman had already left the city and were far away, but that she could take me there. A place where everyone would love someone like me, she said; and you were going there, too."

Catherine cannot look at him, then. Cannot make real what has forever seemed unreal, despite what she knew of his own life. But she gasps into her daughter's hair, little puffs of air, over and over, rocking and rocking their bodies together until at last Antoinette says, "*Maman*, let me *go*," and wriggles away.

THERE IS A CREAKING among them as they set out again from Basel, like deadwood branches rubbing together overhead. Petrus kisses Catherine's brow when she cannot stop weeping, but his eyes slide away, slick as minnows, when she tries to catch them with her own. He mounts his horse with a protestation of saddle and boot leather, and is off before Catherine has the children fully settled in the coach.

The first hour or so, as Basel's cobbled streets taper into pitted dirt roads outside the city, she is occupied by handing out the dense dark bread, studded with chestnuts, and the hard, crumbling cheese, smelling of thyme, which the innkeeper's wife had pressed upon them. She listens to the soft smacks of their lips as her children chew and swallow; she ignores Antoinette's restlessness, curling an arm around her, tucking her close against her own side, that she might feel the press and fall of her ribs as Antoinette breathes; as if, in keeping her close now, she might make up for that moment of inattention in the inn yard, when she thought her daughter safe in the sun with a cat.

It is not until several hours after they left Basel that Catherine begins to breathe again herself, a knot in her chest loosening as a little wind ruffles the coach's window curtains. She shifts her numbing sit-bones against the seat and moves the curtain aside. Outside, Petrus rides a little ahead of them, straight and easy in his saddle despite the hours they had been traveling, the gray-white plume of his hat rippling.

They crest a hill; and they are all cramped and ill-tempered. The air is thick with dust from the horses' hooves, and the road is filled with creeping roots from nearby trees, which seem almost to lift themselves a little higher when they feel the foretelling vibrations of a coach's wheels and a team of horses; and with stones, which roll and leave small hollows into which the horses might stumble; and with larger, washed-out places from the sluicing of the rain, so that the entire journey, when they are lucky enough to find a stretch of road that is navigable at all, jolts the spine bones and makes it impossible for the children to nap, no matter how tired they are.

They crest a hill; and Madeleine sits at the coach window, grumbling; and the two younger children each yank at either end of a wooden horse, hissing at one another because they know that if they shout, Catherine will feel forced to intervene, but that if they keep their voices just low enough she might overlook their misbehavior.

They crest a hill; and Catherine, her very skin dry with weariness, her ears aching for silence, her bones for stillness, glances through the parted window curtains with little interest. And there before her lie the soft yellowed grasses near the roadside, and the wildness of the forest just beyond the boundary of the road; and beyond that, mountains, with trees that crowd like teeth, and breathe, and tremble, so thick together that the mountains seem living beings, watchful and waiting. Green here, nearest the road; and softer farther on, blurred into blues, and even farther, grays, so that Catherine squints, as if in doing so she could pick out all the details of them. And then back to Petrus, his gently jouncing back, his hands steady on the reins.

Looking at him, she finds herself, with a sudden swooping sensation—as if she is a bird herself, diving after insects or plunging merely for the rushing joy of it, knowing she could pull herself upward again—standing at an upstairs window of her house in Lyons, leaning a little far over, straining to keep her father in sight for as long as she possibly could. And then, just as quickly, she is in the coach again, the world around her clearing like a window swiped free of water droplets, brilliant, unveiled. Spreading out before her, unfurling like a summer bloom, like a carpet unrolled and laid at her feet. Her toes curl and uncurl in their shoes and stockings, itching, suddenly, to walk, to set out.

She is, she realizes, with a jolt not unlike that of the coach over the road, doing exactly as she has always secretly wished. *Adventuring.* Just like Papa. A leaping in her belly, of anticipation, as if they are about to drop; but it is a drop she leans toward, a drop she wants, aches for, and she thinks, *I have been here before.*

Which is entirely impossible, of course. And yet. In her memories, her fingers trace Papa's journeys, and her imagination conjures thickets and woodlands, mountains and valleys; rivers teeming with fish and ports teeming with people. She stares at the mountains until her eyes ache. The life she has always wanted, and which she had so completely put out of her mind many years ago, has suddenly appeared before her when she was not paying attention; and she fears, if she looks away, it might vanish.

Part Five

Rome

CAPODIMONTE, ITALY
1618

Catherine

Even now, so many decades after, the thought of what so nearly happened in Switzerland sometimes catches Catherine unawares. She will be kneeling in the garden, weeding among the herbs, all the rich and grassy scents of them filling her nostrils and her own vague humming in her ears; and suddenly she will remember that Antoinette was nearly taken from them in the streets of Basel, and her humming will cease and she will suddenly be inhaling the travel-oiled smell of her child's head, and her arms will ache to snatch at her, to keep her close and safely tethered.

When she recalls herself to the garden, to the sun and the bees and the dirt under her fingernails, she also recalls that, although Antoinette was not taken from them that day in Switzerland—although they had another handful of years with her in the sunburned gardens of the Palazzo Farnese in Rome, where she chirped and chuckled to the penned-up animal marvels who lived near enough to their new home that she could, and did, easily toss scraps of her dinner to them—she was taken from them eventually, just the same.

THIS MORNING, HENRI LEAVES on one of his trips to Rome. He goes occasionally in all their steads, a sort of envoy to both the duke and to his brother the cardinal; a human show of gratitude that they consented to release them all to Capodimonte so many years ago. He kisses his wife on the cheek, and she nods stiffly; then he turns to Madeleine and Catherine, who have also come to wish him safely on his way. His embraces are warm but quick, as if he cannot mount his horse fast enough; as if the thronged, sun-hot Roman streets call out to him.

Catherine holds him a second longer than he wishes. “Be certain to give the other Henri my greetings,” she says, their little joke for years; Henri’s portrait, commissioned by the cardinal nearly twenty years ago, hangs in the Palazzo Farnese.

Henri is not so impatient that he does not play his part; the tight fist of her heart loosens a little.

“I think you mean *Enrico*,” he says, grinning. Henri is the only one among them who stubbornly continues to correct anyone who does not call him by the French variation of his name; and yet, poor boy—poor man—his portrait hangs under the name he hates, and he is noted as Enrico in every register.

The painter, she remembers, showed her son like a true wild man, bare but for an odd little cape made of skins, knotted across his chest. Henri’s body was, strangely, painted as if it were another man’s, the hair that covered it so light and sparse it was almost impossible to see. But the face was Henri’s own dear face, the light shining over its curling hair, his soft mouth and wide ears faithfully rendered. He was painted not alone, but with dogs, monkeys, and two other men from the cardinal’s household: a dwarf named Amon, bent nearly in half under the weight of a huge parrot, and Pietro Matto, the court madman. If she remembers very hard, Catherine can see them all clearly; can hear, too, Amon’s gaiety at the lavish feasts the cardinal and duke liked to host in the gardens, and Pietro Matto’s odd lumbering gait and his laugh, which came from his mouth in short bursts of hilarity, like a child’s.

Henri’s skin cape was meant, he explained to Catherine and Petrus, when they stood before the unveiled painting, to evoke thoughts of his Guanche ancestors, who wore similar garments called *tamarcos*.

“My idea,” Henri had said. “You know how His Eminence loves anything barbaric.”

Catherine remembers how her breastbone seemed to crack over her heart—at his words; and at the image before her of her son reclined like a pagan god from some forgotten land, framed in gilt like a nobleman.

"How handsome you are," she had said at last; and her voice cracked, too.

But Petrus touched his own sleeve, as if it abraded him; put a hand to the stiff ruff about his throat; and turned away.

Henri releases Catherine now; turns and mounts. "I will be certain to give *Enrico* your regards," he says from his horse, still grinning down at her. He raises a hand in farewell, chucks to the animal, and they set forth down the road.

IN THE MONTHS SINCE Petrus left her, she has found herself sinking into the soft warm muck of her own memories more and more often. Sometimes she wonders whether she might someday, like so many old women, sink so far that they close over her head, leaving her senses deadened to everything else.

Later that afternoon, Madeleine joins her on a slow, ambling walk about the village. Catherine's daughter has been more solicitous of her since their father's death, as if she senses that her mother might easily slip away from them as well. She couples their arms like links in a chain, skirts intimately brushing. Catherine lets her talk—of Paola's pregnancy, of Henri's latest business endeavor—drift lazy as smoke about her head. Their feet carry them toward the lake, where the water shows green and blue as a peacock's tail. The shoreline here is all big rocks, speckled like birds' eggs, with the softness of sand beckoning farther down the way. All that Catherine can think about is walking here with Petrus when they first arrived, how his face went gentle as the late afternoon sun, his mouth wide as a child's. He did not speak at all, only looked. But later he would tell her that the deep color of the lake; the high jut of the cliffs above it, coming straight up from the water, steep and stunning; and the green of the hills all around—all this reminded him of the place he had lost, the island of his boyhood. That he felt, for a moment, as if he had come home.

ROME, ITALY

1590

Pedro

The Palazzo Farnese seems to glow. It is a great rectangular building of yellow stone with rows and rows of windows, and the sun is so strong here that it turns the warm stone golden, winks off the glass of the windows, dazzling the eye.

The duke's grin when he lays his eyes upon them—and that is what it feels like, his gaze like the laying on of hands, gentle, welcoming—it rivals King Henri's when he first learned that the little hairy boy gifted him could speak. The duke reads Ludovico's letter, but Petrus knows by the upward slant of his mouth, the easy set of his brows, that he would want them here even without it.

"Oh, yes, I remember you," he says, looking with something like love, like reverence, at the children, standing, as they have been trained to do, unnaturally still, allowing him to take in his fill of them. Petrus takes in a breath, feels it loosening the tight and painful muscles of his chest. He and Catherine exchange a glance, quick, furtive; she smiles.

Petrus knows, for Ludovico told him, that the letter contains the history imagined for him by the blue-eyed man who gave him to King Henri so long ago. *I present to you Petrus Gonsalvus, hairy prince of the Canary Islands.* And the duke's next words confirm this: "Don Pietro," he says, after reading, bowing as if he believes Petrus to be a prince in truth, "you and your family are very welcome here."

For a brief, hot moment, Petrus feels his lungs swell, and his mind flies to his time running between the stifling palace kitchens and the king's *salle*, trying to reach the latter before His Majesty's bread, soft and white and thick-crusted, went cold. Perhaps the duke will consent to offer him a position, he thinks—work where he might do something more, where he might be valued beyond his ability to exist in this hairy body.

The duke instructs a servant to guide them to a suite of rooms within the great palace. "A temporary place, only," he says, and his eyes are alight with something only he can see, some scene painting itself upon his mind in great sweeping brushstrokes. "A house," he says as they follow the servants from the room. "I will build them a house—"

They pause together in the great courtyard, high graceful archways bathed in light, the entire palace glowing around them, and Petrus feels, for an instant, as if they must be standing on the cusp of Heaven; golden, impossible, and too beautiful to be true.

Catherine

The duke builds them a house, right in the palace gardens. Catherine and the children watch the builders at their work, watch the stones set upon stones, a place for them, just for them. When it is completed, they run through every room, dashing about the legs of the servants, who carry in stools and chests, tables and linens. They bear heavy rugs between them, brightly dyed, intricately woven; roll them out over the stone floors to the delight of the children, who pause in their explorations to roll over this new softness. *Ours*, they cry. *Ours, ours, ours.*

Catherine and Petrus wander more slowly from room to room. *Here*, she says, *here, we shall put the table for dining. Here, the chairs where we will sit each evening.* Up the steps, his hand on her back, as if to keep her from falling, her hand on the rope of the handrail, the coils tight under her palm. This chamber, they decide, they will take for their own; this one, with its window overlooking the back of the house, away from the busier areas of the palace gardens, shall be Madeleine's; this one Henri's; this one Antoinette's. There is an extra chamber, and Petrus kisses her there, closes the door, grins at her and draws up her skirts, her petticoats.

Come, he says, and Catherine allows him to pull her down, down, and they knot like two hands fisted together upon the floor, there in the empty room. He is giddy, drunk with glee, with joy. *Ours*, he says, an echo of the children, whose running feet they can still hear on the floor below them.

Ours, she answers. *Ours*.

THE FOLLOWING YEARS ARE gilded ones, for all that their new house is not so wholly theirs as they first imagined. The duke expects that they will welcome all visitors he sends to them into their home, at all times of day and night. A pair of visiting cardinals, tipsy on the best wine from His Excellency's vineyards, takes it into their heads to see the duke's wild family long after they have been abed for hours, while the moon is still bright in the sky. Catherine, fine hairs escaping her nighttime plait, flushed in her chemise and mantle, pours them more wine from their own cellar, arranges cheese and olives and fruit on a plate with flustered hands, all while Petrus sits with them in the receiving room, Antoinette sleeping on his lap, Madeleine and Henri yawning on stools beside him, heads bobbing like flowers in a wind.

Their house is like a palace in miniature, with every luxury they could desire. A cook for their meals; servants to fetch wood and clean, to fill tubs for their baths, and to launder their clothing.

This frees Petrus and the children to spend their time at court, or to play in the gardens, that visitors might easily happen upon them and be amazed. The duke encourages the children to wander where they wish, gives them leave to pick fruits from the orchard. Henri chases Antoinette through the grove of orange trees, all the small white blossoms giving way to heavy bright fruits, the air thick with a sweetness that can almost be licked. He scrambles up the tree, quick as a squirrel to evade the notice of the gardeners—not because they would mind the taking, but because evasion was so much dizzy fun—and returns to earth with his arms laden with fruits, which the two of them eat, sitting together beside the fountain that is shaped like the shell of a scallop, scraps of orange peel scattered about their feet, sticky juice matting the hair on their chins. And then they are off again, racing for the evergreen labyrinth; lying on their bellies to watch the waters of the pond, so swollen with fish.

Madeleine prefers, most days, to walk with Catherine and Petrus. They promenade at a more dignified pace than that which is set by the younger children, allowing Petrus to read aloud from the rare letters that come from Ludovico. Catherine waits for a letter from Agnes, though as the months roll into years her hope turns gossamer, tattering at the edges, moth wings broken and useless. Instead, she concentrates her attention upon the light crunch of their shoes over the stone pathways; the raised hands and grins from the gardeners, who hail Petrus as Don Pietro and Madeleine as Maddalena Pelosa—Hairy Maddalena. Under the sun, they meander past the water chain, a channel elegantly shaped like a very long crayfish that cuts between two rustling hedgerows. Into the knot gardens above, where Catherine spreads her fingers over the splayed toes, crusted with lichen, of a sculpted stone river god. She inhales, listens—sunlight on green, and her younger children shrieking with laughter just out of sight.

The duke ordered their house erected in the same part of the gardens where his wild beasts are kept, and it is this which jars Catherine with the reminder that their new home is not just a refuge, but a sprawling, beautiful cage. When important guests visit the palace, if the weather is fine, they are certain to take a stroll to see the leopard in its cage; and if they are lucky, they might have a glimpse of the wild man as well, or one of his cubs.

HENRI IS THE FIRST to leave them.

The duke's brother, a cardinal, has taken a fancy to their boy and wants him for himself. The duke informs them of this one afternoon, sitting in the gardens with Petrus and Catherine and his own wife, who nods and smiles, as if this is the most natural thing in the world, the gifting of a boy, the stealing of a child. Catherine holds her hands over her belly, rounding with new life, and presses her tongue to the roof of her mouth, that she not shout at the man to whom they are so indebted, who keeps them so richly.

It does not seem so terrible when she realizes that Henri will not be going far. The cardinal lives in the palace, after all; and if the cardinal wishes to take their boy for a coach ride through the streets of Rome, dress him in the finest silk and linen, comb his hair to a glossy shine—well, there are certainly worse fates, Catherine tells herself. She kisses Henri's cheek, lets him go; hugs him when he returns, full of gloating over the wonder on the faces of the people to whom the cardinal introduced him.

MADELEINE SEEMS HAPPIER HERE than she did in Paris. In the open of the gardens, they can pretend they are not confined. She wears gowns in the Italian style, which dip low to show her bosom; she plaits blossoms into her hair, and sings when she thinks no one can hear her. Catherine watches her, wondering; her eldest girl is beyond old enough to take notice of men, and for them to take notice of her. She thinks of what the artist said all those years ago, that Madeleine would be pretty, were it not for her hair.

And then, one day, she comes into the house to find Madeleine on a kitchen stool, bent in half over her own thighs, her hands over her face. The cook, in the garden outside, is harvesting lettuce and pretending she cannot hear Madeleine's sobs. Catherine finds herself across the room, kneeling before her daughter, reaching for her wrists, before she has had time to think. And then Madeleine's hands come away, and the sunlight gleams, obscene, upon her bare, shaven face.

She looks roughly peeled, her skin scattered with angry red bumps, with scrapes from the blade. She removed it all, though there are little tufts near her hairline, as if she feared getting too near the hair on her scalp. Even her eyebrows are gone, giving her a startled look. Catherine takes a breath and holds it in her chest; it is as if she looks at Madeleine through warped glass. It is her daughter's face, and it isn't. It is her daughter's face as it might have been; it is Catherine's mother's face, alive again. Rounded cheeks, a deep, graceful sweep between her lower lip and the knob of her chin. For the first time, she knows the line of Madeleine's jaw; the worry lines on her brow. Catherine's chest is filled with that single breath, filled to bursting; and with grief and gratitude and a strange horror at the sight of so much of Madeleine's skin, so pink and tender, like the private bits that no one is meant to see.

Petrus once told them all of the time he used cat urine and walnut oil to try to melt his hair away. All it did, he said, was make him a reeking laughingstock. King Henri shook his head and said, *Now, why would you try something like that? What would we do with you without all that glorious hair?*

"Oh," she says at last, blowing the word out on a desperate exhalation. "Oh, sweet girl, what have you done to yourself?"

Madeleine puts her hands—still hairy—up to her naked face, then jerks them away as quickly again. "It burns!" she cries, and Catherine sighs. Pulls her to her breast, stroking the hair on her head.

"I only wanted," Madeleine says, gulping in breaths, "to see if I was pretty."

Catherine rolls her eyes upward, as if she can find guidance on the ceiling.

"You are even better than pretty, *cara mia*," she says, stroking and stroking, resting her chin atop Madeleine's head and closing her eyes. She thinks of her mother, whose face she thought she would never see again; she thinks of herself, all those hours before the glass. "Prettiness, you see," she says, "it is—well, it is applied like cosmetics, and just as easily lost to time. You, my sweet one, are . . . beautiful. Beauty is different. It's nothing to do with this"—smoothing a hand over Madeleine's blotched cheek. "It is the—the *truth* of someone. And *that* is eternal."

THE HAIR BEGINS TO grow back within a day, of course—little rough stubbles that prick like needles to the touch.

ROME, ITALY

1592

Pedro

Ercole is born in their own house on the grounds of the Palazzo Farnese, born in such a wash of water that it is as if Catherine sucked up the whole of the sea while she carried him. Her great white thighs spread, streaked with red; the midwife's grunts as she pulls the child forth, slick and floppy as a fish, heedless of the ocean that comes with him, how it wets her apron, her shoes. She only stares, chin dropped, at the creature in her hands, and then turns, wordless, to Catherine, who has tried to prop herself on her elbows, and Petrus, crouched silent by her head. She hands the child to Catherine, and Catherine looks at him, and then at Petrus; and Petrus can feel the strain at the edges of his own eyes as they widen. For he can see plainly the flesh of this child, the hairlessness, even his head perfectly bald and smooth as blown glass.

"I did nothing differently," Catherine says. Her voice high and thin; she looks at Petrus, as if pleading.

Petrus's eyes are pinned to his son—to the folds of him, the creases all thick with vernix. Every line and blotch and dimple of him visible. In a strange way, he seems more vulnerable than the others did at birth, with nothing to cover him.

"Petrus," Catherine says again, and he pulls his eyes away from the infant and to her face, which is filled with—fear? "Petrus, I did nothing differently—do you hear me? I did nothing, nothing—"

All at once, he understands; hears the assertion of her innocence, her insistence that this child, like the others, is, in fact, his.

"My own parents were said to be hairless," he says, and shrugs, smiling just a little. He touches her cheek, finds it wet; she leans into his palm.

Catherine

"Do you love him more, Maman?"

It is eight days since Ercole's birth; his thin crying, stinging and insistent as the swipe of a willow wand stripped of its skin, has filled the house nearly every hour of every one of those eight days. Catherine has become almost unfamiliar to herself in her exhaustion, every sweet and pretty thing faded from her face, leaving only swipes of gray and sudden, slashed furrows behind. Her hair is slick with oil, hanks of it escaping its pins to lie like defeat against her neck; her gowns bear circular stains at the breasts, dark at the centers and fading as they widen, like ripples in a pond, stains she is too tired to care to scrub away.

Antoinette has come into the room where she lies on the bed, Ercole peevishly at suck in her arms. Catherine's eyelids had been drooping toward sleep, but at Antoinette's question they snap to her daughter's face; her voice snaps, too, with tiredness. "Of course not," she says. "Why would you ask such a thing?"

Though she is far too old for such infantile comfort, Antoinette still sucks her thumb, as if it were her mother's breast. She puts it in her mouth now as she climbs up onto the bed and points wordlessly to her new brother's skin, soft and wrinkled and yellowed like old paper. Catherine looks down at the babe, then up, face slackening.

"Oh no, *cara mia*," she says. "Oh, no." Awkwardly, she shifts so that she can tuck her arm around the curl of Antoinette's body. "We love our children as they are, little one," she says, slowly, carefully. "I love you and Madeleine and Henri for yourselves, and I love this little one for whomever he proves to be."

A damp *pop* as Antoinette's thumb pulls free. "And for his skin?" she asks.

"And for his skin," Catherine says, and then, with a firm look, "but

I certainly do not love him for his skin more than I love you for your beautiful hair."

"Do you love Papa for *his* beautiful hair?"

A sound from the doorway—an involuntary grunt such as a man might make if he were jostled. Catherine looks around to find Petrus there, hovering.

"Yes," she says, without taking her eyes from his face. She watches him swallow, put out a hand to hold himself upright against the doorframe. Smiles, very small. "Yes, I love your papa for his beautiful hair." She looks down at Ercole, at Antoinette. "People are people, Antonietta," she says at last, letting her head drop back, her eyes close. "That is all. People are people, however they appear."

CATHERINE WAKES LATER FROM a doze to the sound of Antoinette playing in the garden below. Gently, she lays Ercole upon the bed; he sleeps on, mouth open, hands thrown up above his head as if in surrender. For a moment she can only look at his discolored skin, listen to the wheeze of his sleeping breaths.

Then she steps to the windows, drawn by the high call of Antoinette's voice. Antoinette is just below, head bent as she hops from one foot to the other, her voice raised in a singsong rhythm, the words carrying up on the hot breeze through the open casement.

People are people are people are people, she sings. *People are people are people.*

Pedro

His Excellency, disappointed when his wild man failed to sow another wondrous seed, offered no congratulations, and certainly no gifts, upon Ercole's birth; but sends a bottle of wine and a basket of oranges at his death.

Catherine, not even yet churched, stares into the fire, wordless, after the burial, Madeleine and Antoinette beside her, Antoinette pinching the fat, tender places on her own arms as if in punishment. Henri, given leave by the cardinal to stay in the garden house for a little time, looks at the bottle of wine, his face suddenly grown hard.

Petrus waits until Catherine has gone to bed, and then he takes the basket of oranges to the back of the house. Takes one—the weight of it in his palm, the smooth, dimpled skin. The wrench of his muscles as he hurls it at the stone wall—and another, and another—the smack and bursting of them, the ruined pulp, the juices running down the stones. When at last the basket is empty, Petrus is breathless, and his face is wet, his beard streaked as if with orange juice.

A SORT OF LETHARGY comes over him, after; and does not consent to leave. It steals into his marrow and his veins, heavy and suffocating. He is aware enough to be briefly grateful that his role in the duke's household requires little from him beyond hairiness.

SOON AFTER CATHERINE IS churched, Petrus is summoned by the duke.

"I have the best of news for you, Don Pietro," His Excellency says. He stands with his feet apart, his shoulders thrust back and his chest puffed out. With all his body, he seems to stake a claim to the room, and to the land beneath it. To the very Earth itself. Petrus, feeling the sad slope of his own shoulders, the tired bend of his spine, straightens.

"I would be glad to hear it," he says, though in truth he wants only to return to his house, to his books and his rest with the soft gray cloud that enfolds him.

"With your permission—I have found a husband for Maddalena."

A jolt of surprise. It must show on his face, for the duke says, "Surely you did not think I would neglect to do so? Our Maddalena is a fine girl. She deserves a husband. Children." His tongue lingers over this last word, as if it tastes of sugar. "But, of course," he adds, "it is your right to refuse. You are her father, after all."

Petrus is not certain whether he imagines the sharp edge to His Excellency's voice on this last sentence. And there is a springing inside his mind, from fear to hope and back again. Perhaps some visiting dignitary caught sight of her as she walked in the gardens. Perhaps there is a secret romance, about which Madeleine has kept her mother and father in ignorance. What sort of man would woo Hairy Maddalena? Or is this union entirely blind, like Petrus's own?

For a moment, he could be standing in front of France's queen mother rather than the Duke of Parma, and his stomach sickens; his carefully tall stance slips. And then he blinks, and it is the duke after all, the duke watching him with a blank expression, waiting.

"I will of course supply her dowry," the duke says after a moment, a prompting.

"This is all so—unexpected, Your Excellency," Petrus says, stumbling over the right words, the familiar gestures, as if he is a green young courtier, a country lad with no manners at all. The skin of his face grows hot. "So generous. I thank you. May I ask—is my daughter acquainted with her intended?"

Already, his mind spins dizzy nightmares. A man who would cage

Madeleine and cart her from town to town, fattening his purse by showing others her hair; or one with a fascination for the unusual, the shocking, to whom Madeleine might be little more than a hairy body; or a man who would take the dowry His Excellency offers but despise the wife to whom it is attached.

"She has met him, I believe," the duke says. "Giovan Avinato—master of my kennels. He says she has always enjoyed visiting new litters of pups."

His words thump against Petrus like clods of earth. He examines them as they fall, tries to discover how they are intended. A joke—the hairy girl, wed to the master of dogs? Or a coincidence, a freak of fate? Or is he, Petrus, merely looking too hard for something to be amiss, for something offensive, when really he should be glad, delighted that his firstborn daughter might have found a life's companion, as he has?

"I have met Signore Avinato," Petrus says slowly. "My Antonietta likes to visit the kennels as well." The kennel master, who must be ten years or more Madeleine's senior, has never seemed to Petrus to show any particular interest in his children, though Antoinette's enthusiasm for the newborn pups always makes him smile. Thinking of that smile, Petrus forces his spine straight again, makes it rise like a tree from its root. "I would ask my daughter first before agreeing, if Your Excellency allows. But the match has my blessing."

The duke nods after a moment. "It is a fine match," he says; and again, Petrus cannot decipher the nuances to the statement—or even if there are any nuances there at all to *be* deciphered. "I suspect our marvelous Maddalena will agree."

AS SOON AS HE returns to the house, Petrus seeks out Madeleine. He finds her outside, reading to her mother while Catherine mends a tear in one of Antoinette's gowns.

"Married?" Madeleine says when Petrus tells them the reason for his summons from the duke. "Me, married?" Wonder and fear and joy flit across her face, bright and brief as falling stars.

Petrus glances at Catherine, whose face is carved in lines of worry. But she presses her lips together, keeping her thoughts carefully inside, leaving space for their daughter's feelings.

"I think you must at least speak to the man before we agree," Petrus says; then hesitates. "Child—I want a good husband for you. A devoted husband. We do not know Signore Avinato's reasons for agreeing to this match." He glances at Catherine, who smiles at him a little sadly, and Petrus finds he cannot speak most of his fears aloud, after all, as if doing so might summon them in truth, solid and terrible. At last he says merely, "If he has agreed for the dowry alone—"

But Madeleine flaps her hands, impatient. "Then I will be just the same as most other wives," she says.

Almost, Petrus objects; but then Madeleine says again, "Just the same," and now she is grinning, all her teeth showing, and she is so beautiful that Petrus's chest hurts, all the protective bones of it shattered.

Catherine

Madeleine's wedding feast is nearly as elaborate as Catherine's own. Catherine sits beside Petrus, Antoinette half-asleep in her lap, and watches as Madeleine and her new husband dance a stately pavane, Signore Avinato a little stiff, as if he has only recently learned the steps, Madeleine's steps precise and graceful. Her wedding dress is gray silk, covered in an ocean's worth of pearls that seem almost to glow in the gentle light of the many-branched candle sticks. She is seriousness and serenity at once, a moon whose movements Catherine watches as she feels herself beginning to bleed inwardly as her daughter tears away from her a second time, some invisible cord, strong and pulsing with life as her daughter's birth cord once was, snapping.

She pulls her eyes away at last when the dance is ended, when Madeleine and Signore Avinato go to the duke and duchess and make their bows. Even so, she does not miss the way Madeleine's new husband moves away from her soon after, taking a cup of wine and drinking from it a little too quickly. But he also smiled at her during the ceremony when Madeleine's voice faltered, nervous, over her vows; and if his smile was nearly as stiff as his dancing, Catherine dares to hope that it still promises something, a chance at sweetness in their marriage. Sweetness and stiffness; laughter and sorrow. Isn't that life, after all? Catherine hopes, hands tightening around her youngest daughter, that her eldest, in this marriage, has achieved something approaching a balanced scale.

Henri sits a little down the table, at his ease beside the cardinal. As Catherine watches, her son says something that makes the people around him laugh. Tonight, he shows none of the aversion to this marriage that he displayed in private to his parents. A natural courtier, Henri, from his head to the tips of his toes.

Long tables are laid out, filled with what feels to Catherine like half the nobility of Rome, invited by the duke to enjoy his table, his wine, the spectacle of one of his hairy wonders, married. The food is light and rich in equal measure: chicken broth in which moon-shaped pasta floats; pies filled with ox tongue, the delicate pastry tops adorned with the Farnese crest; olives from the Farnese fields, stuffed with salty cheeses. The wine, purple-red, stains the guests' lips. At the ceremony, five of His Excellency's favorite dogs accompanied Madeleine to the altar, dressed in ruffs and with bells jingling at their tails. And yet Madeleine smiled—is smiling still. She is speaking with a knot of noblewomen who, Catherine chooses to believe, are admiring her gown, her headdress, and not the fine thick hair beneath them.

Catherine's own gown is uncomfortably tight, laced over her belly, which still hangs a little distended after hosting Ercole, and over her breasts, which are still tender and leaking. If her eyes leak, too, a muddle of sorrow and happiness trickling over the rounds of her cheeks, she supposes that is common enough, for a mother whose daughter has just been wed.

ERCOLE IS GONE, HIS sweet, small body shrouded and taken from her; Madeleine is married and living in the fine house gifted to her and her new husband by the duke. Henri is with the cardinal, touring the vast lands controlled by the Farnese. It is only Catherine and Petrus and Antoinette in the house in the garden now, among the bees and the leopards and the visitors who are all eager to be astonished, to exclaim; and Petrus is far away, deep in his own head, his own misery, from which Catherine cannot seem to draw him. It is a cloud, gray and damp and shutting out all joy, this thing that seems to cling to him. And Catherine, trying to rouse him from his sad stupor, to tempt him with a morsel he might enjoy or with talk of Madeleine's happiness, finds her chest feeling tight, her spine aching as if ropes are twisting around her, tighter and tighter. Soon they will have wrapped themselves down over her hands; soon they will stick her legs together. Soon they will strangle her throat and then up over her mouth, her nose, if she does not tear herself free, if she does not speak, if she does not start screaming. For she, too, has lost her son—her boy, her *boy*—and not just Ercole himself, but all the possibilities his life might have held.

Petrus told the children stories, sometimes, stories that he said had been passed down from the ancients, the scholars of the world. Stories of philandering gods and spiteful goddesses. Tales of wisdom and foolishness. Of Pan, the half-goat god, the tripping rhythm of his hoofed hind feet, the merry sailing notes of his piping.

(*Some gods*, he said, a hand touching their children's cheeks, their backs, *some gods used to look like us*.)

And, too, he told them the story of Hercules—the strong, the bold, who killed the Hydra with its nine heads and wrestled even death itself. Hercules—Ercole, in the Italian. It was this name that they gave to their child, the child they have lost, whose final exhalation Catherine still hears, sometimes. Such anger, burning her up from the inside out, when Petrus will not speak to her now, when he only sighs and turns away. She lost Ercole as well as he, it is *their* loss, *theirs*. His name was a prayer in both their mouths; as if in naming him after a demigod, they might will some of that ancient hero's strength into their son's weak, pallid limbs, his watery lungs, his disenchantment with life from the first.

PETRUS USUALLY KEEPS AWAY from the penned-up animals here as much as possible, just as he did in France, where, he once said, had King Henri not seen the intelligence in him, the boy and not the beast, he might have languished all his days in a cage beside the lions' den. But today, one of the duke's guests wanted to speak with him as she and her husband strolled through the pens, and so he and Catherine come with them, past the leopard, the peacocks, until they find Antoinette before the monkeys' cage.

Back in France, Henri and Antoinette's bond was set by their mutual love of the menagerie. Now that she is the only one left, Antoinette spends her days pestering the keepers here at the palace to let her help with the creatures' feedings. She winds her hands around the bars of their enclosures; holds, for long minutes, the dromedary's dull, long-lashed stare.

Today it is the near-human gazes of the monkeys she holds, those keen eyes under funny tufted brows; and as the duke's guests cry out with delight, one of the monkeys reaches through the bars. Its hand is so much smaller than Antoinette's, but perfectly formed, four slender fingers and a tiny jointed thumb, the skin shiny; with those fingers, it explores Antoinette's, bringing them to its lips as if to taste her. She laughs.

And then the visiting lady says, "Look at the funny little monkey!" and hurries forward. Antoinette turns when she is bid, releasing the monkey's hand only at the last moment, and, with practiced patience, allows the lady to take her hands and explore her fingers with her own.

Beside her, Catherine senses Petrus's sudden stiffness.

"WE ARE ANIMALS TO THEM," he says later, when Antoinette is sleeping and they are alone in their house, the doors and windows firmly shut. Catherine watches as he paces their chamber, as his fingers tear at the lacing of his ruff, struggling with the knot until it finally releases. He flings the stiff pleated circle away from him as if it were a rope, a noose, and Catherine is silent, uncertain what to do, what to say. This is the most animated she has seen him in months upon months; but the way that he and their children are viewed by much of the world is hardly news.

He does not say anything more but is restless beside her in bed, fingers tapping against his lips, as if in thought.

Pedro

All through the night, he lies hot and agitated, his mind far too unquiet for sleep. As Catherine breathes softly beside him, dreaming, Petrus moves wakeful through the world inside his own head, peering into windows and doorways, watching men at work. Blacksmiths and wheelwrights, musicians and merchants. Scribes, butchers, fellers, cheesemongers, bakers, tailors, cobblers, goldsmiths, glovers, painters. Life upon life into which he tries to imagine himself, to fit himself, each and every one like a too-tight shoe, uncomfortable because he does not possess the skills needed for it to be a good life, a successful one; or because he fears to try.

Sometime in the darkest hour, that time when it is neither truly night nor truly morning but some dark and watchful nether place between, he begins to fall asleep. His eyelids drooping, blinking, falling slowly once again; his jaw slackening. Sleep mere moments away.

And then his eyes open again, fling themselves wide and wondering. *Tutor*, he thinks, and begins to smile. Slowly at first, a testing of the expression, a slow curling of lips, a gentle crinkling at the edges of his eyes, and then he speaks the word aloud, into being—"*Tutor*," quietly at first and then a little louder so that Catherine shifts and snuffles beside him and he falls at last, grinning, to sleep.

THE NEXT MORNING, HE dresses with purpose in a doublet of black velvet, which—he hopes—lends him an air of scholarly seriousness. He does not tell Catherine of his hopes, his plans, his skin itching at the thought of having to tell her should he fail.

He goes in search of the Duke of Parma, hoping that he is not closeted with business, with family, with anything upon which Petrus would feel he was intruding. But luck is with him, for he finds His Excellency breaking his fast on a terrace overlooking the gardens, and when Petrus approaches, he is greeted with a smile and an offer of a seat at the little table.

"Don Pietro! A fine morning for a stroll," His Excellency says.

"It is, it is," Petrus says, and oh, his voice is unsteady, trembling. He clears his throat. "I am—it is fortunate that I came upon you, Your Excellency, for I have been thinking about something that I would like to discuss with you."

The duke smiles, makes a gesture of generous welcome, arms spread wide. "Of course," he says.

For a moment, Petrus cannot speak. Only once—*once,* in all the years since he was taken—has he asked for anything, and he can still remember the humiliation, the way his very skin seemed to tighten, as if trying to shrink him down to nothing. King Henri dead, and Petrus's position as bread bearer given to one of the new king's favorites. The faint amusement on King Charles's face when his father's pet asked him for something, anything, to do. The laughter that ran in circles around the room, from throat to throat. The way the boy-king turned from him without responding, as if the request were nothing at all and not Petrus's pride, his worth, laid at His Majesty's feet, an offering and a plea.

He swallows and swallows around his throat's sudden stickiness. "I was hoping—if it would please Your Excellency—that I might be given a position here. I would like to—to work. And I thought—as you know, I was given a nobleman's education in France. I thought perhaps you might know of a family in need of a tutor. I can teach Latin, or Greek, or French. Philosophy, history, geography. I'm a fair swordsman. I—even small children. I could teach them to write a fair hand, to read . . ."

The duke has been looking uncomfortable throughout this awkward speech, his fingers drumming upon the tabletop, his lips pulled in. But at this last, his eyes go pitying.

"You don't think," he says, his tone gentle, "that your . . . unusual appearance might frighten small scholars?"

Petrus's blood thunders. He grips the edge of the table, that he mightn't topple over; tightens his teeth together to keep himself from the mortification of tears.

"I am a man," he says, voice tinged with panic, with desperation. "I would earn my family's keep like one."

As quickly as it showed pity, His Excellency's face transforms itself into a mask of irritation, and Petrus realizes that he was meant to take the escape the duke thought he was offering with those words; that the other man did not actually wish to refuse Petrus outright, but that he will, now he has been pressed.

"I do not know any families in need of a tutor," he says, and now his tone is a lid slamming down, a key turned in a lock. Petrus nods and pushes back his chair, bows hastily and mutters a thick-voiced thanks. Takes his leave, feeling the duke's eyes upon him as he stumbles away.

MANY HOURS LATER, PETRUS has dragged a stool from his own house to sit before the monkeys' cage, and is watching the quick little creatures. The sun is hot overhead, and he is sweating, but he cannot seem to move. Twice, Catherine has come to offer him food, water, but both times he shook his head and she returned to the house with a touch to his shoulder.

"Many men would be glad of so easy a life as you enjoy, Don Pietro," a voice says from behind him, and the surprise of it is enough to make Petrus turn, look, to see the Duke of Parma standing a few steps away, his face shadowed by the brim of his hat, expression lost. Petrus stands and bows as His Excellency approaches, and tries not to let his own face show the jumble of his emotions: the springing hope, the mud pit of embarrassment, the sword-slash of anger.

"I hope you never think that I am ungrateful, Your Excellency," he says. "But—"

But the duke interrupts him. "Something occurred to me after our discussion," he says. "If it's work you want, I might have something that will suit."

Petrus curls his fingers into his palms. "I—would be very grateful."

"Your request might be a solution to both your problem and one of my own. Providential, you might say. I've a property in the village of Capodimonte whose overseer only recently left quite abruptly; there's a temporary man there now, but he won't do for long. You are a man of integrity and intellect—and initiative, which I had not realized." The duke looks at him for a long moment while Petrus listens to the glad and terrified whoosh of his own blood. "The position is yours, if you'd like it."

HIS FIRST GLIMPSE OF the lake at Capodimonte is like being netted and dragged, stunned, back to his childhood, when he would sit watching the sea. All the brilliant, shifting colors—blue to green, gold and orange dappling the swells, all the foam so white and seething at the crests.

The lake is little like the sea, of course; it is far more placid, and far less noisy. But it is almost as bright as the waters of Tenerife, that peculiar blue that Petrus has only seen once before, in a Turkish stone of smooth green-blue worn by a Paris nobleman; and fishing boats bob along the water here, just as they did in Garachico. He allows Catherine to guide his footsteps, for his eyes are moons again, too full from looking and looking to mind where he walks.

Their house here is smaller than their home in the Farnese garden, but there is a great hearth, wide enough that he could lie stretched out full within it. There is welcome in its width, perhaps; a promise of warmth, of full bellies. Of conviviality. There is space enough to draw up chairs for every one of their family before this fire. Petrus puts his hands to the smooth pale walls, pressing against them, as if to assure himself that they will not topple; that they are real.

From the highest window, he can see the gentle undulations of the patchwork hills and the ruffle of the wood beyond. Fields of wheat the color of Catherine's hair; a grove of olive trees with their trunks twisted, as if they have been sculpted by the very wind, silvery leaves at their crowns and plump green fruits dangling from their boughs. A vineyard, too, the berries sweet bunches of blue on the vines. Beyond his line of sight lies the village and the beauty of the lake.

He feels again like a young boy, new-come to a brilliant court; but this is a court of earth and water and air. His to tend; his to make prosperous. His.

HERE, THEY WAKE AND sleep to the rhythm of the farm's needs. Petrus has been entrusted with the cultivation of the fields and orchards; the harvesting of the fruits; the breeding of the duke's fine cattle. And, too, the collecting of coin from the villagers in Capodimonte, who must pay the Duke of Parma for the right to use his woodland, his pasture, for grazing their animals. For this, he receives a fine stipend, along with wine and wheat from the farm's bounty for his family's use. For the first time since crossing the sea in a ship sailed by pirates, he refuses to let fear and self-doubt make themselves his masters. He has much to learn; but he has a brain that is more than equal to the task, a brain that has been longing, all these years, for something to *do*.

He has a wife, too, a wife of intelligence and practical knowledge.

They will set themselves to this great task with all their combined energies; and they will succeed.

Henri and Madeleine remain at court, but Antoinette comes to the farm, though she and Catherine wept a little as they packed their things, as the door to their garden house closed behind them. "We will be back, we will stay here whenever His Excellency requires us in Rome," Petrus reminded them, and grinned, for he could not help himself. They were off—off! Off to a place away from court, to a house where no one would expect to come inside to see how the hairy family lives. Off to work, honest work, for which he must be respected. No longer curiosities.

THE VILLAGERS STARE AND whisper and cross themselves when he and Antoinette come to church for the first time. The men and women who work the farm's fields and orchards mutter at first when Petrus walks among them, when he records their harvests in his ledger. The creases of their hands and the wells of their fingernails filled with earth, their mouths with songs that lift over the vines and the groves as they bend and pluck. But Catherine's presence smooths his way; she asks them about their families, their children, and speaks of her own, easing their fears, their superstitions. And Antoinette, too, who misses her friends in the duke's menagerie, but who finds new ones among the goats and the cows; who watches the children of fishermen as they splash at the edge of the lake. Petrus watches her watching them and thinks he understands what she must be feeling. The simultaneous push and pull of longing to join and wanting to pass unnoticed. The ache of difference.

And then his daughter is stripping off her stockings, leaving them abandoned on the shore. Raising her skirt to show her hairy ankles. Stepping into the water with a gleeful shriek.

HE FINDS CATHERINE STANDING at the cusp of one of the farm's high hills. She is very still, her fingers flexed, as if poised to catch the wind. The sun bright upon her face. She looks, he thinks, like the captain of a ship, feet planted wide and eyes on the horizon.

He thinks, then, of mussels, of the seawater scent of them, the click of each shell against the others when he dropped them into his bag. The jounce of the bag against his shoulder blades as he ran back from the sea through the winding streets. He sees, clear as anything, Isabel's grin when he returned with his bounty.

Part Six

Ninnananna

CAPODIMONTE, ITALY

1618

Catherine

Sleepless, eyes dry with tiredness, Catherine twists like a corpse from a tree, trying to remember.

The rise and fall of Ercole's chest; watching it in the night. The peculiar vulnerability of it, slightly concave at the center. How Antoinette slipped her fingers into the hollows under Catherine's arms at night, worrying at the hair there as if it were a favorite blanket, ragged-edged from so much holding; as if she were comforted that even her smooth-skinned Maman had hidden hairy places.

Falling asleep curled on her father's lap when he arrived home from a months-long journey, the unwashed smell of him, the firmness of his arms holding her in place. Her mother stroking her hair. Dried sprigs of rue among folded linens.

If only she were like the queen, with paintings of all her children through each stage of their lives. Resentment curdles, that the cardinal keeps her son's grown-up image on his wall; and she wonders where those long-ago sketches went, the ones of herself and Petrus, Madeleine and Henri; whether they were, indeed, copied by other artists; whether other kings and queens paid to have her husband and her children in their collections. Wonders whether Antoinette's likeness has ever been taken, and if the artist managed to capture her mischief, her intelligence, the beauty of her smile.

She sits and stares hard at the wall, blank but for a carved wooden cross. She tries to recall the particular expression that used to tramp over Henri's face when he was angry as an infant; the tip of Madeleine's head when she was pretending to listen to her lessons but really was woolgathering; Antoinette's grin, alight with silliness, stretching her cheeks and showing every one of her little teeth; Ercole's fists, pressed together under his chin as he slept; Petrus's eyes, holding hers steady. But she cannot, quite; all she remembers now is the feeling of those things. The things themselves elude her, shadows that move away when she tries to catch them in her hands. She misses them as she would miss air.

SHE HAS A LITTLE glazed pot, brought with her from France to Italy, kept safe in her trunk among her petticoats and bodices. All of her children's milk teeth are kept safe inside that pot, jumbled together like buttons in a sewing box. Antoinette had lost only four before she left them, and Ercole's, of course, had never come in, were tucked away like secrets inside his mouth. Catherine wishes, now, that she had kept better account of which teeth had come from which child; for some reason, she had imagined she would know, that she would remember the shapes and sizes of their early teeth, which seemed as individual to her as the children from which they fell.

But she cannot see her children in them now. She has taken them out tonight, spread them across the table in the candlelight, a gruesome scattering. That one sharply tipped; this one still rusty red at the root.

If only she had taken a length of Antoinette's hair, to tie up tight and keep safe. All she has now are teeth, four of them, and they are strangers to her. She picks them up one by one, rolls them in her hands, closes her eyes and tries to remember which four belonged to her youngest daughter, which, which, *which*—

But the teeth do not speak to her.

ALMOST, SHE WISHES SHE had done the unthinkable and pried Petrus's teeth from his jaw before sewing closed his shroud. The thought rolled like a marble through her head as she sewed, as the needle shushed through the cloth and Madeleine wept nearby, and in the strange padded stillness after his death, this thought seemed less terrible than it should have. She poked the needle in above his navel, imagined how easily she could tug his teeth from his mouth one by one. He had so few by the end, and they were so loose in his gums—it would be the work of a moment. Sewing higher, over his chest, she could hear in her mind the patter of each tooth into the pot with the others, but these teeth—bigger, grayer, she would always know instantly. Up to his chin, where her hand nearly paused, her eyes nearly darted to Madeleine to see whether she watched; but no. Peering down over the stern line of his mouth, she suddenly could not bear to part his stiffening lips, much less reach inside.

Shush shush shush. She sewed the fabric together over his face, gulping in air as she did so, feeling her vision narrowing, her breath growing shorter, as if she wore her mother's visard once more, as if it were she who was going to her grave.

DO I HAVE A SOUL? Antoinette once asked the queen, when she was still too small to truly understand her own question. Catherine, standing a little aside, her body tensing at first, then easing as the queen lifted her daughter onto her knee, her hand gentle as it tipped up Antoinette's chin, her smile holding nothing but kindness.

Oh, my sweet one, she said, smiling. *No, you do not.*

CATHERINE WAKES FOR THE third night in a row with Antoinette's name upon her lips. She dreamed again of that afternoon in the brightness of the queen's receiving room. Her daughter's question, the queen's response. In her dream, Catherine felt once more the flood of helplessness she'd felt in life, the volcanic fury, to hear her daughter spoken to so, her humanity dismissed to her own face, dismissed with a smile, with a gentle touch, cruel words and kind touches jumbling together and leaving Antoinette bewildered, uncertain, lost.

After—after the queen relinquished Antoinette to Catherine's care, dismissed them all that she might have her royal rest—Catherine carried Antoinette outside, unable to bear the high stone walls of the palace, the echoing of voices, of footsteps, the lingering of eyes upon her child's face. She carried her through the grounds until they reached a deserted stretch of lawn, sun-drenched, warm; and there she lay her daughter down, and herself beside her. They turned their faces up, eyes slitted, and Catherine pointed to the sun, so brilliant, and said, "Your soul, *cara mia*—it is as bright as that. As bright as the sun."

Rising now, she goes to the window; but the sky is moonless, and there is nothing to see. She remembers that day, the warm ground, the warm air, how Antoinette curled against her. She rubs her arms, dotted like gooseflesh; lights a candle; paces a little. Sits on the stool in the corner.

Her words, on that long-ago day, were spoken fiercely. But still they were not, she thinks now, enough. How could one mother's words, however fiercely and often they were spoken, negate the words, the messages her daughter received from all the rest of the world? And still, how stupid, how impossible it seemed, that Her Majesty could not *see* Antoinette's soul, the brightness of it. It was there, just there, in her eyes, her smile, the eager way she listened and played and spoke. Bright as the sun.

Now, Antoinette fades for her with each day; Catherine can only just grasp the smallest recollections, holding them in her mind for moments only, before they blow away, leaves on the wind, bubbles from a reed.

"Come back," she says now, aloud, for there is no one left to hear her, she is alone in the house. Her elder daughter and son are warm in their own houses, her husband and youngest son are bones in the earth.

It is only Antoinette who is adrift, who she cannot fix safely in a specific place, a specific time. *What happened*, she thinks. *What happened to you?*

Antoinette never got to see her father's hair moon-touched; her mother's skin grown papery. Catherine does not allow herself to think of the things about which Agnes sometimes spoke when she was sad, or tired, or had drunk a little too much wine: hands that touched when she did not wish them to, that grasped and lifted; mouths that murmured sweet words, that said, oh-so-gently, *Come, sit upon my lap. Let me feel the weight of you.*

Instead, she remembers her daughter's delight in the big yellow eyes of the leopard; in the sprawl of Capodimonte's green hills. Wherever Antoinette has landed, Catherine hopes that it is very beautiful.

Sometimes, like the upside-down of clouds in water, she is certain she can feel Antoinette in truth. She is somewhere near, just out of sight. If Catherine were to round the bend of the stairs, she might find her there, playing with her doll; if she were to turn her head swiftly enough, she might find Antoinette standing just behind her, a woman grown and slyly smiling. *I am here*, she says, swirling around Catherine, less substantial than breath, less sure than memory. *I am here, I am here, I am here—*

And then the feeling is gone, and she is left scrabbling through her own mind, her own memories, for a turn of head, a smile, a high calling voice, a thumb puckered from sucking. A voice—her mother's, her own—singing an old *ninnananna*, familiar from all their childhoods, generations of song. She looks down at her hands and remembers them younger, clutching either side of her daughter's small face, finger ends digging too hard into her temples.

I will see you soon, cara mia*—so very soon.*

Antoinette's baffled tears, until those words; and then her face clearing. The touch of her small hands, her soft cheek. How Catherine had to hold tight to the arched doorway to keep herself from flying after her and the smiling, grand woman whose hand she held.

Now she holds tight to the points of her own elbows. Presses her folded arms into the soft give of her belly, bending forward, rocking. Decides she cannot stand the silence in her house any longer, and begins singing.

Lullaby, lullaby, oh
Who do I give this child to?
If I give her to the witch
She keeps her for me for a week
If I give her to the black-cloaked man
He keeps her for me for a whole year
Lullaby, lullaby, oh
Who do I give this child to?
If I give her to the white wolf,
He'll keep her so long.
Lullaby, sleep fairies
My baby is sleeping

ROME, ITALY
1593

Catherine

The first time Catherine sees the Marchesa di Soragna, the marchesa is wearing a mantle of velvet and fur, despite the autumn warmth. She sits stroking the fur in an absentminded way on the balcony of a small garden house at the top of the water chain, built exclusively for the duke and cardinal to entertain their friends and most important visitors. Below, the knotted hedges spread in a sumptuous maze, dotted with fountains and sculptures, leading down to the steps and the fountain, and then to the wood, where the trees glow like fire with the season.

Catherine and Petrus come through those burning trees, he wearing a stiff wide ruff and a suit of black, she a gown the shadowed green of deep forests, the neckline low but for a collar at the back, a spray of intricate lace. Upon her head a small green hat, and attached to it a veil that hangs down in points, whispering around her elbows.

They have not been to court from Capodimonte for many weeks, and it is strange to be back. She can feel anew the constraint of the place, of all the expectations, the eyes here. Here, their story is the old, tired one: the primitive prince, tamed; his wondrous children, here for the petting. When each of Catherine's children emerged bloody and squalling from her womb, they were swaddled in this story as if it were a blanket. She thinks of the painter in France, how he had heard of her family; wonders how their story might have changed over time, telling after telling, the details become more exaggerated with each repetition. She had not realized, until they returned to Rome, how freeing it was to cast the tale off for a time, to live as themselves.

Antoinette walks between them, her gown a twin of Catherine's own, a neat way to show their bond, which the duchess thought would be appreciated by their visitors. Many years later, when she remembers this day, this moment, Catherine will see the way her daughter's veil longed to snag upon the rough stone of a sculpture as Antoinette ran close to it to trail her palm over its base; will see her own hand darting out, catching at the thistledown fabric, conscious of its costliness, of the need to appear neat when they meet the duke's guests. She will remember all the particulars of that afternoon, what they wore, how they acted, and she will wonder, sometimes—if she had allowed Antoinette to run and play as she wished, and the veil to snag and tear; if she had allowed her daughter to appear to be what she truly was, a wriggling child, all motion, all loudness, except when forced into stillness by the presence of noblemen and women—if Catherine had allowed this, and if the marchesa had seen Antoinette as an unruly child rather than as a well-trained beast, would everything have been different? The thought a hole into which she could fall and fall, forever.

THE MARCHESA'S FOOT TAPS a little upon the painted tile floor of the balcony, though she smiles as the duke and her husband speak, a tilted smile that promises flirtation and masks the boredom implied by the tapping foot. Catherine sees all these details through the balusters, her head tilted back as they approach. She sees the marchesa's gown, which gleams the earthy red of garnets, and her fur mantle, and the thick curls of her pinned-back hair. She sees, as the marchesa spies them and her face lights like a lamp, that she is beautiful in the same way Catherine's mother had been beautiful, every line and curve of her face graceful and pleasing. She leans her weight upon the balustrade, the better to see them as they come near, her mouth a delighted round, her eyes skimming over Catherine entirely and swallowing Petrus and Antoinette whole.

Power, Catherine thinks, looking up at her. Just faintly, the word there and gone between one breath and the next.

When they are shown onto the balcony, she claps her hands as they make their bows. The duke beckons Antoinette to him, and she comes forward with a little leap, sitting sweetly on the bench beside him with her hands folded like the cherub she isn't. He offers her fruit from his plate, and she eats with the dainty, nibbling bites of a rodent. The marchesa watches with her wide blue eyes, thoroughly charmed.

Pedro

The duke calls for Petrus on a day of blue sky, of orange leaf; a day in which it is a pleasure to stride out from their garden house, to make his way to the palace proper. Through the courtyard, over colored stone floors that gleam with polishing, with the labor and aching knees and shoulders of servants. Under ceilings tipped with gold, past frescos of naked revelry, bodies at play, at dance, at love.

Petrus feels the pull of muscles in his thighs as he walks, hears the slap of his shoes against marble. He is shown into the duke's office, where the man himself sits frowning over a book of numbers, lips pulled to one side, a luminous quill twisting between his fingers, the sooty feather of a crow, with its fine point.

The duke looks up as Petrus bows. "Ah, Don Pietro!" he says, smiling as if Petrus's presence is a happy surprise, as if he did not order him to come here. "Come, come, sit. I have something to discuss with you."

Petrus sits, conscious of the creaking of the chair under his weight. A leopard from the duke's menagerie, recently dead, now crouches beside a tall shelf stuffed with books and papers, its yellow glass eyes fixed somehow upon both men at once.

The duke folds his hands together under his chin. "The Marchesa di Soragna," he says, still smiling, "is enchanted by our little Antonietta."

"Well," says Petrus—and he can hear the courtier's drawl to his voice, the arch inflection—"she is an enchanting child, if you'll forgive a doting father saying so himself."

Another smile, a chuckle. "I can hardly fault you." He runs a palm over his head. "The marchesa was so enchanted that I have decided to give Antonietta to her."

His words are senseless. There are more of them, but Petrus cannot comprehend them. He stares, narrows his eyes; shakes his head and tries to understand. "I," he says, but no more, for the duke is rising, is gesturing for Petrus to rise as well, to make his way to the door. Petrus does—he is halfway across the rug, halfway gone, before the duke's words become something like corporeal inside his head, as if they have just been scrawled there in ink with the duke's sharp-tipped quill.

"Your Excellency," he says. He feels the press and give of the rug under his heel as he turns. The duke has already sat once more, taken up his quill, bent his head to the book he had been studying. He raises his brows when Petrus approaches once more, hands behind his back, clenching, clenching.

His throat is dry and sour, as if he had only just woken after a stretch of fevered sleep. He says again, "Your Excellency," but cannot fumble quickly enough for words to finish the thought. *You cannot mean it. It cannot be true. I cannot allow—you cannot make her—*

Cannot. Cannot. Cannot. Mad words, to speak to power. To the man upon whose generosity Petrus has thrown himself and his family. Who has fed them, clothed them richly, housed them, denied them no luxuries. The children have had toys, books. Antoinette has chosen a pup from the duke's own kennels, a speckled thing so small its eyes are still squeezed closed, its wee feet paddling the air. She is to have it in a few weeks, when it is weaned.

His mouth fills abruptly with saliva, and he has to swallow and swallow. The duke strokes his quill along the bearded line of his own jaw, *scritch, scritch, scritch*, as Petrus stands immobile. There is a swelling in his chest, in his throat. He remembers the roar that came from him in Basel, how he charged bull-like at the woman who held Antoinette's hands. How he *stopped* her.

But roaring will not serve him well here, now. He speaks softly instead, his tone, his manner a courtier's delicate balance of strength and deference.

"I would wish—I would like to keep Antonietta with us a little longer, Your Excellency," he says. "She is young, yet—not even ten years old. She loves the vineyard, the farm, at Capodimonte. I would like her to have that, the open space she so enjoys." His heart thumps, and he fears his voice has lost its courtier's drawl; that it pleads, wheedles, begs. "There is so much time ahead for court life."

The duke sets his quill down slowly, deliberately. His face, usually so genial, puts Petrus in mind of Henri's face when he was a still child, scowling when thwarted. "The marchesa is well connected; her husband is powerful. They have offered your daughter a place with them, a place where she will be appreciated for her remarkable self. Your refusal, Don Pietro, smacks of selfishness, of ingratitude. Have I not treated your family with respect? Did I not take you in when you had need of a home; have I not provided you with a house of your own, with work when you requested it? Is Maddalena not pleased with her new home, her husband? Does Enrico not enjoy traveling with, learning from, my brother?" His Excellency's voice rises with each word, until he is nearly shouting. A flush of red rises from under his beard, smearing his cheeks and brow.

Petrus can feel himself shrinking away, closing up. When he blinks, he sees their place in Capodimonte, the vastness of the hills, the broad sweep of the lake, the vines and groves. So beautiful; and not really theirs. Nothing is truly theirs. All that beauty could be snatched away with a single word from this man's mouth, this man in front of Petrus who has always, as he said, treated Petrus and Catherine and their children with respect, with kindness and generosity.

But then Petrus thinks of the pulpy fruit, the oranges the duke sent upon Ercole's death, the sickly sweet scent of their juice as they smacked against the wall, one after another. A sack of sweetness offered upon his death, but nothing except sullen silence at his birth, at the smooth evidence of Petrus and Catherine's failure, their one task so spectacularly bungled.

He breathes out. Shadows, like those cast by the high stalks of sugarcane, close over his head. The illusion of escape from the life he so easily might have had, if Isabel had not rescued him, if he had been bought, at that market, by anyone other than a man who wished to give a gift to a king—it is slipping, that illusion, falling away, revealing the truth that he has never wanted to acknowledge, and all at once he is dizzy with it, so dizzy that he nearly puts out a hand to steady himself upon the duke's broad desk. His enslavement might be different from the one so many of his people have lived; it might come with clothes of velvet, bearing books bound in leather for him to read, figs for him to eat, wine to drink. But it exists, still. It stole him away from his almost-grandmother, just as her brothers, her mother, were stolen away from her. And it has come now for his child.

Helplessness is a rope around Petrus's lungs, crushing all his ability to roar. And as if he can sense that the fight has left his wild man, the red recedes from His Excellency's face, and his lips take an indulgent turn.

"Think of it as fostering out," he says, gentle now. "If I am blessed with children, I've no doubt some of them will travel to other courts for education, for social opportunities. Eight, nine years old—this is not so young. Younger children than Antonietta have been sent away from home, and they grow up the stronger for it. And Soragna is not so very far from Capodimonte—only a few short hours by coach. It is possible that you and your lovely wife can visit Antonietta very often."

Petrus nods, a jerky, instinctive motion. The ropes tighten and tighten.

"She will not be far, as I said. And the marchesa keeps the very best company—senators and scholars and artists. Antonietta will no doubt be a great favorite of them all."

PETRUS STAGGERS LIKE A man drunk back through the gleaming halls and out into the autumn sunlight. He flinches away from it, makes for the gardens with their sheltered, shaded copses.

Every word His Excellency spoke was true. The children of courtiers are forever being sent—younger than Antoinette—here and there, for education, for finishing, for the alliances they might form. That he and Catherine have had so many years with their small brood, so many years of their strange and wonderful life—it is a gift, and one that Petrus realizes, hand to chest, breath wheezing, that he has not fully appreciated. Tucked away from all the world, except when they are asked to stand before it, that others might have the benefit of seeing their sublime hair.

When he and Catherine and their children first arrived in Rome, they pressed tight together in the coach, taking in the dizzying rush of the city, the grandeur and the squalor of it. They presented themselves at the Palazzo Farnese, and oh, the widening of the duke's eyes when he saw them, the breadth of his grin. How eagerly he read Nevers's letter; how immediately he invited them to stay forever at his palace.

To grace my gardens with your illustrious presence, Don Pietro, he said, and bowed, as one nobleman to another.

Every night on the road, while his wife and children slept, Petrus felt himself caught once more in the grasping arms of the pirates; but this time, he clung to them as they tried to fling him out to sea. Clung with his hands, his fingers, his toes, his nails, leaving hot red furrows behind on their skin when they finally succeeded in releasing him to the waves. And then he was kicking, moving his arms, his legs, trying to keep his head up, gulping in air against the inevitable closing of the water over his face. As it finally overcame him, dark and cold, stinging his eyes with its saltiness, almost he wanted to let himself sink.

And then his sleeping limbs would spasm, and he would come awake; would touch the soft leather case in which he kept Ludovico's letter safe, close to his breast. If it did not work—if the Duke of Parma refused to have them—

But then they arrived; and the duke bowed to him; and all felt safe.

Catherine

"No," she says when Petrus tells her. She shakes her head. Every bit of her numb, as if cast in ice; and yet her voice crooks back, yanked by some unseen force; and her hands, when she raises them, shake like an old woman's.

"We must," he says, bending the short distance, that their faces be on a level. "Catherine, we *must*. She will be well cared for—"

"*No!*" A splitting open of her throat with that word. "No—"

His hands upon her shoulders; his voice a desperate pleading. "You must see," he says, as if it is the most reasonable thing in the world; as if they are not all mad—or rather, as if *she* is the mad one, the one who must be reasoned with, spoken to as one would speak to a child who simply cannot understand. "You *must* see that this is the only choice we have."

"It is not a *choice*," she says, ripping away from him. "It is no choice at all—we are *told* she is to go, we are *told*—as if she—as if she is not *ours*—" As if she is a creature to be given away. A fine horse, a hunting dog bred for its nose, a lion, a monkey.

His hands upon his head, fingers curled as if they would tear the hair from his scalp.

"Petrus," she says. "Please—*please*—she is our baby—she is *my baby*—"

Her voice rising until it fills the room and sails beyond, and he is again before her, brow close to hers. "*Stop it*," he says, eyes wide and frightened; he looks over his shoulder, as if expecting the duke to appear behind them. "*Stop* it." And his palm is over her mouth and oh dear God, she cannot breathe, she cannot draw in a single breath, she will die, she will *die*—

Her teeth break his hold; he pulls away with a wild look, one hand cradling the other to his chest. They face each other, panting like duelers, and she can see from his eyes that he means to say something terrible again; and she wishes she had bitten harder. She wants to taste his blood in her mouth.

"There is no other way," he says, after the silence has stretched until Catherine thinks she could rend it with her fingernails as easily as if it were pastry dough. His shoulders are limp, like a very ill man's; and now he does not meet her eyes. "We are under the duke's protection. We are *his*, Catherine. His to do with as he likes. And if we deny him this—if we should displease him—what shall we do then? We have *nothing* without his protection—nothing. We will lose our home—our livelihood—"

The words are hammer blows; but they seem to pound Petrus into the ground, each one shrinking him. If he were to meet her eyes, Catherine knows she would see within them the deep roots of his self-hatred. But she does not care; her own hatred sprung like a woodland well from nowhere. It bubbles over, trickles through her, the frothing force of it in the ends of her toes and fingers. Her husband's impotence, her own impotence—a snarl, a snare, a trap.

She folds like a discarded gown then, crumpling where she stands. The weave of the rug abrades her chin; and when she opens her mouth, fibers fill it, tasting of ash from the fire, of dirt from their shoes. Her cries are the only sound in the room.

"She will be cherished," Petrus says. "The marchesa is enamored of her. You saw, Catherine, you *saw* how instantly she loved our girl. Antoinette will be cherished as I was, and we will see her again soon—His Excellency told me himself the marchesa promised this. And Henri hopes to join us soon, you know, and Madeleine, too—the rest of us can be safe together in Capodimonte."

HIS WORDS ARE NOT inaccurate; but still, they sting, an entire nest of bees come swarming over Catherine's body. But when she has calmed;

when she has cleaned and bound her husband's hand, the marks of her teeth stark on the fleshy palm; when they have talked through the night and fallen asleep and woken with the larks only to begin speaking again—she finally acknowledges that they have little choice. Catherine thinks of the marchesa's fur mantle, her bored expression. Will she let their daughter run, when Antoinette feels the need to exert herself? Will she allow her a dog, a companion in her new home? Will she truly introduce Antoinette to artists, philosophers, senators, poets? It could be the beginning of a truly lovely life. She and Petrus, speaking gently to one another once more, clasp hands and say this to each other in the soft of dawn.

Later that morning, this is what they tell Antoinette, as well. *You will be safe. Cherished. You will meet so many interesting people, little love—you will have every advantage, every opportunity. And we will visit you, and you will visit us—*

Antoinette looks at her father, face blank with incomprehension. She looks at Catherine, whose own face, stiff, still, with last night's dried tears, creaks itself into something like a smile.

"It will be an adventure, *cara mia*," Catherine says; but now her voice cracks like twigs underfoot, dry and startling.

But *adventure* clears the shock from Antoinette's face like a hand brushing away cobwebs. She wriggles a little where she stands, and Catherine thinks of how her beautiful daughter charmed the queen mother of France, and the Duke of Parma, and now the Marchesa di Soragna. Who else might she charm? Where might she go? Just for a moment, *adventure* pulses in Catherine's fingers and toe-tips, shivers down her arms and legs; and in that moment, when she looks at Antoinette, she is able to smile in truth.

BUT ON THE DAY that the marchesa claims her child, Catherine cannot smile, however she tries. Antoinette sits very still upon the bed in

Catherine and Petrus's bedchamber and sucks her thumb. Catherine has been moving since she woke before the sun, folding and refolding Antoinette's bodices and skirts, putting fresh bread and hard cheese and three bright, perfect apricots into a sack for her to eat on the journey. There is a suspended feeling behind her breastbone, as if her heart, her respiration, have paused and are waiting until it is safe to begin working once more. Her hands and feet fly, stillness too painful, her thoughts too close.

But at the sight of that thumb in that mouth, she stops moving. Just stands and looks at her daughter, her girl, the bright of her eyes, the round of her face. She has been trying to break Antoinette of thumb-sucking for years, and thought she'd finally managed it; but now, she cannot, will not, scold. For now, she can only look, trying to hold the image of her child in her mind, clear as a painted portrait.

They eat breakfast, the three of them, silently, and there is more food left on their plates than in their bellies when the time comes to bring Antoinette up to the palace. Servants arrive to carry her trunk; Antoinette slips her feet into her shoes. She walks between Catherine and Petrus, hands bunched in the fabric of her skirt, breathing a little too quick, though she does not cry. Catherine's own eyes are dry as well, so dry they burn.

They are met in the palace by the duke and duchess, and by the marchesa, who smiles at Antoinette, all her teeth showing, and who does not glance once at Catherine. And suddenly, Catherine cannot see anything at all; the world has gone wet, blurred, and it is all she can do to swallow the sobs back down her throat; to weep silently, that her grief might be easier to ignore.

But then—*oh!*—her daughter has tugged away, has turned back to her. And then all of Catherine's senses fix themselves upon this moment, Antoinette's arms around her neck, both their voices gabbling together. Her daughter's sobs, wracking her. The feel of her cheek, wet and soft, under Catherine's lips for the last time. The gasp and shudder of her, the weight, the warmth. There; and then gone.

AFTER, SHE CANNOT SPEAK to him for weeks. The anger is so complete it is a fog; she can neither see nor feel anything through it. It is unfair to him, this anger. But it is better, warmer, than the grief that catches her at times unawares, slicing into her chest when she visits Madeleine at the fine house the duke purchased for her and her husband; when she stands talking with the duke and his wife; when they return to Capodimonte without Antoinette and she lies in bed, engulfed by fury at the sound of Petrus's snores, until suddenly the fury dissipates, melted away by a wracking sadness that rushes through her open, soundless mouth, a long, long moment of suspended breath until at last she is forced to inhale, with a sound like something tearing. There is no Antoinette—crawling up between them, taking Catherine's hand in her own, mumbling about bad dreams and then falling asleep again almost instantly, her thumb in her mouth. She aches, now, to feel that wet thumb poking at her in the morning, waking her, Antoinette's insistent voice saying it was time for breakfast, her belly was being so loud, couldn't Maman hear it?

Petrus's arms come around her then, his chin tucked into the dip between her neck and shoulder. She wants to push him off, wants to bite him again; she wants him to draw her closer, to feel the familiar curl of his body around hers. Never, not even when she first knew of him, that he was to be her husband; not even when she feared that his hair would also cover their children; not even when that fear was realized—never has she hated him for what he is. Until now. Now repulsion curdles suddenly at the back of her throat; something sharp catches her under the ribs, jabbing with terrible fury. If he were not what he is, if he were a man like any other man, all the smooth planes and craggy blemishes of his skin clearly visible, then their daughter would not have been so utterly lost to them.

And then disgust melts as suddenly as ice in hot spring sunlight; rushes from her eyes, her nose, her open mouth, leaving a slop of sadness behind. He cannot help his hair any more than she can help her skin, and her chest aches with the thought of how hard he tries, still, to believe that his captors have had true affection for him, for their children. She presses her brow to his forearm, letting her tears drop upon him, refusing to stopper them, hoping they burn. Instead, she feels wetness running down her own neck, and the quake of his chest against her back.

CAPODIMONTE, ITALY

1604

Pedro

Henri spins a fine tale to the duke and the cardinal: of the pull of his savage roots toward the open air, toward sprawling vistas, toward mountains. *My kind do so much better in the countryside than we do cooped in the city. My father thrives, now; we are meant for fresh air; for fresh water.*

And the duke and his brother, charmed, offer him a house in Capodimonte; and, months later, when he has fixed his eye upon a beautiful girl from the village, the duke offers to pay two hundred scudi for her dowry, to which the cardinal adds a number of jewels—a fine price for the daughter of a bricklayer, and no matter that she is rumored to be in love with another man.

A year or so later, Henri charms the duke into relinquishing Madeleine and her husband, that the entire hairy family might be together in the countryside; that they might not wither.

It is only Antoinette whose absence mars Petrus's happiness. When he wakes, shouting, for the third night in a row from a dream of sea monsters, he pads down the stairs and opens the front door, breathing in the night air. This dream has not tormented him for many years; but it makes sense, he supposes, that it would return now, when his child has been stolen away. When he allowed the stealing.

His greatest fear, realized. And yet somehow, that day when Antoinette was nearly taken in Basel seems more true than the day she left holding the marchesa's soft, beringed hand. He can still feel the thump and jolt of his heart as he searched for her; the animal fury when he found her, as a stranger tried to lead her away. But this—this new taking happened so gently—a word from the duke, a reluctant nod from Petrus, and then a smiling noblewoman taking his child by the hand. He can almost forget, sometimes, that it happened at all. Forget that his daughter is not here with them.

In the groves where she loved to run, he imagines he sees her, sometimes, a haunting, the swish of her skirt, the flash of the ribbons in her hair. Sometimes he thinks he feels her curling about his neck like a ruff; tucking herself between him and Catherine in their bed. He hears her voice, raised in childish song, among the placid cows and between rows of vines. She is there, sometimes, he is certain; the sounds so close, the sensations so true. She is there, just there—

But when he puts out a hand to touch her, when he chases the ghost of her through the vineyards, she never is.

Catherine

When Henri's son is born, Catherine takes the babe in her arms whenever his wife, Girolama, will relinquish him. She sings and rocks, walking the floors of Henri's house as she used to walk with her own babes, remembers how she used to sing these songs even when her children were too old for rocking, when they piled together like puppies on her bed. The dip of the mattress under her weight as she sat beside them; the stroke of her hand over their backs. Their breaths all interweaving as the fire burned low, and how she sometimes fell asleep there with them, still in her clothes, the song unfinished. How she wept, once, when she could not recall the words, words that her mother sang to her, and her grandmother to her mother, and back and back and back.

Girolama watches, eyes dark and impenetrable as closed doors. She is often miserly with her thoughts and feelings, but she holds her son—who is as hairy as his father—with such tenderness that Catherine cannot dislike her.

They should be better friends, she and her daughter-in-law, for their stories are near-perfect twins. Just as Queen Caterina de' Medici paid Catherine's dowry when her father could not, so did the Duke of Parma pay Girolama's when Henri spied her in the square and decided he wanted her. Catherine's bold, audacious boy, a notched arrow, always eager for release; but still more eager for the impossible, to be the one who decided where he was to go. He demanded to be seen, to be heard, luxuriating, as a child, in the attention his hair brought him—along with the sweets court ladies popped into his mouth while he sat beside them, allowing them to stroke his head.

She cannot approve of what he did to this girl, this woman, his wife; roping her all unwilling into a life with him. Thoughtless, as she had not thought he could be. Insensitive, as he never was before.

She wants to sit before Girolama and tell her of Henri's sweetness as a boy. How he played at seek with Antoinette, always pretending he could not find her even when she stood in plain sight with her hands over her face. How he cried when one of the lions at the Paris menagerie died.

It took two keepers to drag it from its cage by its great clawed paws; and then they let Henri play with it, to Catherine's horror. The beast's eyes were open and rolled mostly back, its tongue protruding from between its yellowed teeth. She had thought the creatures magnificent when she first saw them, but in death they were as bloated and stiff as human corpses, and monstrous in their massiveness.

Henri had stroked the fur over the lion's ribs, murmuring something that Catherine could not quite hear, but which sounded in tone like something soothing she would say to him and his sisters if they were tucked up in their beds with illness. He then explored the tuft at the end of the lion's tail, and trailed his fingers upward along its spine, ruffling the fur in the wrong direction until he reached the deep expanse of its mane. But then he paused, noticing for the first time the flies that landed and circled about the creature's head, their movement making more obvious the lion's own unnatural stillness. He drew his hands out of the mane as if it had caught fire.

She had to explain death to him, then; and what words existed to convey the well of misery and mystery? They did not exist; or if they did, Catherine could not find them. Death, to her, was still entirely sewn of wrongness. Priests and scholars might go on about its natural cycle; its ultimate beauty. But she could not see it.

So she did the only thing she could do, and wrapped her arms tight about her son as he wept.

"Will you die?" he cried.

"Yes, sweet boy." Smoothing his hair; heart splitting like the shell of an egg. And then, with a silent prayer that she would not be made a liar: "But not for a very, very long time."

This calmed him, but only briefly.

"Will *I* die?" he said, the horror of the thought writ large upon his face; and then he shook his head before she could answer, as if the idea were simply too big to keep.

"But what if you do die?" he said then. "Who will play with me?"

"I have no intention of dying until you are a grown man, my sweet," she said; but his brow furrowed, as if she were being stupid.

"But who will play with me *then*?" And then, narrow back heaving with his sobs, "What if you die and I want you to sing to me?"

SHE WANTS TO PLEAD with this woman who has given her a grandson to see the sweet boy under Henri's arrogant facade. But then she thinks of Papa—how he released her to Petrus, how he did not say goodbye—and of the amethysts that hung so heavy from her ears. The terror of being thrust into a life she had never once wished for, or even imagined. Of her daughter taken from her, and no word, none at all—Petrus has written to the duke, has asked for news, and always the same reply, that the marchesa has not corresponded, that his wife attended one of her famous gatherings and there was no sign of a little hairy girl. The frantic scratch of it in Catherine's chest, the clawing of it, of not knowing where her child is, what she is doing, if she is well and whole and happy. The rending of it, and how, too, it has rent great tatters in the cloth of her marriage. She can see through them, as if her marriage is a sheet on a line, and all the sparkling sunlight winking through the holes as it does through tree boughs in summer. In her head, they both try to sew the tatters closed again, little patient stitches; but she is not certain they will ever quite succeed.

And then she wants to shout at her son; to grasp his wife's hands and beg forgiveness on his behalf.

CAPODIMONTE, ITALY

1608

Pedro

They bend together over a hornbook lent to them by Madeleine, whose daughters no longer use it. Bible verses, familiar and comforting to Catherine; these, he thinks, will make the learning easier for her.

He is teaching her to read.

It is a slow and laborious progress. She stumbles and curses over how *this* letter is so like *that* one; how stupid, she says, to make them so alike. But she comes back to it every night, the candlelight showing the threads of silver in her pale hair, their fingers tracking each sentence in unison.

THESE LAST YEARS HAVE been strange ones. Strained ones. She has not wanted his company as she used to; except in those rare moments when she seemed to forget his part in their daughter's leaving. When she smiled at him and it was a true smile, warming, soft. When her neck bent, showing the tender spot where it met the shoulder; and she glanced at him over the curve of it, as she used to, when she loved him unreservedly.

And then, sometimes, she beckons him closer. Murmurs the words in her hornbook aloud in his ear, breath warmer than the air around it. Smiles that true smile, as if she cares what he thinks of her progress. Cups his palm against her own when she reads an entire page without stumbling, the give of flesh against flesh, the young and giddy feeling of rightness in the world. And he wonders if, despite this thing that he did, this thing for which he has long thought she might never forgive him—for which he still struggles to forgive himself—if time has at last allowed them to find each other again.

AFTER THEIR YOUNGEST DAUGHTER left, Petrus woke almost nightly to the soft shaking of his wife's back as she cried. But this has not happened in a long time, longer than he can think to count. This morning, she dropped a casual kiss upon the top his head when she passed him sitting at the table.

SHE WRITES, NOW, A LOOPED and childish hand. Forms the letters again and again until she has the feel of each one, just as she learned their sounds. One night she cups her hand around the paper so that Petrus cannot see the words her pen is forming; when at last she shows him, the quavering letters, the slanting list of names, he finds himself robbed of speech, of breath. He takes her hand in one of his and presses the base of her thumb as he reads:

Catherine
Petrus
Madeleine
Henri
Antoinette
Ercole

Part Seven

Forever After

CAPODIMONTE, ITALY
1619

Catherine

She hurts in all of her parts, but she does not want to go inside her house. After church, she decided to take a walk, and without intending to—as has happened so often, of late—found herself continuing, when she reached the edges of the town, down the road as it curved away from the lake. She walked until her knees protested, and only then did she turn back, her right knee clicking all the way in time to her asymmetrical rhythm. When the pretty, jumbled roofs of the town came into view, she had the strangest feeling, as if she were pressing onward through swamp water, which caught at her skirts and dragged her back, each step forward a struggle. And now she has reached her own door, she stands staring at it, unwilling to open it and step inside.

A voice from behind her says, "Signora!" Catherine turns, trying to keep her weariness from her expression.

"Oh, Signora, I've been meaning to come by and see how you have been," says the women standing behind Catherine in the street. She is a short, round woman, her dark hair white-streaked down one side, as if touched by a painter's brush. Signora Ricci, who, with her husband, owns a little farm where they make the hard, salty cheese that used to be Petrus's favorite. He ate it with bread and olive oil and a little salt; he claimed, whenever Catherine served it to him, that this was the best meal he had ever eaten. "We don't see you so much now."

Catherine tries to smile. "I don't go through so much of your delicious cheese as I used to, I'm afraid."

The other woman's mouth pulls down, an exaggerated expression of concern. "Yes, I imagine it has been difficult, adjusting." A pause. "But there is something of a . . . well, I would never say *blessing*, of course. But still—I imagine there is a . . . *relief*, perhaps?"

Catherine stares at her. "Relief?"

Signora Ricci puts a hand on Catherine's wrist. "Marriage can so often be a trial, even under ordinary circumstances. And yours was anything but ordinary." She gives a little nod. "We all of us have said it at one time or another—you have borne up astonishingly well. No one, I think, could have endured what you have with more grace, and you have earned a little peace, a little happiness." She pats Catherine's wrist, as if it were a cat.

Catherine's step backward is almost a shudder, a wrenching away from the other woman's touch. Her words. She thinks of Petrus, praising this woman's cheese for years—*years*—and wants to weep, to scream.

"By endure," she says, "I suppose you mean my husband's presence, rather than the loss of it?"

Signora Ricci's eyes widen; her hands flutter like frightened hens. "That is," she says, but Catherine steps away again.

"Excuse me," she says, and enters her house, closing the door behind her with a sound of finality.

The house's thick walls keep much of the day's heat at bay and muffle the noises of all the life outside. Catherine stands, the sudden silence all around her like shoving hands, and folds in upon herself, a crumbling tower, down and down until her brow touches the floor. When she begins crying, the tears are hot and startling, and she has the abrupt, disorienting sensation that she has fallen here before, cried here like this before.

But no—it was the fine tile of their home at the Palazzo Farnese upon which she once wept. With Petrus behind her, and the specter of Antoinette's arms about her neck. She feels, now, that same anger tear through her like a gale; but this time it is not focused solely upon her husband. A little, yes, for Petrus has left her to endure the stares and whispers all on her own, whispers that will likely never cease entirely while she lives in this village, where she was, and always will be, the hairy man's wife; the mother of hairy children. That they are nothing to what Petrus endured all his life—well, that does not dampen her anger at his leaving.

But nearly all of her sudden fury swirls about the figures in the village who think—who *dare* to think—

The road she walks so often now curves away from the lake, away from the village, curling itself like a sun-washed snake away, away, away. Petrus made a feeble jest once, near the end, about leaving her free to wander, to adventure, to claim the life she dreamed of as a girl.

Unencumbered, he said, all self-deprecation; and at the time Catherine had thought he meant by his age, his illness. But now she knows, and thinks how stupid she was to misunderstand him. And all the village, it seems, is thinking exactly as he did: that she is fortunate to be burdened by his hair no longer.

SOMETIMES, SHE DOES NOT mind her house's silence. Does not mind eating exactly when and what she wishes to eat, with no thought for the whims and tastes of others. Does not mind always having the most comfortable chair to herself, the one that long ago molded itself to the shape and weight of her husband's body.

But other times, like earlier today, it is difficult to face the silence and stillness of his absence. And so she walks—not to escape his memory, or others' memories of them together, but to escape the lack of him.

The anger simmers as she chops onions, the heat of them stinging her eyes until her vision is blurred by a wash of tears, and as she removes the delicate bones of a fish and cooks the flesh with the onions and fragrant parsley. As she chews and swallows, though, the anger changes. It does not fade but bleeds itself into something else, something quieter.

It is a heavy sadness, the thought that no one else understands what she and Petrus shared. All marriages endure their trials—children born and dead again; sickness; poverty; inconstancy—but to come through, so many decades later, and still want to turn to one's partner in life, to speak to him about your day, about the dreams that wake you in the night—it is a miracle of sorts, she thinks. A miracle, a marvel, a wonder; but not one that anyone around her seems to recognize. She thinks of the kings and queens she has known, and all the kings' mistresses and other lovers; of so many couples at court who spent enough time together to get an heir in the wife's belly, but who otherwise lived their lives entirely apart.

She thinks, too, of Agnes, of her friend, and the song she once told Catherine she would write—about the wild, hairy man and his beautiful bride. Perhaps she wrote it after all; perhaps it is widely sung where she now lives. Perhaps she is hailed for her brilliance with words.

As far as Catherine knows, Agnes never did let anyone read her scribblings, as she called them, and she wishes now that she had begged her friend to read them out to her. A single song, even. Wishes even harder that, now she can read and write, herself, she knows what became of Agnes, that she might send a letter across whatever distance lies between them.

The thought stirs something in her, and she rises, finds pen and ink and paper, and then she sits at her table, curled over her work as Agnes once curled over her own, and writes and writes until her fingers are numb and her eyes ache. She crouches at the hearth when she is finished, poking at the fire. A small flare; she puts her papers to it, ignoring the wastefulness. One directed to Agnes, and the other to Antoinette. She watches them catch, bright and true; watches them burn away to ash.

And then she returns to her chair, to what is left of the day, to the thickets of her thoughts. She sits and listens to the quiet of the house, and her memories tinged with blue but also with pink and orange and the green of growth. Her husband's stiff reserve at their wedding, which gave way at last, under gentle, patient pressure from their twining lives, to his beautiful smile. To romps with their children, and arguments in hushed voices at night, and kisses from his warm mouth. That so few others knew how deeply human Petrus was—it is an ache. But she knew. She knows.

The urge to flee from her solitude has passed. Now, she sits with a glass of wine from the bottles she and Petrus stored in the cellar, bottles from the vineyards they oversaw. It is enough, in this moment, to remember his imperfect beauty, and theirs together. Almost, she pities those who cannot understand.

CAPODIMONTE, ITALY

1618

Pedro

His children come to see him one by one. The illness that plagued him all winter has not eased with the spring. It is a tiredness that lingers no matter how much he sleeps; a pain in his bones that makes tears leak from the corners of his eyes. He who once carried each of them in his arms now cannot even rise to greet them. Old age has arrived like a storm and blown him all off course.

Madeleine comes and stays by his side as often as Catherine will allow. She spoons broth, boiled from bones and rich with golden circles of fat, into his mouth, patting his beard with a cloth when a little trickles from the corners of his lips. She must be more than forty now—so hard to fathom—and wears her thick hair pinned back severely. Her lips seem thinner, with age or sadness; they look like flowers pressed between the pages of a heavy book until all the life has been squeezed from their petals. Petrus looks away from them, blinking hard.

He tries to push himself upright whenever Henri comes. His son always arrives with little gifts of wine or cheese, kissing his mother's cheek and letting his sister lean her head against his shoulder. He speaks briskly of his business matters, asks them all brief, polite questions about their days, and then departs. Once or twice he repeats his tired old complaint, that despite having lived in the village for so long, no one except his wife, Girolama, will call him by the name he was given at birth.

"*Enrico!*" he says, exaggerating the Italian curl of the word.

Petrus does not even reply. He looks up at the ceiling, turned brown at the edge where a little water must have seeped during the last big rain. Since they came to Italy nearly thirty years ago, he has been Pietro to almost everyone but his family; Catherine, Caterina. Madeleine was known affectionately at the Farnese court as Hairy Maddalena. When Antoinette lived in Rome, she was Antonietta; and still is, he suspects—hopes, prays—if she remained with the marchesa.

But *this* son of his—so adept at kneading people into the shapes that best benefit him—cannot accept that in some things, people will always do as they themselves wish. Made more comfortable by a name they recognize, a name they can easily pronounce, they will use it. Henri has changed his life—his wife's life, too—without ever once wondering whether it was his right to do so. But he rages against anything he cannot change.

AT LEAST THEY KNOW where Ercole's bones lie. Small as they were; little as they knew of the person he was. There is comfort in knowing where someone rests.

Petrus sent Ludovico's coach and horses back to France, and sent letters galloping there as well, many letters over the years, and received Ludovico's replies months later, crumpled and travel-stained from their journey to Rome.

His friend's letters stopped coming entirely six years after they parted, and there was always such a long wait between sending a message and receiving an answer that Petrus did not at first realize that anything was amiss. The news of his death came from a most unlikely source—his wife, Henriette, who found a half-penned letter in her husband's room and sent it off with a note of her own, a single line: *My husband fell ill several weeks ago, and has died.*

Catherine found him weeping, wrapped her arms about his shoulders, held on through the tremors. When the tears finally stopped, Petrus tucked his sorrow away, along with his friend's final, unfinished letter. The thought of Ludovico's bright-dark eyes closing, his sturdy heart ceasing to beat, after only fifty-nine years in the world, seemed impossible; a sadness so thick that Petrus could not entirely take it in, could only sip at it a little, here, there. Easier, by far, to keep most of it plugged away, poison in a stoppered bottle.

I think of you often, old friend, Ludovico wrote. *I think of your happiness, hold it tight as my own in my thoughts, and my own shall only be complete when we are able to see each other again.*

He remembers Ludovico often now, more often than he has allowed himself in years; but only when Catherine is gone from the room. Now that he is old, it is easier to let the fog of his memories close over the things that he would rather forget, and so he thinks now of his friend only softly, letting the fog conceal all memories of the terrible things Ludovico and his schemes helped to set in motion. Petrus thinks of him, and all the others who have also journeyed onward. Whispers their names, each a drop of vinegar and sugar together on his tongue. Isabel, surely; Manuel, almost certainly, for he would be nearly a century old, if he still lived. King Henri, Queen Caterina. Ercole.

And Ludovico Gonzaga. When Catherine is elsewhere, when there is no danger of hurting her, for she seems to see everything in his face, Petrus sometimes remembers that single kiss: how warm and dry Ludovico's lips; how odd, the brush of another man's beard against his own. Almost, perhaps, like the brush of the beard of the girl in the pamphlet, the one he kept until its creases turned fibrous and the paper finally rotted all away.

He had not wanted his friend's kiss, precisely; but he welcomed it all the same. And he thinks of it now with the sting of words unsaid, of a time he can never get back, all the time of his long life rolled out behind him like a bright bolt of silk; but no matter how he tugs, he cannot roll it back up, cannot begin again, however hard his fingers scrabble, however loudly he screams at the skies for a little longer, for a moment returned, for a chance to hold his children again as children, to couple with his wife again when they were young, to let his friend kiss him again and again, because he was the first, the only, person to see Petrus and want him, just as he was, from the very beginning.

CATHERINE COMES OFTEN TO sit beside their bed in the chair with the worn upholstered seat. She takes up some sewing, but he knows, from how slowly her needle moves, that her mind is elsewhere. Eventually she rises and comes to bed, though it is not night and she still wears all her clothing from coif to shoes.

They do not speak of what is coming, except in hand clasps while they pretend to sleep, as the sun sinks low until at last stars shine bright and cold outside their window. They do not speak at all, but breathe together. *In*—recriminations. *Out*—forgiveness.

Or so he hopes.

ANTOINETTE'S ABSENCE FROM HIS sickbed is like a sickness itself. It covers everything with its stench; with the sound of its heaving breaths.

He remembers, again and again, like a play from which he cannot escape, how she was taken from them; how he let her go. Remembers her feverish little head when she was ill in Basel; her smile, sly and sweet at once. Though even those memories have frayed until he cannot be certain whether they are at all true, or whether his mind is merely trying to patch the holes that have worn through them over time.

The heat of the sun, like hands cupping his face, his shoulders. Antoinette licking pastry and sweet almond filling from her fingers. Catherine inside, nursing Ercole. Madeleine and Henri bickering, the noise of it like flies, rising, rising, until at last he stands, says loudly enough to cut across the sighs and the quarrels:

"I crossed the sea in a pirate ship."

And then he waits, stroking his chin hair, for them to turn, to face him, to ask, Why, Papa?

Instead, Henri: "No, you didn't."

Madeleine's admonishment; from himself, a mild, raised brow. "No? Then I suppose you mustn't wish to hear the tale."

Antoinette, with a glare at Henri: "Tell us, Papa! Do tell!"

"I crossed the sea in a pirate ship, from a land of erupting mountains and beaches of black."

Antoinette's thumb finding its way into her mouth; even Henri, his eyes narrowed, not bothering to tease her.

"I lived with a good woman and her grandson in a small, stout house. The grandson was a builder, and the woman made the loveliest necklaces you ever saw. Like something a sea queen might wear, of beads bright-painted and shells that snicked together like music.

"There were caves full of bones, and people tight preserved, as if they lived still; except that their skin clung too closely to their bones, all the fat and meat of them gone. Sacred places, where our very own dead rested. There were a few defiant shepherds in the mountains, who refused to conform to Spanish law and lived as they pleased; as their people—our *people"*—*said firmly*—*"had done for centuries. There were rocks formed by the cooled mountain fire, at once beautiful and grotesque."*

"Like us," Antoinette says, releasing her thumb, as a crack opened inside Petrus's chest. "Like us."

AND HE DREAMS OF her often now. In his dreams, she is in a trunk. Playing, perhaps, just as she and Henri used to when they were children, when they heaped all the clothes upon the bed so they could pretend at rowing a boat, driving a coach. Going, always going, somewhere else. Catherine never allowed them to close the lid, though they always begged, longing to secret themselves inside, to retreat into the wood-scented cave of it.

Waiting. Humming to herself. Waiting for someone to find her; or hoping they will not. A fetus-shaped thing all salty and damp as sand where the waves have been lapping. The air not salt tinged and fresh but stale as old bread, and yet she cannot get enough of it, gulping and gulping, devouring it too quickly.

And then she is floating, flying, sailing away. He reaches, tries to catch her but she is ahead of him. *Here*, she calls, *here is the place you came from, Papa; and oh, it is just as you always described it. Your memory did not fail you. The sea, so blue—the hills, so green. There is a white church just where I expect it to be.*

IT IS THE NOT knowing that is the worst of all. Or best, depending upon what there is to know. For after Antoinette left them, they never saw her again; nor could the duke, when Petrus and Henri both begged him to do so, find a whisper of her anywhere. She had disappeared like breath into the air; like greasy smoke from the candles Catherine still lights for her at church. Gone.

HE WAKES NOW AND looks at Catherine, who has fallen asleep in her chair. Some mending lies spread, pale in the dim, setting light, across her lap, the needle and its fine thread dangling from her fingertips. It is one of his shirts, Petrus realizes; the tear at the shoulder seam is nearly repaired, only the smallest of holes remaining to be closed. His throat fills with water, and he lies there, looking at her—at all the familiar particulars of her face and form; at the pale hair, escaping its tight plaits, the strands more gray than gold, now. His daughter has haunted them both since she disappeared; but suddenly Petrus knows that it is the sight of his wife slumped just so, the light wind of her sleeping breaths, the faint frowning turn of her mouth and the loose curl of her fingers, which will haunt him forever once he is gone.

As if she senses his gaze, Catherine stirs and opens her eyes, the lids drooping more at the corners than they did when she was young, the eyes themselves taking a little longer to adjust.

When they have, she leans forward, the shirt dropping from her lap. "What do you need?"

Petrus finds that the words take their gentle time slipping from his ear to be deciphered in his brain; and while he waits, he looks at her, a small smile curling at his mouth. And then he pats the bed beside him, one hand fumbling with the bedclothes.

"You're tired," he says, his voice a quiet rasp. "Rest with me."

Catherine hesitates, then nods. He watches as she picks up the fallen shirt and folds it carefully, as if she intends to take it up again tomorrow, as if he might wear it again when the seam is mended. Then she undresses, fingers quick upon her laces, until she is wearing only her chemise, and Petrus has the sudden, reeling sensation that it is their wedding night again, that again he watches with furtive glances as she unclothes herself to lie with him.

The mattress dips a little with her weight when she joins him on the bed. And unlike that first night, she is warm and soft and right beside him. Their fingers lace, the pillows of their palms touch.

More time, he has been thinking, all these last weeks. More time, please. More time.

And yet.

If time were his to command, he knows now, he would not use it to travel across the sea. He would not use it to return to the places he remembers or even to those he always wished to visit.

He would stay here, he thinks. If he could have, he'd have remained in the inn at Basel, with Madeleine and Henri on the floor at the foot of their bed, and Antoinette curled between him and Catherine. He'd have remained, suspended, in that moment—of all their shared breaths in that close room; of the softness and solidity of his wife and smallest child beside him. But as that moment has long since passed, and as it is the woman beside him who made it possible, he thinks he will stay here until his end. Catherine is not sleeping, he knows; she is not relaxed enough to be asleep, even the curve of her hip indicative of her wakeful tension.

All those years, those decades, ago—when they slept beside one another for the first time—he has long suspected she did not sleep at all. He would return to that girl, if he could; he would tell her instantly how glad he was to have her by his side. He would not doubt the stoutness of her heart, or the steadiness of her head; he would not judge her by her beauty, or assume that she judged him; and perhaps, then, she would not have done.

All the time he wasted. All the hours lost to uncertainty, self-consciousness; to coveting the lives of other men. And all the while, he might have been perfectly happy if he had only reveled in these moments of quiet, in the easy familiarity of their two bodies touching, rolling together to meet at the center of the mattress; of the comfortable tangle of their calves and ankles and toes. The forever of these moments so stupidly lost on him, when he had days upon days of them to anticipate.

And oh—he would answer her differently, now, if she were to ask him again what he wished to be called, by which name he wished to be known. For very suddenly, he knows it—he *feels* it—under his bones, *Pedro* lives still, small and hairy, wearing outsize shoes, shells clicking together inside the bag that bounces against his shoulder blades as he darts minnow-like around carts and market stalls, around old men who rouse dust from the road with their shuffling and people who cry out as they catch a glimpse of a hairy face rushing past them, grinning with all its teeth. This boy, this Pedro, is light in his chest, his breath moving quick and easy through his lungs, his legs pumping, shoes flapping at the heels. Above him, rising over the town, are the hills, thick with green. Behind him is the sea, the smooth cresting waves tipped with red as the sun sinks into them. And inside him is a joy as vivid as that sun, its warmth radiating outward from the shallow valley at the center of his chest, joy at the prospect of going home—but the home to which he runs with such eagerness is not just the little house where his almost-grandmother waits, but this house, this place, this day so many years after he thought *Pedro* was gone from him forever, dampened like a fire nearly stamped out. But Pedro never left him after all, was not subsumed by all the things he has learned since Tenerife, by the ache to be accepted by a king and his court. Pedro has been here; and inside him, still, is a small, warm sun, a joy built tipsily of toes in the sand, the smell of salt on the air, the burn of muscles carrying him home. The knock of a pair of knee bones against his own, gentle, familiar. The insistent, pressing eyes of the woman beside him. He shifts a little so that he faces her. Feels tiredness tugging at him, though he struggles against its pull. And then Catherine touches her brow to his, hooks her smallest finger around his thumb. He sees her eyes upon his face, steady, before his own close.

CAPODIMONTE, ITALY

1619

Catherine

She dreamed of Antoinette last night, and her daughter was warm and safe and well and living very far away. The land where she lived was humped with mountains that sat stoic as the ancients, their craggy sides softened here and there by trees growing together thick as a pelt. Antoinette—wearing a gown as rich with pearls as any Agnes ever owned, and crusted with silver embroidery that flashed and dazzled like a fish's scales in the sunlight—was tall, taller than either Catherine or Madeleine, taller even than Petrus's slight height, and narrow as a sapling, and with a sapling's supple strength. She walked, indeed, with a sinuous rolling motion that brought to mind some elemental thing, roots through the soil, fish through water, birds across the vastness of the sky. But her feet, incongruously bare of shoes and stockings, padded down a pebbled shoreline to the water that lapped with white-foamed tongues at the dark sand; and she buried her toes deep in the muck, pulling one foot out with a sucking sound and a laugh like an echo of her childhood self. The toes, mud-smeared, wriggled; the head turned, eyes laughing, too, to look at someone Catherine could not see but whose silhouette, dark against the sun's brightness, was somehow familiar.

In her dream, Catherine said, *Oh! Of course. That is why we have not found her*, and found herself before a map like Papa's, all the wide world, great hunks of land surrounded by the monstrous sea. Her finger traced the path of her daughter's voyage, over land and then water and then land again, to a place whose name sat like marbles in her mouth, and which she cannot remember now, upon waking.

It does not matter. She wakes with a smile, the sort of smile that makes all the muscles of her body soft and easy, and turns to tell Petrus about the dream.

HISTORICAL NOTE

This story is, above all, a work of fiction.

Though I tried to stay faithful to the facts that are known about the Gonzales family, as well as to those that scholars have deemed most likely, for the sake of a more coherent narrative I did take liberties with history. In places, time lines have been blurred and historical sites, and even people, combined. The song that Catherine sings is a modified translation of a traditional Italian lullaby.

Animal-husband tales have appeared in cultures all over the world for centuries upon centuries. One—Gabrielle-Suzanne Barbot de Villeneuve's *The Beauty and the Beast*—has spawned countless variations. Whether the historical protagonists in this book might have been the inspiration for Villeneuve's story is—like so much else about their lives—a matter of conjecture, though one that sparked my imagination.

Very little is known for certain about Pedro Gonzales, the hirsute boy brought to the French court around the time of Henri II's coronation, and much of what we "know" is very likely the sort of potent mixture of fact and fiction from which legends are birthed. Still less is known about his glabrous wife, Catherine, though there are documents indicating that her father was a textile merchant. So on the basis of the sparse and sometimes contradictory information available, I had to be inventive, though I am deeply indebted to several works of nonfiction on the subject, particularly Merry Wiesner-Hanks's *The Marvelous Hairy Girls*, Touba Ghadessi's *Portraits of Human Monsters in the Renaissance*, and Roberto Zapperi's fascinating biography of Pedro, *Il selvaggio gentiluomo: l'incredibile storia di Pedro Gonzales e dei suoi figli*.

The history of sixteenth-century France is a turbulent one. Because

I was more concerned with the Gonzales family life than with religious and court politics, I touched on only some of it, and only on that which I felt would have been most likely to affect them personally. And again, liberties were taken; Ludovico Gonzaga, the Duke of Nevers, was a real person, and believed to have been one of the minds behind the Saint Bartholomew's Day Massacre, which set off a series of decades-long wars between Catholics and Huguenots. Gonzaga was fostered at the French court around the same time that Pedro Gonzales was a child there, but their friendship is entirely my invention. For anyone interested in a deeper look into the complex history of this time and place, with all its intrigues and bloodiness, I highly recommend the works of Robert J. Knecht, who has written a number of books about French Renaissance monarchs, the French Wars of Religion, and French Renaissance court life.

We do know this much: a hairy child, approximately ten years old, arrived at the French court in 1547 and was educated at the behest of the newly crowned King Henri II. This child was born with what we now know was a form of hypertrichosis, a genetic condition causing excessive hair growth all over the body. (This form of hypertrichosis is also sometimes known as Ambras syndrome, named for the castle in Austria where some of the Gonzales family portraits were discovered.) Many years later, he was married—according to lore, at the whim of Queen Caterina (Catherine) de' Medici, though this is unsubstantiated—to a much younger woman, also named Catherine. Some recent scholarship indicates that Pedro may, in fact, have earned a law degree and become a lecturer at a Parisian university, which would have afforded him more freedom, status, and financial security than if, as has long been believed, he was only ever a bread bearer for Henri II. Regardless, however, what we do know almost without doubt is that he and his children were subject to the whims of their royal protectors.

Pedro and Catherine lived as part of the French court until sometime after the death of Caterina de' Medici, and went from there to the protection of the Farnese in Parma. Along the way, they may have stopped at other royal courts, though we don't know this for certain. They did stop in Basel, where at least two of the children were examined by Felix Platter, a physician and university lecturer.

Pedro did ask the Duke of Parma for work, and ran a farm for him, though not for long, and the farm was not in Capodimonte as I have it in the novel—though the family did, in fact, live out the ends of their lives in that town—but in Collecchio.

Catherine bore Pedro at least seven children in all, not just the four who appear in this book. Their names, to the best of our knowledge, were Madeleine, Paul, Henri, Françoise, Antoinette, Orazio, and Ercole, though there may have been others, as recently discovered baptismal certificates attest. Of these seven, five are known to have been as hairy as their father; one, Paul, is believed to have been glabrous. Whether Ercole was hairy or not is unknown; he almost certainly died as an infant, and nothing else is recorded about him.

Pedro and Catherine were together from their marriage around 1570 until his death sometime after 1617. Their portraits, which were likely not painted from life, and those of their children were displayed in various scholarly works as well as in the homes of princes and nobles who collected images of "monsters." We know what happened to all of Pedro and Catherine's children except for Antoinette, who disappears almost entirely from the record after she leaves her parents as a child to live with the Marchesa di Soragna. Only her painted image remains—the striking portrait described in the opening to this book, painted by the Italian artist Lavinia Fontana when Antoinette was about eight years old and living with the marchesa—to remind us that she lived.

ACKNOWLEDGMENTS

I began writing *Marvelous* around the time that the COVID-19 pandemic hit the United States. Under perfect circumstances (and with my dream travel budget!) I'd have been able to physically visit all the places Pedro and Catherine lived, to walk where they walked, to experience, as closely as possible, their lives in the palaces of France and Italy and in the towns of Garachico and Capodimonte. To visit their portraits, and those of their children.

Of course, given the state of the world, travel wasn't even a faint possibility. But the pandemic did do one favor for struggling historical fiction writers—a number of museums decided to throw open their doors, virtually speaking, to online visitors, meaning that exhibits that would usually require a plane ticket and the price of admission to see were suddenly free and easily accessible. I am particularly thankful for the staff video tours posted on social media by Château de Fontainebleau, which gave me the sense that I was *almost* right there in the grotto, the galleries, the halls, and the grounds, seeing what my characters would have seen. All books are a product of much more than just their authors' hard work, and I am indebted to a lot of people who were incredibly generous with their time, their knowledge, and their space. As I mentioned already, *Marvelous* was written during the pandemic, and all my usual away-from-home writing spots—the public library, local coffeeshops, our food co-op—were shuttered. I found myself at home with three kids, struggling to write during my youngest son's naps, constantly interrupted. But my mom and stepdad, Chris and Abbie Innes, offered me space on Sundays in their little upstairs landing area (my "writer's garret," we took to calling it), in addition to providing bottomless cups of coffee and home-cooked meals. Thank you both for quite literally fueling my writing—and also for being early readers! I'm so grateful.

Thank you to my other early readers as well, including Ashley Barbour for your careful sensitivity read (and for talking me down from a panic multiple times when I found myself stuck in the course of writing!); Rebecca Howe; and Natalie Jenner. Natalie, this book would be so much poorer without your insights.

Thank you to Merry Wiesner-Hanks and Touba Ghadessi for sharing your expertise about Pedro and Catherine's day-to-day lived experience in the French Renaissance court.

Thank you to my agent, Jennifer Weltz, for helping me keep the heart of this story in mind as I wrote, and for never being afraid to gently but firmly tell me when something wasn't working!

Thank you to the entire team at William Morrow—it absolutely takes a village to raise book babies, and I'm so glad to have landed in this one! Thank you, in particular, to Dill Werner for your thoughtful sensitivity read, to Shelly Perron for your careful copyedits, and to my brilliant editor, Rachel Kahan; your editorial choices always make my writing so much stronger.

As always, I have to thank my husband, Stuart Campbell. I am so lucky to have married a dreamer—one who believes in my dreams as fully as he believes in his own. Thank you with all my heart for your belief, and for so unstintingly giving me the practical space and time I need to make my dreams a reality.

And to my kids: I know you don't always like or understand it when I need time to myself to write, but know this—you are never, ever far from my mind, even when I'm at my desk with the door firmly closed. As I wrote this book about love and marriage and family, you were with me the entire time.

ABOUT THE AUTHOR

Molly Greeley is the author of *The Clergyman's Wife* and *The Heiress*. She lives with her husband and three children in Traverse City, Michigan.